NO LONGER PROPERTY OF
SEATTLE
D0391145

SOMETHIN

Cocking her head, Rory took a couple of steps toward the counter. The corner of a small box stuck out from behind a display. "Why would they leave something...?"

Suddenly, everything clicked. The answer flashed in her brain, lit up with bright warning lights.

"Out!" she yelled, whipping around to start shoving the firefighters toward the door. "Go! Move! *Bomb!*" She finally shouted the important word, but they weren't responding right. The guys didn't panic and rush for the nearest exit. Instead, they all concentrated on getting everyone else out of danger first, and she found herself propelled forward until she was at the front of the pack, closest to the door.

Ian! her brain screamed. *Get Ian out!*

"Ian!" Hands and bodies pushed her toward safety, and she fought them, trying to turn, unable to leave Ian behind. He'd just saved her from her self-imposed exile. How could she return to life without him? "*Ian!*"

FAN THE FLAMES

KATIE RUGGLE

Copyright © 2016 by Katie Ruggle
Cover and internal design © 2016 by Sourcebooks, Inc.
Cover art by Craig White

Sourcebooks and the colophon are registered trademarks of Sourcebooks, Inc.

All rights reserved. No part of this book may be reproduced in any form or by any electronic or mechanical means including information storage and retrieval systems—except in the case of brief quotations embodied in critical articles or reviews—without permission in writing from its publisher, Sourcebooks, Inc.

The characters and events portrayed in this book are fictitious or are used fictitiously. Any similarity to real persons, living or dead, is purely coincidental and not intended by the author.

Published by Sourcebooks Casablanca, an imprint of Sourcebooks, Inc.
P.O. Box 4410, Naperville, Illinois 60567-4410
(630) 961-3900
Fax: (630) 961-2168
www.sourcebooks.com

Printed and bound in Canada.
MBP 10 9 8 7 6 5 4 3 2 1

To the marvelous siblings: Bridget, Chris, Teresa, Beth, Monica, Jenny, and Matt. Growing up with all of you really developed my sense of humor.

Love, Katie

Prologue

It had started out as such a promising day.

"What?" Ian bellowed when the roar of the fire and the rumble of the pump-truck engine drowned out the chief's words.

"The homeowner said he stores a propane tank in the northeast corner of the barn!" Fire Chief Winston Early yelled.

Closing his eyes for a moment, Ian sighed. *Of course he does*. "This barn? The one that's on fire?"

"That would be the barn."

A torrent of profanity rose in his throat, but he clamped his jaw. A few weeks ago, he'd promised Steve's youngest, Maya, he'd stop swearing. Once he gave his word, Ian stuck to it, even if he and his firefighting brethren were all going to be blown to bits thanks to a flame-happy serial arsonist Ian couldn't even call a *fucking asshole*.

Swallowing the curses that desperately wanted to escape, Ian yanked on the hem of his borrowed, too-small bunker coat. "I'm on it."

Soup fell in next to him and spoke over the radio incorporated into their SCBA—self-contained breathing apparatus—gear. "Got your back, Beauty."

The hated nickname deepened his scowl. With a wordless growl, Ian stalked toward the flaming barn. The heat was incredible, and sweat beaded beneath his mask. A backward glance showed Steve and Junior at the trucks, hurrying to hook up the hoses.

"What's the plan?"

Studying the barn, Ian noted that, although the south side of the old storage building was fully engulfed, the northeast corner looked relatively untouched by the fire—it wouldn't stay that way for long, though. The house where the homeowner and his two grandkids lived was only ten feet north of the burning barn. If the propane tank blew, they'd be screwed.

"Hey? Ian?" It was like Soup was incapable of silence for more than a few seconds at a time. "Plan?"

"We go through that door"—Ian pointed to the entrance on the north side—"get the propane tank, and get out."

"Short and sweet." Soup's good-natured chuckle echoed through the speaker in Ian's mask. "I like it. Let's go save the day…again. Because we're awesome like that."

This time, Ian was unable to hold back a snort of laughter. That was Soup—cracking jokes right before walking into a burning building. Despite Soup's tendency to run away at the mouth, Ian couldn't ask for a better, braver partner.

Heat scorched his skin, even through his bunker gear. The door was locked, so Ian kicked it, cracking the ancient wood and sending the door slamming into the interior wall. He blocked it with his body before the door could rebound and slam shut again.

"Aww," Soup complained. "You get to do all the fun stuff."

"The next door is yours," Ian promised before

stepping into a burning building for the second time that month. After six years with the Simpson Fire Department, it still surprised him how dark it was inside a structure fire. The smoke in this one was especially thick and black, probably due to what appeared to be a pile of smoldering tires covering most of the east wall.

Once inside, he moved as quickly as possible across the debris-strewn floor. Stacks of boxes and other junk obscured the northeast corner, and Ian clenched his jaw as he started shoving them aside.

"Fucking packrats," Soup grumbled, breathing hard as he shifted boxes, helping to clear a path.

Tossing an armful of lumber, Ian snapped, "Watch your mouth!" He moved another stack of boxes and uncovered the propane tank...the hundred-pound propane tank.

"Why? You were the one who told Steve's girl you'd stop swearing. I made no such promise." Soup groaned, obviously spotting the container. "Hell. It couldn't have been a twenty-pounder?"

Ian was already bending, preparing to hoist the cylindrical tank onto his shoulder.

"Heads up!" Soup shouted as Ian started to rise, looking up just in time to see a large chunk of burning plywood falling right on top of him. With the weight of the tank, his shift to the left was turtle-slow, and he braced himself for impact. Soup lunged forward, knocking the flaming wood aside, so it only grazed Ian's free shoulder before falling to the floor. Pieces of what had been the roof crashed down around them, smoldering chunks of wood and asphalt shingles blocking the path they'd just created.

"Thanks, Soup," he said, breathing hard. Adrenaline was ripping through him.

"No problem." Despite his words, Soup's voice was tight, and he was holding his right arm against his side. "Let's get out of here before the *rest* of the roof crashes down on us."

Knowing that he couldn't do anything about Soup's injury until they were clear of the fire, Ian adjusted the propane tank on his shoulder, feeling his muscles bulge under the strain. *This* was why he worked out religiously, even on days he would've killed for an extra hour of sleep instead. In his job, that little bit of extra strength could mean the difference between life and death—his own or someone else's.

Soup moved as fast as he could, using his good arm to clear a new path around the burning debris. Following, Ian tried not to obsess about how the tank of explosive gas he was carrying was just a spark away from turning into a bomb. Smoke thickened around them as the flames leapt closer.

The barn was burning quickly, red and orange light smothered by the rolling black smoke. His boot caught on something, making him lurch forward and almost crash into Soup's back. The tank slid, threatening to overbalance him. As he heaved it back into position with a grunt, he squinted through the darkness. The barn had looked so small from the outside that he hadn't bothered to bring a hose with him to help them find their way back out. Ian was regretting that decision now.

"What's the problem, Soup?" Even to Ian's own ears, the strain in his voice was obvious.

"Just trying to find the shortest route to the door." He paused. "Or any route to the door."

"Need me to lead?"

"Nope. It's straight ahead." There was a pause before Soup spoke again, this time with a lot less confidence. "I think?"

"I'll lead." As Ian passed Soup, peering through the gloom, his heart pounded in his ears. Being in this barn—being in any structure fire like this—always made him understand why images of hell included fire. The blackness, cut only by eerie flickers of orange, the constant roaring, and, worst of all, the intense heat…everything combined easily brought to mind eternal torture.

A crash in front of them made Ian lurch to a halt, the tank sliding forward again. He caught it and shifted it back into place as his muscles groaned. The sound of splintering wood came again, loud enough to be heard over the fire's roar, and Ian craned his neck to look at the roof, expecting to see it falling on them. If something hit and damaged the tank… He quickly cut off that train of thought. There was nothing to be gained by allowing deadly scenarios to run through his brain. The only thing he could see above them was a heavy layer of smoke.

He refocused on the darkness in front of them and saw a glimmer of light fighting through the gloom.

"There!" Ian readjusted the tank on his shoulder before charging forward. After each smashing sound, the light got bigger, until it was almost the size of a doorway. A hulking figure, silhouetted by the light, filled the hole.

"Get your dawdling asses out of here *now*!" Steve's voice echoed through the radio speaker in his mask.

Relieved, Ian couldn't hold back a gasp of a laugh as he carried the tank toward the backlit, ax-swinging rescuer. "Hey," he complained. "You're her dad. If I can't swear, then you definitely can't."

"I'm a single father of four kids." Steve helped them through the improvised opening and away from the barn, giving Soup's cradled arm a concerned look before turning back to Ian. "If anyone deserves to swear, it's me. You need a hand with that?"

"I'm good," Ian said, although "good" might have been overstating it. Now that they were out of the burning barn, the pressure of the tank made him realize that his shoulder and back were screaming protests. Ignoring the discomfort, he carried the tank a safe distance and then went another twenty feet, just for good measure. As he lowered the tank to the ground, he couldn't hold back a grunt of effort.

Another gloved hand reached out and steadied the wobbling tank. "Nice job, Walsh," the chief said, clapping his free hand onto Ian's shoulder. Unfortunately, it was the shoulder that had carried the brunt of the weight. Ian swallowed a pained sound.

"Thanks." His voice was only slightly choppy. "Where do you need me?"

After a sharp look—as if checking his physical status—the chief gestured toward the tender truck. "Can you and Steve dump the water into the portable tank and then refill the tender? We might not need it, but I want to make sure not to leave any hot spots."

"That's a go, Chief." Ian jogged toward where Steve had already started setting up the portable tank. He scanned the scene until he saw Soup, standing next to the ambulance. Even from thirty feet away, it was pretty obvious that Soup was flirting with the EMT. With a huff of amusement, Ian refocused on the tank. Soup would be fine.

Hours later, after mopping up was done and they were absolutely positive no embers were left to flare to life after they'd gone, Ian straddled his motorcycle. All the strength seemed to have oozed out of his body, and he was trying to force his arm to lift and start his bike.

"Beauty!" Soup yelled from the passenger seat of the engine. "Leave that beast and hop aboard this lovely vehicle. It has an enclosed cab, a heater, me—everything your little heart could desire."

"It's supposed to snow. I don't want to leave it out all night."

Soup frowned in exaggerated confusion. "Why not? It's an old piece of junk."

Forcing himself not to react to Soup's goading, Ian kept his face expressionless. "It's not old. It's a classic. And it's not *junk*." Despite his best efforts, Ian heard his voice dropping to a growl on the last word.

"Why'd you ride it here anyway? Spring's still months away."

"It was nice earlier." It had been one of those rare, balmy days that hinted of warmer weather to come… right before winter slammed back into place. He'd been unable to resist a ride, just a short one to tide him over until spring arrived for real. Unfortunately, he'd been far away from the station when the fire call had come in, resulting in borrowed bunker gear and the prospect of a chilly ride home in the wee hours of the morning.

Obviously hearing Ian's irritation, Soup grinned.

"Fine. Freeze your ass off, Beauty. Just know I won't be bringing you any chicken soup when you get sick from riding that piece of crap in the snow."

"Don't call me that." Ian didn't know why he bothered protesting. The more he complained, the more the guys teased. "And no. I'll take my *vintage BMW work of art* home."

As soon as the engine rumbled down the drive, Ian started to regret his decision. No good wasting time mulling over it, though—he had miles of freezing highway to go before he was safe in bed. He pulled off his fire helmet and ran his hand through his hair, grimacing when he found it still damp with sweat.

"That bunker gear covering up your gang colors?" a snide voice interrupted, making Ian stiffen. Now he *really* wished he'd taken Soup up on his offer of a ride.

"Lawrence," Ian greeted the deputy, wanting, as usual, to wipe the smirk from the man's face with his fist. Suppressing the urge took a heroic level of restraint. "Run into any bison lately?"

Deputy Lawrence turned an unhealthy shade of purple that clashed with his reddish mustache. "I was responding to a call. A short response time is critical. People's *lives* depend on it. That crash wasn't my fault."

Although Ian tried to behave, he was tired, and his shoulder hurt from carrying the tank. Baiting the deputy was just too tempting. "It was a bison-in-the-road call. Didn't that give you a hint that there might be, I don't know, a large animal standing in the middle of the highway you were speeding down?"

Lawrence narrowed his eyes. "At least I'm not killing people and tossing their headless bodies into a reservoir."

Exhaustion forgotten, Ian stood abruptly, sending the deputy scurrying back a couple of steps. "Yeah," he said, straightening and crowding closer. "I heard there was some 'evidence' linking me to Willard Gray's murder. Tell me about that."

All color disappeared from Lawrence's face. "What? How did you… Who told you that? It was that bitch at the coffee shop, wasn't it? She twisted my words. I never—"

"Watch your mouth." He shifted forward, forcing Lawrence back another step. It had indeed been Lou who'd shared the information, but Ian wasn't about to let Lawrence know—or allow him to insult her. "The source doesn't matter. What matters are the details. Exactly what did you find in that reservoir?"

"I'm not telling you anything." Lawrence turned to leave but Ian shot out a hand and grabbed him. A quick glance around showed that the sheriff, fire chief, and the few deputies still milling around the scene weren't paying any attention to them.

"Yeah," Ian snarled, tightening his grip until he felt Lawrence flinch beneath the pressure. "You are. Let's start again. What did you find that made you think *I* was involved?"

"You're a member of a motorcycle gang," the deputy blustered, although his darting eyes gave away his nerves. "Killing is what you people do."

"No." Ian let his voice go silky smooth and felt Lawrence begin to shake. "There was something else. Some physical piece of so-called evidence. What was it?"

"You'll find out at your murder trial."

A small smile touched Ian's mouth, and Lawrence cringed. Sometimes, fear was stronger than a very real threat. Shifting his body, Ian let a fist swing toward the deputy's midsection, trusting fear to do his work for him.

Sure enough, before he could connect, Lawrence yelped, "Okay! Okay! I'll tell you."

Ian pulled the punch, barely touching the deputy's doughy belly. By the way Lawrence whimpered, it was as if Ian had pulled off his arm.

"It was your necklace," he wheezed.

"My necklace?" Ian repeated the unexpected words. Ever since Lou had informed him that the sheriff's office had found something linking his MC to the murder, he'd racked his brain, trying to figure out what it could be. He'd never considered that his lost pendant would come back to haunt him.

"Yes, your necklace, the one with your gang's symbol on it," Lawrence spat, regaining a little of his bravado when Ian let his fist drop to his side. "The chain was caught on the weight holding down the body. Everyone in town has seen you wearing that thing until you...*lost* it." The deputy's accusing gaze lowered to Ian's chain-free neck. "Maybe next time you kill an innocent man, don't drop any identifying jewelry at the crime scene."

Yanking free of Ian's grip, the deputy hurried away, heading toward the sheriff. Ian watched him, a small part of his brain wondering if Lawrence was getting reinforcements to return and arrest him for assault. The rest of his mind was running over this new information.

"Damn it," he growled under his breath. And damn *him*, for not trying harder to get that pendant back.

Lawrence was talking to Sheriff Rob Coughlin, and both men were looking at him. Although Ian was ninety percent sure that Rob, a stand-up guy, would take his side over Deputy Lawrence's, he figured they could chase him if they really wanted to drag him to jail. Besides, he needed to talk to Lou and Callum. Not only were they unofficially looking into Willard Gray's—the headless dead guy's—murder, but they were two people he knew for sure were on his side in this whole mess.

After donning his helmet, Ian started his bike. Despite everything—the murder investigation, his inconveniently missing pendant, his exhaustion and aching shoulder, the threatening snow—Ian felt a thrill at the familiar sound of the engine firing. He'd done that. He'd taken a broken-down bike and rebuilt it, giving it new life.

Too bad not everything was that simple to save.

With a final glance at the blackened ruin that had been a barn earlier that day, Ian roared off into the icy mountain night.

Chapter 1

If Zup didn't decide on the rifle within the next two minutes, Rory was going to shoot him.

Unfortunately, because he was the son of the local motorcycle club's president, killing him—or even just putting a hole where no hole had been before—would pretty much guarantee severe consequences. Since Rory was moderately content with her life at the moment, she'd rather not have it end abruptly. Drawing a long breath in through her nose and praying for patience, she employed her subpar salesmanship skills.

"What's the problem?"

Zup looked up from his scowling appraisal of the SUB 2000. "Maze said he had a Kel-Tec, and it jammed all the time."

"Tell Maze to quit using crap ammo." He just frowned at her. With another deep breath, she tried again. "These rifles are built to use common pistol magazines."

"I know." He held the rifle to his shoulder again. "That's why I want one. That, and it can fold in half, so it'd be small enough to carry around in a laptop case."

"Well, the recoil spring and bolt are heavier than in a pistol." With a great effort, she kept most of the condescension out of her voice. Rory hated having to explain things to people, especially guys like Zup, who just ignored her anyway. This was why she hadn't become a teacher. Well, that, and she'd most likely fail the background check—and probably the psych exam. "If you use poor quality rounds, you're going to get some failures."

Zup's frown turned from the rifle to her. "Maze loads all our ammo. Are you telling me he's fucking it up?"

"What I'm *saying*," she gritted through clenched teeth, "is that if you run good ammo through this rifle, it's going to be reliable."

After eyeing her suspiciously for a few seconds, he grunted and brought the stock to his shoulder again. He shifted his position several times as he peered through the sights, and then complained, "This steel pipe sucks as a cheek rest."

"That's it." She jumped off the counter where she'd been sitting and held out her hands. "Give it to me."

Instead, he turned away from her while tucking the rifle close to his chest. "Hang on," he told her. "I'm still deciding."

"No, I've decided for you." Rory flicked her fingers in a "gimme" gesture. There was a beep indicating someone had just come through the front door of her shop, and the last of her patience disappeared. "If you can't appreciate an accurate, dependable, *untraceable* Kel-Tec SUB 2000 because it's not *comfy* enough, then you don't deserve it. Hand it over."

Reluctantly, he relinquished the rifle. "I do want it. How much?"

"Nope. Too late." She pulled down on the trigger guard and swung the barrel assembly up and over the receiver, marveling at the ingenuity it took to completely redesign a rifle so it could fold in half. As she gently placed it into its case, she couldn't refrain from stroking her fingers over the gun's practical shape. It wasn't the most attractive of rifles, but it did its job. She'd take functional over pretty any day.

Zup watched the gun disappear. Although it was hard to tell under his bushy beard, she was pretty sure he was pouting. "Ro-ry…"

"What are you whining about now, Zup?" a low voice asked.

It took all her willpower not to look. If she glanced at Ian Walsh in all his dark, muscle-bound glory, she'd start stammering and blushing. Every time he walked into her store, his melty brown eyes focused on her, black hair mussed by his fireman's helmet or a motorcycle ride, those full, beautiful lips curving into a friendly smile, she marveled that this incredible person was in her life. They were just friends, of course, but she told herself that it was enough—more than she could expect, really. With his model-perfect features and body, he looked as if he should be attending photo shoots, not leaning on the wall behind the counter, chatting with plain, weird Rory Sorenson.

Plain, weird Rory Sorenson, who right now couldn't even look at him.

After that first breath-stealing moment when she first saw him, she could usually turn on casual-and-friendly mode, but not after the dream she'd had the night before—a dream that had featured her, Ian, his bike, and not many clothes. Her cheeks flamed at the memory. Keeping her gaze focused downward, she latched the case with more care than was required.

"Rory won't let me buy the Kel-Tec rifle I want."

Ian's amused snort almost brought her gaze to him,

but she resisted. "Maybe if you are a good boy and save all your paper route money, Rory will let you buy your toy."

"Fuck off, Walsh," Zup snarled, stomping into the front section of the shop. After a few seconds, the beep sounded again, indicating he'd left.

She wasn't about to open the concealed compartment where she kept her not-quite-legal inventory to put away the rifle with Ian watching. Once the shop was empty, she'd come back to stow the gun. But that meant that now, with the case latched, there was no avoiding looking at him. When Rory glanced up at Ian and saw he was grinning, showing off his single dimple, she mentally swore and clung to her impassive expression.

"What'd he do?" Ian asked, boosting himself onto a counter.

Memories of her dream flooded her mind. The back room was too small, too…intimate, for the two of them to be alone.

"Let's go," she said, flapping her hands to shoo him off his perch. "I need to be up front."

Ian didn't more. "Why? If someone comes in, the sensor will beep."

"Move." She scowled, irritated that she didn't have a good reason—or at least not one she could tell him.

"Fine." Hopping off the counter, he gestured for her to precede him. "And you never answered my question."

"Which one?" Although she would've preferred taking up the rear, it wasn't worth the argument. Instead, she just moved quickly, giving a silent sigh of relief when she could settle on a stool behind the cash register. Since the nearest chair was across the counter, she'd regain some of her much-needed personal space if he'd only sit in it.

The only problem was that Ian didn't take the chair but leaned against the wall next to her. "I asked what Zup did to get the boot."

"He whined and bitched and moaned until I couldn't take it anymore. He's lucky I just refused to sell him the rifle. I really wanted to shoot him."

Ian laughed, crossing his arms over his chest. "You know he'll just go running to Daddy and cry about how you were mean to him."

"I know," she said, ignoring the dual assault of bulging biceps and that stupid dimple with some effort. "Billy will come storming in here, demanding I sell Zup the gun. I'll put up a fight, but eventually give in, and charge Zup double what I would've if he hadn't been such a baby in the first place."

With another laugh, Ian pushed off the wall and began to prowl around the shop, peering into the glass display cases. "I can't believe it's been only a few years since Billy first came in here and got that Beretta for his old lady. Did you ever think you'd be this casual about a pissed-off Billy?"

"Casual's not really the right word." That had been Ian's first of many visits to the store—although not the first time they'd met. Three years ago, her parents had been gone only a couple of months, and everything from that time was a little hazy. The memory of Ian walking into the store, though—that was etched sharply on her mind. She pulled herself out of her thoughts when she realized Ian was looking at her curiously, as if waiting for her to elaborate. "That'd be dangerous, like getting too relaxed around a pet bear. No matter how friendly he acts, I always have to keep in mind what he's capable of."

His expression grew serious. "Good point. You're smart not to let your guard down around him—or any of the Riders."

"Even you?" Her attempt at friendly teasing came out awkward, as always, and she busied herself with smoothing the curled corner of a sticky note stuck to the counter.

"Even me." He didn't sound like he was joking. When she glanced at him, surprised, he quickly changed the subject. "So what do you have that's new and interesting?"

"Oh!" She jumped to her feet, hurrying toward the back. "You're going to love this. Hang on a second—I'll go grab it."

After retrieving the case she wanted and returning to the front, she set it on one of the counters and opened the lid.

"Check this out," she said.

Ian leaned closer to look. Instead of displaying the appropriate amount of awe, he laughed.

"It's so...little."

"That's the point." She picked up the tiny gun that measured just over two inches. "It's a SwissMiniGun. It's a functioning revolver."

"The latest trend in rodent control?" he teased, taking the gun from her and letting it rest in his palm. It looked even smaller in comparison.

"It's amazing," she huffed, although she couldn't completely stifle her laugh. "So intricate and so tiny."

"It actually works?"

"Yep." Taking the miniature revolver back from him, she placed it in one of the display cases. "It shoots .09 caliber bullets."

Ian shook his head. "You have everything in here."

"Pretty much." Rory eyed the placement of the tiny gun and moved it to a different area of the shelf. Then she closed and locked the case. "If I don't have it, I can probably get it. Speaking of that, did you need something, or did you just stop in to check out my new SwissMiniGun?"

Without warning, his easygoing expression hardened into a look she'd rarely seen on him. Her stomach twisted as she steeled herself for his request. She hated the high-risk orders. If she could have made a living off the front of the shop, she would've been happy to close the back room for good.

"I need information, actually," he said.

Rory stared at him. That…wasn't what she'd been expecting. "Okay," she said slowly. "About what?"

"Julius. Has he been in here recently?"

Propping a hip onto the stool behind the counter, she eyed him thoughtfully. "I don't like reporting on my customers—even to their own families. Maybe especially to their own families."

Ian grimaced. "I know. I don't like asking. But he's been acting squirrelly lately, ever since…" He swallowed, anguish peeking through before his expression smoothed into granite. "I need to know what kind of firepower he's tucking away."

"Ian. His wife died six weeks ago. Give him a little time." As soon as the words passed her lips, she felt like an insensitive idiot. Of course Ian knew exactly how long it had been since his own mother lost her long-fought battle with cancer.

When he stalked a few steps away from her, Rory thought for a moment that she'd offended him enough to make him follow Zup's example and slam out of the shop. Instead, he pivoted around and paced back to where she was half-perched on her stool. "I'm trying to keep him from doing something stupid while he's not thinking straight," he growled, scowling. "I took his key to the armory and cleared all the weapons out of his house."

"If he wants to kill himself," Rory warned, "he'll find a way to do it, no matter what you take away from him."

"I know that." His voice was a snap. "I'm just trying to make it hard enough that he'll have time to think about it first." Pinching the bridge of his nose, he squeezed his eyes closed for a moment. When they reopened, he looked calmer. "C'mon, Rory. Help me out here. I just need to get him through the next couple of months. With this whole pendant-and-murder thing, I just want one part of my life not to be dissolving into sh—I mean, crap."

She was silent for a second, unsure if she'd heard him correctly. "Murder?"

"Long story. One you'll hear as soon as I figure out what's going on. Right now, though, I'm more concerned with keeping Julius alive."

Frowning, she tapped her fingers on the counter. Her brain was still focused on the mention of murder. It wasn't something he could just throw into conversation and then ask her to forget. He seemed honestly tortured about Julius's mental state, though, so she decided not to press him for an explanation…for now, at least. "Fine. But just this once. I'm not going to become your informant about who's packing what."

Ian looked relieved as he echoed her words. "Just this once."

"Good." At his expectant look, she continued, "Julius has been in twice since January. The first time was three days after Suze died, and I told him to get his grieving butt out of here—nicer than that, of course." A little nicer, at least. "The second time was last week. He wanted a handgun, and he wasn't too choosy what kind. That raised all kinds of red flags, even more than were already up and flying. Before Suze got sick, Julius would come in here and talk guns for hours." She met Ian's somber eyes. By the look in them, she could tell she wasn't saying anything he hadn't already suspected. "I know he wouldn't pass the background check at any legitimate dealer, but I didn't want him to start hunting around for a private sale. So I told him I'd already special-ordered a Springfield 1911 TRP for him. He'd mentioned wanting one a while back. I said I'd requested a standard-length recoil spring guide and plug system instead of the two-piece, full-length guide, so it might take a little extra time to arrive. I figured I'd hide it in back for a few months after it got here, or at least until Julius showed up sober. And started showering again."

Ian was quiet for several seconds, his expression unreadable. When he suddenly strode toward her, she jerked in surprise, knocking the stool out from under her and almost falling. Ian caught her, pulling her into a fierce hug.

"Thanks, Rory."

All she could do was grunt in response, since shock and his tight grip had squeezed most of the air from her lungs.

"I'm trying to be there for him," Ian said, his breath warming the top of her head. "I really am, but it's hard. He's either drunk off his ass or won't leave his bedroom, and I have to keep reminding myself that he's just lost his wife. Sometimes I'm so tempted to shake him and tell him to quit acting like an idiot, but then I feel guilty for being impatient. But, Jesus, I just lost my mom. I can't lose anyone else." Rory felt a few strands of her hair flutter as he exhaled shakily. "Sorry. Don't mean to dump this on you."

His grip loosened, and he stepped back.

Once her arms were free to move again, she didn't know what to do with them. How were normal people supposed to act when their friends were obviously hurting? Should she give him a conciliatory pat? Rory mentally swore at her impaired social skills. She blamed isolation and home schooling—well, that and the fact that her parents had been full-blown nuts.

Instead of offering him any kind of sympathetic gesture, she settled for an awkward smile.

"It'll get easier," she babbled. "For Julius, I mean. Uh, and you too. It doesn't feel like it's going to at first, but it eventually does. After my parents—" She closed her mouth abruptly, appalled that she'd almost dumped a messy load of emotions on Ian Walsh, of all people. Sure, he was her friend, but he was also her perfect, gorgeous, unattainable, long-term crush, and he didn't need to know exactly how messed up she was.

"After your parents...?" Despite his nudge for her to finish her sentence, Rory pressed her lips together.

"Never mind." Her gaze darted around the shop as she wished desperately for someone to arrive. She'd even be happy if Billy came storming in with Zup in tow. "Did you need anything else?"

When he didn't answer right away, she risked a glance at his face and immediately wished she hadn't. He was looking at her in that way he sometimes did, like his X-ray vision could see all the way to her hidden, insecure, terrified depths. Rory quickly shifted her eyes to the glass beneath her tapping fingers. Seeing the SwissMiniGun nestled in the display case settled her. After Ian finally left, she decided, she would pull out the Glock 21 that had been brought in that morning for cleaning. The familiar process would be soothing.

"No." The belated answer to her question made her jump. "But since when did I need a reason to visit?"

"You don't. Of course you don't. I'm just..." She didn't know how to finish that sentence. She was what? Panicked? Clueless? Socially stupid? Silence stretched until it moved beyond awkward and into agonizing.

He still didn't leave.

"I have a Glock to clean, so..." Rory took a step toward the safety and comfort of the back room.

"Then I better get going." Moving slowly, reluctantly, Ian headed for the front door and then paused, looking over his shoulder at her. His smile was small and a little sad. "Thanks again."

She watched as the door swung shut behind him, her heart still beating just a little too fast.

To Rory's surprise, Billy hadn't arrived by closing time.

At ten minutes after six, she turned the key in the front-door lock. *Something to look forward to tomorrow*, she thought with a wry smile, twisting the dead bolts and placing the bar across the door. After setting the alarm and turning off all the lights except those she kept on for security, she moved to the back room. Grabbing her coat from the rack, she headed outside.

Rory immediately shivered and zipped her coat. The wind was tossing sharp BBs of snow around her three-acre patch of evergreens, rocks, and scrub. As she pulled a stocking hat from one of the voluminous pockets, she glanced around at the property. Everything seemed quiet, except for the wind and the hard pellets of snow pinging off her ten-foot chain-link boundary fence—topped, of course, by razor wire.

Over by the chicken coop, her German shepherd mix lifted his head. Heaving himself to his feet, he shook off the snow clinging to his fur and trotted over. Although he occasionally would hang out in the shop with her during the day, he preferred to stay outside and watch over "his" chickens, barking at any hawks that ventured too close.

"Hey, Jack." She rubbed his ears as he pressed his head into her hand with a low groan of delight. With a final pat, Rory headed around to the front of the shop. Jack followed her through the small gravel parking lot as she made her way to the front gates. Snow had settled into the tracks, and she kicked it free before pulling the gates together. Wrapping the chain around both where they met, she fastened the padlock.

Jack knew what came next, and he led the way back to the chicken coop. Dusk had fallen, and the last of the light was slipping away. Her hens had already abandoned the greenhouse and their expansive run for the warmth of the coop, so Rory just had to close and latch the door, keeping out any critters that might manage to circumvent the fences.

Returning to the back door with Jack close on her heels, she double-checked that the shop alarm was on. Rory removed her coat, shaking off the snow before hanging it on the coatrack. She jammed her hat back into her coat pocket and then engaged the dead bolts. Once her nightly routine was finally done, she moved over to a set of shelves lined with tools and cleaning equipment.

A hidden latch released a section of shelving, allowing it to swing toward her. Behind the shelving was a steel door, designed to resist forced entry. She entered the eight-digit code on the keypad next to the door, waited for the beep, and then pressed her thumb onto the biometric reader. When the light next to the screen glowed green, she used a key to manually open the lock. Each step was smooth, practiced—drilled into her by years of living in the bunker with her parents, before…

Well. *Before*.

The door swung open to reveal stairs descending into darkness. Brushing past her legs, Jack trotted down the steps. Rory hit the light switch before the steel door closed behind her. She heard the familiar and comforting solid *click* as it relocked. After engaging the manual deadlock, she followed Jack down the stairs.

When she reached the bottom, she automatically turned off the stair lights as she illuminated the living room. Her entire childhood, she'd been taught to conserve electricity whenever possible. Her photovoltaic and wind system was expansive now, and she had two back-up generators in case of system failure—or even just a stretch of cloudy, calm days—but saving power was second nature.

All of this was second nature.

Wandering over to her fridge, she frowned as she pulled out some leftover soup. Normally, she enjoyed this part of her day, when work was done, the animals were warm and safe, and she could unwind in the peace of her underground bunker. This evening, though, Rory felt unsettled.

She blamed Ian Walsh.

As she absently heated the soup on the stove, she thought back to how idiotically she'd acted with him at the shop. They'd been friends for years. Why was she still getting panicky and stupid in his presence? She was twenty-five, too old to keep hanging on to an adolescent crush.

But Ian was just... He was so...

Rory realized her hand not stirring the soup was rubbing her breastbone, as if to assuage the ache beneath it. She quickly lowered her arm to her side, hating how a visit from Ian left her raw, stripping away her usual contentment and leaving only loneliness in its place.

A steady beeping made her drop her spoon, splashing the broth over the side of the pan. Rory frowned as she turned off the burner and hurried over to the desk in the corner of the living room. There, the monitor displayed footage recorded by the security cameras scattered around her property.

When she'd taken over the gun shop three years ago, she'd had some trouble. For the first time in her life, she'd actually been grateful for her late parents' rampant paranoia. She'd even added on to the security system after the local militia group tried to break into the shop. A few flashbang grenades and a carefully placed rifle shot that had knocked their ringleader's weapon from his hand had sent the would-be burglars fleeing into the night. Although Rory sold guns to the militia members who'd sheepishly returned to her shop—this time as paying customers during regular business hours—she never forgot the lesson they'd taught her. She was young and small and female, and there were some who'd always see her as an easy mark sitting on a pile of guns.

A pile of guns they'd be only too happy to shoot her to get.

The alarm had been triggered at the front gate, so she pulled up the live feed from Camera Three. As she scanned the screen, a human-shaped shadow darted out of camera range. Inhaling sharply, she jerked back from the monitor. Despite her worries, she'd honestly thought she'd see a mule deer or a fox, not a person. Her heart pounded as she shifted to Camera Seven, which was aimed along the west boundary fence. She couldn't see anything except for grainy snowdrifts.

Reaching for the mouse, she rewound the video twenty seconds. Her knee bounced as adrenaline rushed through her. Although she was always prepared for the worst, she hadn't really expected it. Rory watched the playback with her nose almost touching the screen, but she still couldn't tell if the shadow was a person or just that—a shadow. Since the alarm had sounded, she decided to assume it was a person. Plus, her gut was screaming at her, telling her that someone was out there—someone looking for trouble.

Opening the desk drawer, she pulled out her baby, a Colt Python .357 Magnum revolver with a six-inch barrel. It was as accurate as Rory could aim, had a soft kick, and was just plain pretty, with its mirror-shined, stainless-steel finish. As soon as she wrapped her fingers around the grip, her nerves settled slightly. Jack watched her, his ears pricked and eyes alert.

"Let's see who came to visit," she said, surprised by her calm voice when her insides were all jittery. As she moved toward the stairs, Jack followed with an eager whine. She flicked off the lights in the living room but didn't turn on the stair light. Instead, she moved through the darkness. Even as her feet found their way with the ease of long familiarity, the utter blackness made her imagination go wild. All sorts of bogeymen hid in the lightless spaces around her, making her jump at the sound of her foot scuffing against a stair.

Despite the way her fingers itched to reach for a light switch, she kept her hands firmly at her sides. The front of the shop had glass blocks lining the tops of the walls to allow natural light to enter. Although she'd be opening the door in the enclosed back room, she didn't want to chance any light seeping out and alerting her intruder that she was on the move. Panic was her enemy. She needed to keep calm and do what she had to do with a clear head.

At the top of the stairs, she paused to check the monitor set to the left of the steel door. The screen was divided into four sections, each showing a different angle of the shop, front and back. Everything looked quiet, so she unfastened the dead bolt locks with shaking fingers and let herself into the back room, closing the steel door and pushing the camouflaging shelving back into place.

After disabling the alarm, she took a minute to slide into her coat and hat. Her aim wouldn't be improved if she was shivering with cold as well as nerves. She picked up a small flashlight from the shelf by the door and slid it into her left coat pocket before she unbolted the multiple locks on the back door and slipped outside, Jack close on her heels.

The wind slapped her immediately, peppering her exposed skin with sharp flecks of snow. She tucked her hands in her pockets, her right one still holding the Python, and her left fingers wrapped around the flashlight.

Instead of heading for the front gate, she followed the line of pine trees past the greenhouse and chicken coop, allowing the shadows to help hide her from any watchful eyes. Her footfalls were almost silent, except for the slightest crunch as her boots compressed the frozen snow, and her heartbeat was thudding in her ears. Deep, even breaths didn't help. As much as she didn't want to admit it, Rory was flat-out scared. She may have been prepared and well-armed, but she was just one person sitting on an arsenal every criminally minded group in the area would kill to get their hands on.

The waxing moon was almost at the halfway point, casting an eerie blue light that was reflected by the windblown drifts of snow. She circled around the pole barn that housed her vehicles but then hesitated, reluctant to leave the shelter of the trees for the more dubious cover of the wooden walls. Fifty feet separated the pole barn from the west fence line—fifty feet of exposure, fifty feet in which she'd present a clear target to anyone hiding in the trees beyond the fence.

Her fingers tightened around the grip of her revolver. She needed to *move*. She could imagine her father's disappointment if he were still alive, the impatient push he'd give her to break her paralysis. Shaking off all thoughts of militia snipers and fatal gunshot wounds, Rory forced herself into the open space surrounding the pole barn.

That first step was the hardest. Keeping her body low, she moved quickly but quietly, as she'd been taught, until she was standing in the narrow shadow cast by the pole barn. The darkness that pooled around the pines could easily hide someone—or multiple someones—from view. Rory waited, trying to be patient, her eyes trained on the line of trees. Nothing moved. Besides the wind, there was no sound. The human-shaped shadow in the camera feed started to feel more and more like a figment of her paranoid brain.

Her heart didn't agree, though. If anything, it beat even faster.

Rory glanced at Jack. He'd settled next to her, lying in the snowdrift like it was a cushy, warm dog bed. His pricked ears were cautious, but he didn't seem to be fixated on anything or anyone beyond the west fence. Still, she hesitated to leave her hiding place. But when an extra-cold, extra-strong gust of wind cut through her clothes to rake her skin, she shivered and stepped away from the pole barn.

She half-expected the crack of a firearm, but there was nothing. She moved quickly across the exposed section until she reached the fence. Feeling almost as vulnerable next to the fence as she had walking across the snowdrifts, Rory hurried toward the gate, her eyes constantly scanning her surroundings.

When she got close enough to see the padlock, her breath stalled. She jogged the final few steps to the gate for a closer look. Although it and the chain were intact, the lock had been flipped over to the other side, so it hung in the small crack between the gates. Frowning, Rory eyed the ground in front of the gate, but plowing, tire tracks, and a warming sun had reduced the snow on her drive to a patchy assortment of icy clumps. There was no way to leave boot prints in what remained.

Someone had tried to break into her home. Bile rose in her throat as she retraced her steps along the west fence. This time, she concentrated on the snowdrifts just beyond the boundary line, but there were no breaks in the even crust. Although she knew she should open the gate and explore the area beyond her fence for evidence that someone had been there, her caution overruled her curiosity. She circled around the pole barn to her line of pine trees, instead.

Her feet kept wanting to run, but she kept her pace even and deliberate, thanks to relentless childhood drills. Her gaze moved constantly, her head turning so she could catch any threat before it jumped out at her. But when the shop door grew closer, she let out a silent exhale of relief. As she took another step toward home, she heard it—the muffled sound of snow falling…or being knocked…from an evergreen bough.

She whirled, pulling her Python from her pocket as she crouched behind the closest concealment—a squatty pine tree. Peering through the branches frantically, she tried to get a glimpse of whoever was approaching. Between her pounding heart and her rapid, shallow breaths, she couldn't hear anything else, and frustration at her inability to stay calm vied with fear.

Movement at the edge of her peripheral vision brought her head and her gun around to focus on the oncoming threat. A low-lying shadow shifted, morphing into the shape of her dog.

Her breath came out in an audible whoosh. She didn't return her revolver to her pocket, though. Instead, she kept it out and ready until she and Jack were inside the shop, and the back door was closed and locked.

Only after she was inside her underground bunker-home, all locks secured and alarms set, did she reluctantly place the Python in its drawer. Rory would've liked to hang on to the gun, since her nerves steadied when her fingers clutched the familiar grip. She kept reminding herself that she was safe in her home. No one could get through the steel door at the top of the stairs.

Still, with the gun tucked in its drawer, she felt a little naked, her fingers twitchy without something to hold. She turned the burner on under the now-cool soup, making a face. Her fruitless walk around the property had not reassured her. Something had set off the alarm, and the lock hadn't moved on its own. Not knowing what—or who—had triggered the motion sensor made her stomach jumpy and destroyed any trace of hunger.

Once the soup was hot, she forced herself to eat it, despite her clamped-down belly. Ingrained childhood lessons stuck with her, even though her parents had been dead for three years now. Part of being prepared was keeping her body rested, fed, and strong, so she'd be ready for whatever came next. A nervous stomach was no excuse not to nourish her body.

Once she was halfway through a bowl, though, even those hammered-in lessons couldn't keep her eating, and she gave the rest of her soup to Jack. After measuring out his nightly ration of dog food and dumping it in his bowl, she tried to get lost in the thriller she was currently reading.

Within twenty minutes of reading and rereading the same two sentences, she gave up and tossed the book onto the end table. She lasted another five minutes before she hurried over to the desk and pulled out the Python.

Returning to the couch, she held the revolver and let her mind bounce from scenario to scenario. It wasn't helpful, she knew that, but she still couldn't stop. When her eyelids started to droop, she carried the handgun into her bedroom.

The Python stayed on her bedside table that night. Before she drifted to sleep, she gave a humorless smile. Some little girls had teddy bears. Growing up, she'd learned to find her comfort in weapons.

A psychologist would have a field day with her.

Chapter 2

Rory narrowed her eyes at Billy. Despite his MC president's patch and the scar that spread like a sunburst over his left eyebrow, the guy looked a lot like Santa. His hair and full beard were white, and his middle had settled into a definite gut. He should've appeared harmless...but he didn't. There was nothing harmless about Billy.

"Any idea who was lurking around my place last night?" Rory asked, watching carefully for his reaction. Her hands were sweating, but she was happy that none of her nerves about confronting Billy were evident in her voice.

Billy's face showed nothing except for irritation. "No."

"How about you?" Her gaze turned to Zup, who was standing just behind and to the side of his father.

"No." He sounded sulky, but Rory didn't see any signs of guilt or evasion.

"What the fuck are you talking about?" the third man, Rave, demanded. "*You're* the princess bitch, jerking Zup around, telling him you'll sell him the rifle, and then deciding you won't. Now you're accusing us of stalking you or some shit—" He broke off when Billy lifted his hand without looking at Rave.

"She asked, and we answered. It's done." Billy raised his bushy white eyebrows, but the stiff scar tissue on the left side didn't allow his skin to wrinkle. It looked as if he'd had Botox injections in only half his forehead. The flatness this lent to his expressions added to the feeling of menace radiating from him. "What's not done is the situation with the rifle."

Rory crossed her arms and propped a hip on her stool, feigning confidence. She'd dealt with the MC long enough to know it was best not to let them know they could get to her. "I gave Zup a considerable amount of time to make up his mind on whether he wanted the Kel-Tec or not. When he couldn't decide on his own, I made an executive decision."

Turning his frown on his son, Billy demanded, "What was the problem? I told you to come here, take a look at the SUB 2000, and then buy it if it was in decent shape. Kel-Tec guns are a pain in the ass to find—plus this one is a ghost. Was it defective? Did Rory ask too much for it? What kind of fucking decisions did you have to make?"

Zup flushed and lowered his gaze, appearing to drop a decade in age as he muttered at the floor. "It's just… fuckin' ugly."

The irreverent part of Rory's brain, the part that wasn't occupied with the almost unbearable tension that came from being trapped in a room with three pissed-off Liverton Riders, waited for him to mention how the pipe wasn't comfortable on his cheek. He must've had a tiny bit of sense, though, since he stayed quiet after that.

"What the hell?" Billy reached up and smacked Zup across the back of the head, ignoring the fact that his son had four inches and fifty pounds on him. "Ugly? Since when do we give a shit if something is pretty? If we did, your ass wouldn't be in the club, would it?"

Casting his son a final glower, Billy turned to Rory. “Well, show me this ‘ugly’ rifle, then.”

With a tip of her head, indicating that they should follow her, she led the way into the back room. The back of her neck prickled as her instincts screamed for her to *never* turn her back on those men, but she had to do it to show them they didn’t intimidate her.

Since she’d been expecting Billy and company to show that morning, she’d already taken the Kel-Tec rifle, still snug in its case, out of the hidden compartment in the top of the cabinet where she kept the less-legal merchandise. It was sitting on top of the table where she cleaned firearms. Walking over to the rifle, she unlatched the case and opened it, turning it toward Billy as if she were showing off precious jewelry.

Giving a satisfied nod, Billy picked up the rifle and unfolded it, running experienced hands over the gun. “How much?”

“If it were a normal SUB 2000, I’d say five,” she said. Her stomach twisted again as she spoke. Rory always hated bargaining, especially with Billy. She just wanted the sale to be done and these three hard-eyed men out of her store. She should’ve just sold the gun to Zup in the first place, but she’d let irritation win. “Since it’s untraceable, let’s go with twelve.”

“Eight.”

“One thousand.”

“Done, if you throw in two boxes of ammo.”

“One box.”

“Fine.” He twisted his head so he could glare at Zup, who was leaning against the wall next to the door. His expression hadn’t changed. “See how simple that was? Now Rory has the cash, and we have the rifle. Easy-fucking-peasy."

Zup didn't answer. He just glared at the gun.

"I don't know why we keep dealing with this temperamental bitch," Rave grumbled, as if Rory wasn't even in the room.

"Feel free to shop at Walmart instead," she shot back. Her nerves were stretched almost to the breaking point, which made her snappy.

"Better just to take you out," Rave said so flatly, so matter-of-factly, that Rory knew he could kill her with little remorse.

"I said that's enough!" Billy barked. "Rory's not the problem. If my son had pulled his head out of his ass when he was here yesterday, this wouldn't have been a fucking issue."

Zup slammed out of the back room, followed closely by Rave. As they left, Billy tucked the rifle back in its case, apparently unbothered by the other men's anger.

"Like two hormonal teenage girls," he grumbled, but then grinned at her. Somehow, that friendly smile just made him all the more unsettling. "Have anything else worth checking out back here?"

"I just got a SwissMiniGun," she told him, the thought of her new acquisition making her relax slightly. "It's up front."

His smile faded into a grumpy pout. The resemblance between father and son was suddenly striking. "One of those tiny things? Why would I want to see that?"

"Because it's an engineering marvel." When he continued to frown at her, Rory snorted. "Why do guys only like the big stuff?"

"Overcompensation," he said, straight-faced.

She forgot how dangerous Billy was for just a few seconds as she laughed.

"I want the little one," the woman whined, pointing at the Phoenix HP22A while tugging on Phil's arm with her other hand. "It's cute."

Phil winced slightly. "You need something with more stopping power than a .22. A .38 at the minimum. Better to go with a nine millimeter."

His latest fling was obviously not listening. "Do you have anything with some bling? Something flashy, with crystals, maybe?" she asked Rory, who suppressed a grimace with enormous effort. It wasn't as if she wasn't used to this. Phil, one of the rescue dive-team members, dragged his latest infatuation into her shop every couple of months, and he definitely had a type—blond, stacked, and high-maintenance.

"No." Rory couldn't hold still anymore. She gave up her position perched on her stool and paced behind the counter. Phil was a great customer, but after spending the past half hour dealing with his newest girlfriend, Rory's patience was fraying.

Phil gave her an apologetic look and tried to tug the blond woman away from the "cute" gun that had caught her fancy. "Maybe a Glock 17," he suggested, not for the first time.

She pulled the same face she'd made when he'd first pointed it out to her. "It's so plain and…masculine looking. I want something with a little more flair."

"There's nothing with flair here," Rory said flatly,

ignoring Phil's pleading look. After a sleepless night and dealing with Billy, Zup, and Rave that morning, Rory was quickly reaching the end of her rope.

"Do you have a restroom?" the woman asked, and Rory wordlessly pointed to the door clearly marked "restroom" in the corner.

Phil's girlfriend giggled. "Oh! There it is!" She headed toward it, taking small steps in her four-inch heels. Rory wasn't sure how she'd made it across the gravel parking lot in those shoes. Maybe Phil carried her.

As soon as the door to the bathroom closed behind her, Rory turned her glare on Phil.

"I know! I know!" he said in a hushed voice, his hands raised defensively. "She's really sweet, though."

"Phil," Rory said between gritted teeth, "I don't care who you date. I don't care that she's the fiftieth blond clone you've dragged in here. If that's who you want to be with, more power to you. But you need to quit *arming* these women!"

"She needs to know how to protect herself," he protested, his voice still quiet as he kept one eye on the closed restroom door.

Rory took a calming breath. "Phil. I'm all for everyone understanding how to handle and shoot guns. If I thought for one second she would take that cute, blinged-out pistol to the range, treat it responsibly, and become a competent shot, that's one thing. But it's a whole 'nother ball of wax if she walks around with a loaded gun in her purse and has no clue how to use it. She thinks it's a fashion accessory!"

"I'll teach her." Phil was so earnest it was almost painful to look at him. "She can use that shooting range down the road from the station, and I'll give her tips and..." He trailed off, hope fading from his expression. "She'll never do that, will she?"

Shaking her head, Rory reached over the counter to give his slumped shoulder a quick pat. "You need to either appreciate these women for who they are, or date someone who enjoys the same things you do. Quit trying to change them into NRA Barbies, for God's sake."

Although he nodded, she fully expected he'd return in a couple of months with a new trophy woman looking for a bedazzled handgun.

The front door flew open just as Phil's girlfriend emerged from the bathroom. As soon as Rory saw the blond's predatory expression, she knew who'd arrived, even before Ian started bellowing.

"What the fuck, Ror?" He charged behind the counter and caught her shoulders, eyeing her up and down as if checking for damage. "Billy said someone broke in here last night?"

"Ian. Customers."

When Ian glanced at the couple watching their interplay with keen interest, Phil's girlfriend gave him a flirty wave. Without responding or reacting in any way, he turned back to Rory. "It's not customers. It's just Phil. Tell me what happened."

"And I thought *I* was supposed to be the rude one," Rory muttered, glancing at Phil. He, thankfully, looked more amused than anything, although his girlfriend appeared miffed at Ian's blow-off.

"Rory." He gave her a small shake. "Details. Now."

"Ian." Grabbing his wrists, she pried them off her

shoulders and brought them back to his sides. "Stop trying to bruise my brain. It's none of your business."

He actually growled.

"We'll just be going, then," Phil said, ushering his girlfriend toward the door. "See you at the station, Ian."

"I thought you were going to buy me a gun," the blond protested.

"You heard the owner," Phil said, glancing over his shoulder as he opened the door and shooting Rory a wink. "There's nothing with flair here."

His girlfriend's response was lost as the door closed behind them.

Ignoring Phil's farewell and the pair's departure, Ian leveled an impassive stare at Rory. "At least tell me if you were hurt."

"No. I'm fine." She crossed her arms over her chest. The events of the previous night had pushed her sexy Ian dream to the back of her mind where it belonged. It was a relief to be able to talk normally to him again. "Whoever it was didn't get past the front gate."

That seemed to calm him down a little, although a muscle in his cheek was still twitching with tension. "Good. Any idea who it was?"

"My main people of interest, Billy and Zup, denied it, so no."

Ian began pacing. "I don't like it. First someone dumped that body in Mission Reservoir, and then Lou's stalker burned her cabin and tried to kill Callum. And now someone's lurking around your compound? Seriously bad sh—uh, stuff keeps happening around here."

"The stalker is dead, though," Rory said, attempting to make her tone soothing, but probably failing miserably.

She'd never been very good at soothing. "Wasn't he an ex-boyfriend of hers from back East? That has nothing to do with someone testing the lock on my gate."

He came to a stop and folded his arms across his chest, mirroring her stance. "I still don't like you being out here by yourself."

She couldn't hold back a laugh as she swung an arm, indicating the shop and all its contents. "Right. Me, by myself, with hundreds of guns, knives, and other weapons. I think I'll be all right."

His gaze swept over the store, but he didn't look any happier. "I wish you'd tell me where your apartment is. We're friends. I should know where you live."

"You do know where I live."

"I have a general idea. Friends should know *specifically* where their friends live. There are only two doors in the back room—that one," he pointed to the opening between the front and back rooms, "and one that leads outside. Do you stay in the pole barn? In some pit you dug under the chicken coop?"

"No." Her stomach jumped at the idea of anyone but her or her parents knowing about the underground bunker. That had been the first rule drilled into her head as a child: trust no one, not even friends. Not that she'd been allowed to have friends until her parents were gone.

Not that she had any friends besides Ian.

Trying to hide her panic, she turned the conversation toward him. "What's with you, anyway? Why'd you come blasting in here, all crazed just because I had a wannabe trespasser?"

He eyed her for a long moment, and she was worried that her distraction hadn't worked. After a long silence, he finally spoke—although about a completely random topic. "I remember seeing you for the first time at the grocery store when we were kids."

That first meeting had been seared into her brain for over a decade. "It was my birthday."

He smiled. "You were just a tiny thing, like ten or something, and you were staring at this bakery display with huge eyes. From the look on your face, you'd have thought those cakes were magical."

Rory started to smile. "My parents hated going to the store. Everything we ate or wore was either homemade or grown or raised or traded with a neighbor. My mom loved Colorado peaches, though, and Harry, the guy who usually had the roadside stand—remember him?" Ian nodded. "He never showed up that day, but the grocery store was carrying those peaches. My mom's code of ethics didn't hold up to her craving. It was the first time I remember being in there, and those princess birthday cakes were so pretty. I asked my mom for one, and she acted like I'd asked for a sealskin coat lined with the fur of innocent puppies. Instead of a cake, I got a lecture on corporate greed and rampant consumerism. I didn't care about any of that, though. I just really, really wanted a pink-and-white cake for my birthday."

He laughed. "I could tell."

"I saw you watching," she admitted, remembering noticing that beautiful boy and being so ashamed. She'd been the weird, oddly dressed kid, and he'd been gorgeous, even as a gawky fourteen-year-old. "And then, in the parking lot..."

With a bashful shrug that looked strange on him, he said, "I wanted to get you a big cake, but I didn't have enough money. I'd just bought a part for a bike Julius was helping me fix up."

"The cupcake was perfect."

It had been. She remembered every second of that encounter, from him touching her arm while her mother was talking to a neighbor, to the detail of the pink and white frosting hearts on the cupcake in his hand. He'd held it out to her with an awkward, "Happy Birthday." As soon as she'd accepted it, he'd hurried away, leaving her staring at his departing back. That was the start of a thirteen-year crush.

"I was older than ten, though," she said, shaking off the nostalgia that wanted to cling. "I'd just turned twelve."

"Even as a kid, you were so pretty." Reaching over, he caught a few pieces of her hair between his fingers, running the full length of the strands until they slipped out of his hand and dropped across her shoulder. "Still are."

She'd been too shocked to move away from his touch, and now she could only stare at him, not sure what to say. Rory had always figured she was attractive enough, but nothing special—straight, light brown hair and muted blue eyes. The way Ian was looking at her, though, made her feel more than just average. Much more.

But...what was he doing? What was he trying to say?

And what the *hell* had brought it on? The attempted break-in? Something else? Rory was barely equipped to deal with Ian on normal days. She had no idea how to respond to the look in his eyes.

"Ever since that first time I saw you, I've tried to get your attention." The twist of his mouth was wry. "Never had much luck with that. Hell—heck, even that cupcake held your interest more than I did."

Her mouth was open, but no words emerged. Rory couldn't wrap her head around the idea that gorgeous Ian Walsh, whom she'd crushed on forever, was seriously attracted to her. Sure, he'd flirted, but she assumed that was just his way. He was perfection, and she was just average—and weirdly hermitlike, to boot. Now, though, he was calling her pretty, touching her hair, and acting like someone who was interested—*romantically* interested.

As it started to sink into her brain, she closed her mouth and frowned.

"What does *that* look"—his finger made a circle in the air, indicating her face—"mean?"

She shifted back a step, stopping only because she bumped into the counter. "It means that I have a lot going on here. The shop, the back room"—she gave him a meaningful look—"dealing with certain customers—*including* your family."

"Yeah? So?" His forehead was still wrinkled in confusion.

"So, you split your time between hanging out with criminals and working with cops."

Ian leaned against the wall and crossed his arms. "I wouldn't drag you into anything. Besides, the Riders aren't involved in anything illegal—anything serious, at least."

"Ian. Billy just walked out of here with an untraceable rifle. Is that so he can use that gun for hunting, to keep the mule deer's family from tracking him down and getting revenge on him for shooting their loved one?"

"You just sold it to him!" His voice rose.

"*I know.*" Tucking her hands into the back pockets of her jeans, she moved her gaze around the shop, focusing on anything except the man standing a few feet away from her. "That's my point. Most of the money I make is in there." Rory jerked her head at the door to the back room. "I don't want to get in any deeper than I already am. And I definitely don't want to attract any attention from law enforcement. Right now, the cops pretty much leave me alone. I'd like that to continue."

As he stared at her, his expression changed to something closer to thoughtfulness.

"What?" she finally snapped, not able to take the charged silence for another minute.

"I just realized you're full of shit—er, baloney."

"Excuse me?"

"I've been trying to figure it out. You're nervous about us getting together," he said, watching her closely—too closely for comfort. "But it's not because of what I do. It's not Fire, and it's not the Riders."

Making a scoffing noise, she pulled her hands out of her pockets and went to move past him. "I have work to do. If you want to stand here and play gun-shop psychologist, have at it."

He caught her arm, turning her to face him. Meeting his eyes with a defiant gaze, she tried to ignore the way her heart was thudding in double time. It wasn't from fear—which made it so much scarier.

"In the three years we've been friends, haven't you ever wanted to be more?"

Yes! The answer echoed in her brain so loudly that she worried for a second she'd actually shouted it. The images from the other night's dream replayed in her head, heating her cheeks—and other body parts, as well. For an instant, she allowed herself to consider it. Could she and Ian actually be a possibility? Then Rory imagined walking through Simpson while the locals whispered and laughed behind their hands, wondering what the crazy gun-shop lady was doing with the motorcycle-riding, lifesaving picture-of-beauty that was Ian Walsh.

Her nerves quickly smothered that spark of hope. It was ridiculous to even consider that she was good enough for Ian. Firmly squashing her secret thirteen-year-old dreams, she tugged her arm free of his gentle grip. Her expression must have given her away, though, because his eyes lit.

"Ror," he said softly, hopefully, taking a step closer. "You do want me."

"No." It sounded weak, even to Rory's own ears.

"You do." His voice was certain. "I know you're scared, though."

"I'm not scared," she snapped.

"We'll take it slow," he assured her, ignoring her obvious lie. "As much time as you need. I can wait." His laugh was short but happy. "I'm good at waiting."

She didn't know how to respond, so she didn't. Averting her eyes, she hurried toward the back room, keeping her gaze focused strictly in front of her. If she looked at him, she'd waver. Just a conversation with him yesterday had made her restless and unsettled. Ian Walsh had the power to completely dismantle her safe life if she let him.

As she closed the back-room door behind her, Rory turned and let her forehead press against the cool metal. It felt good on her flushed face.

She knew perfectly well that he could make her miserable, so why did she feel like she'd just made a mistake by walking away?

Chapter 3

When the alarm started beeping for the fourth night in a row, Rory swore vehemently enough to startle the dog. Stomping over to the desk, she grabbed her revolver and headed for the stairs. Her precautions stayed the same as the previous three nights, though—no light on the stairs, checking the shop cameras before opening the steel door, staying in the cover of the trees. Although she wasn't sure what the trespasser's endgame was, she couldn't allow repetition to dull her response. The intruder's plan could be to make it routine so Rory would start to disregard the alarm, or at least lower her guard while checking the perimeter. She couldn't allow that to happen.

It was a nasty night, too. The wind whipped the snow that had fallen that morning into blinding clouds, ruining her visibility and stinging her face. As she walked the west fence line, she peered into the neighboring trees, blinking the flying ice crystals from her eyes.

Rory had been tempted to wear her night-vision goggles, but it was too easy for someone to temporarily blind her with a flash of light. Although she'd regain her vision in a short time, that might be too late. She'd keep her unenhanced night vision, as poor as it was with the cloudy sky and blowing snow.

It was also hard to hear anything besides the howling of the wind. Rory didn't like having her two main senses so impaired. It made her feel exposed and vulnerable. As she approached the gate, Jack loping ahead, the trees on the other side of the fence thinned. A dark form darted across an open space between the shadows of two trees, making her suck in a breath.

Rory had dropped to a crouch, her Python out and aimed, before she even realized what she'd glimpsed. She strained to see, staring so hard at the spot where she'd last caught the shape that her eyes stung. There was no more movement, though.

Staying low, her eyes on the trees, she retreated ten feet to one of the several blinds she'd constructed the day before. Although the wooden shield wouldn't offer cover from gunfire, it would provide some concealment. Something moved next to the first tree. Her heart hammering, she aimed her revolver through an opening in the blind at the shifting dark shape. Her breath escaped in a long, silent exhale of relief when she realized it was just a pine tree branch bowing in the wind.

Peering through one of the peepholes, she watched the trees for a long time. When she finally accepted that the intruder had either slipped away without her seeing or had frozen to death, she stood, her muscles protesting the movement.

As she headed toward the gate, Rory tried to move quickly, but her cold-locked joints made her hobble. Sweeping her gaze from left to right and back again, she hurried as best she could to the gates to check the padlock. As she tugged on the steel loop, the material of her glove snagged on something.

She kept her eyes moving, conscious of her surroundings as she felt in her coat pocket for her flashlight.

Cupping her hand over the front to block the light, she pushed the button on the end to turn it on. Allowing just a sliver of light to peek through her fingers, she quickly glanced down at the light before returning her gaze to the area beyond the gate.

There were two grooves on either side of the steel loop, as if someone had pressed down with a heavy-duty bolt cutter. The lock was still secure, but seeing the evidence that the intruder had tried to get through her gates made her flush with anger and her stomach knot with fear.

With her attention still focused on the area beyond the gates, Rory hurried into her shop, returning to the gates with three additional chains and locks. After securing all of the extra chains, she gave the surrounding space a final once-over before retracing her steps to her door.

For the first time in her life, however, her bunker didn't feel secure. Rory spent the night with her eyes glued to the security camera monitor, hardly allowing herself to blink.

The next morning, she regretted her sleepless night. Rory stared at the paperwork in front of her, but no amount of blinking could keep the print from blurring. Giving in, she folded her arms on the counter and let her head sink down to rest on them.

"Rough night?"

She sat up abruptly and had to catch herself before she toppled off her stool. Ian was standing by the front door, smirking at her. Despite herself, her first feeling was relief. After she'd run away from him, she figured he'd give up on her—and as nervous as the thought of *more* made her, she couldn't bear the idea of losing his friendship. Her next thought was panic that he'd gotten into the store without her hearing the alarm.

Logic pushed aside the last of her sleepiness, and she felt silly as common sense took hold. With a shake of her head, she tried to slow her pounding pulse. The front-door sensor sounded only in the back room. When it was installed, she'd assumed that she wouldn't need the sensor in the front room, since she'd actually hear and see the person walking into the shop.

"Not a rough night?" Ian must have taken her *I'm an idiot* head shake as an answer to his question.

"No. I mean, yes." She rubbed a hand over her face, surreptitiously checking for any nap drool on her chin. "Never mind. What did you need?"

"Just wanted to check on you." Moving behind the counter, Ian took his usual position leaning against the wall. She swiveled around on her stool until she was facing him. "Any more trouble with your trespasser?"

Her yawn turned into a grimace. "Every night." When Ian's face went hard, she immediately regretted her words. "The deer cameras I ordered should be arriving today, though. Hopefully, I'll get a shot of this guy's face tonight. I've come to the realization that my security cameras are crap."

"Rory." The news about the deer cameras didn't lighten his scowl. "Has he—or they—gotten in your fence?"

"No. They tried to cut the lock on the front gates last night, though."

He eyed her face closely. "How long's it been since you've slept?"

"A while." She bit off another yawn. Despite her

initial joy at seeing Ian, now she kind of wished he'd leave so she could take a nap.

"You're staying at my place tonight."

"No. I'm not leaving my shop and all my inventory so whoever it is can go nuts at the gun buffet. I need to be here."

He obviously didn't like that. "I'll stay here, then."

"No." She rejected the idea immediately as panic coiled in her belly.

"Why not?"

"Because." Rory couldn't give him a reasonable answer, because her feelings weren't reasonable. If she tried to explain, she'd just end up sounding as loony as her parents had been. She didn't want Ian to see her like that.

A smile curled up one corner of his mouth. "What if I promise to behave?" Ian practically purred.

The suggestiveness in his voice threw her off balance and woke a whole herd of butterflies in her belly. Images of Ian in her home—in her bedroom!—flashed through her mind, and she opened her mouth and then closed it again. It was hard enough to banter with a sexily smiling Ian on a good day, much less when she'd been functioning on little to no sleep for the past four nights.

Ian's grin broadened. "I'll come over around six, then."

"No."

"Earlier? I can probably get here around five thirty."

Rory pressed the heels of her hands against her eyes. "No. No sleepover." The word "sleepover" brought up all the tempting mental pictures again. She sighed. *Stupid brain.*

"I'll pull up to your gate and spend the night in my truck, then."

"Ian…" Lowering her forehead, she hid her face in the safe darkness of her folded arms. Her breath created a layer of condensation on the countertop. "Why can't you just let me handle this by myself, like I've handled everything else in my life?"

He touched her upper back, the heat from his palm soaking into her spine. "Why can't you let me help?"

Any physical contact was rare in her life, especially after her parents had died. The weight and warmth of his hand made her stomach clench with longing. How was she supposed to argue when he touched her like that?

"Please, Ian." Even to her own ears, she sounded tired, defeated almost. "Give me one more night to figure out who it is."

He went still, then sighed. "Fine. One more night. After that, though, if they're still coming around, you'll just have to call me your roomie. I'm not going to stand by and watch you get hurt."

She couldn't find any words. His protectiveness warmed her even as her instinctual response to him scared her silly. All she managed to do was groan.

Melvin, the UPS driver, brought the deer cameras just before noon. As soon as he drove away, she grabbed her toolbox, coat, and a ladder, and headed for the front entrance.

After closing the gates, she set up two cameras along the top, pointing them down at different angles. To test the position, she stood in front of the gate and held her hand approximately six inches above her head. It might've been a sexist assumption, but she was fairly sure her intruder had been a man. Grabbing the memory stick after the cameras took several pictures, she hurried inside to download the contents onto the shop computer.

The camera on the left side needed a slight adjustment. After that, the second round of pictures were clear shots with her hand centered in the frames. The second pair of cameras went in two spots on her west fence, pointed into the trees.

Only one customer, George Holloway, interrupted her installation, but he just wanted to pick up the laser sights she'd special ordered for him. To her relief, he was his usual taciturn self and didn't want to hang around to chat. Usually, Rory didn't mind talking with her customers, but she wanted to get the cameras set up before dark. The threat of Ian Walsh invading her bunker hung over her head, providing even more motivation to figure out who the trespasser was that night.

By the time she'd finished hanging and checking the cameras, it was late afternoon. The light was fading, and the cameras flashed with each test shot. Rory was happy with them, though—the resolution was great and the pictures crisp.

Giving them one final, satisfied look, she headed for the coop to tuck in the chickens for the night. Jack ran ahead, his tail swinging. That afternoon, he'd been torn between his responsibilities, trotting back and forth between Rory's ladder and the poultry, his ears flat with anxiety. Now, with his feathered charges safely perched in the coop, he relaxed and bounded through the snow.

Rory smiled as she watched him play. Although exhaustion still pulled at her, she felt a little more relaxed with the cameras in place. Just one more night, and, with any luck, she'd have a face to put on the shadowy figure she'd seen in the woods. The intruder obviously knew where her security cameras were; he'd avoided them since that first night. Plus, anything out of the limited area illuminated by the lights at the gate blended into the night. With the deer cameras, by the time the flash went off and the trespasser realized his picture had been taken, it'd be too late for him to prevent it.

With a surge of renewed energy, she bounced through the new drifts left by the previous night's winds. Now all she had to do was wait for him to show.

The alarm never sounded that night.

Although Rory was disappointed that her trespasser didn't get caught on camera, the uninterrupted night did allow her to snatch a few hours of sleep. When she checked them in the morning, the memory cards were blank, except for a few pictures of a passing coyote.

She was still frowning at the computer screen when Belly Leopold, the Field County Coroner, shoved open the front door and clomped inside the shop. Rory swiveled her stool around to face Belly, amazed at how much racket the tiny woman could make when she moved.

"I'm doing it," Belly said as she stomped over to Rory and leaned on the counter.

"The Ethos?"

"Yes. I need a new shotgun like I need another hole in my head, but I can't stop thinking about it." She scowled. "It's just so darn comfortable to shoot."

Belly's disgruntled look made Rory want to smile. "That it is. Benelli really managed to soften up the recoil on that gun. Do you want the plain black or engraved silver receiver?"

"Since when have I ever wanted my guns fancy?" Belly demanded.

Amused, Rory held up her hands. "Okay! Plain black receiver it is, then. Just for the record, though, there's nothing wrong with liking shiny things."

Belly made a rude noise before changing the subject. "Nice shot."

Since her brain was focused on guns, Belly's comment confused her until the other woman pointed toward the coyote's photo still displayed on the computer screen.

"Oh!" Rory said. "Right. It wasn't the predator I was hoping to photograph, but it is a pretty nice wildlife picture, isn't it?"

"Were you hoping to catch a mugshot of whoever's been lurking around here?"

Rory stared at the coroner, frowning. "How did you know?"

"Please." Belly rolled her eyes. "First off, this is Simpson. Everyone knows everything. And second, I'm me. And I know even more about everything than the average Simpson resident."

Blowing out a frustrated breath, Rory leaned back on her stool and rubbed her eyes. "I've lived here all my life. Why am I surprised to find out that everyone's in my business?"

"Because," Belly answered, although Rory had intended it to be a hypothetical question, "you've never been what I'd call a participating member of the Simpson community. Since you leave everyone else alone, you figure they'll leave you alone, too.

There's your mistake. Being all mysterious just adds to your allure."

"My allure?"

"With the gossips." The corners of Belly's mouth twitched. "And possibly a certain fireman."

Rory gaped at the other woman. "What? How did…? I can't believe…" With a groan, she tipped her head back and closed her eyes. "Is there any way you could use your powers of gossip for good and report back that there is nothing—I repeat, absolutely nothing—going on between me and Ian Walsh?"

"Well…" When Belly trailed off, Rory opened her eyes and looked at the coroner. "You could throw in the silver receiver for the price of the plain black one."

Her eyes narrowing, Rory stared at Belly for several seconds. "Half."

"Deal." By the way Belly was grinning, she would've taken a quarter.

"For that," Rory said, her voice stern, "you will quash all rumors about any type of relationship between me and Ian."

"Got it." With a businesslike nod, Belly reached a hand over the counter.

After shaking the other woman's hand firmly, Rory closed the coyote picture so she could pull up the special order form for the shotgun.

"So who's been tramping around here at night?" Belly asked.

Rory shrugged, her focus on the screen. "No idea. I was hoping to catch a shot of his face, but I got Wile E. Coyote instead."

With a grunt, Belly digested that for a minute. "I

don't know what this place is coming to. As soon as one woman kills off her stalker, another one appears. They're popping up like cockroaches."

Rory gave an amused snort. "Mine hasn't done anything except set off alarms and put a dent in my front-gate lock. I don't think he qualifies as a stalker. Yet."

"Must aggravate the hell out of you, though."

"That he does."

~

It must've been Ladies' Day at the gun shop, because her next customer was Louise Sparks. Although Rory had seen Lou in passing a few times—and she'd definitely heard the stories about Lou's stalker and her corpse discovery—they'd never really exchanged more than polite smiles.

"Callum is appalled," Lou began as soon as she breezed through the front door, "that I don't own any firearms. Zero. Not even a starter's pistol or a squirt gun. He's decided to get me a gun for my birthday in April. I'm supposed to try out a bunch and let him know which one I like the best. It's kind of killing the surprise, but honestly, I didn't want to hear him whine about it anymore, so here I am."

With a slow blink, Rory digested the load of information Lou had just dumped on her. "Okay. Have you ever shot a gun before?"

"Nope."

"What are you planning on doing with it?" At Lou's confused shake of her head, Rory elaborated. "Target shooting, skeet shooting, hunting, home defense, keeping Callum in line?"

Lou laughed. "Definitely the last one. And I'm not really a hunter, so probably target shooting and home defense. Not to sound like an idiot, but I'm not sure what a skeet is."

It was Rory's turn to laugh. "Shooting clay pigeons with a shotgun. It's fun, but if you're looking for home defense, I'd recommend a handgun instead of a long gun."

Lou shrugged. "Fine with me. Small is good."

The comment reminded Rory of Phil's girlfriend's insistence on a cute gun. She narrowed her eyes. "You don't want anything with crystals, do you?"

"God, no." Lou cocked her head. "Do guns seriously come with crystals?"

"Not in my shop," she said, and then gestured at the display cases. "Why don't you look around and let me know if anything catches your eye." Rory had a few handguns in mind already, but she wanted to see which guns drew Lou to them.

Lou began to examine the contents of the cases, providing a running commentary of her impressions as she slowly walked the length of the counter. "That one has a real cowboy feel to it. Hmm...I don't like the look of that one. It's too short—squished, almost. You know, the ones with the wood and silver and all that are pretty, but I kind of like these plain black ones. It's like they're so badass, they don't need to be flashy."

With a grin, Rory pulled out the Glock 21 Lou was eyeing and offered it to her, keeping the barrel pointed away from both of them. "Glocks are great guns. Really reliable. You picked a big one, though. This is a .45 caliber."

"Is big bad?" Lou took the gun tentatively.

"Definitely not. You're going feel a bit more recoil, and the grip on this gun can be a little big for small hands. Plus, you're going to pay more for ammo."

Lou turned the pistol in her hands, and Rory gently redirected it so the barrel once again pointed away from her.

"Never point a gun at anything you're not willing to destroy," Rory said.

"Oh!" Lou stared wide-eyed at the Glock in her hands, her expression as horrified as if the gun had turned into a poisonous snake. "Sorry! I thought it wasn't loaded."

"It's not. See?" The slide was locked open, and Rory pointed to the empty chamber. "You always want to treat every gun as if it *is* loaded, though. It's just good to get into the habit."

"Right." She let out a shaky breath. "Do I lose badass points if I admit that the thought of shooting a gun makes me nervous?"

"Of course not." Rory picked out two more Glocks, a sub-compact and a full frame .40 caliber, as well as a Beretta M9 and a Ruger revolver. She packed each one into its case for the trip outside to her shooting range. "That'll go away with practice and familiarity. Spend some hours on the range, and you'll get to know your gun."

"You're really comfortable with them," Lou commented as she relinquished the G21 to Rory so she could place it in its case.

"I should be." Rory focused on latching the case. "I grew up with guns. My parents had me target shooting before I could read."

"That mental image is kind of freaky." Although Lou laughed, her thoughtful gaze made Rory a little uncomfortable.

"Ready?" Rory asked, glad to change the subject.

Lou grimaced. "Yes?"

With a laugh, Rory handed her a stack of ammo boxes. Lou's eyes widened as she sagged under the unexpected weight. "You'll be great."

"That was awesome!" Lou's cheeks and nose were pink with cold, but her grin was huge. Every third step or so, she skipped in excitement as they headed back to the shop after a half hour on the range. "I love shooting!"

"Great," Rory said, although she winced at the volume of Lou's voice. "You can take off your ear protection now."

"Right. Sorry. Hey, is that Ian?"

Rory's heart jumped as her head whipped around, and she immediately flushed at her reaction. If she kept acting like that, no amount of Belly's gossip control would quell the rumors about them.

Ian was indeed leaning his shoulder against the locked front door, next to the sign that read, "At the range—back soon."

"Ian!" Lou called. "I've been shooting, and I was magnificent!"

Despite her agitation, Rory had to laugh. As different as they were, she couldn't help but like Lou.

Ian was grinning. "That's great, Lou."

"I'm going to tell Callum to get me the big one for my birthday. The Glock..." She shot a look at Rory.

"Glock 21," Rory filled in for her.

"Isn't that grip a little large for your hand?" Ian asked doubtfully.

"Are you saying I can't handle a big gun?" Lou demanded, but then laughed, ruining her show of indignation. "It felt good, actually. *Right.*"

"The Gen 4 grip is more manageable," Rory added, feeling a little defensive at the criticism, which wasn't like her. She didn't know why she was surprised. Ian seemed to excel in bringing out odd and unexpected reactions from her.

He didn't respond but just stepped forward, taking the stack of gun cases from her arms. She felt as if she should protest, but then realized how much easier it was going to be to unlock the door with her hands free.

"Thanks," she said instead, hurrying to shove the key in the lock. She refused to think about why her hands were trembling. The key finally turned, despite her nervous fingers, and she pulled open the door, holding it for Lou and Ian. Once inside, she shed her outerwear, tossing it into the back room to hang up later, and then busied herself with placing the guns back into the display.

"Shoot!" Lou said, and then laughed. "Get it? Shoot? Anyway, I have to run. If I'm late for work, Ivy will cut off my fingers and shove them into the coffee bean grinder."

Rory blinked. "That was…vivid."

"Sorry." Lou was already at the door. "Thank you so much. This was amazing."

"Glad you had fun." By the time Rory had finished her sentence, the door was already closing behind Lou.

"I think you've created another gun nut," Ian said as he circled around to her side of the counter.

"She did great." Rory was placing the Ruger into the display and panicking a little. It was the last gun to put away, so she was actually going to have to look at

Ian in just a minute. Keeping her eyes off him helped keep the butterflies and giddy feelings under control. "She's a natural. Once she had the feel of it and wasn't nervous about the upcoming bang, she got a nice, tight grouping on the target." She laughed a little too loudly. "As soon as she tried that .45, she wanted nothing to do with the smaller calibers. She just said, 'Go big or go home.'"

"Maybe she should've gotten a gun a few weeks ago when her stalker was a problem."

"I don't know. She seemed to do just fine without it." Her mouth twisted wryly as she put the last case away. Unable to delay the inevitable any longer, she perched a hip on her stool, half-sitting and half-leaning, and met Ian's gaze.

"True." He eyed her closely. "You're looking better today."

"I actually got some sleep last night."

His brows rose. "Did the deer cameras work, then?"

"They worked fine," Rory said with a grimace. "Or they would have if the guy had actually shown up. I did get a nice background wallpaper out of it, though." She moved the mouse to wake up the computer, revealing the coyote.

Frowning, Ian drummed his fingers on the counter as he scowled at the photo. "This was the first time he didn't show in how many nights?"

"Four."

"Huh." The rhythmic noise was driving her crazy. Without thinking about it, she reached over and covered his hand with her own, stilling him. When the warmth of his skin seared her palm, she froze, realizing what she'd done. He flipped over his hand and laced their fingers together.

It was the first time she could remember that she'd ever held someone's hand. Usually, she was self-conscious about her blunt-cut nails and fingers stained with gun oil. In Ian's grip, however, her hand looked feminine, dainty even.

"We'd be good together, Ror," he said quietly, in what she was starting to think of as his gentling-the-wild-Rory voice.

She swallowed, staring at their intertwined hands for several seconds before pulling away with a nervous jerk. The movement unbalanced her position on the stool, and she had to grab the counter to steady herself. She instantly missed the warmth of his hand.

"Uh..." she started, swallowing again. For some reason, her throat was really dry. "I...um, think he might have given up on breaking in here."

He watched her for a long moment. Worried that he wasn't going to accept her panicked change of topic, she waited with a pounding heart. After what seemed like forever, he shifted back slightly and gave a skeptical grunt. "Who saw you setting up those deer cameras?"

"George Holloway," she said after thinking for a moment. "That's it."

"You mention what you were planning to anyone but me?" When she shook her head, his face darkened. He looked pissed...really pissed. "I'll be back."

"Where are you going?" He didn't hear her, though, since he was stomping to the exit. After he slammed through it, the door settled back into its frame with a rattle. She stared at it for a long time, thinking about the feel of his hand on hers. That connection had felt nice—more than nice. Everything about Ian made her warm inside, from his protectiveness to the intense way he looked at her, as if she were the only person in his universe. It had been a long time since anyone had cared about her. As uncertain and ill-prepared as she was, it felt so very good to be seen.

When she finally tore her gaze from the closed door and returned to her paperwork, she was smiling.

Chapter 4

THE REST OF THE AFTERNOON WAS QUIET, SO RORY had a chance to switch out the plastic safety button on Fire Chief Winston Early's Mossberg shotgun with a steel replacement. As usual, working on the gun soothed her, although she couldn't completely shut off her rambling thoughts. To her, the intruder's absence the past night was a good thing. She wasn't sure why it had provoked Ian's anger.

Once she was done with the replacement, she called Chief Early and left a message that his shotgun was ready to go. It was after four by then, and the shop was still dead. Rory eyed the pile of paperwork she hadn't quite managed to complete, but she knew she was too twitchy at the moment to concentrate. Anything she attempted to do would only need to be redone later.

She was dusting—not a great distraction, but it was something she couldn't really screw up—when Ian returned. Feeling the usual stomach lurch of excitement, Rory studied his face. Although he didn't look much happier than he had before he'd left, he did appear more controlled. She turned back to the display case and squirted the top with the vinegar and water mixture in her spray bottle.

"Did you accomplish what you set out to do?" she asked, wiping at the glass with her rag.

"No," he grumped. Since she was standing on the

other side of the counter, he took a seat on her usual stool by the cash register.

Wiping the glass with more force than was probably necessary, she tried to wait him out. After a solid minute of silence, she couldn't take it anymore. Dropping her spray bottle and rag onto the top of the display case, she demanded, "Well?"

"Well, what?" His hard expression had softened a little, and the corners of his mouth twitched.

Rory gave him her best glare. "Why'd you go storming out of here earlier, all mad and cryptic?"

That killed any amusement in his expression. "I had told Billy."

"Told him what?"

"About the deer cameras. That I was going to stay with you if they didn't work."

She looked at him for a few moments before her brain clicked into gear. "So you thought Billy was the one trying to break into the shop?"

Ian shook his head. "Not Billy. We were standing next to the bar in the clubhouse when we were talking about it, though. Some of the other guys were close enough to overhear."

"So you think one of the Riders is my trespasser?"

"Maybe." His frown deepened as he tapped his fingers on the newly cleaned counter. "They could've talked to someone else, too. They gossip worse than the guys at the station."

"Seems to be a county-wide epidemic." When he looked at her, she elaborated, "Gossiping."

His laugh was gruff. "No kidding."

"I comped Belly a hundred bucks to shut down the

rumors about…" She belatedly closed her mouth when she realized what she was admitting.

"Rumors about…?" he echoed, cocking his head.

"Never mind." There was no way to stop the heat from warming her cheeks. "So you went to the clubhouse this afternoon?"

This time, his chuckle was low and knowing. "I'll just have to guess what those rumors were, then. And, yeah. I talked to Billy, but he doesn't think any of our guys is the one who's been coming around here at night."

"Do you? Suspect any of the Riders?"

That brought the return of his frown. "Not anyone in particular. I wondered if Zup was trying to get back at you for making him look like an idiot, but I doubt he could avoid getting caught four nights in a row. He'd be more likely to stick his stupid face right up to your gate and smile for the security camera."

She laughed, and a snort escaped. "Oh, man. I can just imagine it."

After his grin faded, he asked, "Do you have any idea who it might be? Anyone giving you trouble?"

Taking a moment to flip through her mental directory, she finally shook her head. "Nothing out of the ordinary. Rave's a little bitchy, and Zup is…well, Zup, but most of the Riders are polite and low-maintenance. They know what they want and how much they're willing to pay for it. Easy." The Riders, as a whole, could also be very, very scary, but that was nothing new. Since she'd taken over the store, she'd regularly dealt with people who frightened her, and had gotten pretty good at hiding her reactions.

Ian glanced around the shop. "I can see the temptation. To stock an armory for the price of a pair of bolt cutters."

With a scowl, Rory protested, "It's a little harder to get past my security than *that*."

"I know." He held his hands up, as if deflecting the heat from her glare. "And whoever's setting off your alarm is figuring that out, too."

"But you don't think he's given up on the idea."

"No." He was once again leaving fingerprints on her freshly de-printed glass as he drummed his fingers slowly. "I don't."

Crossing over to stand across the counter from him, she grabbed his offending hand. "I'm going to tell Ivy at The Coffee Spot to put *your* fingers in the grinder if you don't quit smudging my counter."

As quickly as before, his hand flipped over and he captured hers. "Bloodthirsty." Tugging her fingers toward him, he kissed the tips and released her hand. "I like it."

"Uh..." Rory couldn't figure out why he had this kind of effect on her, that the simple touch of his lips to her fingertips could reduce her to a blathering idiot.

"Fire training's tonight at seven."

She blinked at the non sequitur. "That's nice."

"I'd like you to come."

"No." Rory was already shaking her head before he'd even finished his sentence.

"Why not?"

"I have to watch the shop."

"You have the deer cameras, your regular security cameras, a big dog, four dead bolts on each door, and I saw at least three chains and padlocks on your gate. The only other thing you could do would be adding land mines and electrifying your fence."

"I looked into the electric fence," she admitted, a little wistfully. "The soil is too dry and rocky to get a good ground, though, at least for the voltage that would provide the greatest deterrent."

He eyed her for a long second. "You didn't mention the land mines. I'm hoping that's because they're not even an option."

"Of course I don't have land mines." Rory examined her polish-free, close-trimmed fingernails.

"Ror..."

"No land mines." Unable to hold his steady gaze, she stared at his shoulder. "Maybe a trip wire or two."

"Hooked to what?"

"Nothing lethal," she said defensively. "A couple CS gas grenades and some flashbangs."

Although he sighed, Ian looked to be fighting a smile. "So you can come with me tonight then."

She tried to hold her exasperated look, even though she wanted to laugh. "You are as tenacious as a badger."

"Yup." He stood up and stretched. "Lock up, and let's go."

"I need to take care of the chickens."

"So take care of the chickens, lock up, and *then* we'll go. If you get a move on, we'll have time to get some dinner."

"Dinner?" She'd been moving toward the door, automatically obeying his authoritative tone, but the word brought her to a standstill. "So, is this a...date?"

"Of course not. It's training."

"And dinner." Rory eyed his innocent expression with suspicion.

"We both have to eat. Look at it more as a biological need than a social interaction."

The term "biological need" did not soothe her ruffled nerves in the slightest. "This is a bad idea. Why do you want me to go to training, anyway?"

"You might find volunteering interesting." His expression was ultrasincere, but she didn't trust his motives for a second. "We learn lots of fun stuff at training."

"Uh-huh." Eyes narrowed, she crossed her arms over her chest. "What's the real reason?"

His choirboy expression dropped away, and his frown returned. It was a relief to see that familiar scowl. "I don't want you here alone."

"What about the locks and alarms and cameras?" she mocked. "Didn't you just talk about how safe it was?"

Ian leaned on the counter, adding forearm smudges to the fingerprints already there. "All this"—he jerked his chin, indicating the shop—"is replaceable. You're not. There are too many people who wouldn't hesitate to kill you for what's in your shop."

"But if I'm here, pointing my Python at some intruder's face, neither this"—she swept a hand toward the shop's contents—"nor I need to be replaced."

"Ror. Quit being stubborn and go do your chicken thing. I'm hungry."

She didn't move at first, but she was hungry too, and she knew that Ian was not going to leave until she agreed to go with him. Plus, although she didn't want to admit it, a big part of her was thrilled at the thought of spending more time with Ian—though if she called it a date, even in her head, nervous excitement would short out her brain. But going to a restaurant with a good friend—that was something normal people did, wasn't it?

Taking a deep breath, she accepted that she was

going to be eating a meal with Ian Walsh at a place that was not home. For tonight at least, she was going to be *normal*.

"Fine." Pivoting toward the exit, she stomped outside. When the cold air hit her face, she realized she was just in jeans and a long-sleeve T-shirt. Muttering to herself, she reentered the shop. As she hurried to the back room to get her coat, she tried her best to ignore Ian's smirk.

"Isn't the whole point of a motorcycle club to, you know, ride *motorcycles*?" Rory asked, eyeing Ian's SUV. The older Ford Bronco sat alone in the shop's parking lot.

Instead of taking offense, he gave an amused snort. "Out here, we get four months to ride, six if we're masochistic. Either way, March is not one of those months. I tried on that nice afternoon last week and ended up spending most of the day at an arson call in borrowed bunker gear." He opened the passenger door and waited. Jack, the traitor, followed and sat on Ian's foot. Her dog, apparently, had a full-blown crush on the man. Honestly, Rory couldn't blame him.

"Um…I think I'll take my pickup." Rory's nervous gaze darted toward the pole barn where her vehicle was stored. Ian had opened her door. That was intimidatingly date-like.

"Ror. Get in."

With a last, longing look at the pole barn, she moved toward the Bronco's open door. She blamed her compliance on all the survival drills her parents had run. When Ian barked orders in that drill-sergeant tone, she had to obey, thanks to twenty-two years of her parents' conditioning. Rory ignored the tiny part of her that said she got in the SUV because she actually wanted to go on this not-date date.

After Rory climbed in, Jack put his front feet on the running board, prepared to jump into the SUV with her.

"Jack. Off."

With flattened ears and a pathetic whine, he returned all four feet to the ground and slunk a few feet away from the Bronco. Ian closed her door and circled the truck.

Chewing her bottom lip, she looked at her unhappy dog. Jack wasn't used to being left at home without her, and his bewildered expression made her nerves return with a vengeance. What was she thinking? She needed to get her behind back to her bunker and cook the meatloaf she'd planned for tonight. There was hamburger thawing and everything.

"This isn't a good idea," she said when Ian hopped into the driver's seat. Her right hand felt for the door handle.

"Yes, it is. We'll eat, maybe talk to another human being or two, see if you like fire training, and then head home. You might even have fun." He cranked the engine. "Rory, don't even think about bailing."

That stupid commanding tone worked its magic again, and her hand returned to her lap as he drove through the gate. When they came to a halt right outside the fence, she reached for the door handle again.

"I've got it," Ian said, opening his door and jumping to the ground. "Do you have your keys?"

Patting her coat pocket, she felt the lumpy bulge of her key ring. "Yes."

"Good." He gave her a grin. "Be right back."

The SUV was angled so she could watch him in her side-view mirror as he pulled the gates closed, then locked them with the multiple chains and padlocks. While he worked, the deer cameras flashed as they photographed him.

By the time he returned to the Bronco, he was scowling. "I hate those cameras," he growled, releasing the brake. "They've completely fu—uh, messed up my night vision."

"At least we know they're working." Now that the gate was secured behind them and the option of running was, if not impossible, at least more inconvenient, Rory relaxed a little. "I might have a new picture to use as wallpaper for my computer, too."

At Ian's grunt, she bit her lip to hide a smile.

They ended up at Levi's, as did most of Simpson's residents. There wasn't much choice, really, with most of the other restaurants closed until May. Rory made a beeline for an open booth in the back, grabbing the bench on the far side of the table so her back was to the wall.

"Shove over," Ian grunted, trying to sit next to her. When she didn't budge, he used his body to slide her along the seat until she was wedged between the closed end of the booth and Ian's substantial bulk.

"What's wrong with that side?" she asked crankily, waving a hand at the empty seat across from them.

"I don't like to have my back to a crowd," he said, his gaze sweeping over the small, but busy, restaurant.

"Me neither," she admitted, shifting back and forth on the seat in an attempt to claim more room. It didn't work. All Rory managed to do was brush her hip against Ian's. Flushing, she tried to focus on her menu.

"Ian," a deep male voice said, making her raise her head. Sheriff Rob Coughlin and his teenage son, Tyler, stood next to their booth, and Rory mentally chastised herself for getting so distracted that she hadn't paid attention to her surroundings. Her parents would've been so disappointed. It was especially surprising that she'd missed Rob's approach—with his formidable build and rugged, striking features, he was not a man who was easily ignored by any woman with a pulse.

"Sheriff." Ian, his face expressionless, gave the other man a stiff nod. He warmed visibly as he turned to the teen. "Hey, Tyler."

"Hey," the boy responded, keeping his head down.

After returning Ian's nod, Rob focused his gaze on Rory. She wanted to squirm, but forced herself to remain still under his careful scrutiny. "It's Rory, right? Rory Sorenson?"

Although it had been phrased as a question, Rory was sure he knew perfectly well what her name was. He'd even visited her shop a couple of times, needing a part his usual source in Denver hadn't been able to supply immediately. Both had been innocuous visits, during which Rory had struggled to keep her gaze from darting to the back-room door, where her less-than-legal inventory was hidden. It hadn't helped that talking to a good-looking guy, especially one who could arrest her, made her tongue-tied on the best of days. The sheriff hadn't ever expressed more than a polite but cursory interest in Rory or her shop, and she was really hoping to keep it that way.

"Yes," she belatedly replied, flushing. "How are you?"

"Busy," he said easily.

"I'm sure." Rory still felt awkward. Once again, she resisted the urge to wriggle in her seat. "With the fires and that dead body in the reservoir and...uh, Lou's stuff and everything." Her flush heated even more. Stupid nonexistent social skills. Ian's laugh didn't help, even if he did try to turn it into a cough halfway through. Under the cover of the table, she pinched his leg. Hard.

He jumped, covering her hand with his so her fingers were flattened against his thigh and unable to repeat the pinch.

"You're the lady with all the guns?" Tyler asked suddenly, jerking Rory's attention away from the rock-hard thigh muscle under her palm.

Why did the kid have to bring up my semi-illegal business in front of his sheriff dad? Resisting the urge to send Rob a nervous glance, she kept her gaze on Tyler instead. "Yeah. I mean, I have a gun store."

"Awesome. Do you have, like, Uzi machine guns and shit?"

"Tyler!" Rob barked. "Language."

"No." Again, she stopped herself from sending the sheriff a nervous look. "I wouldn't sell any fully automatic weapons unless they were registered in the U.S. before the 1968 Gun Control Act was passed." As Tyler stared at her blankly, she risked a peek at Rob. He rubbed his hand over his mouth as if hiding a smile, and Rory relaxed slightly...at least until Tyler asked his next question.

"So, are you two, like, dating?"

"Yes."

"No!" She glared at Ian before turning back to Rob and his too-nosy son. "This isn't a date. It's just us satisfying a biological need."

Rory wasn't sure if Ian was choking or laughing. Just to be on the safe side, she patted his hunched back. When she looked up at Rob's face, his startled expression had her reviewing her last comment in her head.

"Oh!" Her blush before was nothing compared to what was burning her face now. "No! Not that kind of biological... I mean, eating! We were both hungry. That's it."

Tyler made a muffled sound, his hand hiding his grin in an unconscious imitation of his father. Squeezing her eyes closed, Rory wondered how she'd stumbled into blurting unintentional sexual innuendo in front of a teenage boy. Her gaffe shouldn't have surprised her, though. She was clueless when it came to kids. They baffled her. Even when she'd been young herself, they'd seemed like an alien species, complete with their own language. She avoided them when she could. Owning a gun shop helped with that, since her customers were all over eighteen and rarely brought their offspring along.

Rob cleared his throat, and she realized she must have missed a chunk of conversation.

"Sorry. What'd you say?" she asked, tucking a section of hair behind her ear. In a fit of vanity, she'd pulled it out of her usual ponytail and brushed it out before their date—or non-date, or whatever it was. Now it kept tumbling into her face, annoying her. Rory wished she'd brought the ponytail holder along.

"Just that we'll see you later."

"Okay. Yes. Good-bye." This was why she stayed

home. Unless guns were the topic, Rory felt like she was wandering around a conversational swamp, complete with quicksand and alligators.

Ian turned to Rob, the humor in his expression slipping away as he lifted his chin in farewell. "'Night, Sheriff. Tyler."

They were quiet until Rob and Tyler had reached their booth.

"You can let me go now," she muttered, tugging fruitlessly at her captive hand.

His hold didn't ease. "Are you going to assault me again?"

"It was just a pinch. You're acting like I caught you in a leghold trap or something."

"Maybe you have." The corners of his mouth curled up as his eyes heated. "I don't see myself escaping your clutches anytime soon…or ever."

Although she hated to admit it, smoldering-gaze Ian Walsh was even more appealing than smiley Ian Walsh. In the fluorescent glare of the restaurant, Ian didn't look washed-out and pale like everyone else. His olive skin gave him a year-round tan, and his short but still unruly black hair caught the light in the most photogenic way. It was like he had a spotlight on him all the time, his startlingly good looks and magnetism pulling people's attention. Instead of feeling even plainer in comparison, though, she almost felt like some of his beauty reflected back on her. The way he watched her with those heavy-lidded dark eyes made her feel like the female lead in a romantic movie. For once in her life, she could be the one people looked at with envy, rather than pity and curiosity.

Rory dragged her attention away from his too-tempting beauty. "It was just a pinch. You're sort of being a big baby about it."

He laughed, squeezing her hand and then finally releasing her. "I wasn't talking about that."

"Then what?"

"Never mind."

Rory opened her mouth to demand an explanation. She hated when things went over her head. It made her feel stupid. Since the waitress chose that moment to arrive at their booth to take their order, Rory wasn't able to get any clarification.

"Good to see you out of that shop of yours," the server commented after she took their orders and then their menus. "You're too young to be a hermit."

"Thanks?" Rory said to her retreating back.

They had only a few seconds of peace before a scowling Belly Leopold was sliding into the empty seat across from them.

"Hi, Belly." When the other woman just grunted in response, Rory asked, "Is everything okay?"

"How am I supposed to have any kind of success when the two of you are getting all cuddly at Levi's?" the coroner barked.

"We're not cuddling!" Flushing, Rory tried to create a cushion of space between her side and Ian's, but there was nowhere to go, unless she climbed over the side of the booth. She seriously considered it, since she was reaching the limit of how much awkwardness she could take.

As if he could read her thoughts, Ian laid his hand on her leg right above her knee, letting its weight hold her in place. The warmth spread through her as her breaths came faster. Ian's touch seemed to be directly wired into her nervous system.

Completely ignoring Rory's protestations, Belly frowned at both of them. "Our bargain was just for the old rumors. You two are responsible for any new gossip you manage to stir up by getting handsy where anyone can see."

"What?" Despite the weight of Ian's hand on her leg, Rory practically levitated. "We're not getting handsy!" It wasn't until several people in surrounding booths turned their heads that she realized how loud she'd gotten. Even Tyler was grinning at them. Her face flaming, Rory sank back down in her seat, wishing for invisibility.

Glancing around at the interested faces, Belly threw up her hands. "I give up. There's no controlling the rumors now." She pointed a finger at Rory's humiliated face. "And you're still paying for half of that silver receiver, too." With that, Belly slid out of the seat and stalked back to her own table.

"So…" Ian stretched out the word, turning what should've been a single syllable into four, all filled with innuendo. "You paid Belly to stop the rumors about us."

Her shoulders twitched in an uncomfortable shrug. "Maybe. Not that it did any good."

"Rory! And Ian! Awesome." It was Lou's turn to sit across the table from them, tugging Callum in after her. "I'm so glad you guys are here. Callum thinks I got the gun name wrong."

The tightness in Rory's stomach eased a little. Gun talk she could do. "It's a Glock."

"The 21, right?"

"Yes. The Gen 4 fit your hand the best."

Frowning, Callum said, "That's a big gun."

With his stiff posture and perma-scowl, Callum intimidated Rory a little—actually, more than a little. She tried to shift in her seat, but Ian's hand still held her in place.

"Yes." Lou's grin was filled with glee. "It gives a big, satisfying boom." Rory had to admire her resilience. In the past month, Lou had discovered a headless corpse, been stalked, had her home burned to the ground, and had almost been killed—twice. Rory imagined it took a lot to bounce back from all of that.

Callum didn't look convinced of Lou's choice of firearm. "Sure you don't want the G36?"

When Lou sent Rory a questioning look, Rory said. "She didn't like the sub-compact she tried."

"Is that the one with the short barrel?" At Rory's nod, Lou made a face. "Nope. It was too flippy."

"Too what?" Callum glanced at Rory, apparently looking for a translation.

Rory obliged. "She found it hard to keep steady after she fired."

"Yep. Too flippy." Demonstrating, Lou pointed her index finger forward, mimed a trigger pull, and then popped her finger up toward the ceiling.

"I could take you back to Rory's shop if you want to try a few other models," Callum suggested.

For some reason, Lou looked positively infuriated at his suggestion. "Didn't we have this discussion?" she asked sweetly, her tone not matching her deadly glare. "Something about me continuing to make my own decisions about trucks and, oh, I don't know, what kind of gun I like?" By the end, the sweetness had faded, and her voice had deteriorated into something close to a growl.

"Fine," Callum snapped, glowering right back at his girlfriend. "I'll get you the 21."

"Fine."

The two of them stared at each other for a long moment. Then, as if they'd both heard a silent signal, they slid out of the booth.

"Bye!" Lou called over her shoulder, giggling as Callum grabbed her hand and towed her to the exit.

Rory stared after them, looking away only after they disappeared out the front door. "That was weird."

Ian's smirk was back in place. "Not really."

She was seriously sick of his cryptic statements. "Explain."

"Sure you want me to?" His expression was odd and hard for her to read.

"Of course," she gritted. "That's why I asked."

"It was more of a demand than a request, actually."

She wanted to kill him. Since she was unfortunately not armed at the moment, she settled for trying to murder him with her glare.

"They're going to find some privacy."

"To finish their argument?"

He gave her a look. "The fighting was over. They've moved on to making up."

When comprehension finally dawned, a flush crept up her neck and over her face. She wasn't sure if she was more embarrassed about the topic, or because it took her so long to get it. "Oh."

His eyes were lit with humor and something else, something hot.

Even though she desperately wanted to drop it, Rory couldn't stop the words from tumbling out of her mouth. "Why do they have to make up from that? It wasn't much of a fight."

He chuckled, but his expression still held that banked fire. "They're new. Anything's an excuse to make up."

"Oh."

The server arrived with their food, and Rory was so relieved by the interruption that she could've leapt over the table and kissed her on the mouth. Instead, she settled for thanking her with a little too much fervor.

"You're welcome," she said, although she gave Rory a wary glance.

Rory shoveled brisket in her mouth so she wouldn't continue revealing how ignorant she was about relationships. After a few bites, she realized that Ian hadn't started eating. Instead, he was still watching her thoughtfully.

"What?" she asked through a mouthful. Obviously, filling her mouth with food was not going to stop her from embarrassing herself.

"You were homeschooled, right?" he asked, finally taking a bite. His gaze stayed on her, though.

"Yes." She focused on sliding her fork into her greens. The question felt like a criticism, but she knew she was sensitive about her lack of social skills, so she tried to keep the defensive scowl off her face. Ian was probably just asking to get to know her better. Wasn't that why people went on dates? Or non-date dates?

"Did you go to college?" Even though they'd met

over a decade ago, they'd been able to be friends only after her parents had died. She supposed there were still lots of things they didn't know about each other.

"I didn't go away to school, but I've taken some online classes. Mostly business ones—marketing, accounting, that type of thing. Stuff that can help me with the shop."

"Huh." That one syllable was loaded with meaning.

Narrowing her eyes, Rory turned her head to look at his profile as he studied his plate. "What?"

His gaze met hers. "Have you ever had a boyfriend?"

Her blush returned. She kept holding eye contact, but it was hard. She forced a shrug, hoping it appeared casual. "Not really."

"Not really?"

Rory answered with another shrug. She turned back to her plate, stabbing her fork into a piece of meat.

After a short silence, he asked, "Have you been on a date before?"

The unchewed food went down with her panicked gulp, painfully scraping her esophagus and making her choke. Ian slapped her on the back with enough force to shove her toward the table and almost plant her face in her plate of food. Coughing, she turned her head to glare at him.

"Is that what you consider first aid, Mr. Fireman?" she rasped between coughs.

He lifted one shoulder. "It worked. You're not choking anymore."

"No thanks to the body blow," she said, taking a drink of water. Her throat still ached, but the positive part of almost choking to death was that it had changed the topic, and she didn't have to answer his humiliating question.

"So, *is* this your first date?" he asked, and she almost growled.

"You okay, Rory?" For the second time that evening, she was tempted to kiss someone who'd interrupted them. This time, it was Winston Early, the fire chief, standing by their table. The lines on his usually cheery face drooped a little with concern.

"Fine, Chief," she told him with a smile. It was impossible to be rude to Chief Early. It'd be like kicking a puppy.

After a close scrutiny of her face, he returned to his normal jolly self. "Good. How've you been? I heard you had an unwelcome visitor a few nights ago."

Her molars clamped together. Everyone in town seemed to have a direct line into the details of her life. Still, this was the kindly chief, so she tried to sound as nonannoyed as possible. Rory thought she probably partially succeeded. "Yes. I think that's over with, though." She ignored the quiet scoffing noise from Ian. "Stop into the shop when you get a chance. The Mossberg is ready to be picked up, and I just got in a Colt Peacemaker I think you might like."

His eyes lit with interest even as he winced. "If I bring home one more, I'll be sleeping on the couch indefinitely. Doris called me a gun hoarder the other day."

"Okay." Rory held back a smile. "Feel free to stop in and just look at it, though. It's really pretty. Ivory grips."

Squeezing his eyes closed as if he were in pain, Early groaned. "You're the devil, Rory Sorenson." Pivoting around, he took three steps away from their booth before tossing over his shoulder, "I'll be in tomorrow." Then he stomped back to his table, where Doris was waiting.

Ian huffed a laugh. "You're like the antimarriage counselor."

"Not really. Doris is okay." She gave Mrs. Early a little wave. "She doesn't really hate his guns. Doris just knows she's the only thing keeping his addiction in check. If she didn't fuss over every gun he bought, there'd be no holding him back. They'd end up living in a tent in the yard, because their house would be so packed there'd be no room to even move."

He didn't laugh at that like she'd expected. Instead, his gaze turned distant. "There are worse addictions than gun collecting."

It was clear where—or to whom—his mind had gone. "Julius isn't doing any better, huh?"

"No."

Rory grimaced. "Sorry."

"Has he been in the shop this week?" When she shook her head, he turned back to his food, jabbing at his meat as if it had offended him. "Figured. Don't think he's left his armchair for days. Someone's supplying him with booze." A muscle in his cheek flexed as he poked at his food some more.

Completely at a loss about what she should do, Rory reached out to pat his forearm awkwardly. He went still under her touch, and she wondered if he felt the same surge of awareness she did whenever he touched her. The moment stretched as they stared at each other. His focus on her was so complete, so intense, it felt like the imaginary spotlight that followed Ian had turned its beam on her. For a short time, she believed that she was the center of Ian Walsh's universe, and it felt wonderful—and terrifying. The clatter of a dish broke the spell, and she pulled back her hand, returning it to her lap. Heavy silence covered their table, and she looked anywhere but at Ian. For some reason, people had been interrupting them for the entire meal. Why had everyone chosen *now* to leave them in peace?

"Dessert?"

Seriously, Rory thought, smiling at the expectant waitress, *the people in this town have the* best *timing*.

Chapter 5

Dinner at Levi's had been awkward. Entering Station One was its own special brand of uncomfortable.

"Uh..." Rory's feet stopped a few steps inside the door. The whole idea of her volunteering to be a firefighter seemed outlandish now. "I think I'll wait in the Bronco."

Ian's eyebrows shot up. "For two hours?"

"Sure. I'm a patient person." She turned to face the door, but Ian grabbed her arm.

"You'll like volunteering. Just try it. If you hate it, I won't push it anymore." He didn't listen to any of her objections, but just dragged her into the main training room.

"Hey, Beauty!" Soup called from across the room. His name was actually Mercer Warhol, but no one called him that. "You bring us a new recruit?"

Before Ian could answer—or Rory could pull her arm free and make a run for it—Junior Higgins said, "Rory! What are you doing outside the compound?"

Steve Springfield gave Junior's shoulder a shove. Since Steve was a burly monster of a man, and Junior, at five feet, six inches, lived up to his name, he stumbled back several feet before catching his balance.

"What?" Junior asked plaintively.

Steve gave him a stern look. "Don't be rude."

"Rory." The chief walked toward them, smiling. "Thinking of volunteering?"

Feeling uncomfortable under the curious stares of a dozen pairs of eyes, Rory gave Early a tight shrug, trying to return his smile. "Ian invited me to training. I thought maybe I'd give it a trial run."

"Great!" The chief gave her a boisterous pat on the upper arm. Rory had to firm her stance so she didn't go flying like Junior had. "For tonight, I just have a waiver for you to sign. Then give it a few training sessions and see if it's for you. We could use some women in the ranks."

"Yeah." Junior's eyes lit. "Feel free to recruit any friends. Especially the hot ones."

This time, Ian cuffed the back of Junior's head. "Knock it off."

As Junior rubbed the back of his skull and sulked, Steve nodded at Rory and gave her one of his rare, sweet smiles that were usually directed only at his kids. Despite his size and normally serious expression, Steve had a gentle way about him and an old-fashioned sense of gallantry. It was impossible not to like him. "Good to see you."

"You, too." She racked her brain for a conversational topic and seized, as always, on guns. "How's that Kimber rifle working for you?"

Steve grimaced. "Haven't been able to touch it. Brady, my thirteen-year-old, used it on our elk hunt last fall. He liked it so much, he's claimed it as his."

Smiling, Rory relaxed a little. "Come in sometime, and we'll find you a replacement."

Before Steve could reply, the chief handed Rory a clipboard holding a release waiver and called for everyone's attention. "Got a new portable tank we need to get wet. A couple of people"—he eyed Junior, who dropped his gaze to his boots—"need a refresher in how to operate the trucks, especially where to find the tank-to-pump switch. Steve, you're heading up training tonight. Soup, get the lights. Go."

As the firefighters scattered, Rory signed the form and handed it back to the chief. After that, she just tried to stay out of the way, but Ian gestured for her to join him. She climbed into the cab of the truck he'd just started, and she eyed the unfamiliar controls with interest. He drove into the parking lot, joining two other trucks.

"This is one of our tenders," Ian explained as he backed the truck toward the portable tank some of the other guys were setting up. The tank looked kind of like a large kiddie swimming pool. "It carries water to the scene."

"Not many places out here with hydrants, I suppose," she said, and he shook his head.

"Exactly. We're going to set up the portable tank and draft water from that to the engine."

Rory frowned. "Why not just hook the tender to the engine and skip a step?"

"Sometimes we do," he agreed. "With the tank, though, we can dump the water and then take the tender back for more. That works the best when we're a ways from the nearest water source."

"Do you get the water from the reservoirs, then?"

"Reservoirs, creeks, rivers, plus we have underground tanks scattered around the district." Ian opened his door, and the noise of the truck engines made it impossible to hear anything quieter than a yell.

Rory climbed out of the cab, jumping from the bottom step to the ground. Her feet slipped on the packed snow when she landed, and she had to grab the open door to catch her balance. As soon as she was stable again, she glanced around to make sure no one had seen her almost bite it. To her relief, everyone was focused on setting up the tank or connecting hoses to valves on the trucks.

She carefully made her way to the rear of the tender, just as Ian opened up the back, allowing water to pour into the portable tank.

"We'll be pumping the water from the tank to the engine," he yelled over the noise. "Then pumping it from the engine to the tender."

Eyeing the setup, Rory frowned. "That seems… pointless."

He flashed his single dimple. "At a real call, we'd send the water from the engine to the fire, but there's no point in wasting water on an exercise."

Opening her mouth, Rory was about to ask another question, when a sharp whistle from the chief interrupted her. He was trotting toward them across the parking lot.

"Got a call," he shouted. "Pickup versus elk on Highway Six, mile marker one-seven-four. Unknown injuries, unknown damage. Higgins and Lowe, stay here for cleanup. The rest of you, it's go time!"

"Come on," Ian said, jerking his head at Rory as he and all but two guys hurried back toward the station.

"Me?" she asked, but obviously not loudly enough, since his quick strides didn't pause. She rushed after him, catching up when he reached the door. Ian held it open, and she ducked inside. "You want me to go?"

"Yes. Grab one of those blue helmets from that shelf

and meet me at Rescue Two." He pointed at one of the smaller trucks.

Once again, her childhood drill training had her hurrying to grab a helmet and rush to the passenger side of the truck he'd indicated. Steve joined her, so she slid to the middle seat and buckled her seat belt.

"Ready for your first call?" Ian asked.

"No."

He laughed as he eased the truck through the open overhead door. "The blue helmet means you're new. The scene commander won't ask you to do anything hard."

Suddenly feeling fond of the blue hard hat she was clutching in her lap, she pulled off her stocking cap and exchanged it for the helmet, buckling the strap under her chin. As Ian fell in behind the chief's SUV, Steve reached in front of her and flicked a few switches, turning on the overhead lights and the siren.

The sudden wail made Rory jump, and Ian turned his head to grin at her before returning his attention to the road in front of them. She eyed him with interest. This was a different Ian from the one she'd thought she'd known. It was as if one of the switches on the truck's instrument panel had turned a light on inside him. Ian looked more alive than she'd ever seen him.

Once they turned onto the highway, the truck picked up speed—a lot of speed. Rory was tempted to grab something and hold on, but the only things close enough were Ian and Steve's thighs. She flattened her gloved hands over the tops of her own legs.

"Fun, huh?" Ian sent her another smile, and she could only blink at him, too focused on how they were hurtling through the darkness to think of an answer.

Steve reached in front of her again, this time to grab the radio mic. There had been almost constant chatter coming from the radio, but Rory could catch only the fifth or sixth word. She wondered if interpreting radio-speak was an acquired skill.

As Steve gave their location, the brake lights on the chief's SUV lit. Ian slowed the rescue truck, and Rory got her first glimpse of the scene. A light-colored pickup with a crumpled front end and cobweb-cracked windshield sat diagonally across both lanes, and the carcass of an elk cow was stretched out on the road in front and to the right of the vehicle. Although it was hard to see through the broken windshield, Rory could tell there were two people in the cab.

The chief's voice came through on the radio. "Fire 201 on scene and establishing 174 Command."

"Copy," the dispatcher answered.

Ian parked the truck, killing the siren but keeping the overheads flashing. He and Steve hopped out of the truck while Rory fumbled to unlatch her seat belt.

She finally won the battle and wrestled free. Steve had left the passenger-side door open for her, so she slid along the seat and climbed out. As soon as she rounded the front of the truck, the chief bellowed at her.

"Rory! Grab the battery kit. Left side, top left section."

"Yes, Chief!" she yelled back over the engine noise and the approaching sirens. Hurrying to the driver's side, she continued to the first top storage section. It took a few seconds for her to figure out how to unlatch the door, and then to realize that it opened upward, rolling into the top like a garage door.

The area was lit, and Rory quickly spotted the tool

bag marked "Battery Kit." She grabbed it and a flashlight hooked to the other side of the section. When she hurried back to the chief, she held up the kit.

"Soup!" the chief yelled. "Battery!"

One of the guys clustered around the open driver's side door of the pickup turned his head at the chief's shout and hurried to the smashed front of the vehicle. Even though he'd been in her shop numerous times, it took her a few seconds to recognize him. At night with the disorienting flashing lights, all the firefighters looked alike in their bunker gear.

When she got close to Soup's side, she held up the battery kit.

"Got to get it open first," he said, taking the kit and setting it on a semiflat portion of the ruined bumper. "Grab me a crowbar."

"Where?" she asked.

"Rear of the rescue. Bottom left, unless someone didn't put it back right last time." His voice was calm, raised just enough so she could hear him. In contrast, her heart was pounding in double-time. She'd drilled for a lot of emergency situations, but this was a whole new experience for her. This was real.

She found the crowbar where Soup had told her it would be. As she headed back to the pickup, an ambulance passed the parked fire trucks in reverse. She moved aside so it could back up close to the damaged pickup.

With the help of the crowbar, Soup pried open the hood. It took him only a short time to disconnect the battery.

"Is that so the truck doesn't blow up?" Rory asked, holding the flashlight so Soup could see what he was doing.

"That, and so the airbag doesn't deploy while we're working on the patients in there."

Once the battery had been disconnected, Soup returned to the rescue workers clustered around the pickup doors. Rory glanced at the chief for any further instructions, but he was focused on the two victims in the truck, as well. She moved closer to the chief's SUV, well out of the way of the rescue work.

She watched as both the driver and the passenger were fitted with cervical collars and strapped to long spine boards. It was impressive how quickly they were removed from the smashed pickup and loaded into the ambulance.

Once the injured couple were headed to the Connor Springs hospital, all the rescue workers seemed to lose some of their urgency. Although they still moved efficiently, it felt as if everyone had released a breath, and a good portion of the tension had seeped out of the atmosphere.

A state trooper took pictures of the scene before using spray paint to bracket the beginning and ends of the skid marks left by the pickup's tires. He measured the marks as Rory watched, curious.

"He can use those to figure out how fast the pickup was traveling when the driver started to brake." Ian's voice next to her made Rory jump.

"Oh." She glanced at him and then back at the trooper. Ian was front and center in her thoughts way too much already. Seeing him in his bunker gear, glowing from cold air and leftover adrenaline, was just overkill. "Will the couple from the truck be okay, do you think?"

"Should be. From the quick assessment we did, it looked like they both had just minor injuries."

Something inside Rory that had been twisted into a tight knot since she'd gotten her first glimpse of the smashed truck relaxed. "Good."

A couple of firemen were dragging the elk to the side of the road. "I'm going to go help," Ian said.

"Will someone get a tag for that?" she asked, following him. Moving an elk carcass was one of the skill-less tasks she felt confident she couldn't mess up.

"Already called it." Steve looked up from the carcass and grinned at her. "You going to fight me for it?"

"Nope," Rory said. "I'm not crazy about elk. It just seems like a waste of a hundred and fifty or so pounds of meat."

"I've got four growing kids," Steve said. "It definitely won't be wasted."

Ian waved her away when she bent toward the elk. "We've got this."

As she watched the others drag the elk to the side of the road, an odd feeling curled in her belly. Growing up as an only child, she'd never been excused from any task because she was a girl. At the gun store, most of her customers treated her as one of the guys. She felt like she should be offended, that she should insist she was just as capable as the guys. In actuality, though, she was kind of pleased. Ian respected her abilities, but he also went out of his way to help her. That kind of old-fashioned chivalry was nice. Rory couldn't stop a smile as her gaze followed Ian.

The arrival of a tow truck interrupted her musings, and she hurried to retrieve the battery kit, flashlight, and crowbar from in front of the wrecked pickup. She returned them to their original locations and then circled the truck to make sure that all the compartments were closed and latched.

"Rory." The chief met her at the back of the truck. "Good job. We'll make a firefighter out of you yet."

"Thanks, Chief," she said, a little uncomfortable with his praise. "I didn't do much."

"You followed orders and kept your head. That's a lot more than most newbies."

She gave him an awkward bob of her head, relieved when he left her to finish her circuit of the truck.

"Ror," Ian called, climbing into the driver's seat. "Get the wheel chocks, would you?"

She pulled the chocks from their position under the rear tires, stowing them in one of the storage compartments. Once she retook her spot in the center of the truck cab, Steve climbed in after her, heaving his big body into place with a groan.

"I'm getting too old for this," he complained, buckling his seat belt. "And I still need to pick up that elk tonight."

"Do you need help?" Rory asked.

He shook his head. "That's what my kids are for. It'll do them good to work for their supper. My brother and nephews will help, too—both with the pickup and with the eating."

"So?" Ian asked, giving her a nudge with his elbow.

With a confused look, she echoed, "So…?"

"How'd you like your first call?"

Rory considered that for a long moment, trying to sort through the muddle of emotions swamping her. "It was…terrifying, but satisfying at the same time."

Both men chuckled.

"That's a good description," Steve said.

Ian didn't say anything, but he reached over and squeezed her knee, adding a flare of heat and confusion to her already mixed-up mind.

They returned to the station after a quick stop to gas up the truck, and Steve gave Ian hand signals from the ground to help direct him in backing the truck into its spot. The two firemen who hadn't gone on the call had finished cleaning up from training, so it didn't take long before everyone was calling their good nights and heading to the parking lot.

Rory stared at Ian's Bronco, her stomach twisting. In the excitement of the call, she'd forgotten that he'd driven her into town. All she wanted to do was hide in her bunker and process the evening—or maybe just hide in her bunker, full stop. The processing could wait.

"Ready?" Ian opened the passenger door and waited for her to get into the SUV. With a sigh, she swung onto the seat, appreciating the relatively short climb in comparison to the rescue truck. He closed the door and rounded the hood while she watched him, feeling like a rabbit crouched in a woodpile as a coyote circled her hiding spot.

Shaking her head to clear it of her fanciful thoughts, she kept her eyes off Ian as he got into the driver's seat. Instead, she focused intently on fastening her seat belt, impatient with her ricocheting emotions. Somehow, just the act of getting into his vehicle had transformed the night back into a date.

"Does it ever make you nervous?" she blurted, desperate to put off the awkward silence she just knew was waiting to descend.

"Does what make me nervous?" Giving her a curious look, he cranked the engine.

"Driving. After seeing so many accidents."

"Not really nervous." He paused, thinking. "More cautious, maybe."

She snorted. "Or maybe not. I saw how fast you were driving the rescue truck."

With a grin, he said, "It's different heading to a call. Lives are at stake."

"Plus, you just like to drive fast."

That brought an actual laugh. "True."

The silence hit, and Rory released a soundless sigh. She'd known it would get quiet and awkward sooner or later.

"You'd be good at this," Ian said.

Turning her head, she eyed him curiously.

"You should sign up to be a volunteer firefighter," he clarified. "You were calm and took everything in stride."

Rory snorted. "If you'd have taken my pulse, you wouldn't have called me calm."

"Doesn't matter what's happening on the inside. As long as you keep thinking, you'll be fine."

"I'll consider it." That would mean a heap of social interactions she'd managed to avoid all her life—training, team bonding, summer potlucks, Christmas parties. She winced, not able to stop the curl of panic rising in her stomach at the idea. "I'm not that great at, well, group activities."

She expected him to laugh, but the look he gave her was thoughtful, instead. "I think you'd like it. They become your family."

That wasn't the most appealing thought. Her last

family experience wasn't anything she wanted to re-create. Since Rory didn't know how to share this in a way that didn't make her seem damaged, she just made a noncommittal sound and changed the subject. "The Riders are kind of like a family, too, aren't they?"

"Yeah." His laugh didn't contain much amusement. "A dysfunctional family."

Rory opened her mouth and closed it again, not sure how she'd managed to direct the conversation from slightly uncomfortable to completely awkward. "Julius?" she finally asked.

Ian was quiet long enough for her to think he wasn't going to answer, but he finally said, "Mostly. Plus Billy's been acting erratically, Zup's being sulky, Rave's flipping out about the stupidest shit, and someone's sneaking booze to Julius, like they're doing him a fucking favor or something." He blew out a hard breath. "Sorry. About the swearing."

"It's okay. I've heard worse."

"You shouldn't have to hear that sh—uh, stuff."

Sending him a sideways glance, she said, "You do know that you're encouraging me to volunteer for the fire department."

"Yeah?"

"The fire department, containing firefighters, whose dirty mouths are second only to cops?"

His laugh was grudging but more authentic than the hollow sound he'd made earlier. "Okay, you might have a point. I think the Riders win for most profanity, though."

"True. It really doesn't bother me though."

His grimace looked to be part rueful and part pained.

"Last time I babysat Steve's kids, I stepped on a Lego and let loose. Maya, his littlest one, started crying. The only way I could get her to stop was to promise I'd quit swearing. I'm trying, but it's fu—uh, really tough."

The sweetness of his explanation twisted her heart. Rory had always thought of herself as unromantic, but the mental image of big, manly Ian attempting to comfort a little girl just made her melt.

Ian turned onto her drive, pulling up to the triple-locked gate and setting off the deer cameras in a battery of flashes. As Rory opened her door, he caught her arm.

"Wait," he said when she looked at him, startled. "I'll unlock it. Give me your keys."

"Don't be stupid." She hopped out of the SUV, digging the keys out of her coat pocket. It just made sense for the passenger to be the one to get the gate. There was chivalry, but then there was plain inefficiency. Apparently, Ian didn't agree, since he got out of the truck as well.

As she opened each padlock and untangled the chains, he watched the area around them. After they pushed aside the gates, Ian jerked his head toward the Bronco.

"Drive through, and I'll shut these."

With a shrug, she did as he asked. It was only when she was sitting in the idling truck, waiting for him to finish relocking the gate, that she realized he was going to be locked in the compound. Her spine stiffened, her fingers clutching the steering wheel. Did that mean he was planning on staying the night? Because that was not going to happen.

In a full-on panic, she opened the driver's door and jumped out of his Bronco, nearly crashing into him.

"You can't stay," she blurted. Although she immediately felt a flush rise on her cheeks, she was freaked enough by the idea of someone—even Ian—invading her home, to ignore her embarrassment. "I'll unlock the gate again so you can leave."

"Nope." He stepped around her and got into the driver's seat. "You asked for one more night, and you got it. Time's up." As she watched, anxiously chewing the inside of her lip, he drove the short distance to the shop parking lot and backed into a corner spot. Jack hurdled out of the darkness toward her. Sitting on her boots, he smacked his tail against her legs in his excitement. She automatically rubbed his ears. Giving a low moan of pleasure, he leaned into her touch.

"What am I going to do about him, Jack?" she muttered. "How do I get him to leave?"

A blissed-out groan was the dog's only response.

"I don't suppose you could bite him? Or just show some teeth and chase him off the property?" Her hopes on that front were dashed when Jack spotted Ian getting out of the Bronco. With an excited yip, the dog tore over to Ian, greeting him with as enthusiastic a welcome as he'd given Rory, the creator of his food. With a defeated sigh, she walked over to the pair.

"Let's go, then," she grumbled, heading for the narrow path that led to the back entrance of the shop.

Chapter 6

Once she'd unlocked the door and disabled the alarm, she took a long time removing her outerwear to give herself a moment to think. As long as he didn't see her alarm codes—and cut off and steal her thumb—it wasn't as if he'd ever be able to get inside without her permission. Plus, she did trust him.

Ian watched her slow-motion boot removal with a raised eyebrow before glancing around the back room. "Where do you sleep? Those chairs don't look all that comfortable." He gestured toward a couple of straight-back wooden chairs next to her worktable.

"They're not." Taking a deep, hopefully calming breath, she braced herself to open the door of her home to a stranger.

Rory caught herself—Ian wasn't a stranger. He'd be the first person besides her and her parents to ever step foot in the bunker, though, and the idea was strangely terrifying. With another bracing breath, she moved toward the shelves hiding her steel door.

He was quiet as she swung open the shelves. Although she didn't look at him, she knew he was right behind her, watching. Rory had the sudden impulse to check out his expression, but she quickly quashed the idea. She didn't think she could handle it if he was looking at her like he thought she was crazy.

Her body blocked his view of the keypad as she typed

in the code, which made her feel a tiny bit more secure. After finishing the unlocking process, she opened the security door with a hand that shook. Oblivious to Rory's distress, Jack bolted past her and down the steps.

It was hard to move away from the yawning entrance of her real home to reset the shop alarm. Having the door open with someone there, even if that someone was Ian, made her feel raw and vulnerable.

It wasn't any better when they'd both crossed the threshold. Rory closed and relocked the door automatically. To cover up her insecurity, she waved Ian toward the stairs. He stood back and gestured for her to precede him. Too shaky to argue about who would go first, she started descending the steps with Ian at her back.

It felt as if it took forever to reach the bottom. When she turned on the living area lights, Ian's low whistle made her jump.

"This is great," he said, moving past her to walk farther into the main room, his eyes scanning the space, his open examination making Rory even twitchier. Shifting the strap of his duffel bag off his shoulder, he dumped it next to her couch. "You could survive a zombie apocalypse down here."

Her laugh sounded nervous to her ears, so she quickly swallowed it. "That's the idea. Zombies, nuclear winter, pandemic—one world-ending disaster is pretty much like another."

Ian shot her a grin over his shoulder as he prowled around the room. "Well, however it happens, I know whose house I'll be visiting when the end comes."

Although she smiled back, it was strained. Rory couldn't seem to make herself move from the base of the stairs. It was as if Ian had completely taken over her home just by being in it.

"Would you…um…" Her hesitation brought Ian's attention away from the display of throwing knives decorating one wall.

"What?"

Rory's gaze bounced around her living room like she was the one seeing it for the first time. "Could you not… uh, tell anyone? About my place?"

"Of course not." He sounded a little disgruntled that she thought he might blab.

"Thanks."

"I won't say anything."

"Okay."

He must have heard doubt in her voice, since he frowned. "Don't you believe me?"

"I do." After a pause, she continued, "It's just that… well, you *are* a firefighter."

"So?"

"You guys are the worst gossips in Simpson. Everyone knows that."

Ian looked utterly offended. "I know how to keep my mouth shut."

"Okay, okay!" She held up her hands, palms facing out. "I believe you."

His affronted scowl eased. "Why don't you want anyone knowing about this place? It's amazing."

She shrugged, her frowning gaze fixed on the knives adorning the wall. "It's not very…well, normal, is it? Plus, my parents were really strict about not letting anyone in here. Even though they're gone, it's hard to break that habit."

"Fu—uh, forget normal. This is Simpson, after all. You're not even in the top hundred weirdest people. Besides, this is great." He swung an arm to indicate the entire living room and kitchen before refocusing on Rory. "*You* are great."

The tension in her chest eased a little, although it didn't disappear completely. To distract herself, she took a step away from the stairs. "Want to see the rest?" She could almost hear her parents shrieking their objections from the grave, but she firmly ignored the voices in her head.

"Sure."

There wasn't much else to see, but she showed him the small bathroom, complete with composting toilet, and her parents' former bedroom that she'd turned into a storage room.

"It's like you have your own Costco," he said, eyeing her stacked cases of toilet paper.

"I don't actually think the world is going to end soon, but if something did happen, there are some things I wouldn't want to go without," she said. "I like being well stocked. It's…comforting."

"I get that."

Despite his words, the way he was examining her supplies made her uncomfortable. She ushered him out of the room, shutting the door behind them, hiding what was probably another sign of her unbalanced mind.

"That's my room." With a tip of her head, she indicated another closed door and then tried to hurry past it. Her efforts were for naught. Ian gave her a wicked grin and reached for the knob.

"Wait!" she said, moving to block his entrance, but it was too late.

He stepped into her room and stared. When he was quiet for a long moment, she closed her eyes, dreading his reaction.

"I don't think I've ever seen this much pink in one place. It's like falling into a bottle of Pepto-Bismol."

"Okay." By the heat in her cheeks, she knew her face was pinker than her bedroom. "You've seen it. Let's move on."

Ignoring her efforts to shoo him out of her room, Ian took another couple of steps away from the door. He eyed the pink walls, the pink and white bed, the white dresser with pink accents and, to top it all off, the fluffy pink bunny perched on top of the pile of pillows at the head of the bed. "I'm guessing you haven't redecorated since you were…what? Eight?"

Her blush intensified. Dropping her gaze, she glanced around the room and then wished she hadn't. It really was an extreme amount of pink.

"What?"

Her eyes snapped back to his. "What?"

Leaning a shoulder against one of the four posts supporting the pink and white canopy, he watched her like a hawk would eye a chubby ground squirrel. "What's the story?"

Rory knew she should shut him down and get them both back to the relative sanity of the living room. For some strange reason, though, her mouth opened, and the truth popped out. "I just decorated this room a couple of years ago."

The corners of his mouth tucked in, as if he was holding back a smile. "When you were twenty-three, then? So not eight."

"Not eight." Her face was going to burst into flames if she blushed any more. Good thing she had a firefighter in her room.

"You…hmm, like pink, then?"

"Yes."

"A lot."

"Yes!" Her humiliation turned a corner and morphed into anger. "I love pink, okay? Do you know what color my room was when I was a kid?"

He shook his head, watching her in apparent fascination.

"Brown. And beige." The words kept tumbling out, as if Ian had opened the door to an overfilled closet in her brain. "And do you know what color almost all of my clothes were?"

This time, he just raised a questioning eyebrow.

"Camouflage. Mossy oak and desert sand, to be precise, depending on the season and where we were going to run drills that day. I'm a grown woman, and I like pink. So shoot me."

Ian scratched his nose. She couldn't tell for sure, but Rory was fairly certain it was to hide his smile. When he lowered his hand, his face was completely serious. "That's probably not something you want to say in a gun shop. Well, in the bunker beneath a gun shop."

"What?" Confusion killed a good portion of her indignation, and she deflated a little.

"'So shoot me.' It's probably not a good habit to use that particular phrase with all these guns around." A smile was definitely trying to break free.

"Out." She pointed toward the door. A full-on grin slipped across his face as he turned to leave. With a huff, she gave his shoulder a shove. It didn't move him off balance in the slightest, but it did make her feel a tiny bit better.

He looked back at her, his expression growing serious. "It's okay to like pink, you know."

Her gaze dropped to the floor. She startled as his hand cradled her jaw, tilting her face so he could meet her eyes again.

"I mean it. Having a pink-loving, girly side doesn't make you any less of a gun-toting, zombie-smiting badass." His smile was so tender that her eyes began to burn. "And I like both sides—all sides of you, actually."

Looking into his beautiful, earnest face…she almost believed him.

Pulling away before she did something crazy, like tell him she'd been crushing on him for years, she squeezed by him and rushed back into the living room. The monitor on the desk caught her attention.

"Let's check tonight's camera footage," she suggested.

Without waiting for him to respond, she sat in the desk chair and flipped the power button on the monitor. Ian leaned next to her, one hand on the back of her chair and one on the desk. Rory shifted in her seat. His position put him close enough to smell, a mix of leather and motor oil and wood-smoke and the clean, crisp scent of winter. All good things, but his scent made her too… aware. She started to rise.

"I'll grab a chair for you," she said, but her upward movement was halted by his hand on her shoulder.

"I'm fine." He gently pressed her back into her seat.

"Okay," she muttered, although she definitely wasn't feeling okay with him hovering over her. Twitchy and too warm and off balance, yes. Okay, no.

Rory was happy for the distraction of checking the video. One by one, she scrolled through each camera's footage of the evening, but nothing of interest caught her attention. The photobombing coyote managed to get captured by the south camera, trotting along the outside of the fence line.

It was a relief to find no sign of the intruder for the second night in a row. After finishing her scan of the last camera's recording, she turned to Ian. His face was much too close to hers, and she jerked back to put some space between them.

"Um..." She couldn't think when she was staring at his mouth. Quickly shifting her gaze to meet his brown eyes, she didn't know if that view was any less distracting. Giving herself a mental shake, she forced her brain to concentrate on something besides the all-too-pretty Mr. Walsh. "I'll check the pictures caught by the deer cameras tomorrow. It doesn't look like there were any unwanted visitors while we were gone, though."

"Good."

"So...there's probably no reason for you to stay here," she said, her gaze darting toward the base of the stairs and back to Ian.

"Are you trying to kick me out?" he grumbled, although there was a note of amusement running through his words.

"Yes."

He laughed. "Won't work. I'm staying. I don't think this is over, and you shouldn't be here by yourself."

"I'm not." Rory gestured toward Jack, who was stretched out on the rug, snoring softly. One back leg twitched, as if he were dreaming about chasing ground squirrels, and then he settled.

"As ferocious as he appears"—his mouth quirked a little—"a dog is too easy to…subdue."

His careful word choice almost made it worse. She cleared her throat, shoving away the mental image of someone harming Jack in their effort to break in. "I'm not easy to subdue. I'm also very well armed."

He grinned. "I know. I'm still staying."

"Fine." The word was almost a groan. It was late, and she was tired. Having Ian there had kept her adrenaline hopping, but that nervous edge was beginning to fade, along with the last of her energy. "I'll dig out some blankets for you."

Once the bedding was arranged on the couch, Ian eyed it. "You weren't kidding about the camouflage."

With a snort, she shook the mossy oak pillowcase in her hands so the pillow dropped in the rest of the way. "I was not." She tossed the pillow to the end of the couch, which was draped in a mossy oak sheet and two matching blankets. "Once you're tucked into bed, I won't even be able to see you."

He laughed. "Your love for pink is starting to make sense."

"Yeah." Clearing her throat, she concentrated on straightening the pillow. "That's another thing to keep to yourself."

When he stayed quiet, she looked at him. His teasing grin made her close her eyes, as if in pain.

"Ian," she said through set teeth. "If you even whisper one word about what you saw in my bedroom, I will use each and every knife on that wall to cut you into teeny-tiny pieces and then feed you to the chickens. Understand?"

If her threat had intimidated him, his expression did not show it. In fact, she was pretty sure his smile had widened. "You're kind of hot when you're making very specific and graphic threats."

She made a sound somewhere between a groan and a growl. "I'm going to bed."

Stalking away from him, Rory went into her bedroom and slammed the door. Although the sound from the living room was muffled, she was pretty sure Ian was laughing.

Chapter 7

The alarm woke her instantly, her body jackknifing into a sitting position before her brain even registered the beeping. After a disoriented second, she shot out of bed, scattering pillows and bedding in her wake. She'd almost reached the bedroom door when it opened, forcing her to stumble backward so she didn't get slammed in the face.

"Which alarm is that?" Ian asked, sounding wide-awake.

"Move, and I'll check," she snapped, shoving past him into the living area. When she hit the power button on the monitor, the cameras' live feeds filled the screen. A quick scan didn't show anything amiss. She checked the alarm panel next.

"It's the southwest corner," she said, and began scanning the recorded footage.

Ian paced toward the stairs. "Let's go."

"Give me five seconds," she said, her eyes fixed on the screen. "We need to know what we're dealing with before we charge out there, guns blazing."

Although he made an impatient sound, he returned to watch the monitor over her shoulder.

"There." She reversed the video and pointed to the shadow that moved in and out of the far side of the frame. Not much of the intruder had been captured by the camera.

Squinting, Ian leaned closer to the screen. "Play that again." After she did, he shook his head. "What is that, someone's arm?"

"Think so." She replayed it a third time.

"The resolution on that camera is crap."

"Yeah, that's why I was hoping the deer cameras would get a better shot." She straightened and opened the desk drawer, grabbing her revolver. "It does tell us there's at least one person out there, looking to cause trouble, so we're not just dealing with our coyote friend."

Ian followed her as she charged up the stairs. "Is that a Colt Python?"

"Yep." After checking the store cameras, she unlocked the door.

"Nice. Can I shoot it sometime?"

"No." She automatically closed the door and covering shelves behind them, then punched in the code before the store alarm could sound. After jamming her feet into her boots and yanking on her coat, she unlocked the back door and charged into the night. Jack ran in front of her.

"Rory!" Although Ian's voice was low, he managed to pack an entire yell into his whisper. "Wait for me."

Without pausing, she headed for the trees. They would provide cover for most of the trek to the southwest corner where the alarm had been triggered. She heard Ian swearing under his breath as he followed. Rory was a fast runner, but he was faster. It was just a few seconds before he caught up with her and took the lead. She wanted to roll her eyes at his protective insistence on being the first to encounter any danger, but she couldn't do that and watch where she was going.

They'd just passed the greenhouse and chicken coop when a loud *boom* echoed through the night. Through the trees in front of them, a bright flash illuminated the darkness for a blinding moment. Ian jerked to a halt, whirling around to grab Rory and pull her into his chest, his back to the detonation. With a pained yip, Jack streaked toward them and cowered next to their legs.

"What the hell?" Ian growled. "I thought you didn't have any explosives out here."

"I didn't say that." Her voice was muffled, since her face was pressed against his chest. Despite the situation, she couldn't help relishing the comfort and security of his hold. It was a novel feeling to be protected—novel and addicting. "I said I didn't have any land mines."

"Rory..."

"Relax." Reluctantly, she tried to push away from him. After resisting for a second, he released his tight grip, allowing her to take a couple of steps back. "It was just one of the flashbangs."

When she said the words, a delayed realization hit her: something activated the grenade. That meant someone had made it inside the fence. Her eyes widening, she turned and ran, once again ignoring Ian's demand that she wait.

A man was sitting in front of the trip wire, hands pressed flat against his ears. Without pausing, she ran full speed toward the intruder. She would have closed the distance and tackled the guy if Ian hadn't shouted, "Gun, Rory!"

Skidding to a halt ten feet from the crouched interloper, she raised the Python and pointed it at him. The trespasser raised his head, turning a startled face to her, and Rory couldn't hold back a sharp inhale as she recognized him. It was Zup.

"Hands up!" she yelled, too amped to be embarrassed by the cliché. Jack stayed behind her and barked.

"What?" Zup shouted, and she realized he was still feeling the effects of the flashbang.

"What are you doing here?" she asked, biting back a frustrated snarl when he shrugged, pointing to his ears, which were most likely still ringing. "Jack, enough."

"Rory." Ian's sharp tone made her glance at him for a split second before she refocused her gaze and gun on Zup.

"What?"

"Zup didn't plan this. This dumbass couldn't figure out how to break into his own house." Ian spoke quickly. "He's just the distraction. You didn't lock the back door."

As she realized the implications, her eyes widened. "Watch him," she snapped, half turning toward the shop.

"And let you face who knows how many Riders?" he scoffed. "I don't think so."

Striding to Zup, who cringed as Ian approached, he tucked his pistol in the back of his BDUs and crouched in front of the other man. Rory shifted to the side so she could keep her gun aimed at Zup. From this angle, she could see Ian yanking the laces out of Zup's boots.

"Sorry, man!" Zup was still yelling. "He's lost his fucking mind! I didn't have a choice."

"Who?" Ian didn't pause his swift movements. Once he had a bootlace free, he jerked Zup's hands behind his back and tied them with the lace.

"What?" Zup shouted.

Finishing his knot with a hard, final yank that made Zup wince, Ian moved around so the other man could see his face. "Who?" he demanded.

"Rave."

This was not surprising to Rory. Judging by his lack of reaction, Ian was not too shocked, either. He removed the second bootlace and used it to tie Zup's ankles together.

"How many?" Ian shoved his face right up to Zup's.

He didn't even try to pretend like he didn't understand. "Three. Rave, Lester, and Duke. Duke's the only one not carrying."

With a tight nod, Ian stood and gave Zup a shove that toppled him back onto his bound hands. "Let's go."

Rory didn't hesitate, turning and running after Ian. Even if Zup managed to get out of his bindings, it would occupy him for a while. The more urgent issue was the three men who were probably in the process of clearing out her shop—her entire livelihood. When they reached the greenhouse, she skidded to a stop and grabbed Jack by the collar. The memory of Ian's comment about how easy dogs were to "subdue" echoed in her head, and she shoved a resisting Jack into the greenhouse and closed the door. As soon as it latched, she took off toward the shop again.

As they got closer, her stomach twisted at the sight of the open back door. Ian cut toward the rear wall, staying close as he moved silently toward the black rectangle of the entrance.

"Where the fuck's the good shit?"

Rory didn't recognize the voice coming from the back room, but the thought of Riders digging through her shop made rage flash through her.

"Keep looking, Les." That sounded like Rave. "That bitch has to have some hidden compartments or something."

"What if she comes back?" Les again.

"Blow her brains out."

Ian was flat against the exterior wall next to the open door. Tucking up behind him, Rory gave his shoulder an "I'm ready" squeeze. He darted into the entrance, and she immediately followed, going left as he went right, her gun up and ready.

It all happened so fast, there was no time for fear.

Something flashed to her right, but her eyes were locked on Rave and the tactical shotgun he was lifting. She reacted before he could take what was obviously intended to be a fatal shot. Aiming for center mass, she pulled the trigger twice—and both the shotgun and Rave dropped to the floor.

There was another body sprawled near Rave's, thanks to Ian's quick response, and she swung around to scan for the third burglar. Ian met her gaze, then jerked his head toward the half-open door to the front room. Staying close to the wall, she moved toward the door until she was pressed next to the opening. There was no one visible from her vantage point.

Ian had taken position on the other side of the doorway. His fingers closed carefully around the doorknob. She couldn't see his face because of the angle of the door, but his index finger tapped once, then twice. Rory grimly adjusted her grip on her gun. At the third tap, he jerked the door open.

Darting through the doorway, she went right this time, aiming toward the corner and then swinging around to check the rest of the room. In the dim glow of the security lights, the shop appeared to be empty.

After a quick glance to see Ian on her left, she padded forward toward the counter. The store had two rows of glass display cases, one on either side of the room. On Ian's side, he would have a clear view of the aisle behind the displays, so the only place someone could hide would be at the far end.

The layout was a little trickier on Rory's side, since the counter with the cash register turned the row of display cases into a stubby "L" shape. The counter could easily hide their third intruder if he crouched.

When she reached the side of the cash register, she moved quickly, pointing her gun at the inside corner. There was no one there. She paced down the row, checking the blind spot at the end. It was empty, as well.

Raising her gaze to Ian, who had rounded the end of the row on his side, he tipped his head toward the restroom. Rory wanted to smack herself for her stupid mistake. She'd passed right by the closed door without a thought. It would've served her right if she had been ambushed.

Moving quietly back to the restroom door, she moved past it and put her back against the wall as Ian mirrored her on the other side of the door. Holding her revolver ready in her left hand, she closed her fingers around the door handle, careful not to jiggle it and give away their presence. Meeting Ian's eyes, she silently mouthed, "One, two, three!"

On "three," she pushed down the handle and yanked open the door, rounding it in the same movement. The tiny room didn't allow for the usual entry, so she stopped behind and to the right of Ian.

"Don't shoot! Don't shoot!" The man was crouched between the toilet and the wall, his elbows bent and his hands hovering, palms front, on either side of his head. Rory vaguely recognized him, with his skinny frame and bulbous blue eyes—probably from occasional encounters around town. He'd never been in the shop, though. She was sure of that.

"What the hell are you doing, Duke?" Ian demanded, tucking his gun into the back of his BDUs. Rory kept hers aimed at the cowering man. "This is a big step up from shoplifting and stealing from unlocked cars. Are you trying to get yourself killed?"

"I know, Walsh." Duke dropped his chin, tucking his hands closer to his head, as if to protect himself. "I know. But Rave told me it'd be an easy score, and he said he'd sponsor me with the Riders if I helped him with this."

"Shit, Duke." Ian rubbed his hand over his mouth, looking suddenly tired. "Stand up." When Duke sent a nervous glance toward Rory, Ian added, "She's not going to shoot you unless you do something stupid. Something *else* stupid."

Duke shakily pushed himself to his feet, keeping a wary eye on Rory's revolver. She backed out of the doorway, allowing him to exit, followed closely by Ian.

"You packing, Duke?" Ian's gaze ran over the other man's baggy jeans and coat.

"Nah. I never mess with guns."

Ian's laugh exploded in a sharp crack that made the other two jump. Rory sent him a quick, chiding glance. She made a mental note to mention to him later that it was a bad idea to startle the woman holding the gun. Ian swept an arm to indicate the shop. "What the hell are you doing here, then?"

"I told you," he whined. "Rave—"

"Stop," Ian cut him off, frisking Duke quickly and not very gently. He pulled a folded knife out of Duke's pocket and dropped it into his own. "Ror, have you got any duct tape?"

"Who doesn't?" She jerked her head toward the cash register. "Behind the counter, second drawer on the right."

He retrieved it and quickly returned with the roll. As Rory kept her gun aimed at the skinny man, Ian strapped his wrists together behind his back. After telling him to sit on the ground, he taped Duke's ankles, as well.

"Roll onto your stomach."

Although Duke gave a protesting whine, he complied, and Ian taped his bound wrists and ankles together, hog-tying him. Rory figured he wasn't much of a threat in his current position, so she slid her revolver into her coat pocket.

"I hate to say it," Ian said once he finished, "but we're going to have to call the sheriff."

Although she made a face, Rory said, "I figured. There are two bodies in the back room, after all." As she said the words, the image of Rave crumpling to the ground flashed in her brain. Bile rose in her throat, and she swallowed.

"What?" Duke yelped. "Bodies?"

"Quiet," Ian ordered.

"I'll call on the store phone," she said, walking on suddenly shaky legs to the counter.

Ian's sharp gaze focused on her. "I'll check on the two in back. You okay?"

"Of course." The phone rattled against the base as she picked it up, contradicting her words. It took a couple of tries before her shaky fingers could hit the right numbers. As the phone rang in her ear, she met Ian's concerned eyes and tried to force a smile. "Don't be nice to me, or I'll get all weepy on you."

"It's okay if you do."

Since someone on the other end answered, she only shook her head at him. He frowned, but turned and headed toward the back room. "Hi, Libby. It's Rory Sorenson." The dispatcher had been in the shop two months before, looking for a muzzle loader for her brother's birthday. She had a squeaky voice that was easy to recognize. "Could you send some deputies this way? My shop was burglarized."

"Oh my goodness, Rory!" She could hear the rapid tap-tap of keyboard strokes as Libby typed. "Are you okay?"

"I'm fine." Letting out a shaky breath, she closed her eyes. She *was* fine—well, she would be eventually.

"Is there a possibility that they're still in the building?"

"They are, but I'm pretty sure two are dead, and one's tied up."

There was a pause. Not even typing broke the silence for a long moment. "Oh my goodness." The keystrokes resumed with a vengeance. "Deputies are on their way, and I've paged the sheriff. Medical is en route, as well, although they'll just stage nearby until they get the all clear from law enforcement that it's safe to come on scene."

"Thanks, Libby." Ian returned and gave a grim shake of his head. She felt the bile creep up her throat again.

"No problem, hon. Stay on the line with me until the deputies arrive, okay?"

Rory remembered something. "I need to run out and unlock the gate, and I'm on a landline. Can I call you back in five minutes?"

Ian held out his hand for the keys, but she shook her head. It might be wimpy of her, but Rory did not want to be left alone in the shop with a trussed-up Duke and two dead bodies.

"I'd rather you didn't go outside until the deputies clear your property and make sure there isn't anyone else nearby," Libby said with worry evident in her voice.

"There is, but he's tied up, too. With his bootlaces." It was probably just a stress reaction, but Rory suddenly wanted to laugh.

"Oh my goodness."

After a short discussion, both Rory and Ian ended up going out to unlock the gate. When they returned to the shop, Rory reached for the phone to call Libby again but hesitated, looking at the back-room door.

"What?" Ian asked, following her gaze.

"I should probably check that they didn't…um, disturb anything." She gave the listening Duke a wary look.

"I can do that." Ian started to move toward the door, but she hurried after him.

"No," she said, catching his arm. "I'll be able to tell if anything's not right."

Watching her carefully, he didn't move from his position blocking the door.

"It's fine," she said, wondering how many more times she would use the word "fine" that night. "I'll just do a quick check and then get out of there."

After another hesitation, he stepped back. Straightening her spine, she forced her legs to walk forward. At the threshold, she paused. The smell was already terrible. She didn't remember her parents' bodies smelling so strongly, although shock had messed up her memory of that event.

There was a lot of blood. It was pooled around the bodies and even sprayed over the walls and her worktable. She wouldn't have guessed that two bodies could hold so much blood. A strangely detached portion of her brain thought of how much cleaning was going to be required before her back room was usable once again.

Forcing her gaze from the bodies and blood, she focused on walking over to the cabinets lining the far wall, carefully placing her feet in spots clear of blood and other matter she didn't want to think about. The cabinet doors had been opened, but the secret drawers had not been disturbed. After checking each one, she picked her way back to the front room.

"Okay?" Ian asked.

Unsure if he meant the state of the cabinets or of her mind—one of which appeared to be fine while the other was still up for debate—Rory just answered, "Yes."

Ten minutes later, the first sheriff's department squad flew through the gate. As Rory opened the front door to let Deputy Chris Jennings inside, she noticed that the mountains in the east were edged with pink. The sun was starting to rise.

Since Chris had bought a couple of hunting rifles from her, she was on friendly terms with the cheerful deputy. Despite that, he had both her and Ian handcuffed and weaponless within minutes. He sat the two of them on the floor, their backs to the shop wall. Once they were secured, he grimly ventured into the back, pulling on blue latex gloves as he went.

The deputy quickly returned to the front area, looking a little pale. Although his voice was low, she heard him speaking into his shoulder mic.

"Neither victim has a pulse, and there are signs of lividity in both bodies, so I did not begin CPR. I have two people in custody, and there is a third who was restrained with duct tape before I arrived on scene. None are complaining of any injuries." He paused and then continued in an urgent tone that contrasted to the calm, objective way he'd delivered the previous information, "Please tell Rob to hurry his ass up."

Chris eyed Duke. "As soon as another unit arrives, I'll get you out of that duct tape."

"That's okay," Duke said. "This tape's actually more comfortable than cuffs, anyway."

Although Chris gave him an odd look, the deputy just said, "That's…good, I suppose."

While Jennings's focus was on Duke, Rory caught Ian's attention and mouthed, "Zup?"

"Hey, Chris." The deputy turned toward him. "There's a fourth guy. He's on the southwest side of the property. He was tied up, but he might've managed to get loose by now."

Chris's gaze shot to the door, as if Zup was going to be charging inside at any second, and his hand reflexively touched the butt of his holstered gun. "Shit, Ian," he groaned. "Could this be any more of a cluster?"

Ian just shrugged, the motion abbreviated by his cuffed hands.

"Um…I know it's not a priority right now," Rory said, glancing across the room to the countertop where Chris had placed her beloved revolver after clearing it, "but do you think I'll ever get my Colt back? It was my sixteenth birthday present from my parents."

"You should, eventually, if you're not charged with anything." After a pause, Chris added, "I'm not sure if that's the best sweet-sixteen gift ever, or if it's completely messed up."

Rory huffed a laugh, but her amusement didn't last long. "Me neither." She realized Ian was watching her closely. "What?"

"You okay?"

"Yes. Quit asking." There was a tremor in her voice that made her flush with shame. She wasn't dying, wasn't even hurt, so there was no reason for her to be shaking.

"I will when you quit lying."

"I'm not lying." She bit out the words, glaring at him. "I'm not injured. Therefore, I am okay."

Ian made a frustrated sound. "That isn't—" Whatever he was going to say was interrupted by the arrival of the sheriff. Rob looked around the room, his sharp gaze taking in everything within a few seconds.

"Bodies are in the back."

With a nod, the sheriff moved to the door leading to the back room and looked inside. When he turned back to Chris, his face showed grim resignation before it returned to his usual implacable expression.

"I'll call the state investigators again. Damn it."

Chapter 8

Before the BCA investigators made it to the scene, a lot of other people did. Once several more deputies arrived, the sheriff sent a group to collect Zup. They returned in short order with the shivering and furious man, the bootlaces around his wrists having been replaced with handcuffs.

After turning Zup over to the sheriff's care, the deputies swept the property, looking for any other suspects. When their search turned up only Jack and the chickens, the scene was declared secure, and the coroner was allowed into the shop.

Belly was in a cranky mood. "So you two are the reason for my being yanked out of bed at the ass-crack of dawn. Why am I not surprised?"

Too tired to think of a clever comeback, Rory just gave the coroner a poor attempt at a smile. Ian offered Belly a silent lift of his chin in greeting. After eyeing the two of them balefully for another moment, Belly turned and stalked toward the back room.

"Rory." Rob crouched down next to her. "I need to get your statement."

She'd figured this was coming. He'd already talked to a de-taped and newly handcuffed Duke, as well as Zup, who'd gone from raging to sullen. He was currently cuffed and sitting against the opposite wall, glaring across the room at Rory and Ian.

With her hands behind her back, she struggled a little to get her feet underneath her. Rob held her upper arm to help her stand. Once she was upright, Rory swayed, lack of sleep mixed with the shock of the night's events making her light-headed. She must've looked pretty pale, since Rob didn't let her go once she was standing. Instead, he kept his fingers latched around her arm as he escorted her across the room to the makeshift interview area.

Since outside was freezing cold, and the back room still contained bodies, the sheriff had quietly questioned Duke and Zup in the front corner of the shop, as far as he could get from the other witnesses and suspects. After helping her take a seat on a stool, Rob pulled out a pen and small notepad, and turned on the digital recorder hooked to his duty belt.

"Why don't you tell me what happened?" he said.

The idea of going through the whole story made exhaustion flood over her, but Rory forced her shoulders to square. *Not dying*, she reminded herself. *Not even bleeding, so there's no reason to whine*. Taking a deep breath, she told the entire tale, from the first night the alarm was triggered to her call to Libby.

When she finished, Rob glanced around the shop and gave a puzzled frown. "Where are your living quarters?"

This subject made her even more uncomfortable than talking about shooting Rave. "Uh, downstairs."

"Where's the entrance?"

First Ian found out how to get into her home, and now the sheriff wanted the details. Rory didn't like it. "In the back."

"I didn't see it."

"You were probably distracted. By the bodies and blood and stuff."

"No, I would've—"

"Shouldn't we talk about last night?" She knew it was probably stupid to interrupt the sheriff to demand a change in the direction of his questioning, but Rory was tired and not up to revealing her secrets to a stranger. It was hard enough with Ian, and he was... Her brain refused to define exactly what Ian was to her. He was not a stranger. She decided to leave it at that.

Rob was eyeing her curiously.

"Sorry, did I miss a question?" she asked, flustered. "My brain shut off for a minute."

"It's fine." He gave her a small, encouraging smile. "I asked what your relationship was with Erwin Banks."

"Who?" Rory stared at him blankly.

"Also known as Rave."

"His name was Erwin?" He so did not look like an Erwin. Hiding a wince, she mentally corrected herself. He *hadn't* looked like an Erwin. Thanks to her, Rave was in the past tense now.

"Yes. Answer the question, please."

Rory had to think back to remember what the question had been. "Oh! Um...we didn't have a relationship. He was kind of a jerk."

"But you knew him."

"Yes. He used to come into the shop with Billy."

"William Wysocki?"

She lifted one shoulder in a shrug, dropping it when it tugged the handcuff against her wrist bone. "Uh, I suppose. I never knew his last name. He was just Billy."

"So, Billy and Rave were customers?" His

expression attempted to be casual, but there was a sharp edge to his look, and she knew to tread carefully, despite her exhaustion.

"Billy liked to stop in and look at the guns."

"Did he buy any?"

Although she tried for an innocent look, she wasn't sure how well she pulled it off. "I doubt he'd pass the background check."

"Uh-huh." Apparently, her guileless expression needed some work. "What about the guns in the back room? The ones not requiring a background check. Did he buy any of those?"

Big-mouthed Zup. "Guns in the back room?" Shaking her head, she let her eyebrows draw together in confusion. "I have a couple back there that are in for cleaning or repairs, but they're not for sale."

"Come on, Rory," he said, almost gently. "It's the worst-kept secret in Field County. Everyone knows about the guns you keep in the back."

"Sorry." She forgot about the cuffs and shrugged again, then held back a wince. "I don't know what you're talking about. Shouldn't we be focusing on the burglary?"

Rob looked tired, but he didn't push any further. "Why do you think Rave and the others targeted your shop?"

It seemed like such a stupid question that she paused to think how it could lead to a possible verbal trap. She couldn't think of any, so she answered, tipping her chin at the front room and all its contents. "The guns."

"These guns?" He glanced around at the display cases.

"Yes."

"Hmm." After studying her for a long minute, he

moved to a different question. "How many times did Rave visit your shop?"

The questioning continued for what felt like hours. The sheriff would ask one thing, and then ask it in a different way a few minutes later. He went over what happened and then over it again, until she started swaying in her chair. Rob brought up the back room several times, but she kept up her protestations of confusion and innocence.

"Rob," Ian finally called from his spot across the room. "Enough."

Rob sent him a reproving look. "We're almost done, Ian."

"Look at her. She's about to fall off her chair."

Rob directed his gaze back at Rory and frowned, then reached down to turn off the recorder. "Okay. We can finish later." To her relief, he helped her off her stool, since she found she needed the support to stand and then walk in a semistraight line. Once back in her original spot, she slid into a sitting position and watched as Ian shrugged off the sheriff's helping hand.

"I've got it, thanks." Ian stood and walked with Rob to the interview corner.

Although she was hoping to strain her ears and overhear parts of Ian's statement, her eyelids were not cooperating. With a sigh, she rested her head back against the wall and gave in to sleep.

Someone was shaking her shoulder. Rory had the distinct urge to punch this person for pulling her out of wonderful unconsciousness and back into the reality of dead people and exhaustion and sore wrists. Reluctantly opening her eyes, she saw Ian's face come into focus. He looked pissed.

Sitting up abruptly, she shook the last tendrils of sleep out of her brain. "What's wrong?"

"Nothing." When she didn't say anything, he shook his head. "Rob just has some fu—uh, messed-up theories, that's all."

Glancing down at the hand that had been shaking her shoulder, she said, "You got the cuffs off, at least. That's a good sign."

"You're next." Ian tipped his head toward Chris, who smiled at her.

"Come on, Sleeping Beauty," the deputy said. "Let's turn you loose."

"Does this mean we're cleared, then?" With Ian's help, she scrambled to her feet and turned her back toward Chris.

"It means you're not getting arrested right now," he hedged while easing the cuffs from first one wrist and then the other. "I'll let Rob talk to you about the rest of it."

"Thanks." Rory rubbed her wrists, although her flinch came more from the pulling ache in her shoulders than from any bruising from the cuffs.

With another smile, Chris headed for the door, and Rob moved toward them. Rory didn't miss the way Ian stiffened at his approach. Once she'd gotten some sleep and was thinking rationally again, she needed to ask Ian what was going on between him and the sheriff. Until recently, Rory had been under the impression that the two men got along well. The memory of Ian's cryptic mention of the murder investigation rang in her head.

"Your shop is going to be off-limits for several days while the crime-lab people do their stuff," Rob warned, breaking into her thoughts.

Although she should have expected the news, the realization hit her like a physical blow. She barely caught herself before taking a step back. If she couldn't be in the shop, then that meant her home was inaccessible, too. Rory wondered if she could sneak down to the bunker and hole up like a mole until the invasion was over.

"Can I stay downstairs?" The question popped out before she could reconsider it. She restrained a cringe.

Rob jumped right on that. "Depends on where the entrance is. I'm not really clear on how you get down there. Why don't you show me?"

"That's okay." It really, really wasn't okay, but it was a better option than revealing her home to anyone. "I'll stay at the Black Bear Inn."

"No." Ian's hard, implacable tone brought her gaze to him. "You'll stay with me."

She blinked, holding back the arguments that immediately rushed to her lips.

"You still at Julius's place in Liverton?" Rob asked.

Ian shook his head. "I'm checking in on him several times a day, but I've moved back into my house."

"How's he doing?"

"Not great." A muscle twitched in his cheek, but his tone was even when he asked the sheriff, "Can we go now?"

After a slight hesitation, Rob said, "Sure. Go get some sleep. I'll need to talk to both of you again over the next few days, though."

A small smirk curled Ian's lips. "So we shouldn't leave town?"

Rob didn't smile. "Exactly."

So many people trailing about the place meant that Rory couldn't get downstairs to grab any basic necessities. That meant she was going to her first-ever sleepover unarmed. She didn't even have a toothbrush.

Ian had turned his Bronco into the driveway of a small Victorian house on the southeast side of Simpson. After parking her pickup next to his vehicle, she turned off the truck but didn't move. Jack, riding shotgun, waited patiently on the seat next to her.

A knock on her window made her jump. She rolled down the window with the hand crank.

"You getting out?"

"Yes," she said a little defensively, but she didn't make any move to open the door.

"Today?"

That didn't even deserve an answer, so she changed the subject. "Why do you live here if the Riders are based in Liverton?"

"I'm close to Station One." He seemed to take the switch in topics in stride. "Sometimes I'll spend my days off at my mom's—well, at Julius's house in Liverton. I was staying there up until a few days ago, but I don't think it was helping Julius. It made it too easy for him to…check out."

Since she couldn't think of a response to that, she changed the subject again. "Is Billy pissed?" Rory had heard Ian's phone buzzing in his pocket like a swarm of angry bees when they'd been sitting, handcuffed, on her shop floor.

"Yeah." His shrug was nonchalant, as if Billy's anger was nothing to cause concern. Rory knew better. "He thought I should've called him before the sheriff, so he could've cleaned up first."

"Gotten rid of the bodies, you mean?"

"Maybe." He folded his arms and rested them on the top of the open window. "He definitely would've gotten Zup out of there."

"Will this cause problems for you? With the Riders, I mean."

"Nothing I can't handle. I'm used to being the odd man out."

"Really?" She cocked her head as she eyed him. "Because you're with the fire department?"

"Yeah."

Rory opened her mouth to ask him another question, but he took a step back and opened her door. Apparently, he was done sharing.

"Out."

Reluctantly sliding out of the truck, she moved aside so Jack could jump to the ground. She cranked the window closed and locked the door. The old beast of a truck was stiff, and she had to use both hands to slam the door hard enough to get it to latch. When she turned around, Ian was eyeing her with amusement.

"You lock that thing?"

She stared at him. "Of course. Don't you lock the Bronco?"

"Why? There's nothing in there to steal." He ushered her toward the side door of his house with a hand on her lower back. Jack trotted around the front yard, exploring.

He was obviously dealing with their temporary relocation better than she was. "Besides, this is Simpson. If someone broke into my truck, I'd know exactly who it was, and then I'd go to Benny's trailer and kick his ass."

She smiled a little at that, although the thought of leaving her truck open and vulnerable to anyone who wanted to crawl around in the cab made her truly uncomfortable. Ian held open the door for her. Before she went inside, she glanced around at the few neighboring homes within view. There was a flash of movement from the upstairs window of a cedar-sided house.

"Your neighbor is watching," Rory said in a low voice, tilting her head toward the offender.

After glancing in the direction she indicated, Ian shrugged and nudged her through the doorway. "That's just Daisy. She doesn't leave the house, so we're her entertainment."

"She doesn't leave? Ever?"

"Nope. Hasn't for years."

"Wow. Guess I'm really not the only strange one in Simpson." Rory was distracted by the large kitchen they'd entered. Brushing by her legs, Jack walked into the room, as relaxed as if he'd lived at Ian's all his life. The decor was dated but cute, with avocado appliances, white cabinets, and a tile floor. A window over the sink let in the sunlight, and she couldn't stop looking at it.

"Doesn't that make you feel... I don't know, exposed?" she asked Ian.

"What?" He followed her gaze and then looked back at Rory. "The window? Not really. It has curtains."

Eyeing the frilly lace covering the bottom half of the window, Rory said, "I see that. Did you pick those out yourself?"

"They came with the house, smart-ass." He turned her shoulders toward the arched doorway leading to the living room and then gave her butt a slap.

Whirling to face him, she gave him her best glare. "Watch it. I've shot people for less." As soon as the words left her mouth, the slow-motion movie of Rave collapsing to the floor played in her mind, and she flinched.

As if he could see exactly what was going on in her brain, he didn't respond to her poor choice of words. Instead, he turned her again, more gently this time. "Time for bed, Ror," was all he said.

She allowed him to guide her through the living room, where the large, plentiful windows made her a little sick to her stomach, and up a staircase. Jack followed. Running her fingers along the banister, Rory admired the ornate rails. The house was an odd mixture of masculine furniture and fussy details, but it was charming and strangely welcoming.

Ian led her into a small room holding just a double bed, a small dresser, and a nightstand. There was an oval rug next to the bed, and Jack stretched out on it with a low groan. The ceiling sloped to the wall with the windows, creating angles that made the otherwise bland room interesting. When he saw where her gaze had landed, Ian moved to close the blinds covering both windows. Sunlight still peeked around the edges of the coverings, illuminating the room.

He frowned. "You going to be able to sleep with it this light?"

With a snort, she reminded him, "I was sleeping sitting up on the floor of my shop with my hands cuffed behind my back. I think I'll manage."

"Okay." He hesitated, his gaze bouncing around the room. "Bathroom's down the hall on the right."

He took a step toward the doorway and then paused. "Sorry about the colors."

Rory looked at him blankly, and he gestured toward the bed. It took her a few seconds, but then she realized the bedding was differing shades of brown. She huffed a laugh.

"I'll survive an absence of pink for a few days," she said.

He didn't smile, but just nodded solemnly, as if it had been truly in question. "Do you need anything else?"

"A water bowl for Jack. And do you mind if I shower?" she asked, feeling suddenly grubby. A deputy had checked her for blood spatter and hadn't found any, but she could feel phantom blood on her skin. "And borrow some clothes?"

"Go ahead." He waved toward the doorway. "I'll see what I can dig up. Everything I own is going to be huge on you."

"That's fine. At least it'll be clean." She sent him a sideways look. "It'll be clean, right?"

"Yes," he said with mock offense. "I do know how to do laundry."

Too tired to respond beyond an amused snort, she moved past him into the hallway. When she entered the bathroom, she cringed at yet another window.

"Who needs a window in the bathroom?" she muttered, checking that the blinds were closed before starting to undress. It took her a minute to figure out the shower controls, but she managed to get it operating. As she waited for the water to heat, she shivered, her teeth chattering together more from nerves than from cold. It was strange to be naked in someone else's house, especially surrounded by all those windows. Rory sent a glare at the blind-covered glass.

After testing the water and finding it warm, she stepped under the spray. It felt wonderful, and she stood still for several minutes, letting the jets pound against her skin. Although much of the house's decor was older, his bathroom had obviously been updated. The shower was huge compared to hers, and she spent a moment thinking about how it would fit two. Her brain immediately pictured a naked, wet Ian. Somehow, she knew just how the water would trickle over his skin, running down the grooves between his pecs to his ridged abdomen, and then lower… She flushed from her cheeks to her toes.

Shoving the blush-inducing fantasy away, she reached for the soap.

"Rory." Ian's voice on the other side of the shower curtain made her freeze in place, her hand outstretched toward the soap. "I'm putting some clothes on the counter for you."

She didn't say anything. She couldn't. Her lungs felt like they'd frozen, right along with the rest of her.

"Rory?" Oh, jeez Louise, now he sounded even closer. "You okay?"

"Fine!" The word came out high-pitched and fast. Her eyes closed in humiliation. She had actually *squeaked*. "I'm fine." That had been a little better, although she was still in the rodent-family range.

"Sure?"

His voice was really close to the curtain now, and

Rory panicked. What if he looked in to check on her? "Yes! Fine! Go away!"

"Okay." Now he sounded amused. Rory didn't care, as long as he was stepping away from the shower curtain. "I'm going."

"Thank you." Now that the crisis had been averted, embarrassment at her overreaction began to warm her cheeks. "For the clothes, I mean."

"You're welcome." He was definitely holding back a laugh, the bastard. To her relief, she heard the click of the door closing behind him.

Once he left, she hurried to finish, washing her hair and body at warp speed. Rinsing quickly, she turned off the water and peeked her head around the edge of the curtain.

Her clothes were gone. She figured that Ian had probably grabbed them to wash, which was good, except he'd taken her underwear. The idea of him handling her underwear, even just enough to toss it into the washing machine, made her flush.

As fast as possible, she toweled off and dressed in Ian's sweatpants and top. The clothes were enormous on her, as Ian had warned, and she had to roll up the pants and fold the waistband over a few times before she could even manage to walk. Avoiding the mirror, she ran her fingers through her damp hair, picking out the worst of the knots.

Once that was done, there was no more delaying. Rory wasn't even sure why she was nervous about facing Ian again. Frustrated with herself, she squared her shoulders and opened the door.

Ian was framed in the doorway, his fist lifted as if

he'd been about to knock. With a quick inhale of surprise, Rory stopped herself before she took a step back. Instead, she held her position and raised her eyebrows in question.

"Just about to check on you." He lowered his hand to his side.

"I'm fine," she said for the hundredth time that day. "Ready for bed."

Stepping to the side, he gestured for her to move past him. Her arm brushed his chest as she left the bathroom, setting off a buzzing feeling under her skin.

"Stupid," she muttered.

"What?"

"Nothing." It seemed that embarrassment was her constant companion when she was around Ian. "Good night."

It was an odd thing to say, considering that the afternoon sun illuminated the hallway, but he took it in stride. "'Night."

With great effort, she didn't look back at him as she hurried toward the guest room. She felt the heat of his gaze burning her back the entire time, until she rushed into the room and closed the door. Jack swiveled an ear toward her, and his tail thumped against the rug, but otherwise he didn't move. Leaning against the door, Rory let out a relieved breath. She'd survived being naked in Ian's home. After that, the rest of this sleepover would be a breeze.

Even though she was exhausted, her sleep was uneven. Half-awake memories of the previous night mixed with dreams, creating a nightmarish mishmash. Occasionally, she jerked completely awake. Each time, she was relieved to be out of her restless doze, but she was too tired to stay alert, so she'd fall right back into it. The room didn't help, with all its windows. It would be too easy for someone to watch her. She could almost feel the pressure of eyes on her, of Billy's rage-filled glare. He could be outside right now, determined to get retribution for Rave. Her tired brain ran over everything she'd sold to the Riders. Hadn't Billy bought that SR-25 sniper rifle from her? He could be aiming it at her head right now. Startling to full consciousness, she barely resisted the urge to crawl under the bed.

She longed for the safety of her bunker. Giving up, she dragged her exhausted body out of bed, along with the brown-toned comforter and a pillow.

The closet was small. Even the most optimistic real estate agent couldn't call it a walk-in. Rory managed to squeeze inside, though, and made a nest on the floor. The wooden boards beneath her were not comfortable, but the security she felt after closing the door between her and the windows made the hard floor worth it. In less than a minute, she was asleep.

Chapter 9

"RORY!"

Her eyes popped open at Ian's shout. It was so dark! She never slept without the glow of the security lights. She sat up abruptly, one arm swinging instinctively toward an imaginary attacker as the other groped for a gun that wasn't there. The back of her hand connected with a wall, sending a shock of pain through her and reminding her of where she was. *Ian's. Windows. Closet. Right.*

"What's wrong?" Her voice sounded croaky, so she cleared her throat as she shifted positions. Her body protested, her muscles complaining about the time spent on the hard wood floor.

The closet door swung open, and light from the fluorescent bulbs in the overhead fixture blinded her. Covering her eyes with her hand, she flinched away.

"Why are you in the closet?" Ian demanded.

Blinking as her eyes adjusted to the light, she peered at his silhouetted figure. "It was too bright out there. Plus, you know, windows."

"Windows?"

"Yes."

"What about them?"

"I don't like them. Anyone could be looking in. They're glass, so someone could throw something through them, like a Molotov cocktail or a grenade.

Plus, they let in the light." She stretched, and her spine popped several times.

There was a pause before Ian spoke again. "They had blinds over them."

She shrugged. "Still don't like windows."

"Every house has windows." When she just looked at him, he amended his statement. "Every house except yours has windows."

"So?"

"So haven't you stayed anywhere with windows before?"

"No."

He paused again. "Are you telling me you've never stayed anywhere except your house?"

For some reason, she was embarrassed to admit that. She wasn't going to lie about it, though. "So?" she demanded, her voice sharp.

"That's..." He trailed off as he watched her like she was a strange species of bug. That made her feel lonely and a little sad. She stood abruptly, shoving past him to get out of the closet.

"It's what?"

Ian shook his head. "Nothing. I have to go to work. Did you want to join me or stay here?"

"Join you." Her answer was immediate. She didn't even have to consider whether she'd rather stay in this fishbowl of a house alone or spend the night at Station One with Ian. "I need different clothes, though."

"I washed yours," he said, nodding toward the end of the bed where he'd left her things in a folded pile. "I'll let Jack out in the back. It's fenced. There's some leftover chicken and rice—would it be okay to feed him that?"

"That'd be great. It's pretty close to the homemade dog food I make for him, actually."

"Can you be ready to go in ten minutes?"

"Sure." She stretched again as he headed for the door. After pulling on her clothes, she made a quick trip to the bathroom.

As she passed him in the hall, Ian said, "There's a spare toothbrush in the top right drawer."

"Thanks." That drawer, she discovered to her delight, also held toothpaste and a comb. It was funny how the absence of simple things made her appreciate them more.

"Two minutes!" Ian called from the hall.

"Ready." She opened the door and walked out to join him.

"Speedy," he said with an approving nod. "Good."

Shrugging off his praise, she followed him down the stairs. "What time is it?"

"Quarter 'til seven."

"Your shift starts at seven?" Their boots were lined up next to the door. As Ian reached for his, Rory eyed the two pairs of footwear. It was oddly cozy, seeing the boots together like that. She thought of her bunker, and how there was only one of so many things—one pair of boots by the door, one coat, one plate to wash after dinner, one dent in the pillow in the morning.

"Yeah. Seven to seven. We have four twelve-hour shifts, and then we get four days off."

Twelve hours would be a long time for her dog to stay alone in an unfamiliar house. He was normally well behaved, but she didn't want to come back to find he'd eaten Ian's couch. "Can Jack stay in the yard while we're gone?"

Shaking his head, Ian said, "It's still pretty cold, and I don't have a shelter for him back there. He can come to the station with us."

"Good." She moved to pull on her boots, thinking of her other animal dependents. "I'll take my truck and meet you at the station. I need to close the chickens up for the night." That morning, she'd let them out and fed them before they'd left for Ian's house.

He frowned. "I don't want you out there by yourself."

"I won't be by myself," she argued, pulling on her coat. "There will be several law enforcement officers there, as well."

"You don't know that for sure." Pulling out his cell phone, he tapped the screen a few times and then put it to his ear. "Hey, Squirrel. You free? Great. I need a favor."

When he eventually ended the call and moved to put his phone back in his pocket, she stopped him. "You'd better give the sheriff a heads-up that some strange guy's going to be on my property, messing with my chickens."

"Good idea." He made the call. His tone was quite a bit stiffer talking to Rob than it had been during the conversation with Squirrel.

Once he put away his phone, they headed out to the Bronco, collecting Jack on the way.

"I thought you and Rob were friends?" she said, raising the end of the statement to turn it into a question.

"Never really *friends*," he answered as they climbed into the SUV. "Usually we get along pretty well, but lately the sheriff's department has developed some jacked-up theories about me and the Riders. It's made things tense."

"Is this about the murder?"

His jaw grew visibly tight. "Yeah. Supposedly, something that used to belong to me ended up by the body Lou found in Mission Reservoir."

Her eyes growing wide, she stared at his grim profile. "So the sheriff thinks you killed him?"

"Maybe." He drummed his fingers against the steering wheel. "At the very least, he suspects the Riders are involved."

"Why do you stay with them—the Riders, I mean?" she asked. It felt like an extremely intrusive question, but she'd been wondering for a while, and something about the dim interior of the Bronco made intimate conversation easier.

"I grew up in the club. They're family. I can't abandon my family, even if some of them make piss-poor decisions."

With a frown, Rory asked, "Are you angry that I killed Rave?" She tried to keep the words from turning into full-color images in her mind, but she wasn't successful. The movie in her brain flared to life, and Rave crumpled to the floor again in grisly detail. Swallowing down bile, she wondered if the memory would ever lose its vividness.

"No." Ian sounded surprised. "In another two seconds, he would've killed you. The fu—ah, jerk deserved what he got."

"But he was an MC member, part of your family."

"Just because he was a Rider doesn't mean he deserved to keep living, not when he was ready to point a gun at you and pull the trigger." Ian turned into the Station One parking lot, his movements jerkier than normal on the steering wheel. The abrupt turn made her shoulder bump the passenger door. Putting a hand on the dash, she steadied herself as he whipped the Bronco around and backed into a parking space.

Thinking about Ian's response, Rory jumped out of the SUV and circled around to the back to release Jack. Ian had made it there first.

"Was Lester a member?" she asked as he opened the hatch to let Jack jump out of the Bronco.

"No. Just a dumbass Rave pulled into his scheme." Despite his even tone, Ian's mouth was flattened into a hard line, making Rory wonder whether he had a movie of Lester's death playing on a loop in his head, too.

"Have you talked to Billy again?" They headed for the station door with Jack bounding circles around them.

"Briefly." Opening the door, he held it for her. The gesture threw her, and she wondered if she'd ever get used to Ian's courtesies. Jack brushed past both of them, making a beeline to the training room. Her dog, obviously, had no problem with men holding the door for him.

As soon as she entered, there was a small shriek.

"Rory!" Lou ran over to grab her in a hug. Although Rory tried to step back to avoid the embrace, there was nowhere to go with Ian right behind her. She had no choice but to accept Lou's hard squeeze. Luckily, the hug was quick. "I heard about the break-in at your shop. I'm so sorry!"

"Why?" When Lou looked at her, obviously puzzled by the question, Rory elaborated, "Why are you sorry? It wasn't any of your doing."

"No, I'm just sorry you had to go through that." Although Rory was instantly embarrassed she'd missed the obvious meaning, Lou didn't seem annoyed about explaining. "Are you okay?"

"Fine. How'd you hear about it already?" A quick glance around the group of firefighters and dive-team members showed that everyone knew. Rory could tell by their expressions, a mixture of avid curiosity and awkward condolence. Jack had zeroed in on Soup, who had gone down on one knee so he could rub the dog's upturned belly. Jack was always able to pick out the biggest dog lovers in the crowd.

Lou snorted. "With this group of gossipmongers? I'm sure they were glued to their radios early this morning, listening to the play-by-play, and then they activated the phone tree."

"There's a phone tree?"

Although she grinned, Lou said, "Nope. Well, not to my knowledge, anyway. I was just kidding about that part, although I wouldn't be at all shocked if they did have one in place."

Obviously, Rory needed more sleep, since she couldn't seem to carry on a conversation without missing social cues left and right. Usually, she could at least *pretend* to be normal. "Right. Of course there's not."

"Sparks!" Callum barked. When both women looked over at him, he was scowling and tapping his watch. Even though she wasn't even a part of the dive team, Rory had to restrain the urge to fall into line. Lou, however, just rolled her eyes.

"I'd better get over there. Looks like training is starting." Lou gave Rory another quick hug. "Let me know if you need anything. I have an idea of what you're going through, and I know it sucks. Even if you just want to talk, stop in to The Coffee Spot some afternoon."

"Okay." Rory was touched but not sure how to respond. She settled on a stiff nod. "Thanks."

"No problem. Like I said, I've been there." With a warm smile, she headed toward the group of dive-team members. A simmering Callum looked about ready to go nuclear. Within less than a minute, his scowl had disappeared, and he even smiled at something Lou said. Rory sighed, wishing she had even a fraction of Lou's easy way with people.

"Who are you looking at?" Ian's voice in her ear startled her, and she jumped and flushed. Her reaction immediately made her irritated with herself. What was it about the man that regressed her back to her tongue-tied, twelve-year-old self? Ian must have followed the direction of her gaze, and his grunt sounded displeased. "You won't have much luck with that. He's completely gone on Lou."

"What?" Confused, she turned her head to look at Ian. He was leaning down a little as he looked over her shoulder, so their faces were close—really close. Her blush flamed brighter.

"Callum." He sent a dark look in the other man's direction.

"What about him?" Rory didn't know if her flustered state made it hard to understand the conversation, or if Ian was just not making any sense.

"You were eyeing him like he was a gold-plated shotgun," he grumped.

"What? I was not!"

Still glaring at Callum, Ian just made a sound of disbelief.

"I wasn't! I was watching Lou."

"Oh. Why?"

It would've been a good time to stop talking, but Rory was flustered, which brought on babbling. "I was just wishing I had Lou's social skills."

"Why would you want to be like Lou?"

"She makes interacting with people look so effortless."

Ian threw an arm over her shoulders and steered her toward the back of the room. "You interact with people just fine. I've seen you at your store and at Levi's."

Although she stiffened initially at the unexpected contact, she relaxed after a few moments. The weight of his arm actually felt good, comforting even. "At the store, maybe. If the topic isn't about guns, though, I'm hopeless."

"No, you're not. Everyone was coming over while we were eating last night to talk to you, not me. You know people."

She just shrugged as he ushered her into the storeroom.

"I like Lou, but I don't know how Callum deals," he said. "Her brain and mouth are always going at a hundred miles an hour. She'd tire me out."

"They seem to work well together," Rory said, looking around the storage area. Gear and equipment were piled everywhere, with only a narrow path of floor showing. "She loosens him up, and he keeps her focused. What do we need from here?"

"Yeah, I can see that. He definitely seems happy with her—they both do. And we're getting you some bunker gear to go with that blue helmet of yours."

"Okay," she said doubtfully, eyeing the unkempt

piles. "I don't suppose they're arranged in any kind of logical fashion—maybe by size?"

His snort killed her faint strain of hope, and she sighed, wading into the stacks.

It took some digging, but they eventually found some pants and a coat that fit fairly well. Her boots were a size too large, but they'd work. The gloves, though, were hopeless if she wanted to perform a task that required any dexterity at all.

"I feel like a Muppet," she complained, trying to move her fingers in the huge mitts. "These are really the smallest available?"

Ian shuffled through the bin of gloves again. "Looks that way. We're not prepared for someone with mini-hands."

"I have perfectly normal-sized hands," she huffed, placing the oversized gloves on her hips.

Giving up his search, he returned the bin to a shelf and walked over to her. With a teasing look, he wrapped his fingers around her elbows and slid his hands down to hers. Lifting her suddenly tingling hands, he pretended to examine them seriously. "For a toddler, maybe."

Although he'd touched only her coat sleeves and gloves, heat rushed through her, and she struggled to find a comeback. Even casual contact with Ian short-circuited her brain. "I'll have you know—" To her relief, since she had no idea what she'd been about to say, Rory was interrupted by Lou sticking her head into the doorway.

"Hey, guys. Callum wants to know if you have one of those magnetic pick-up tools in here somewhere?" Lou asked. "Jonah dropped some critical part into the engine compartment of the dive van. Callum would come look himself, but the chaos in here hurts his soul, and the chief has banned him from reorganizing. I guess no one could find anything after the last time he did that."

"Yeah," Ian said, reluctantly dropping Rory's hands before skirting some piles of miscellaneous stuff, a stack of rolled hoses, and a power washer to get to the back shelves. "I think there's one in the toolbox over here."

As he searched, Lou raised her eyebrows at Rory. "So?" she mouthed.

Rory just stared at her. "What?"

Rolling her eyes, Lou pointed at Ian's back and then at Rory, before doing a finger shuffle that Rory couldn't translate. She did catch the general gist, though, and it made her blush. Since there was no way in the universe that Rory could answer the question implied by Lou's charades, she just shrugged and glanced at Ian, mentally begging him to hurry.

As if he'd heard her silent plea, he turned around, magnetic tool in hand, and picked his way back to them.

"Here." Ian offered it to Lou, glancing between the two women, which made Rory blush even harder. "What's up?"

"Nothing," they said in unison, making Ian's frown deepen.

"Thanks, Ian." Lou gave a mischievous grin and ducked out of the room, leaving Rory to dodge Ian's suspicious glare.

"What?" she finally asked.

"You tell me."

"This conversation is making no sense."

"Rory. Good." Chief Early's voice in the doorway made Rory's shoulders sag with relief. "Glad you're here. I have some paperwork for you—if you're interested in being an official volunteer firefighter, that is."

"Sure." She hadn't made the conscious decision until that moment, but the agreement popped out of her mouth without hesitation. Being around other people wasn't as painfully awkward as she'd expected. She could even picture herself getting along with most of them. The strange thing was that the other firefighters—some of them, anyway—actually seemed to *like* her. The idea of having real, live friends was tempting and panic inducing at the same time.

"You all set with gear?" the chief asked, eyeing her enormous gloves.

"Think so." Rory held up her hands. "These are a little big, but everything else should work."

"Once you're done with your probationary period, we'll order everything sized to your measurements." He pushed the door open wider and tipped his head. "Come on. All the paperwork's in my office."

She followed the chief out of the storage room, the back of her neck prickling from Ian's gaze. With an enormous effort, she didn't look back at him.

The first two hours were quiet. While Soup and Ian tinkered with the engine of one of the tenders, she and Junior cleaned and organized all the compartments in the rescue trucks. It was useful, since she got a hands-on lesson on what was where. She hoped she could remember once the adrenaline was pumping when they were on-scene at a call. Jack had stretched out near a heater and fallen asleep.

One-on-one, Junior was a lot more laid-back than he was when surrounded by his buddies. To her surprise, Rory found it easy to make conversation with him as they worked. They were deep in a friendly argument about the must-have contents of a bug-out bag when the guys' portable radios blared in unison.

When the tones quieted, the dispatcher's voice announced, "Medical call at 4689 Deer Chase Court. Complainant is a sixty-eight-year-old female, having trouble breathing. She has a history of COPD. Simpson Fire, do you copy?"

Al Zarnecki, the lieutenant on duty, acknowledged the call, while the others donned their gear with the speed and ease of much practice. Rory's stomach lurched with nerves as she hurried to collect her helmet. Station One was chilly, so she'd kept on all of her gear—except for the Muppet gloves. Those she stuck in one of the many pockets covering her coat.

Jack had raised his head when the radios sounded, and Rory called him over to the training room. Once he was shut safely inside, she headed for the rescue truck that Ian had started. The overhead doors were opening, allowing in the cold wind. Despite her bunker gear, Rory shivered as she climbed into the truck, sliding over to the center so Soup could sit on her right.

The other rescue truck, with Al and Junior on board, rolled out first. Ian followed, activating the lights and sirens as he turned onto the street.

"We haven't heard from Letty in a while," Soup said over the chatter on the radio. The EMTs in Med-One were asking for Flight for Life to be on stand-by. "I was starting to think she'd died on us."

Rory glanced at Soup. "You've been there before?"

"Oh yeah." He grimaced. "Just wait."

The dispatcher spoke again. "Rescue One, Rescue Two. The complainant warned that her driveway is drifted over and is probably not passable."

Ian and Soup groaned in unison as Soup reached for the radio mic. He waited until a grim-sounding Al acknowledged the information, and then said, "Rescue Two copies." He released the button on the mic. "Think we should go back for the sleds?"

Tapping his finger against the steering wheel as he thought, Ian finally shook his head. "Letty's driveway isn't that long. It'll take more time to hook up the snowmobile trailer than it will to walk from the road."

"But I want to play with the sleds," Soup whined, although he was smirking.

"Watch it," Ian warned. "You might get your wish. Lots of winter left."

Ian followed the first rescue truck onto the highway and immediately accelerated.

"Are we not going as fast as last time," Rory asked after a minute, "or am I just getting used to it?"

Soup laughed. "Don't get him started." When Rory looked at him curiously, he tipped his head toward Ian. "Beauty here thinks Al's a granny driver."

"He is," Ian grumbled, frowning through the windshield. "I get it if there's a blizzard, but the highway is dry right now. Why is he driving like an elderly tourist?"

They only went another mile before turning onto a side road. It was snowpacked and narrow, but Ian still complained about Al's speed. Rory was silently glad Al was in front of them. It was nerve-racking enough to fly down the highway with Ian at the wheel. She didn't want to see how fast he'd take the slick side street.

When they turned again, it was onto an even snowier and narrower road. The truck in front of them stopped in front of a gate, and Junior jumped out and ran to open it. If the gate wasn't there, Rory wouldn't have known there was a driveway under the drifted snow.

"Are we going to try to drive down there?" she asked, frowning at the white stretching out in front of them. A small cabin sat about a tenth of a mile away from the gate, surrounded by a sea of unbroken drifts.

"Let's see what the LT does," Ian said.

Soup grinned. "Hey, we didn't get to go snowmobiling, but we might get to do some four-wheeling."

With a huff of laughter, Ian said, "And then we'll get to dig the rescue out of the snow."

"You're always such a Debbie Downer," Soup complained, making Rory laugh.

"I have to be." Ian shot the other man a look. "Since you're Little Miss Sunshine all the time, I need to balance you out."

Leaning closer to the windshield, Soup said, "I think he's going for it."

They all watched as the rescue rolled forward, plowing into the snow.

"He should've gotten a running start." Soup tsked. "They need more momentum."

"I don't think it's that deep," Ian countered. "They're still moving."

"Twenty bucks says they don't make it halfway."

"You're on."

Soup looked at Rory. "Do you want to throw some money into the pot?"

After eyeing the snow still in front of the rescue, she said, "Sure. I think they're going to make it to the cabin."

They all leaned forward, watching as the truck foundered, backed up, and then plowed forward again without getting stuck that time.

"Aren't you going in after them?" Rory asked.

Shaking his head, Ian said, "Unlike Granny Al, I'm going to take it fast. I'll wait until they're stuck or all the way to the cabin. If they get stuck, we'll walk, so the ambulance can get as close as possible."

"Halfway," Rory said as the rescue truck rolled forward through the snow.

"Damn it." Soup didn't sound too upset. "I think you might be the winner, Rory. The worst of the drifts are behind them."

Sure enough, the rescue rolled to a stop in front of the cabin.

"Ready?" Ian asked, and Rory groaned, making him laugh.

He flew through the gate, following the tracks of the other truck as he plowed through the drifts. It felt as if the rear of the rescue had a mind of its own, sliding sideways in the snow before gaining traction and rocketing the truck forward.

Rory closed her eyes and then snapped them open again. It was worse just feeling the motion and not being able to see. When they pulled up next to the other rescue, Al and Junior were waiting for them.

"You didn't go in yet?" Soup asked as he hopped out

of the truck, landing shin-deep in snow. There was a false sweetness to his voice that made Rory suspicious, especially when Al and Junior bit back grins.

"Rory gets to go in first," Al said, gesturing her forward.

"Hey." Ian didn't sound happy, which made her nervous. What exactly was waiting for her inside?

"It's a rite of passage." Soup nudged her toward the snow-covered steps. "We all went through this. Now it's Rory's turn."

Whatever was in there, Rory could tell she wasn't going to like it.

Reminding herself that a woman was struggling to breathe inside that cabin, she forced herself to the front door and knocked.

"Fire department," Al called in a booming voice.

"Go on in," Soup told her.

She opened the door, stepping inside the cabin as her stomach churned with nerves.

The smell hit her like a bullet from a .45. It was cigarettes and body odor and feces and urine, mixed with the stench of decomposing garbage. Even though she immediately started breathing through her mouth, the smell was bad enough to bring bile up into the back of her throat.

Someone behind her gave her a gentle push, and she took several steps forward until she stood in the middle of a tiny, extremely dirty kitchen. There was trash everywhere, with food sitting on the counters and small kitchen table, and piles of junk lining the narrow hall. Since Letty wasn't in the kitchen, Rory moved down the narrow passageway.

“It looks like your storage room,” Rory said, and then immediately regretted speaking, because it required her to take a deeper breath of the foul air than she really cared to inhale.

“Very funny,” Ian said.

Al again bellowed, “Fire department!”

There was a strange sound, and Rory cocked her head to listen. It was a high-pitched, vibrating tone, sometimes louder and sometimes softer. “What’s that noise?”

“That’s Enrique,” Soup said, not very helpfully. “Turn right. Letty, we’re coming in!”

There was a faint sound of acknowledgment. Reaching to grasp the knob Soup indicated, Rory twisted it and pushed open the door.

Chapter 10

A tiny missile flew at her, latching its jaws around her pant leg. Rory tried to take a step back, but the guys were surging into the room, pushing her in ahead of them. Staring down at the Chihuahua hanging off the fabric covering her shin, she asked, "Enrique?"

"Enrique," Soup confirmed, nudging her to the side. "Letty, put out that cigarette. You're going to blow us all to kingdom come."

"I don't have many pleasures in life," the woman lying on the couch wheezed. She was wrapped in a yellow blanket that had several stains that Rory didn't want to examine too closely. "I'll smoke if I damn well want to."

"You're on oxygen," Al said, nodding toward the tank sitting on the floor next to the couch. "You can't smoke when you're on oxygen."

Without a word, she blew out a stream of smoke, glaring at the lieutenant through the haze.

"Letty, if you don't put that out right now, we're leaving," Ian snapped.

Grumbling under her breath, she dropped the cigarette in a jar of yellow liquid. As horrified suspicions of what was in that jar crept into Rory's brain, the dog hanging off her pants gave another muffled growl. She looked down at him and gave her leg a shake, but he managed to keep his grip. It was kind of impressive. The tiny dog must have had the jaw strength of a pit bull.

Junior started asking Letty questions about her health history as he pulled a blood-pressure cuff from the bag he'd brought in with him. Letty levered herself into a seated position, and the blanket slid down to her lap, revealing her naked, sagging torso.

Quickly looking back to the dog still clinging to her like a Christmas-tree ornament, she focused on trying to detach Enrique from her pants. Although she knew she would need to get used to seeing naked people if she was going to be a volunteer first responder, this was only her second call. She wasn't quite ready for full-frontal yet. She'd rather look at the dog.

"I'm going to make sure the ambulance makes it down the driveway," Soup said in a strangled voice as he hurried from the room.

"I'll…uh, supervise." Al darted after him.

"Thanks, LT!" Junior called after him as he wrapped the cuff around Letty's upper arm. "I appreciate the support and leadership!"

When Rory gave her leg another gentle shake, it brought another round of high-pitched growling, but didn't dislodge the dog. His tenacity was beginning to concern her. She pictured having the Chihuahua as a permanent accessory.

"Um…will Enrique eventually let go?" Rory asked, her gaze darting to Ian, since she was avoiding looking at Letty, and Junior was a little too close to naked boobs for Rory to focus on him.

"Just let him hang out there," Ian said, eyeing the dog with an amused twist to his lips. "That'll keep him out of the way until we're done here."

"Out of everyone else's way, maybe," she muttered, but managed to resist another, more strenuous leg shake.

"It's called taking one for the team," Junior added before relaying Letty's blood pressure, pulse, and respiration numbers over his portable radio.

With a sigh, Rory asked, "Can I help with anything?"

"You're on dog duty." Ian grinned at her. "That's your job."

"This one new?" Letty's question made Rory automatically look at the other woman, which she immediately regretted. The blanket had slipped down farther, revealing pretty much everything that should've been covered.

"Uh, yes," she answered, fixing her gaze firmly on Letty's face.

"Huh," Letty grunted. "When did they start accepting women?"

Rory blinked. "I'm a volunteer. I think they take anyone who's willing to do this for free."

Making a displeased face, Letty reached for her pack of cigarettes. "You're not eye candy like the rest of them. Especially not like that one." She jerked her chin toward Ian.

"Letty! No smoking," Ian snapped, and the older woman's hand yanked back, away from the smokes. Although she scowled at him, Letty left the cigarette pack alone.

The sound of boots clomping down the hallway brought Rory's head around. Two EMTs came through the doorway. By the expressions on their faces—a mixture of resignation and distaste—both had dealt with Letty before.

"Hey, Letty," the female EMT said, leading the way into the room. "Having some trouble breathing, huh?"

Letty glared at her. "Didn't I tell you not to come back here?"

"Sorry." The EMT shrugged, not looking at all put out by her patient's animosity. "It's like what they say in kindergarten. 'You get who you get, and you don't throw a fit.'"

The male EMT, tall with dark hair peeking out from under his stocking hat, eyed the Chihuahua decorating Rory's pants and grinned. "You got dog duty, huh?"

"How could you tell?" she asked dryly, glancing down at Enrique. He was still holding strong.

The EMT laughed as he moved toward Letty. Junior rattled off her history, symptoms, and vitals before backing off and letting the two newcomers take over her care.

"So," Junior asked quietly as he moved next to her. "How do you like the glamorous life of a firefighter so far?"

Enrique growled.

"It's…uh"—she glanced down at the dog—"interesting."

After everything, Letty decided she didn't need to go to the hospital. Rory thought her wheezing breaths were alarming, but the EMTs both agreed with their patient. Ian produced some venison jerky and used it to coax Enrique into releasing his grip on Rory's pants. To her relief, it worked. With the meat clamped in his jaws, he ran behind the couch, growling the entire way.

"She's no worse than she usually is," the dark-haired

EMT, who introduced himself as Scott, told her once they'd left the house. "I think she calls us when she gets lonely out here."

Rory studied him thoughtfully. "The eye-candy brigade."

"What?" Scott laughed.

Flushing, Rory explained, "Letty said I'm not eye candy like the rest of you. Um, them."

Leaning in closer, Scott lowered his voice. "Why, Rory. Are you calling me hot?"

"What?" She stared at him in horror, taking a step back. "No! Why would… I mean, of course not."

When he started to laugh again, she turned away and plunged through the snow toward Rescue Two, ignoring Scott calling after her. Climbing into the warm cab was a relief, as both an escape from the cold night air and Scott's…she didn't know what.

Frigid air swirled into the cab as Ian climbed into the driver's seat. He looked at her and raised an eyebrow.

"What?" she snapped, hating that she was embarrassed and confused about why.

"What was that about?"

With an exasperated huff, she tossed her hands in the air. "I have no idea. He was being weird."

"He was hitting on you."

Rory glared at him. "He was not."

Real humor was absent from his laugh. "Want to bet?"

"No." After a moment, she added, "If he was, that was inappropriate."

"Why?" Ian eyed her curiously. "Because we're on a call?"

"I don't know." Shrugging uncomfortably, she stared out the windshield at the snow lit by the truck's headlights. "More because that house was so gross and Letty was naked."

This time, Ian's chuckle actually sounded amused. "Yeah. Both kind of put you off the idea of sex, don't they?"

"Plus, I'm not interested in *him*."

"Good." The single word was thick with male satisfaction.

Her flush burned her cheeks as she stared even harder through the glass in front of them. Rory had no response to that, even if she could have shoved any words past the blockage in her throat.

He laughed again, softly. Something about the husky edge to the sound made her blush flame even hotter. To her relief, Soup yanked open the passenger-side door.

"That place is disgusting. It gets worse every time. Can't someone do something about the state of that house?" he grumbled as he settled his body in the seat next to Rory.

"The county knows about it," Ian said, watching as Al drove the other rescue truck toward the gate.

"What's the problem? Not enough jars of piss in the living room?"

Rory groaned. "I thought that's what the yellow liquid was, but I didn't really want to know for sure. Thanks, Soup, for confirming that."

"No problem." He nudged her with his elbow. "Just sharing the love. Nice job with the dog, by the way."

"That was the 'rite of passage' you guys were talking about?"

"Yep." Grinning, he settled back against the seat. "Don't worry, though. There are more to come."

"Great." Although she rolled her eyes, there was

a warmth in her belly that had nothing to do with the truck's heater. Maybe there was something to this whole "family" thing.

After they helped an elderly man push his Buick out of a snowy ditch and responded to a wildland fire sighting that ended up being someone's porch light, there weren't any more calls for the rest of their shift. By the time they headed out to the parking lot, Rory was finding it hard to keep her eyes open. The early-morning sun reflected off the Bronco's shiny bits, making her squint. As she opened the back hatch so Jack could hop into the SUV, she couldn't hold back a jaw-popping yawn.

"Up for breakfast?" Ian asked.

Rory yawned again. "Mind if we get a few hours of sleep first? I'm afraid I'd doze off and face-plant into my pancakes."

"Sure." He opened the passenger door for her, waiting until all her limbs were safely inside before shutting it. Leaning her head back against the seat, she allowed her eyes to close.

The next thing she knew, someone was nudging her. With a groan, she peeled open her heavy eyelids just enough to see it was Ian bugging her…yet again.

"Why do you keep waking me up?" she complained, fumbling to unbuckle her seat belt.

Reaching across her body, Ian unfastened the belt. His nearness enveloped her in his scent, bringing her to full, instant wakefulness. She started leaning closer, but he stepped back. With a regretful but silent sigh, she climbed out of the SUV.

"Because you keep falling asleep on me," he said. "I'm starting to get a complex."

Despite her flustered awareness, Rory had to grin as she headed for the door. At the thought of the exposed, too-bright guest room, though, her smile faded as she slowed her steps.

"What's wrong?" Ian asked, resting a hand on her lower back to nudge her forward when she slowed to turtle pace.

"Nothing. Just the windows." As soon as the words were out, she flushed. Being around Ian made her a little too honest.

"We'll figure out something," he said, urging her toward the door only to stop abruptly.

She glanced at his furious face before following his gaze to the skinny piece of green plastic looped over the doorknob. "What is that?"

"Get inside," Ian ordered tersely, looking around as he crowded close to her. He unlocked the door and ripped the plastic circle off the knob before urging her into the kitchen. Once inside, he locked the door, tucked her into a corner, and told her to stay. Normally, she would've made a sharp comment about how she wasn't Jack, but Ian's furiously determined expression kept her silent as he searched the house.

After what felt like a very long time to her jittery stomach, Ian returned to the kitchen, looking no less enraged.

"What is it?" She stared at the piece of plastic lying on the floor.

With a wordless, angry sound, Ian swept it up and crammed it into the garbage under the sink. "It's Billy, trying to scare us."

"What?"

Ian closed his eyes for a second, looking like he was attempting to calm down. "A glow-stick. That was Rave's thing. If someone pissed him off, he'd leave a glow-stick."

"But..." Frowning, Rory pictured the harmless-looking item that had been hanging from Ian's doorknob. "How is that scary?"

A muscle twitched on his jaw. "It was a message. Rave would be back to end whoever got a glow-stick."

"Oh." Her fingers were shaking, so she jammed them into her coat pockets to hide their revealing tremors. "So Billy's saying he's going to kill us."

Suddenly, Ian was in front of her, cupping her face in both hands. "He won't hurt you," he promised fiercely. "I won't let him even get near you."

She stared at him, startled and touched by his intensity, by how determined he was to keep her safe. "I believe you," she said, and she meant it.

"Okay." Blowing out a hard breath, he let his hands drop to his sides. "Okay. Are you going to be able to sleep after this?" He gestured toward the closed cabinet hiding the trash can where the glow-stick resided.

The adrenaline was fading, and she felt exhaustion creeping back in. "No windows?"

"No windows."

"Then yes."

During the short time she was in the bathroom, Ian managed to turn his closet into a bedroom.

"Will that work?" Ian asked, frowning.

"Perfect." She was so tired that she was swaying in place. Anything horizontal would've looked perfect to her.

"Sure?" He glanced between her face and the makeshift bed. "I feel kind of rude having you sleep on the floor in the closet."

"It's a big closet. Plus, the camping mattress is a huge step up from yesterday."

Ian had made a bed out of an inflatable mattress and a sleeping bag on the floor of the master closet. She hadn't been lying when she'd said it was big. It could probably sleep a family of eight comfortably.

"It still doesn't feel right—" Ian started, but Rory cut him off.

"Please," she begged. "I'm so tired. Can I sleep now?"

He stopped glaring at the closet bed and looked at her. "Sure." Taking a step closer, he leaned in until she could feel his breath warm her lips. She went still, wondering if *this* would be the time he kissed her. His addictive scent surrounded her, making her realize how familiar it was becoming—familiar and comforting. Oddly enough, as much as he made her heart race, he calmed her, too. He moved, and she held her breath, but he only brushed his lips against her cheek. "Sleep tight."

The second his mouth touched her skin, she felt like she'd caught fire. When she tried to tell him good night, the only thing she could force out of her tight throat was a very unladylike grunt. He grinned at the sound and then left the closet, pulling the door closed behind him.

Once he was gone, the tension seeped out of her muscles, leaving only exhaustion. She was tempted to crawl into the sleeping bag fully clothed, but she knew that what she had on was her only wearable option, besides enormous sweatpants and T-shirts. With a quiet groan, she stripped down to her underwear.

"Here's—" The closet door opened, making Rory suck in a startled breath and twist around so her back was to Ian. "Whoa."

"Do you mind?" she snapped, glaring at him over her shoulder, her arms crossed tightly over her chest. Although she was wearing a bra that was more serviceable than sexy, and panties with enough coverage to satisfy the average grandmother, Rory still felt naked. She reminded herself that a bikini would cover less skin than what she was wearing, but it didn't matter. She'd never been in a bikini, much less in a bikini in front of anyone—much, much less in a bikini in front of *Ian*, who was still staring at her. The hungry look in his eyes made her skin flush with heat, and she swallowed, her throat suddenly dry.

"No," he said, sounding a little dazed. "I don't mind at all."

Obviously, she needed to be more direct. "Get. Out."

Ian blinked and then held out a T-shirt and sweatpants. "I brought something for you to sleep in."

"Thank you." Her tone did not convey much gratitude. Between her mostly naked state and his smoldering stare, she was clinging to her composure by her fingernails. Awareness rushed through her, awakening feelings she didn't even know she could have. Her flush darkened, and she knew she was blushing *everywhere*. "Now will you please *leave*?"

"Right." After running his eyes over her almost-naked back once again, he took a step toward the door. "I knew you had a nice ass, but I'd have never guessed it was *that* nice."

"Out!" she practically shrieked, barely catching

herself before she whirled around to point at the door. If he was mesmerized by her underwear-clad back half, she definitely didn't want to see his reaction to her front side—or *her* reaction to *his* reaction. Her stomach did a flip.

He held up his hands in front of him. "I'm going! I just need to take a mental picture first."

With a growl, she looked around for something to throw at him. Of all the times not to be armed…

As if he could read her thoughts, he chuckled and exited the closet. "I know what I'm dreaming about tonight," he said as he closed the door.

Her growl morphed into a snarl as she grabbed the first thing within reach and threw it where Ian had been standing. The plastic hanger bounced harmlessly off the wood panel, and Rory was pretty sure she heard him laugh again.

Muttering curses, she pulled on the T-shirt and pants, trying very hard not to notice the scent of his detergent clinging to the fabric. She turned off the closet light and crawled into the sleeping bag. She felt warm all over from her whole-body blush.

Although the room and the makeshift bed felt foreign, the darkness of a windowless space was reassuring. With a little effort, she could pretend she was in her underground bunker, only without her security lights. With a quiet huff, she flipped onto her side, trying to cool the embarrassment and uncomfortable excitement that flowed like fire through her veins.

As she closed her eyes, the movie began, rewound, and replayed. Rave crumpled to the floor again and again, until her eyes popped open, and she stared into the dark. She'd take humiliation and unfamiliar arousal over the looping visual of the man she killed bleeding his life away on the floor of her shop.

Instead, she shoved both Rave and Ian out of her head and mentally field-stripped an M16 over and over until she fell asleep.

A knock on the closet door woke her much too soon. With a groan, she yanked the sleeping bag over her head, but she could still hear the second, more insistent knock.

"What?" she demanded.

"State investigator's here to talk to you."

That woke her completely, and she wriggled out of the sleeping bag. "Out in a minute."

Ian had sounded surly. Rory wondered if that was because he was as sleep-deprived as she was, or if his interview hadn't gone well. With a frown, she donned her clothes, wishing she had something a little...fresher. Although they weren't actually stinky yet, the jeans and long-sleeved shirt had had a long night under her bunker gear. Lately, she'd had the foreign and unwelcome desire to look nice for Ian. She'd even considered breaking her self-imposed ban on buying factory-made clothes and stopping into the Screaming Moose for a dress, of all things. The thought of wearing a dress and high heels made her wince—she wouldn't even be able to walk out to feed the chickens, much less run from an attacker. She'd be safer in her jeans and combat boots. Too bad they weren't a little more...well, feminine.

When she opened the closet door, Ian was waiting,

not looking at all happy. His eyes warmed when he saw her, but he didn't smile.

"That bad?" she asked.

His answer was just a short nod.

Making a face, she headed for the bathroom. An unpleasant interview with a state investigator about the man she'd killed wasn't the best thing to wake up to. "Three minutes, and I'll be ready."

He caught her hand, pulling her to a stop. When she turned her head, Ian was right there. He dropped a quick kiss on one corner of her mouth.

"You're even beautiful when you first wake up."

Giving her hand a final squeeze, he walked toward the stairs. Rory, her body on fire from that simple kiss, stared after him.

Chapter 11

It actually took her only two and a half minutes before she was moving quietly down the stairs. Ian, having been preemptively banned by the investigator from being present at her interview, stayed upstairs with Jack. Only one man was waiting in the living room. Since his back was to her, she was able to observe him before he realized she was there. Although he wasn't very tall or bulky, he had a lean strength that reminded her of her father. The similarity made her stomach lurch. Her dad had been the first—although not the last—man to try to kill her.

The investigator's dark hair was neatly combed from the side part, and it was carefully trimmed above the nape of his neck. His clothes were appropriate for the mountains in March—warm and casual layers—but something about how he wore them made Rory feel extra mussed in her recycled outfit.

He turned and saw her then, so she descended the final stairs and crossed the living room, stopping several feet away from the investigator. They eyed each other, and neither extended a hand to shake. His eyes were calm and as cold as the snow outside.

"Rory Sorenson?" he asked, breaking the silence.

"Yes."

"I'm Investigator Paul Strepple with the Colorado BCA."

Since she wasn't sure how to respond to that—as "Nice to meet you" didn't seem appropriate—Rory settled for a nod.

"Have a seat." He gestured toward Ian's couch, and Rory had to restrain a tense smile at the investigator's attempt to claim the space and gain the upper hand. There was no way she was going to sit on the sofa, since it faced a wall of windows, so she headed for the doorway.

"Mind if we talk in the kitchen?" she asked over her shoulder. "I was too tired to eat this morning when the shift ended, so I'm starving."

He followed her. Having a stranger behind her made her twitchy, and she wished Ian could've been there. The thought surprised her. Since when did she consider anyone—even Ian—trustworthy enough to watch her back?

Strepple leaned against the counter as she explored Ian's cupboards. To her surprise and delight, he had the cereal with the marshmallows in it. She'd never tried it as a kid, but the box had fascinated her during their rare trips to the grocery store. After her parents died, she'd bought a box of that cereal and ate the entire thing in one sitting. Afterward, she'd been sicker than she'd ever been in her life, but the taste had been worth it. Grinning, she grabbed the cereal box and started hunting for a bowl.

"New to this place, are you?" Strepple asked, reminding her of his presence and bringing her back to reality with a jarring thump. The cereal find had been distracting. Pausing her bowl hunt, she glanced over her shoulder.

"This house, you mean?" At his nod, she said, "Yes. Ian's letting me stay here until my shop's no longer an active crime scene."

"You two aren't together, then?"

There was a set of mixing bowls in the next cupboard she opened. Grabbing the smallest one—which was still large enough to hold half the box—she focused on closing the cupboard doors, keeping her back turned so Strepple wouldn't see her blush at the question. She didn't want to show the investigator any weaknesses, and the vulnerability and uncertainty that flared up when she thought about Ian definitely felt like weaknesses. "No."

"Huh." His weighted tone made her look at him. "Not what he said."

There was no way to hide her blush at that, but she did her best, diving into the fridge and taking a long time to find the milk. "Oh. Well, we… Uh, he…" Talking wasn't helping, so she clamped her lips together.

When she emerged with the milk carton, she saw a small smile on his face. Scowling, she asked, "Didn't you come here to ask about what happened at the shop?"

"I did." Strepple had an unsettling way of watching her. It was cool, almost clinical, and it made her feel flustered. She tried to hide it, focusing again on her cereal, dumping an excessive amount into the mixing bowl. After pouring the milk and then putting it away, she found a spoon in the third drawer she checked.

The cereal was as good as she remembered. Processed sugar and artificial flavoring were amazing things, and they were a temporary distraction from the piercing regard of the investigator. After a few bites, she waved her spoon at Strepple. "So?"

“How long have you known Ian Walsh?”

Frowning, she answered, “Since I was twelve. What does this have to do with the burglary?”

“I’ll ask the questions.” Instead of sounding hostile, his tone was completely even. Somehow, it still made her want to cringe and apologize. Biting the inside of her cheek, she straightened her shoulders and mentally told herself to quit being weak. “How long have the two of you been dating?”

“We’re not.” When he raised an eyebrow and remained silent, she continued, “We’ve been spending time together because he was worried about someone trying to break in to the shop. It’s not dating, though.”

“So, you’re spending lots of time together, including dinner at a restaurant, and you’re staying at his house, but you’re not dating.”

“Right.” Rory quashed the urge to babble by shoving a huge spoonful of cereal into her mouth.

“Do you know Willard Gray?”

The change of topic made her blink. “Willard Gray? That sounds familiar, but I can’t place him.”

“He owned a shotgun he bought at your shop two years ago.”

“What kind?”

“A Remington tactical shotgun.”

Tapping the spoon against her lips, she thought. “Quiet guy in his fifties or sixties? About your height and weight?”

“Sounds about right.”

“He bought the 870.” Although she didn’t like talking about her customers and their purchases, Strepple already knew what the guy had gotten from her, so Rory figured it wouldn't do any harm to confirm it. Plus, talking about guns calmed her. After another bite of cereal, she added, "Over a week or so, he stopped in three or four times. I was starting to think he was just a lookie-loo, but then he got the Remington. That's a nice shotgun. Dependable. Kind of heavy, though."

"Did you have any other interactions with him?"

Since her mouth was full, she waited to answer until she swallowed. "I didn't see him again after that."

"What about Walsh?"

Rory lowered the spoon still loaded with cereal. "What about him?"

"What was his relationship with Gray?"

"No idea. You'd have to ask him."

Strepple eyed her for a long moment. Feigning nonchalance, she stuffed another spoonful of cereal into her mouth and chewed, not dropping eye contact with the investigator. His questions about her personal life made her babble, but she didn't hesitate when it came to defending Ian.

"Tell me about Walsh's involvement with the Riders."

"No."

His calm expression faltered a little. "No?"

"I don't know anything about that," she said, dumping her leftover milk down the kitchen sink drain. It had turned a pastel green from the dye in the marshmallows. "That's another thing you're going to have to ask him directly."

"You can get into a lot of trouble by impeding an investigation."

Rory took her time rinsing the bowl before setting it carefully in the sink. Turning, she met Strepple's gaze. "I can't tell you what I don't know."

They had another stare-down before the investigator spoke, breaking the tense silence. "Why don't you tell me what happened the night of the shootings."

"You mean the night of the burglary, when an innocent shop owner and her...friend defended her residence and their lives as allowed by law?"

It almost looked as if he were holding back a smile. Inclining his head silently, he gestured for her to proceed.

As she told the story for what felt like the hundredth time, the mental movie started to play, but she shut it down fast. It was hard enough getting through this interview—or interrogation—without the added stress of seeing Rave's death over and over again.

When she finished, Strepple asked a few questions about how she knew Rave, which she answered as succinctly as she could. With her belly full of artificial goodness, she was starting to get tired again, and she didn't want to slip up and say something she shouldn't.

When Jack trotted into the kitchen, followed by Ian, relief surged through her. Rory couldn't hold back a smile when she met his gaze.

"Mr. Walsh." Strepple pushed away from the counter and drew himself up to maximum height. "I thought you were aware that you couldn't be present while I was speaking with Ms. Sorenson."

"And I figured that two hours was a long enough time for you to grill her, when she had a twelve-hour shift at the fire station last night."

As if sensing the tension in the air, Jack's ears pricked forward, and he moved to stand in front of Rory, creating a dog-shaped wall between her and the men. She reached down to scratch him under his collar. Although his tail thumped against her leg in appreciation, his attention stayed fixed on the guys currently locked in a staring contest.

"I think we were about done, weren't we?" Rory asked.

Although he didn't look happy about it, Strepple gave a reluctant nod. "I'll let you know if I have any other questions."

After Ian ushered the investigator to the door, both he and Rory watched from the living room window as Strepple's SUV pulled away from the curb in front of the house. They both stayed silent, standing close enough that their shoulders touched, until the vehicle turned the corner and disappeared from sight. Rory was amazed by the comfort that small contact gave her.

"Why was he fixated on Willard Gray?" she asked, turning to look at Ian.

His expression was grim. "He's the headless body found in Mission Reservoir a few weeks ago—the one Lou discovered during that ice-rescue training exercise. She and Callum are unofficially investigating his death, since the local guys and the state investigators are all running in circles. Will was a reclusive guy who lived in Simpson. Apparently, no one except an old army buddy realized he was missing."

She winced, remembering the quiet man who'd visited her shop. "He's the one they found in the reservoir?"

"Yeah." The muscles in his jaw were tight.

"The Riders are implicated in Willard Gray's murder?"

With a rough sigh, he scrubbed a hand over his face. "*I'm* the one implicated. I owned a pendant with the Liverton Riders' mark on it. My dad—not Julius, but my biological dad—wore it until he died, and then my mom passed it to me when I was fourteen. It was found by the body."

Startled, she blinked at him.

"I lost it a month or so ago. It disappeared while I was showering at the clubhouse. I turned that place inside out but couldn't find it. I have no idea how it ended up next to a dead guy."

She was quiet for a few moments, absorbing this. "So Strepple thinks you killed Willard Gray."

"He didn't actually come right out and say it, but yeah. That's probably a safe assumption."

Looking through the window at the other houses, automatically picking out all the locations a sniper could be positioned, she shivered. It seemed like everyone—the Riders, the BCA, the local sheriff's department—were gunning for them. It wasn't enough to hide in her bunker anymore, though—she had to protect Ian, too. If only his house didn't have so many windows. "Do you mind if we continue this discussion in my closet?"

"Your closet?"

"Fine." She rolled her eyes. "*Your* closet."

"I didn't mean..." He shook his head. "Never mind. Yeah, we can talk in the closet. Can we run an errand first, though?"

"What's that?" Rory took a couple of steps back from the window. She didn't know how Ian could relax surrounded by glass. It was so easily broken and so *transparent*. Anyone could see her.

"I've called him a few times, but I haven't been able to check on Julius in person for a couple of days."

"Oh." She suddenly felt selfish. Her problems had completely absorbed Ian's life. "Of course. Do you mind if I come along?" Although the question made her feel clingy, she didn't want Ian out of her sight with everything going on. "I should check on the chickens, too."

Ian scowled. "I'd rather you not go by yourself. Billy's pissed. He posted Zup and Duke's bail, so those two are around, too."

"Both of them?" Rory could understand bailing out his son, but Duke, too? That just seemed strange.

"Yeah." Ian was still frowning. "Why don't you come with me to visit Julius, and then we'll both go to your place. I'm sure the chickens are fine, though. Squirrel's been taking care of them, and he's like the poultry whisperer or something."

She smiled. "I know. I just want to see for myself that they're okay."

Accepting that with an easy nod, he changed the subject. "Did you get something to eat?"

"Yes." A beatific smile curled her lips as she thought about her breakfast—lunch, really, she mentally amended as she glanced at the clock.

His gaze seemed to be locked on her mouth. "What food caused that look?" he asked, his voice a little raspy.

"Cereal," she told him, her smile growing. "With marshmallows."

Ian laughed, his intent expression fading. "You ate that disgusting stuff? I just got it because Steve's kids stayed over one night."

Frowning at him, she said, "It's not disgusting. It's amazing. And you babysit?"

"Sure. We all take turns helping out. That time, Steve got knocked on the head on a call. They kept him in the hospital overnight, so his four kids crashed here."

"He's a single dad, then?"

"Yeah. His wife died about five years ago."

Rory tried to imagine raising four children by herself and shuddered. Poor kids would be doomed. "How does he do it?"

"No clue." Ian shook his head. "I couldn't even keep a goldfish alive."

"I do okay with the chickens and Jack," she said. "Kids, though…"

There must've been a trace of horror in her tone, because he eyed her with the beginning of a smirk. "You don't like them?"

"Kids are fine." Even to her own ears, Rory heard the insincerity in her voice. "They're just…"

"What?" Ian sounded like he was about to laugh.

"I don't know. Sticky."

"They're sticky."

"Yeah. And there's usually some kind of bodily fluid seeping out of them."

"That's disgusting. What kind of kids have you been hanging around?"

"I haven't really been hanging around any of them. I've just noticed the snot and drool and other stuff from a distance." A large distance, if she noticed them first.

Ian was full-out grinning now. "Rory, are you scared of tiny, innocent children?"

"No." As soon as it was out of her mouth, she knew she'd spoken too quickly to be believed. "Of course not. Who'd be afraid of kids and their stickiness and multitude of germs and their Children-of-the-Corn stares? Not me." Her scoffing noise was weak, very weak.

"Uh-huh." He had a look of satisfaction on his face. "Now I know *two* things that scare the fearless Rory."

"I'm not fearless." She spent most of her time being fear*ful*. "And what's the second thing?"

"Windows."

"Ugh. I do hate your windows. Why do you have to have so many? And so big? And so see-through?"

Ian stared at her. "I'm not sure how to answer that."

Very ready to end the entire conversation, Rory suggested, "Should we go see Julius?"

As the Bronco approached Liverton, Rory thought of the Riders, and her stomach tightened.

"Will anyone else be there? Besides Julius, I mean." Although she tried to keep her voice casual, Ian's sharp glance told her that she hadn't been completely successful.

"Could be." After a pause, the telltale muscle in his cheek twitched, and he looked at her again. "You worried about seeing Billy?"

"No." She made a face when the word came out rushed. "Not really. A little, maybe. Judging from his recent threat, he's not too happy with us." That was an understatement. She wished they'd brought Jack along, rather than leaving him at Ian's. "After all, I did kill Rave and get his son arrested."

With a shake of his head, Ian pulled the Bronco up in front of a barn-red, single-story house. "You didn't get him arrested. The dumbass managed to do that all by himself."

Rory was relieved that, other than Ian's SUV, the immediate vicinity was empty of vehicles. Unless someone had walked over to see him, Julius was alone. "I don't think Billy sees it that way."

"Fu—forget Billy." He set the parking brake with restrained violence. "If he wants to blame you for what Rave and Zup did, then he'll have to deal with me."

Her hand stilled on the door handle as she turned to look at his grim profile. "What do you mean?"

"Nothing." The muscle in his cheek was flexing like crazy, telling her that it was definitely not nothing. When she didn't say anything, he looked at her, and his face relaxed a fraction. "I need to talk to Billy about it."

It wasn't really an answer, but she knew it was all she was going to get right then. Opening the door, she stepped out of the Bronco, landing ankle-deep in snow. Looking at the driveway, she saw that it had been overtaken by drifts that climbed halfway up the closed garage door. The walkway and porch were covered, too.

"If Julius has a shovel or a blower, I can clear this for him," she offered.

"No need." Ian got out of the driver's seat, slamming the door behind him. "Julius isn't going anywhere."

"Why not?" she asked, high stepping through the mounds of snow that rippled in crusty waves, hiding where the yard began and the pavement ended.

"Because," he said testily, taking her arm to help her through the snow, "I have his car keys."

She glanced at his hand, a little startled. No one had ever helped her like this before. It was odd, although not unpleasant. In fact, it was kind of nice.

"I'm not giving them back until he drags his ass out of the bottle." Ian must've taken her silence as criticism, since he sounded defensive and his fingers tightened around her arm.

"Good idea."

"He doesn't—" Her words must've registered. He cut off whatever he'd started to say. When he spoke again, his tone was calmer, less tense. "Thanks."

"Those couple of times he was at my shop," she said, sliding her boot across each porch step to kick some of the snow out of the way, "he drove himself."

"Sh—uh, shoot." The muscle in his cheek was ticking again. "Was he in a blue Ford pickup?"

"No. Silver Oldsmobile sedan."

His hand on the doorknob, he paused to look at her. "Good memory."

"Thanks. I watched him leave the second time he was at the shop."

"Still, not many people would've remembered what he was driving."

She shrugged. "That was part of my training—noticing my surroundings and remembering details."

"Training?"

"Can we go inside?" she asked, not wanting to discuss it. In fact, she was kicking herself for letting that slip. "I'm freezing."

"It's not that cold. What training?"

"It *is* that cold." Rory knew her expression was bordering on belligerent, but she didn't care. The guy was like a dog with a bone when it came to discussing topics she really didn't want to discuss.

"Fine." He shoved open the door and stepped back to let her go inside first. "But we're talking about this later."

"No. We're not." Despite the lack of vehicles

outside Julius's house, Rory stepped forward cautiously, relieved by the empty entry.

"Hey, Julius," Ian called as he followed behind her. "It's me. Rory came along too."

There was no response, and Ian frowned. After toeing off his boots, he quickly moved down the short hallway and passed through an arched opening. Rory removed her boots and followed. The entryway opened to a living room, where Julius was slouched in a worn recliner.

Even in just the few short weeks since she'd seen him, Julius appeared to have aged. Gray stubble covered his sunken cheeks, and the hair surrounding his good-sized bald spot looked greasy. He was a big guy, but he didn't look it at the moment. In fact, his robe-clad body looked almost shrunken. Although he was facing the television, it wasn't turned on. The worst was his expression, distant and dull.

"Julius," Ian said, approaching the older man. Except for the slightest glance at his stepson, Julius didn't react.

"Hey, Julius," Rory said, but he didn't respond at all to her greeting.

"When was the last time you showered?" Ian stopped next to the recliner.

"Fuck off," Julius grunted.

Ignoring the slurred words, Ian leaned down to gently grasp Julius's arm. "Come on, old man," he said, the words filled with affection. "You need to get cleaned up before the flies start to circle."

Julius struggled slightly, but his body soon sagged as he relented, and he allowed Ian to help him to his feet. As he stood, something hit the wooden floor with a thud. All three of them looked down at Julius's feet, where a bottle of vodka had fallen. It was almost empty, the dregs spreading along the side of the bottle rather than spilling onto the floor.

"Julius." Ian tilted back his head and closed his eyes. He looked suddenly and completely exhausted. "Who's bringing you this shit?"

"None of your fucking business," Julius snarled. "I'm an adult. I can have a drink if I want one."

"You—" Biting off with visible effort whatever he was going to say, Ian pressed his lips together, his cheek muscles practically vibrating with tension. After a long moment, he blew out a breath. "Shower. You need to shower."

All the pugnaciousness slipped out of the older man, and he wilted in Ian's grip. Julius allowed Ian to escort him out of the room. Once she was alone, Rory let her own breath escape. Needing to do something, she picked up the bottle and went searching for the kitchen.

It was easy enough to find, just a room over from the living area. She dumped the small amount of remaining liquor down the sink and rinsed the bottle. The kitchen garbage was overflowing, so she lifted out the bag and tied the top, hearing glass bottles clanking against each other. Obviously, Julius was not much of a recycler.

A door on the other side of the kitchen led to the garage, she discovered. In there, she saw the blue pickup currently on lockdown, as well as a large plastic trash bin. As she turned around after depositing the trash into the container, a glinting reflection on one of the plywood shelves caught her attention.

Behind the paint cans, she found three full bottles—vodka and two different kinds of whiskey. Rory bit the inside of her cheek. It seemed wrong to take them, like she didn't have the right to interfere. Then the look on Ian's face when the empty bottle had dropped to the floor flashed through her mind. With renewed purpose, she pulled the bottles off the shelf.

When she reentered the kitchen, Ian was there, opening cupboards and shoving aside the contents.

"I found three bottles in the garage," she said. "Not that he couldn't have more." When Ian took a step toward the door, she stopped him. "Already got rid of it."

"Where?"

"Trash can. Under the garbage bags."

He stood for a moment, staring at her. His arms were limp at his sides, and he looked...lost. It was so un-Ian-like that she couldn't stop herself from crossing the few feet that separated them. Tentatively, she circled her arms around his middle and gave a squeeze. It felt extremely awkward at first, with her stiff and him unresponsive, and Rory regretted the impulse.

Before she could pull away from him to stammer apologies, his arm locked around her, yanking her into his chest. He held her for a long time, pressing his forehead against her hair so it felt as if he surrounded her completely. Like his hand on her arm earlier, it was odd, but not unpleasant. She relaxed into his warmth, and his grip tightened.

Definitely not unpleasant.

He shuddered as he exhaled, his breath hot against the top of her head. "Jesus, Ror. What am I going to do with him?"

"Rehab? There's a place in Connor Springs."

"He won't go. If I drive him there, he'll just leave."

"Not to be all clichéd, but you can't force him to quit." She squeezed him, as if to temper the harshness of her words. "He has to do it himself. And he has to *want* to do it."

"I know." The despair in his voice developed an edge of anger. "I *know* that. It doesn't stop me from wanting to punch him in the face until he sees what he's doing to himself."

A bubble of laughter rose in her throat, but she swallowed it back, since there was a good chance it would emerge as a sob instead. "I get that."

"Yeah?" He pulled back far enough to make eye contact. Rory wished he hadn't. It was easier to talk about private things when she didn't have to look at him.

"Yeah. I want to punch people in the face all the time." When he didn't smile at that—looking disappointed instead—she swallowed and dredged up her courage. "My parents were crazy."

The disappointment was immediately gone from his expression, replaced by a sharp look of interest and empathy.

"They weren't that bad at first, at least from what I remember as a kid. They wanted to be self-sufficient, to be ready in case of a disaster. I get that." She gave him a wry look. "You've seen my supply room."

"The underground Costco? Yeah." His smile was crooked, but real, and she relaxed a little. It was easier to share her messed-up childhood stories if they were actually making him feel better. That way, she didn't feel so much like she was vomiting her issues all over him.

"My mom would even make an occasional grocery store visit for peaches—I told you about that."

The other side of his smile lifted to match the first. "I saw you there, remember? When you first developed your obsession with processed sugar."

Her laugh surprised her. She couldn't believe she could expose the raw mess of her insides and still be able to find humor in it. "Right. So, anyway, they became more and more…militant about everything. Paranoid, too. Everyone was an enemy. Instead of just preparing for a possible what-if situation, they started seeing catastrophes around every corner. They began running drills all the time."

"Training?" His arms had relaxed, but he still held her loosely, his hands resting warmly on her lower back. The heat was comforting.

"Training. As in, yanked out of bed at two in the morning to practice running from zombies."

"Zombies?" His eyebrows shot up. "You had zombie drills?"

She scowled at him without any real anger. "Didn't I mention that my parents were crazy?"

"Well, there's crazy, and then there's zombie crazy."

Her glare dissolved when she couldn't hold back an amused snort. "Quit making me laugh when I'm telling you all the traumas of my childhood."

"Did you ever think about leaving?"

"Sure." One hand had oh-so-casually dropped to her waistband, and the tips of his fingers slipped under the bottom hem of her shirt. The brush of skin against skin raised her voice to a high pitch. Clearing her throat, she tried to ignore the contact, even though it was all she could focus on. For her, being touched was a rare occurrence. Ian's fingers warmed her back in a way she could easily start to crave. "Um, all the time. It would've scared them so badly, though, me being out in the evil, dangerous world. I couldn't do it to them. Everything—the bunker, the drills, the isolation—was to protect me."

Nodding, he opened his mouth, but a crash from the other room interrupted him. She spun, putting herself between the door and Ian, her hand reaching for a weapon that wasn't there. When she realized she was unarmed, Rory straightened her shoulders. Billy was going to have to go through her to get to Ian.

Chapter 12

Ian skirted around her and dashed for the doorway, with Rory close behind. Julius's—and only Julius's—swearing made her realize it wasn't an attack by Billy after all, and she sucked in a shaky, relieved breath. She followed Ian to the bathroom, where the swearing had originated, but stopped a few paces away, not wanting to embarrass Julius if he was in an awkward position—quite possibly naked.

"What happened?" Ian asked.

"Slipped," Julius muttered just loud enough for Rory to hear. She stayed out of sight, pretty sure her decision not to barge into the bathroom was a good one.

"Let me help you up."

"Leave it, boy!" There were a few muffled sounds, which she hoped were Julius getting to his feet. "I can do it myself."

"Okay." Ian's voice was thick with frustrated patience. "At least let me check out your head. It looks like you bumped it."

"I'm fine!" The words were practically snarled. "Go be a do-gooder somewhere else. I don't need help from a fucking traitor."

There was a long silence, until Ian broke it with a quiet, "Traitor?"

"Billy told me what you did. Shooting a brother and turning another one over to the pigs. And all over a piece of tail."

"A piece of tail?" His words were pure ice, his tone so scary that she shivered. "It's *Rory*, Julius. Not a piece of tail. Rory. The woman who saved your sorry life!"

"What the hell are you talking about?"

"I'm talking about you trying to buy a gun after Mom died. This piece of tail kept you from blowing your brains out like the self-pitying, selfish bastard you're being right now."

"I knew she never ordered that gun!" Julius snarled. "Told me she did, lying bitch."

Ian stepped back until he was in the hallway. "I'm done." He was using the soft, scary voice again. "Done. I'll ask Carrie to come over and check your head."

Ignoring Julius's protests that he didn't need Carrie or anyone else bothering him, Ian turned and walked toward Rory. His face was blank as they moved to the front door. They donned their boots and coats in silence.

Ian held her arm as they plowed through the snow to the Bronco, then he opened her door. His movements were carefully controlled, his expression as smooth as a mannequin's. Instead of getting into the SUV, she circled around to the driver's side.

She climbed in behind the wheel and pulled her door shut. Ian was still standing by the open passenger door, staring at her like he wasn't sure what was happening.

"Keys." Rory held out her hand, palm up.

"I'm driving."

"No, you're not." Flicking her fingers in a "gimme" gesture, she gave him her sternest look. "You always drive. This one time, I'm going to drive. Now give me the keys and get in."

Although a hint of anger sharpened his features, he did as she asked. Rory started the Bronco, relieved to see an actual emotion breaking through the dead blankness.

"Call Carrie," she ordered, easing the Bronco into the road.

He reached for his cell phone and proceeded to have a three-sentence conversation, asking Carrie to check on his stepdad before ending the call.

"Do I know Carrie?" she asked, turning onto the highway that would bring them home.

"No." As if regretting his shortness, he added in a gentler tone, "She's Squirrel's wife."

Rory nodded, and they drifted into silence. She drove slowly at first, feeling out the vehicle. It soon felt comfortable—fun even—and she relaxed as they sped along the highway.

"Why are we going to your place?" he asked a while later, just a short distance from her front gate.

"Figured you could use a physical outlet for some stress relief."

"Physical outlet?" The odd note in his voice made her glance at him.

"Yes," she said warily, slowing as she rolled through her gate that the cops must have left open. "Why did you say that so weirdly?"

"I didn't say it weirdly."

Although she shot him a look, she didn't argue as she pulled into her lot and backed into a space between two sheriff's department squads. The deputy lounging by the front door straightened and paled as they approached. His hand rested on the butt of his holstered gun.

"What are you doing here, Walsh? The shop is

closed," the deputy snapped. "We're conducting a murder investigation."

Rory wanted to roll her eyes, but she restrained herself. "It's a burglary investigation, not murder. If anything, it's a justifiable homicide investigation."

The deputy turned an interesting shade of pinkish purple. "I'm going to need to see some identification before I can let you in."

"Quit being an ass, Lawrence."

The purple deepened to a vivid red, making Rory worry that the deputy was going to have a stroke. "Stay out of this, Walsh. It's none of your business. This is official procedure."

With a sigh, Rory unzipped her interior coat pocket, intending to pull out her wallet, but the sheriff and Investigator Strepple rounded the corner of the shop before she could present her ID.

"What's going on, Lawrence?" Rob asked. "How are you doing, Rory?"

"Okay." Strepple was hanging back, eyeing them with a neutral expression. It made her uncomfortable, but she tried very hard not to show it. "How are things going here?"

"We're just finishing up." He raised an eyebrow in Strepple's direction, who confirmed the statement with a small nod.

"Already? Oh. I mean, good." The thought of not having to sleep in the closet anymore was surprisingly bittersweet. She was distracted from her bouncing emotions when the front door of the shop swung open, revealing a woman holding a large case in one hand.

"Harding," the sheriff greeted the woman. "All done?"

"Yep. Got everything cleaned up."

Rory was pretty sure that by "everything," Harding meant the BCA's equipment and not the blood and gore that awaited her in the back room. She barely restrained a wince at the thought.

Harding shivered and huddled deeper into her coat. "I'll be glad to get back to Denver. It's practically tropical compared to Simpson. This place is like Siberia."

Strepple made a vague sound that could've been interpreted as agreement. It was going to be a relief for Rory when the investigator did leave town. He was still eyeing her and Ian a little too intently for her peace of mind.

"You had good timing," Rob said to Rory. "The place is yours again. Unless you want to change your mind and show me how you get to your living quarters?" He raised a teasing eyebrow.

She just shook her head, and the four law enforcement officers made their way to the vehicles parked in her lot. All were facing outward, prepared for a quick departure. It almost made her smile. There was no question they were all first responders. As they climbed into their vehicles, she hurried to the gate, reaching it just as the first one—the sheriff's SUV—approached.

After watching the last car pass through the gates, she secured them. Glancing at the cameras still affixed above her head, she frowned. She'd need to take those down, but she figured she'd leave them up for a little while longer. Her place didn't feel safe yet, and she still hadn't looked at the residual carnage in the back room.

With a grunt of displeasure at her timid thoughts, she turned toward the shop. Immediately, she gave a startled yelp. Rory hadn't realized that Ian had been right behind her, and she'd almost gotten a mouthful of shirt when she'd turned.

Quickly regaining her composure, she asked, "Ready?"

"For what?"

"Your stress relief."

"Right. The physical outlet." He put an obscene amount of innuendo into the last two words.

It was impossible for her to calm the raging blush that heated her entire body. She strode toward the shop, unable to look at him, her eyes fixed forward. As she passed the Bronco, she let Jack out of the back. He took off toward the coop immediately, reminding her of the chickens.

With a grimace, she turned to follow the dog.

"What was that look?" Ian asked, quickly falling in place next to her, his long stride shortening to match hers.

"I just feel like a bad chicken mom."

He gave a grunt that might have been a laugh if it had been any other day. "I told you that Squirrel is a marvel with poultry. They're fine."

"I know." It just didn't make her any happier. "Still feel guilty for neglecting them."

Instead of arguing further, he silently took her arm. She already found it a comforting gesture, which was why she knew she should pull away from him. Instead, she leaned a hair closer as they walked to the coop.

As Ian had predicted, the chickens were fine, content to scratch around in the sun-warmed safety of the greenhouse. She watched them for a moment, relaxing as she took in the rhythm of their simple routine. A glance at

Ian showed a slight lessening in tension. Jack had taken his usual position, sprawled next to the south side of the greenhouse, obviously happy to return to protecting his feathered charges.

"Don't most dogs want to *eat* chickens, not guard them?" Ian asked.

She shrugged. "Jack's always had a thing for the chickens. When my parents were alive, we had a few cows, but he'd never been interested in them. He and the cattle had a truce—if he didn't get too close to them, they didn't try to kick him in the head. He's always loved chickens, though."

"Huh." After a pause, he asked, "Why don't you have cows anymore?"

She hesitated before answering, not wanting to tell him the truth. It felt uncomfortably like she was admitting to a weakness. When she'd paused long enough for the silence to get awkward and Ian's expression to grow curious, she finally blurted, "I can't eat an animal if I've named it."

"So don't name them."

"I can't help it." She looked at the chickens and pointed to a smaller hen. "See that one? I didn't set out to name her, but I couldn't help but notice how bossy she was. One morning, I said, 'Out of the way, In-Charge Marge.' That was it. The name stuck."

"Marge?" A corner of his mouth lifted in the beginning of a smile. This wasn't the stress reliever she'd originally intended, but chicken-watching did seem to be calming Ian.

"Marge." She pointed to a different hen for each name. "Clara. Doughnut. Ms. Sprinkles, Lulu, Peeps, and Dinner."

"Dinner?" He grinned, and her chest warmed at the sight.

"She's cantankerous." Rory sent the hen a warning look, which the chicken ignored. "I keep telling her that if she doesn't watch it, she's going to be dinner."

"Dinner," he repeated under his breath, shaking his head but still smiling.

"Come on," she said, turning away from the coop and heading for the shop. Although she was loath to interrupt their happy moment, she knew they had only a limited amount of time before daylight slipped away from them. "Stress relief is waiting."

"They weren't it?" he asked, tilting his head toward the coop.

"Nope." For some reason, maybe the reassurance of being home—despite the present bloodstained condition of that home—she felt a surge of happiness. "Those are chickens. *Chick-ens*," she slowly sounded out, laughing and dodging when he reached toward her mock-threateningly.

He straightened from his playful lunge and looked at her.

"What?" Her smile faded at his unreadable expression.

"Nothing. I just don't get to see you laugh very often."

"Oh." Once again, she had no idea what to say.

Reaching out, he stroked his fingers from her cheekbone to her jawline. At his touch, she instantly stilled, as if they were playing freeze-tag. "I like watching you laugh. It makes you even more beautiful."

Her skin reddened under his touch.

Dropping his hand to his side, he gave her a wicked smile, as if he enjoyed reducing her to this flustered, speechless state. "Stress relief?" he prompted.

Scowling, she stomped toward the front of the shop. She wasn't ready to see the back room in its current condition. Since neither the sheriff nor Strepple had arrested her, she'd just assume that her hidden arsenal hadn't been discovered during their search. "Quit distracting me."

"Sorry." Ian didn't sound sorry. He didn't sound sorry at all.

"This was great," Ian said, eyeing the side-by-side targets. Both had a large hole where the center had been, as if they'd thrown apples at the target and not bullets. "Thanks."

"No problem." She kept her attention focused on the ground as she gathered the spent brass, dropping the casings into a bucket. "I had fun, too. Normally, I don't get to shoot as much as I want. I'm too busy helping other people pick out guns."

Squatting down next to her, he began picking up brass as well. "I needed this. After Billy and then Julius..." The tense lines started to return to his face. "Never mind. I don't want to think about them right now. Especially since you figured out how to make me forget for a few minutes."

"Shooting does that." She kept her head tilted down to hide her expression, since she couldn't stop the smile that crept onto her face. "Everything else goes away except the gun and the target. It's like really loud meditation."

He laughed, dropping a handful of casings in the bucket.

"Cleaning guns does that for me, too," she admitted, shifting over a few feet to grab the stray brass. "Maybe not quite as much as shooting does, but cleaning does calm me."

"Riding's my escape," he said. "It clears my head. Going on a call, though...that's different. The split second we see that wrecked car or blazing fire or the person lying on the ground, not moving, everything else just goes away. The only thing I'm thinking about is the people in that car or how to contain that fire. And after... If it goes well, there's no better feeling. If it doesn't..." Tossing a final couple of casings into the bucket, he stood and brushed off his hands. "Then the crash is pretty brutal."

Rory realized she'd been staring at him, brass-collecting forgotten. Flustered, she hurried to stand, wobbling a little as her legs protested. Tucking the bucket beneath the bench, she reached for the gun cases, but Ian beat her to it. She settled for collecting the empty ammo boxes.

"Ready?" she asked, and immediately felt like a socially inept idiot. He'd spilled his guts to her, and she'd not even said a word in support or comfort or *anything*. Sometimes—most times—she really sucked at this human-interaction thing.

They silently walked away from the range, stopping to drop the empty ammo boxes in the bin where she kept her burnable trash. Next, they checked out the property and fixed the hole the burglars had made in the fence before returning to the chicken coop. Rory took some comfort in performing those simple tasks. Although she might not be a good friend or *girlfriend*—she mentally choked on the word—she knew how to take care of her place.

All too soon, though, the chores were done, and she couldn't put it off any longer. It was cold, the light was fading, the chickens were tucked into their coop, and both Ian and Jack were waiting patiently behind her. Although she knew she had to do it, Rory still couldn't lift her hand to the doorknob.

"We don't have to do this now," Ian said quietly. "We can get ready at my place, work the shift, and then come back tomorrow afternoon."

"I need clothes."

"We'll stop by the Screaming Moose and grab you a few things."

That made her turn her head to stare at him over her shoulder. "Factory-made clothes?"

He blinked. "Uh…aren't they all? Besides the sweaters that grandmas knit and stuff?"

"I make my clothes." She turned back to her battle with the door. "Except for jeans. My mom used to make our jeans, but they never looked right. I hate sewing denim, too, so I cheat."

"Cheat?"

"I buy jeans."

"Aren't they factory-made, then?"

"No. Organic cotton, natural dyes, hand-loomed, and nickel and chemical free," she rattled off absently, still staring at the door. Why was opening it harder than shooting a man? Gritting her teeth, she forced her hand to grasp the knob.

"Wow. So, no mall shopping for you?"

"No." Although she didn't tell him, the two times she'd been in a mall, she'd escaped to the safety of her truck within minutes of walking through the doors. The crowds, the overwhelming multitude of stores, even the piped-in music made her panic.

For some reason, thinking about her two futile mall visits distracted her enough so she could turn the knob, and the door swung open.

It was almost anticlimactic to see the room without the bodies or fresh, pooling blood. On the other hand, the remaining dried bloodstains were like a fist to her belly. Her head jerked back as she absorbed the dark red—almost black—streaks and spatters painting her walls and floor.

When Ian's hand closed over her shoulder, she jolted again, pulling free of his gentle grip. His fingers returned, finding the back of her neck this time, and he gave a soft squeeze.

"Rory." That was all he said, but it was enough. Her exhale shuddered as it left her shivering body, and she allowed him to draw her back against him. When he wrapped his muscular arms around her midsection, she blew out another lungful of air. For some reason, his touch reminded her to keep breathing.

"I can't stay here tonight."

"Then stay with me."

"Okay." It bothered her to leave the place unoccupied, but not as much as the idea of sleeping so close to all this blood—blood that she'd spilled. Rory paused before blurting, "Tell me about Rave."

"Rory..." This time, his voice was reluctant.

"Please." When he remained silent, she continued, "All I know is that he was a member of the Riders. Well, that, and he acted like a rude jerk at the shop."

"That pretty much describes him."

Although Ian's tone was stiff, she still pressed for more. "Was he married?"

"Divorced."

"Kids?" There was a pause, and her stomach clenched. She'd killed someone's father. "Ian..."

"Yeah." It sounded as if the word was dragged out of him.

"Boy or girl?"

"Both."

"Two kids?" She twisted her neck to look up at him. "How old?"

"I don't know." Shrugging, he held a hand about three feet off the floor. "The girl's about this tall, and the boy's a little smaller. It's been months since I've seen them, though. The mom has full custody and lives in Durango, so Rave got just a handful of weekends with the kids since he split with his ex."

Rory was quiet for a short time as she processed that. "Did he live at the clubhouse?"

"Yeah."

"Did he have, I don't know, any redeeming qualities?"

"Do we seriously need to do this? We have to get going if we're going to get Jack and make it to Station One on time."

"We have time." When he still didn't answer her question, she reached back and poked him. Judging by his grunt, she'd managed to hit a sensitive spot.

When the silence stretched, she reached back to physically prod him again, but he grabbed her wrist. "I'm thinking! Quit jabbing at me."

"Is it that hard to come up with a good trait?"

"For Rave, yeah." He didn't release her. Instead, he absently stroked his thumb over the skin on the inside of her forearm, just under the hem of her sleeve. "He was a good mechanic."

"That's it? What about his personality? There had to have been some good in him."

"He could be funny sometimes. Usually, it was unintentional, but still. He did make me laugh a few times."

Her gaze fixed on the dark stain covering her tile floor, she remained quiet until he took his turn, prodding her to speak.

"Why did you want to know? You feeling guilty?" He rested his chin on her head.

"A little," she said, liking the way his body covered her top and back half. It was like having an armadillo's armor. "Not enough."

"What does that mean?"

"That I don't feel bad." It felt good to say the words out loud, but scary at the same time. Admitting her feelings peeled away that protective shell, so she was just a defenseless slug, so easily squashed. "I mean, I do, but I always thought I'd be completely wrecked if I ever killed anyone. This is too easy."

"I don't think it's easy." Releasing her wrist, Ian wrapped both arms around her, pulling her back tighter against his chest. "Have you been having flashbacks?"

"No." The denial came out too quickly, and she knew he'd caught the lie in her voice.

"Something else then?"

"A movie plays in my head," she admitted reluctantly, more willing to say things with her back to him than she ever could have facing him. "Rave is falling, right after I shot him. The film is on loop or something, so it's the same thing over and over. Him staring at me and then falling to the floor. Should we have started CPR?"

"No. There was still a threat. It would've been risky and stupid to try to save those guys."

The plural reminded her that this wasn't just her trauma. "Do you have flashbacks about Lester?"

"No. I did after the first, though."

"First? You mean the first person you killed?" Once again, Rory was glad she was facing away from Ian, so she could hide her moment of shock. She knew she should have expected it. Although the Riders were proficient at keeping their members out of prison, they were far from law-abiding angels. They'd approached her a couple of years ago about offering their protection services, which, her stomach roiling with nerves, she'd politely declined. She'd known, even back then, that they'd be the reason she'd need protection.

"Yeah." His voice had gone rougher, as if he had gravel in his throat.

"When was that?"

"I was sixteen."

Once again, her eyes widened. "Whoa. That's young."

"Yeah." He gave one of his humorless chuckles that she was starting to hate. "Young and dumb."

"Was it an accident?"

"Sort of. Billy sent me to have a…discussion with a guy who'd been causing trouble for the club. Not sure what kind of trouble—back then, Billy told me when to jump and how high. I didn't ask any questions, just followed orders. The guys were always giving me shi—uh, grief about my looks, so I felt like I had to prove I wasn't just a pretty boy, that I could take care of myself. This guy was in his garage, working on this old red Nova. In my head, I can still see that POS car as clear as day.

I meant just to make him hurt, but the guy fought back harder than I thought he would. He got me down on the ground, and I panicked. I grabbed this torque wrench lying next to us and cracked his skull with it." His chest pressed into her back as he sucked in a deep breath. "What a mess."

"Did you get arrested?"

"No. Some guys from the club cleaned up and got me out of there. I was really twitchy for a while after that. Couldn't get the guy's fixed stare out of my head."

There didn't seem to be anything to say to that. Instead, she covered his hands with her own, giving him a quick pat. In return, his arms tightened, squeezing until his grip was just a little short of painful. After a minute of allowing herself to enjoy the comfort of his embrace, she gave him another tap, this one more purposeful.

"Time to move, or we will be late," she told him.

With a sigh, he released her. Rory carefully picked her way to the swinging bookshelf, not wanting to step in any of either man's remains. It still felt strange to open the bookcase and hidden steel door with Ian watching. Now that he knew about her underground lair, though, it would've been silly to leave him sitting on one of the stools in the front room of her shop while she furtively slunk downstairs.

"Just grab some things, and we'll go," he said, following her down the stairs.

"I want to shower."

"My shower's better."

Since she couldn't really argue with that, she didn't. "Yeah, it is. Fine, your shower it is. Just give me a minute." After jamming a few clothes and toiletry items into a backpack, she returned to the living room.

"That was fast," Ian commented.

As she walked into the kitchen, she gave him an odd look. "I grabbed a few things. What did you think would delay me?"

"I don't know." Looking amused, he shrugged. "Most women would've taken an hour. Don't ask me what they would've been doing that whole time."

Scowling, she yanked open the freezer and pulled out a container of Jack's dog food.

"What's wrong?" he asked.

"I hate being compared to normal people," she admitted, wanting to slam the freezer door but restraining herself. "Especially normal women."

When she turned around to face him, she saw that Ian was watching her with a curious look. "Why? It wasn't a criticism. I like that you're efficient and don't waste time."

"It makes me feel like a freak." Dropping the container of dog food into her duffel and zipping it, she made a face. "*More* of a freak."

"You're not a freak." As she passed him on the way to the stairs, she gave him a get-real look. "Well, if you are," he added, "then I think there should be more freaks."

She couldn't help but smile a little at that. Reaching toward her, he grabbed the strap of her bag and gave it a tug. Baffled, she held tighter to the duffel.

"Give me the bag, Ror."

"Why?"

"So I can carry it and feel manly. Give." He gave a hard tug as she released her grip, the bag smacking against his legs. She watched as he shouldered the strap, but then she shrugged. If he wanted to haul around a bag she was perfectly capable of carrying, that was fine with her.

"What you did here the other night," he continued as if they hadn't just had a mini tug-of-war. "That was amazing. You're strong and brave and smart, and I'd take that over anyone or anything else. Plus, you can shoot almost as well as I can."

With a snort, she glanced over her shoulder at him. "Please. I'm a much better shot than you."

He laid a hand over his heart, as if he were mortally wounded. "When we were shooting earlier, I was *clearly* the winner."

Pausing in the middle of unlocking the steel door, she turned and gave him a narrow-eyed glare. "You're just asking for a beat-down, aren't you?"

He grinned, his eyelids partially lowered in a way that made the butterflies in her stomach go on a rampage. The fact that he was standing much too close to her didn't help. "From you? Anytime."

Frowning, she demanded, "Was that supposed to be flirting or something?"

With a startled, booming laugh, he reached for her and, before she could duck out of reach, pulled her into a fierce hug. "Oh, Ror. I do like you."

Once again squashed in his grip, she wheezed, "Uh…thanks?"

He laughed again and pressed a kiss to her hair before he let her go.

"You're so strange," she said as she finished opening the steel door.

"Yeah, I know." Ian didn't sound too upset about that. "But you like me too. Admit it."

Her face was burning, so she tried to avoid looking at him. "I don't *loathe* you."

"That's a start."

Chapter 13

Joel Becker passed them outside the Station One door as he was leaving and they were arriving. Ian and Rory's greetings were met with a surly grunt.

Rory watched the firefighter cross the parking lot and climb into his pickup. When she'd met Joel a couple of other times, he'd acted completely different. "That was kind of rude."

"If you were here alone, he'd have talked to you." Ian held the door open for her. "He doesn't like me."

"Who couldn't like you?" At his teasing glance, she quickly amended her statement. "I mean, who couldn't not-loathe you?"

"Becker."

"Why?"

"Because I'm hotter than him."

"I wouldn't say that." When Ian shot her a truly affronted expression, she had to laugh.

His shoulders relaxed. "Good. You were kidding." He paused. "You *were* kidding, right?"

It was too much fun to mess with him, so Rory didn't respond except for a noncommittal shrug. "So what's the real reason he doesn't like you?"

"He's never come right out and said it, but I'm guessing it's the club."

They entered the training room. Soup and Junior were already there, and Rory returned their greetings absently. "I don't get why he'd care about you being a member of the Riders."

"There are a few who do," he said, although he didn't really answer the "why" part of her question. Then Soup was there, pounding Ian on the shoulder, and the conversation took a more general turn.

Rory slipped off to the women's restroom. From the dust on the towel dispenser, she could tell it'd had very few occupants. After using the bathroom and washing her hands, she noticed the door on the small cabinet in the corner was ajar. When she tried to close it, the door hit an object and bounced open again, farther this time. In the dimness of the cabinet, something glowed pink.

Apprehension surged through her as she reached into the cabinet and pulled out a glow-stick identical to the one left on Ian's door, except that this one was pink. Her stomach twisted as she glanced around the tiny room, her gaze catching on the window set high in the wall. It was just a dark square, revealing nothing, but Rory suddenly felt exposed and vulnerable. She seriously hated windows.

Dropping the glow-stick into the small garbage can, she yanked open the door and hurried to the safety of the crowd. As soon as she entered the training room, Ian spotted her. From his instant frown, she must have looked as hunted as she felt. Clearing her expression with an effort, she made her way over to him.

"Everything okay?" he asked, his voice low.

"Yes." Her answer came quickly, without thought. She was the one causing all of his problems with the Riders. Ian'd had her back during the burglary, going above and beyond what anyone could expect from a friend. She'd killed Rave and incurred Billy's wrath, and she needed to deal with that. It would be cowardly of her to endanger Ian any more than she already had.

"Sure?"

She firmed her jaw. "Yes."

"Rory!" Junior bounced over to them, beaming. "I ordered a pocket chainsaw."

"Good. It'll come in handy."

"Yeah, you convinced me it was a necessity for the survival bag."

Soup groaned. "So *you're* the one encouraging his crazy."

"You won't call me crazy when you're desperate for a drink of my purified water after the water supply is tainted," Junior said.

"Tainted by what?" Ian asked.

"Do not get him started," Soup ordered. "Once he starts on his conspiracy theory bullshit—"

"It is *not* bullshit!" Junior interrupted. "If you would do a little research, you'd see—"

There was another interruption, this one from the radio. Everyone went quiet as the dispatcher relayed the information for the medical call, a forty-eight-year-old man with nausea and shortness of breath at the gas station on the south end of town. Everyone dashed for their bunker gear, and the night began.

As the EMTs were giving the man oxygen to help with his altitude sickness, another call came over the radio—this one a two-vehicle accident on Highway 36. The firefighters piled into the trucks and headed in that direction.

"Fucking full moon," Soup muttered from his spot in the passenger seat of the rescue truck.

"Watch your mouth!" There was a snap to Ian's voice.

Sending Rory a sheepish look, Soup apologized.

"Swearing doesn't bother me," she said.

"Hey, I'm just saving you from the trauma of Maya's tears when she visits the station and you drop the f-bomb. Learn from my mistakes, Soup." Ian increased the truck's speed, only to have to slow again a moment later. If he hadn't made that promise, Rory was pretty sure he would've been swearing about Lieutenant Al's driving.

"Does a full moon really make a difference?" she asked.

"Seems to." Soup seemed relieved at the change of subject. "People do the nuttiest things during a full moon. Remember Lars Sojn?"

Ian gave a pained groan. "Unfortunately."

"Yeah, I wish I could erase that image from my brain, but it's burned there permanently." Soup shook his head. "This old guy got drunk, stripped naked, and climbed onto his roof. In *January*. Said he was waiting for the aliens to come and get him. As if any self-respecting alien would want some wrinkly, scrawny old dude when there are hot chicks to abduct and probe."

Rory choked on a laugh that died when the truck in front of them started to slow. Their view was blocked, but she assumed that they'd arrived. This was confirmed by Junior's urgent voice on the radio.

Once they jumped out of the truck and approached the scene, Rory slowed, taking in the horror in front of her. An SUV and a sedan were both mangled, crushed into almost unrecognizable shapes.

"Rory!" Ian's shout jerked her out of her daze. "You're with Junior!"

It took her a few moments to spot him. She finally

saw Junior next to the remains of the SUV, and she hurried over.

"What do you need?" she asked when she reached his side. He had the driver's door open and was placing a cervical collar around the neck of the woman inside. A cut along her hairline streaked her temple and the side of her cheek with blood. Her eyelids fluttered open and closed, and she was moaning—a steady, eerie drone.

"Child-sized c-spines, but we're going to have to wait for Med to arrive for those." He moved quickly to the rear and opened the back hatch with one hand while digging in his coat pocket with the other. It looked as though most of the damage had been to the front of the SUV, so the door opened easily. He held out a pair of purple latex gloves. "Put these on and then get in here."

She pulled the too-large gloves onto her chilled and trembling fingers, and then climbed in next to him, kneeling behind the backseat.

"Hey, Buddy," Junior was saying. "My name's Junior. I'm a fireman, and we're here to help you. We're going to hold your head still, okay? It's just for a little while, until the doctors can check you out and make sure you're okay." He jerked his head at Rory, and she shuffled closer.

Leaning over the top of the seat, Rory saw that Junior had been talking to a little kid.

"Support his head and neck like this." He moved behind her and demonstrated on Rory.

Her hands shook as she wrapped them around both sides of the small neck. "Got it."

"Great. You stay with him." He started to exit the rear hatch door.

Rory glanced to the side and yelped, "Wait! Junior!"

"What?"

"There's a baby!"

"I saw. Relax. I'm just going to the side door."

"Okay." Reassured that she wouldn't be left alone with a possibly injured baby and no usable hands, she gave the infant a final worried look and then focused on the little person in her grip. He was trembling and gasping every so often, so she tipped forward to see his face, worried that something was wrong.

To her relief, her upside-down view showed that the boy was crying, which explained the shaking and funny breathing. His eyes widened when they stared at her face.

"Hi."

He didn't answer, just watched her suspiciously, but his crying abated a little. Junior, as promised, had circled to the side door. He was leaning into the backseat, checking the baby's brachial pulse. The infant wasn't crying, which worried Rory a little. It seemed like a situation that would make a baby wail, so the silence coming from the car seat was a little unnerving.

Pulling out a knife and flipping it open, Junior cut the straps securing the baby seat. He closed the knife and lifted the seat.

"I'm going to put her in the rescue truck," he said, obviously feeling the panic coming off of Rory in waves. "It's cold out here and warm in there."

"Should you move her?"

Junior gave her a reassuring smile. "A car seat is a great infant backboard. I'll be right back to check on their mom." With that, he was gone, and Rory was on her own with a little patient who was still staring at her. At least his crying had stopped completely, so that was good.

They looked at each other in silence for a little while. She racked her brain for a child-appropriate conversation starter.

"What's your name?" she finally asked.

He remained big-eyed and quiet for so long that she figured he wasn't going to answer, but then he finally spoke. "Jack." His whisper was so soft that Rory could barely hear him.

"Jack?"

He tried to nod, but she was holding his head still, so he mouthed, "Yes," instead.

"That's my dog's name." He smiled a tiny bit at that. Encouraged, she added, "My name is Rory."

"Like a lion?" His words were actually audible now—barely, but she still took it as a promising sign.

"Uh, sure." She was back to not having anything to say to this kid.

"Are you scared? You look scared."

She blinked, not sure how to answer that. It didn't seem like the most reassuring thing for a firefighter to admit she was freaked out of her mind. She didn't want to lie to him, though, especially because she was pretty sure he'd know it wasn't the truth. "Yes."

His already huge eyes widened even more, and she mentally swore at herself for not lying. "Why?"

"It's only my second day with the fire department," she admitted, although she fully expected her confession to make things worse. "I don't want to do anything wrong."

"Oh." He paused before asking, "Like what?"

A dozen possible horrific scenarios flashed through her mind, but even she knew not to share those with a traumatized kid. "Um…how old are you?"

"Five."

Junior's reappearance by the open driver's door made her jump. Instantly glancing down at Jack—whom she was mentally calling boy-Jack, as opposed to dog-Jack—afraid she'd jostled him, she asked, "Did that hurt?"

"No. Is my mom okay?"

From the quick glance Rory had gotten of the woman, she definitely hadn't looked okay. She decided to let the expert field that question. "Hey, Junior? Is Jack's mom okay?"

"She will be, Buddy," Junior said, tucking a blanket around the boy. "Looks like the ambulance just got here. How would you like to ride in it with your mom and little sister?"

Jack's response was lost when the back door next to him opened, and Ian stuck in his head. He gave Rory a quick, appraising look, then turned to the boy, moving so Jack could see him without moving his head.

"Hey, there. How's Rory treating you?"

"Good."

"Good, huh?"

"Yeah, even though she's scared 'cause she's new and is afraid she's gonna make mistakes."

"Hey, now, Mr. Loose-Lips." Rory frowned at him. "Remind me not to tell you my secret plan to take over the world."

Ian chuckled, even as he snuck a quick glance toward the front seat, where the EMTs were getting Jack's mom out of the SUV. He quickly refocused on the boy. "What's your name?"

"Jack."

"Boy-Jack, though. Not dog-Jack," Rory added, and then immediately flushed. That had sounded all kinds of dumb.

"Thanks for setting that straight." Ian smirked. "I wouldn't have figured it out, otherwise."

"Rory's dog is named Jack, too."

"Yeah." Ian sounded a lot less sarcastic with the five-year-old than with her, Rory noted. "I've met dog-Jack."

"Is he a good dog?"

"A very good dog." Ian smiled at the boy while gently holding his wrist, and Rory realized he'd been discreetly taking Jack's pulse.

"Okay?" she asked, tilting her head to their joined hands.

"Great. Right around ninety." He grinned at the boy again. "You're doing great, staying calm and cool under pressure. I bet you'll be a fireman when you grow up."

"No. I'm going to be a soldier."

"You like guns?" Rory asked, making Ian snort.

"You've found the key to her heart," Ian told Jack solemnly.

The boy's eyes darted between the two of them. "I like guns. I want a BB gun, but Mom says I have to be twelve before I get one."

"I have a gun store," Rory told him. "When you turn twelve, have your mom bring you there, and I'll get you a nice BB gun."

His eyes widened again. "Really?"

"Really. You can meet dog-Jack there, too."

"He lives at the gun store?"

"Yep."

The EMTs returned, and Ian retreated, getting out of their way. Once they put the c-spine on the boy, she tried to move away, as well, but Jack wailed her name, his tears starting again.

"Hang on, kid," she said, moving to the back hatch. "I'll come around to the side so I don't have to look at you upside-down anymore."

Despite her attempt at reassurance, Jack's cries didn't subside as he was strapped to a board and taken out of the SUV. Rory leaned over him so she was in his line of sight. Once he spotted her, his tears abated. Holding his hand, she trotted along next to them as they headed for the back of the ambulance.

"See you later, Jack." Giving his fingers a final squeeze, she pulled her hand free as the EMTs loaded him into the ambulance. At his renewed wails, she flinched.

"He'll be fine." Ian draped an arm across her shoulders and gave her a sideways hug.

"How do parents do it?" she muttered, watching as the ambulance pulled away from them. "When he cried, I just wanted him to stop. I would've given him a pony if that would've made him quit. If I ever have kids, I'll be bankrupt in six months."

With a laugh and a final squeeze, he dropped his arm. She looked around, finally seeing more of the scene than a little boy's scared face. "Were the other people in the car okay?"

"One guy." The humor slipped out of his expression. "He was trapped in that car like it was a smashed tuna can."

She winced at the visual, glancing at the car's remains. "It looks like you took a chainsaw to it."

"Pretty much." He grimaced. "We had to use the hydraulic tools to cut him out."

"Not good?" she guessed, reading his grim expression.

"Not good. He was alive when we got him out and on the helicopter, but barely."

A little startled, she asked, "Flight picked him up? How'd I miss that?"

"You were occupied." He glanced past her. "The first wrecker's here. Let's get this cleaned up so State can open the highway."

Although she knew the call wasn't over, her body thought it was. She helped with cleanup, feeling like she was walking through sludge. Every muscle felt weighted. Her brain was a mess of scattered thoughts and fuzziness, so she was relieved when Al barked orders at her. As long as she was told exactly what to do, she could continue to function.

By the time they climbed into the trucks, she was swaying with exhaustion.

"Tired?" Soup asked kindly.

"Yeah." Resting her head against the back of the seat, she allowed her eyes to close. "How do you guys manage to make it through an entire shift?"

"An iron will," Soup answered solemnly. Opening one eye, she gave him a look before closing it again. "And coffee. Lots and lots of coffee."

"You get used to it," Ian said. "Plus, you haven't gotten much sleep the past few nights—longer than that, even."

"Yeah?" Something about Soup's too-interested tone

had her eyes snapping open. "Why wasn't she sleeping? And how do you *know* she wasn't sleeping, Beauty?"

"Stop." Despite his hard tone, Ian sounded more resigned than angry. "Of all the gossipy old women in this department, you are the worst."

"Just because we like to stay well informed"—Ian snorted, but Soup continued, ignoring the interruption—"doesn't make us gossipy old women."

The three of them rode silently for a moment before Soup spoke again, "So…are you two sleeping together, then?"

All tiredness forgotten, Rory sat straight, grateful that the darkness hid her vividly red cheeks.

"Soup!" Ian snapped. "Enough."

"Better to tell me the whole story." Soup was obviously not deterred. "That way, I can correct any vicious, untrue rumors I hear floating around the station."

"What are you—a tabloid reporter?" Ian demanded. "I'm not telling you sh—ah, anything."

"Not that there's anything to tell yet," Rory blurted, and then regretted opening her mouth when Soup's voracious gaze focused on her.

Ian spoke before the other man could. "Say another word, and I'll let the lieutenant know that you volunteered to clean that tender compartment holding the moldy hoses. On your day off."

Eyeing Ian, Soup appeared to ponder his sincerity for a moment before closing his mouth and settling back against the seat.

"Smart man," Ian muttered.

They'd barely gotten back to the station when the radios blared again. There was a chorus of groans before the dispatcher's voice relayed the call. Even through the radio static, Libby's squeaky voice was unmistakable.

"Caller is reporting that his backyard storage shed was on fire. He believes he put it out, but he would like confirmation that it is completely extinguished. This is behind four-two-two Bison Drive. Simpson Fire, please acknowledge."

"Fire copies the call." Al released the radio button. "You three," he pointed at Ian, Rory, and Soup, "are in Engine One. We'll follow you in the rescue." He pulled out his cell phone and tapped the screen. "Chief, I think you'll want to meet us at this call..."

His voice faded as they separated, heading to their assigned trucks.

"No tender?" Rory asked, climbing into her usual spot in the middle seat.

"No," Ian answered as he started the engine. "Bison Drive is in town, part of the Esko Hill development. They have hydrants."

"A luxury."

He grinned. "Definitely. You know what else is a luxury?"

"What?"

"This time, LT's behind me." The engine truck shot forward out of the station.

Rory and Soup both groaned.

When they arrived, it appeared that the homeowner had indeed gotten the fire under control, but Al had them dump some water on the charred remains of the shed anyway. For Rory, it was a good, low-key training exercise to introduce her to how the trucks and hoses and valves and everything worked.

Once the blackened skeleton of the small structure had been well drenched, she helped pull anything that might be salvageable out of the wreckage. As she dropped the head of a shovel into the pile, she glanced over to where Winston Early was in a three-man huddle with Al and Rob Coughlin.

"Why are the sheriff and the chief here?" she asked Ian quietly. "I know I'm new, but it seems like a pretty minor incident to me."

Ian glanced over at the men and then stepped closer to Rory. In a low voice, he said, "This is the eighth or ninth small structure in Simpson to catch fire this winter, not to mention last summer's wildland fire. We can blame Lou's cabin fire on her stalker, but the rest of these have got to be related."

She turned her head to look at him and was a little startled to find him so close. "Someone's setting fires intentionally?"

"Yeah. It's happening more frequently lately. I can't help but wonder if the next target's going to be someone's house."

Shaking her head, she walked back to the remains of the shed to continue digging. "Sleepy Simpson is turning into a hotbed of crime lately."

Ian had followed her. "Yeah." He rubbed his forehead, leaving a black smear of soot, and then repositioned his helmet. The smudge just emphasized his perfect face, making him look like a model posing as a firefighter. The hard line of his cheekbones and jaw contrasted in the best way with his full, gorgeous lips. The sheen of sweat on his skin caught the light. Despite his almost beautiful features, he looked like what he was—a hard-working, tough, and brave man. He continued speaking, and Rory realized she'd been struck dumb by the sight of him—yet again. "Maybe we should move to sleepy Liverton to get away from the dangerous city," he added.

Tearing her gaze away from Ian, Rory snorted a laugh before returning to her salvage mission.

Chapter 14

Ian wasn't happy she'd decided to return to her bunker, but he had a night shift, and she had to sleep so she could open the shop in the morning. As much as she didn't want to face the back room again, she'd already lost two days of business. Although she enjoyed firefighting, it wasn't a paying job like it was for Ian, and volunteer work didn't pay for chicken feed. Since she had to sleep alone in one of their houses, she'd picked her hidden, reinforced refuge over Ian's fishbowl.

Although it was a relief to return to her bedroom, the oasis of pink didn't relax her as it usually did. Instead, it had a slightly foreign feel, as if two nights—or days—on closet floors had altered her somehow. All the repaired fences and locks in the world wouldn't be enough to keep out worried thoughts featuring Billy and Rave. Even though they hadn't caught any images of the burglars, the deer cameras were still in place and activated—just in case. Closing her eyes, Rory ordered her brain to stop being ridiculous and sleep. It took longer than she expected, but she eventually managed.

A blaring alarm woke her. She sat up abruptly and fumbled for the light switch, disoriented. It took her a few seconds before she realized that what she'd thought was an alarm was actually just the landline phone. The number was the same as the one in her shop, so whoever was calling was most likely a customer. Glancing at the clock, she saw it was almost eleven.

She contemplated letting the phone ring, but the loud trill was jumping up and down on her last nerve, so she answered it. "What?"

"Rory."

"Ian, you'd better have a really good reason for waking me, and it can't have anything to do with your concern for my well-being."

"I'm in jail."

She blinked. "That'll do."

"The sheriff arrested me for Willard Gray's murder."

"The headless guy?" Residual sleep must've been slowing down her brain, because Rory was having a difficult time comprehending. "Well, that's just stupid."

He gave one of his humorless barks of laughter. "Tell the sheriff that. Would you do me a favor and let the chief know that I can't make my shift tonight? And ask Squirrel to get a hold of Tack Sampson. He's the Riders' lawyer, and I've dealt with him before. I know I'm not Billy's favorite person right now, but I'm still family, and the Riders take care of their own. My phone's on the table by my bed. I left the side door of the house unlocked, since I figured you'd need to get in there. See if Carrie can check on Julius, too."

"Whoa." She held up a hand in a "stop" motion, even though Ian couldn't see her. "Back up a step. Can I bail you out? I have some money stashed."

"It's a murder charge, so I'll be held until the arraignment tomorrow, and then they'll set bail."

"Okay." Rory was out of bed and doing her best to dress one-handed. "Then side door, phone on the nightstand, call Chief, Squirrel, and Carrie. Did I miss anything?"

"No." His voice had warmed slightly. "Did I ever tell you how much I like your crisis-management skills?"

"Time's up, Walsh," she heard a male voice say in the background.

"You're such a sweet-talker," she said flatly, although her heart was pounding as she absorbed the information—Ian was in jail for murder.

His chuckle was more authentic this time. "Thank you, Ror."

"I'd say anytime, but I don't want to be getting calls from jail on a regular basis."

He laughed again. "Bye."

"Talk to you soon," she said, making her words more of a promise than the typical sign-off.

She kept the "Closed" sign in the shop window and left Jack to guard his chickens, since she wasn't sure where exactly the day would take her. As soon as she had locked her gate behind her and was back in her truck, she pulled out her cell phone. Once she made the turn onto the county road, her reception improved, and she was able to make calls. While her pickup fishtailed around the turn, she was already dialing the chief.

"Early."

"Chief, it's Rory."

"Hi, Rory." His good-natured voice warmed even more. "I've been hearing great things about you from—"

"Great," she interrupted, really not caring about commendations at the moment. "Ian's in jail."

There was a pause on the other end. It extended long enough for Rory to check her cell-phone screen to make sure the call hadn't been dropped. It hadn't.

"Why?" Chief Early finally asked.

"Willard Gray's murder." She took another turn too fast, grateful that the weather had been relatively dry the past few days. The last thing she needed was a fresh layer of snow and ice covering the road. When the chief didn't reply immediately, she clarified, "The headless guy Lou found in the reservoir."

"I know who Willard Gray is—was—but why do they think Ian killed him?" Early sounded completely baffled.

"Something Ian lost was found by the body, but it's completely crazy to think he could be the killer." A tiny, niggling doubt reminded her that he'd killed before, more than once, but she pushed it away. She told herself that she was in a glass house now that she'd killed someone, as well. Her gut told her that Ian wasn't responsible for Willard Gray's murder, and she'd learned a long time ago to trust her instincts.

"Of course it is," the chief said, after the tiniest of pauses. "He's a good man."

"He wanted me to tell you that they're holding him until his arraignment, which will probably be tomorrow, so he'll miss at least tonight's shift."

"That's Ian for you." Chief Early gave a short laugh. "He's arrested for murder, and his main concern is that someone's available to take his shift. Next time you talk to him, let him know I'm here for him if he needs anything."

"I will. Thanks." Before the chief even managed to

get out his response, Rory ended the call and was dialing Squirrel. He'd texted her a chicken photo earlier, so she didn't need to get his number from Ian's phone.

"Yeah?" he answered. His phone manners were about as good as hers were.

"Squirrel, it's Rory."

"Rory, hey. What's wrong?"

"Ian's been arrested."

There was a long silence, followed by an even longer string of profanity. Rory stayed silent and waited him out. Despite her preoccupation with Ian's situation, she was impressed with Squirrel's creativity. "This is about that headless dude, isn't it?"

"Yes. Do you have the number for the club's lawyer? It's Tack…somebody."

"Tack Sampson? I do, but it won't do any good. Billy said he's out of the country."

Her molars were grinding together, and she forced herself to loosen her jaw before she broke a tooth. "Is there another lawyer who can take his case? His arraignment's probably going to be tomorrow."

"There's Archie Innis." His tone was doubtful.

That actually made her laugh. "He hasn't been sober for probably twenty years. I won't even sell a gun to him when he comes into the shop, because he's either obviously drunk or high. Who're the Riders using while Tack's gone?"

"We haven't needed a lawyer."

"Yet." Forget breaking a tooth—she was grinding them hard enough that her whole jaw was about to snap. "Why am I getting the impression that Billy's leaving Ian to hang?"

"Because he is." Squirrel sounded tired. "Billy's been out of control lately, especially since Rave…" He cleared his throat. "Anyway. I can't produce Tack, but is there anything else I can do to help?"

"Not that I can think of right now."

"Well, call anytime if you think of something. And, Rory?"

"Yeah?"

"Keep me in the loop, okay? Even though Billy's acting like a psycho right now, Ian's still my brother."

"I will."

After ending the call, she tapped the cell phone against her thigh, trying to think of who to contact next. Her brain was spinning, and she tried to organize her thoughts in a logical fashion. The priority was to find Ian a good lawyer. Tack Sampson was unavailable and, after Billy's recent actions, she wouldn't trust the club's lawyer to defend Ian well, anyway. Archie wasn't even a possibility. *Rory* would do a better job representing Ian than Archie would.

Scrolling through her contacts while keeping one eye on the road, she found Soup's name and hit send.

"Rory!" he greeted enthusiastically. "We were just talking about you."

"Hey, Soup. Ian's been arrested for Willard Gray's murder."

After a short silence, he said in a serious voice, "What do you need?"

"The name of a good lawyer, if you have one?"

"I don't, sorry. He's a member of the Liverton Riders, though. I'm sure they have someone with a law degree on speed-dial."

"Tried that." Her teeth clenched at the reminder. "They're not interested in helping."

He gave a whistle. "That's low. He's done a lot for that club."

"Yeah. Are you at the station?"

"Yep."

"Would you mind asking around if anyone knows a good lawyer?"

"Sure."

Rory expected him to hang up, ask the other firefighters, and then call her back. Instead, without moving the phone away from his mouth, he bellowed, "Yo! Any of you know a good lawyer? Beauty's in jail because they think he killed Lou's headless floater."

In the background, there were muffled exclamations and several conversations going on at once, but Rory couldn't make out what anyone was saying, except for an occasional "Yeah?" or "Not helpful, Tucker," or "Really?" As she pulled into Ian's driveway, Soup began talking again.

"So, Lou's a lawyer."

"Seriously?" Hope rose in Rory, but then doubt squashed it. "She works at The Coffee Spot."

"Yep, but she's still a lawyer. Passed the bar exam and everything, according to Callum. Even if she can't defend him herself, she's going to know a shit-ton of other lawyers who might be able to help."

"That's great, Soup." The relief of at least having possibilities washed over her, and she let her head rest against the back of the seat for a moment. "Where's Lou now, do you know?"

"I don't, but Callum will. He probably has her

schedule all mapped out in a flowchart. Hey!" he yelled, making Rory wince and pull the phone away from her ear. "No throwing tools, Cal. That's just ugly."

"Could you ask him?" Her tone was embarrassingly close to begging. It was strange how her pride took a backseat when it came to helping Ian.

"Callum!" he bellowed again. "Where's Lou?" He paused, and Rory could hear a muffled male voice speaking in the background. "She's headed to her shift at The Coffee Spot, which starts at noon. See, I told you he'd know."

"Thanks, Soup."

"Keep us updated, okay? Whatever he needs, we've got his back."

"I will."

After ending the call, she got out of the truck and hurried to the side door. As Ian had promised, it was unlocked. Although that normally would've driven her up a wall, it just gave her a mild twinge now, since most of her brain and nerves were occupied with Ian's situation.

His phone was on the stand next to his bed, and she grabbed it. Carrie answered immediately.

"Ian?" she said anxiously. "Squirrel said you were arrested! What's going on?"

"This is Rory," she said, feeling a little awkward. "He's in jail. Ian asked me to call you to see if you could check in on Julius until he gets out. I forgot to ask when I was talking to Squirrel."

"Of course," Carrie said warmly. "And it's nice to finally speak to you in person, although the circumstances aren't the best. Do you know what's going on?

Squirrel won't tell me anything except that Ian was arrested for murdering that guy found in the reservoir. I haven't ever seen Squirrel this mad, and I've been married to him for ten years."

"I just know that Ian's been arrested. I'm trying to find a lawyer for him."

"What about Tack?" Carrie asked. "He comes off as a greasy used-car salesman, but I guess he's a piranha in court. He's gotten Zup and Nickel off a few times, and Rave was a frequent customer of his until…um. Anyway, he'd be sure to get Ian out of those trumped-up charges."

Rory was beginning to hate the sound of Tack Sampson's name. "He's out of the country."

"But I just saw him at the grocery store yesterday," Carrie said. "That international trip must've started today. I'd bet anything his sudden departure isn't a coincidence. No wonder Squirrel is raving mad. Billy's shoving Ian under the bus, isn't he?"

"Yeah, I think so." In fact, she was pretty positive about it. "Lou's a lawyer. I'm going to go talk with her now to see if she has any contacts who might be able to help Ian."

"Good idea. I'm going to have a come-to-Jesus talk with Squirrel, and he *will* tell me everything he knows about this." Carrie's voice was grim, and Rory almost felt sorry for the gentle, chicken-loving Squirrel. "If I uncover anything useful, I'll call you. Should I use Ian's number?"

"No, I'm calling you from my phone right now." Rory tapped the number from Ian's cell screen into hers and hit send.

"There it is," Carrie confirmed.

"I'll let you know if I learn anything, too."

"Thanks," the other woman said gratefully. "Ian's always been such a sweetie. It broke my heart when Billy used to have him act as an enforcer. Ian just didn't have the meanness he needed to do that kind of shit."

"He really is a good person." As she spoke, the image of him gently holding boy-Jack's arm to take his pulse flashed through her mind. Rory's voice broke in the middle of the last word, and she cleared her throat. If she started getting soft and weepy now, she wouldn't be any use to Ian. "Thanks, Carrie. I'll talk to you later."

"Bye, honey. Ian's been on his own for so long. I'm so glad he has you now."

Rory's heart gave a little flutter, but she ignored it, staring grimly forward. "Me too," she said—and was surprised to realize just how desperately she meant it.

There was a crowd in the coffee shop when Rory arrived. As soon as Lou spotted her, though, the barista put two fingers in her mouth and whistled sharply. Every pair of eyes turned to her, and silence fell over the shop.

"Okay, listen up, ski refugees!" Lou announced in a carrying voice. "Here's the deal. One of our local firefighters has been falsely arrested for murder." Several members of the crowd gasped, and everyone was obviously mesmerized by Lou's words. "This is a good guy, someone who risks his life every day to help save other people. I mean, he'll run into a burning building to save a kitten. Plus, he is about the hottest chunk of manliness whose six-pack has ever been wedged into bunker gear, so there's that, too." Rory felt her cheeks redden. Lou wasn't wrong. "Anyway, I'm asking that you do your small part to help this hero by waiting patiently for five minutes while I talk to my friend"—she waved at Rory, whose blush intensified when everyone's eyes turned toward her—"about finding our innocent fireman a lawyer so he can get out of jail and back to saving lives. Can you do that for me?"

There was a chorus of agreement from her spellbound audience. One woman stepped forward. "I'm an attorney."

The woman next to her gave the speaker a strange look. "You specialize in patents."

"Hush," the first woman hissed. "Hot fireman. I mean, how hard can trial law be?"

Lou and Rory exchanged a quick, appalled look before Lou said gently, "Thank you so much, but I already have the perfect attorney in mind." She raised her voice and addressed the entire crowd again. "Please wait here, and we'll be right back."

At Lou's urgent gesture, Rory hustled behind the counter and followed her into the back of the shop.

"I've already made some calls," Lou said. "It's amazing how much you can get done when you toss customer service out the window. Anyway, I'm waiting to hear back from North Butterfield. He's my number one choice. Next would be Suzanne Zhang. I already talked to her, and she'd be willing to take Ian on as a client. I'd really like it if North could represent him, though—he's brilliant."

Rory's brain was trying to process the information Lou was throwing at her at warp speed. "His name is really North Butterfield?" Instantly, she was embarrassed for asking such an inane question when Ian's freedom was at stake.

Lou seemed to take it in stride, though. "I know, right? His parents did not do him a kindness with that. He admitted to me once that he was called Butterface all through high school."

Shaking her head, Rory tried to focus on the more important details. "His arraignment will probably be tomorrow. Do you think one of the two will be able to get here in time?"

"Suzanne's in Colorado Springs, so she could get here in a two-or-three-hour car ride. North's practice is in Denver, but he's in Chicago right now. I'm hoping to talk to him this afternoon so he can get a flight back to DIA tonight or early tomorrow morning. It'll be tight, but I think we can do it."

"How expensive will they be?" Rory bit her lip, doing math in her head. "I have some money, but if it'll cost more than what I have, I'll need to sell some of my collector pieces, which takes a little time."

"Don't worry about that right now," Lou said, reaching out to give Rory's arm a squeeze. "This is a picture-perfect case for a defense attorney to get publicity. I mean, a hot mountain-man fireman falsely accused of murdering a headless guy? Well, he wasn't headless until after the…anyway. Both North and Suzanne will see that and price their fees accordingly. Plus, you two have a lot of friends in this town. Everyone wants to help get Ian free. If need be, we can throw a pancake breakfast or something. Now, scoot, before there's a mutiny." Lou headed toward the front of the shop.

"Lou." When she stopped and looked over her shoulder, Rory said, "Thank you." She'd said those words so many times in the past hour and a half, and they seemed so ineffective in relaying the full weight of her gratitude.

"Of course." Lou grinned. "We all have our strengths. You set me up with a gun, and I set Ian up with a shark of an attorney. Now go see if they'll let you talk to him, and tell him that we're all rooting for him. Well, maybe not Deputy Lawrence, but everyone else."

Once Lou was out of sight, Rory took a deep breath and released it, glad that no one was around to witness how shaky her exhale was. "Okay," she said after another, slightly steadier breath. "Okay. Let's go to jail."

"Visiting hours are Monday nights from eighteen hundred to twenty-one hundred hours." Of course it had to be Deputy Lawrence manning the jail.

"I just want to pass on some information about his attorney," Rory pressed, although she could already tell by his smug expression that there was no way she was getting to talk to Ian that afternoon.

"Walsh is not above the rules," Lawrence said, as expected. "If you return Monday night, you can visit him for one hour. No revealing or inappropriate clothing is allowed, however."

She followed his gaze to her extremely well-covered chest. With her multiple layers, including a zipped, bulky coat, the only way her outfit could have been less revealing was if it were a hazmat suit. "Uh…okay."

"Rory?"

The friendly voice brought her head around in relief. "Hi...Deputy Jennings, right?"

"Chris." His smile slipped away. "Sorry about Ian."

Lawrence made a choked sound, and they both turned to look at him.

"Hairball, Laurie?" Chris asked with mock sympathy.

At that, Deputy Lawrence turned an unhealthy-looking shade of purple. Except for a glare, though, he didn't respond.

"C'mon," Chris said, guiding her away from the other deputy.

He steered her through a couple of corridors to a small office. After ushering her inside, he closed the door behind them. He gestured toward one of the chairs squeezed in next to a desk, but she remained standing and lifted her eyebrows at him.

With a grimace, he took the chair behind the desk. Leaning back, he dug the heels of his hands into his eye sockets. "Sorry for dragging you in here, but I wanted to talk to you without Lawrence listening."

"Understandable." She eased herself into the chair across the desk from him.

"This whole thing," he sighed, dropping his hands to the chair arms, "is a complete cluster. And now Ian's been arrested—*Ian,* for Christ's sake. *I'm* more likely to be the murderer than Ian Walsh."

"Agreed," Rory said, leaning forward, excited by the possibility of an ally on the inside and only realizing belatedly what she'd implied. "Not that I think you're the killer, either."

His grin was crooked and tired. "Thanks."

"Why was he arrested? There must've been something to make the sheriff think he was responsible."

Chris eyed her for a long moment, his fingers tapping against the desk. "Be careful how you use this information I'm going to share with you. Normally, I wouldn't dream of blabbing to the girlfriend of the main suspect in custody, but this isn't right. This is Ian. We both know he didn't kill Willard Gray. Rob knows that, too, but he's getting pressured from all sides to wrap up this case. Once that pendant with the Liverton Riders' symbol on it was found and identified as Ian's, Rob's hands were tied. He had to bring in Ian."

The word "girlfriend" made her eyes widen a little in protest, but then she reminded herself to prioritize. Mislabeling their relationship was so far down on the list of things to care about that it wasn't even worth mentioning.

"Rob brought Billy in for questioning. The pendant was found by the body. Billy pointed his finger at Ian. Said it had belonged to Walsh's father, and Ian always wore it—never took it off, in fact. Then, sometime last fall, Billy noticed it wasn't hanging around Ian's neck anymore. Said he asked Walsh about it, but he just blew Billy off, mumbled something about losing it, and then changed the subject."

Fury burned at the pit of her stomach, and she squeezed the chair arms until the metal edges bit into her fingers. "Ian called me this morning and asked me to get Tack Sampson to represent him, but Squirrel told me he was out of the country. Carrie said later she'd just seen Tack at the grocery store yesterday."

With a nod, Chris sat up in his chair. "The whole thing stinks like a setup. What are the chances that a clearly identifying piece of jewelry falls off when Ian dumps the body? Not only that, but Ian doesn't notice, and the thing hooks on to the weight holding down the body and stays in place for three to six months? I know it's not a rushing river, but it's hard to believe the water movement in the reservoir didn't shift it around. Someone screwed up when entering items into evidence at the scene, and that weight and pendant didn't get logged into evidence until the next day. And now, right after things get tense between Ian and the Riders, Billy's volunteering this kind of damning information? The Riders protect their own; if this wasn't a setup, Billy'd have refused to tell us anything. It strains credulity, especially when the evidence points to Ian, of all people."

"Do you think Billy is the real killer, then?" Rory asked. "And he used Ian's necklace to frame him?"

Chris looked doubtful. "That doesn't really work, either. Why connect his own MC to a murder with the planted evidence? Besides, I got the impression Billy and Ian were tight until the shoot-out at your place. Now Rave's dead, Zup was arrested, and Billy's pissed. I'm thinking that, once he recognized Ian's necklace, Billy made the impulse decision to get some revenge on Walsh."

"So, who?"

With a huff of laughter, Chris said, "If I knew that, we wouldn't be holed up in here having this discussion. I'd be arresting the killer's sorry ass, and you'd be home in bed with Ian."

The words, or maybe the mental image they conjured, made her jerk in the chair. "We wouldn't be… I mean, it's not…" Trailing off, she tried to ignore how hotly her cheeks were burning. "Anyway, what's the next step in clearing Ian?"

"Get him a good lawyer."

"I'm working on that. Well, Lou's working on that."

He eyed her thoughtfully. "Speaking of Lou, she's been doing her own informal investigation into Willard Gray's murder. You might want to have a talk with her about what she's discovered. She could have some helpful information."

"I will." She stood, wanting to move, to do *something* to help free Ian. "Thanks."

"And you didn't hear any of this from me, right?"

"Not a word." Extending her hand across the desk, she shook his solemnly. "I can pass this on to his lawyer, though, right? I promise not to mention your name."

"Please do."

Chris escorted her to the main doors, and she headed to her truck after a final thanks. The wind had picked up speed during her time in the sheriff's office, and she hurried across the icy lot, half-jogging and half-skating. Once inside her pickup, she started the engine and cranked the heater fan. As she shivered, waiting for the blowing air to change from freezing to warm, Rory tried to plan her next step.

Lou would've called if she had lawyer news to report. As far as information about Willard Gray's murder went, it didn't seem to be something they could discuss in a crowded coffee shop—but there was one person who might be able to refute Billy's story. She eased out of the lot and turned onto the street. Before she'd even realized she'd made a decision, she was on the highway headed toward Liverton.

Chapter 15

She questioned her sanity several times during the half-hour drive. Why was she walking right into the lion's den, especially without any backup? Despite her rational side's objections, she kept her foot pressed firmly on the accelerator.

The wind blew a fine layer of snow across the road, like a silky white flow of water. She slowed a little, knowing that the pavement would often glaze with ice beneath the cloaking snow. Traffic was light, as was normal on this stretch of road. There weren't many people who voluntarily chose Liverton as a destination.

She pulled up in front of Julius's place. No other vehicles were sitting close to his house, so she assumed he was alone. After parking in the street, she waded through the drift-covered yard to his front door. Their tracks from the day before were already filled by the wind-blown snow.

No one answered her knock. Turning the knob, she found that the door was unlocked.

"Julius?" she called as she stepped inside. When there wasn't any response, she kicked off her boots but kept on her coat. Rory had a feeling she wouldn't be there long.

She headed for the living room, not at all surprised to see Julius in the same recliner where he'd been sitting the day before. She thought he probably spent his days there, and possibly the nights, too. "Julius? It's Rory."

"The boy with you?" His voice was rough, from disuse or emotion, Rory wasn't sure. "Thought he'd washed his hands of me."

"I think he just needed a short break," she said, hoping that was tactful enough. "He couldn't come today. He's in jail."

She'd been expecting some surprise, but Julius didn't show any. "Acted like he was better than the rest of us, ever since he got that fireman job. Now he's locked up. Guess he wasn't as perfect as he thought he was."

Forget tact. "Don't be an idiot! Ian's not there because he did anything wrong. Billy was having a tantrum and framed him."

"He killed Rave, his own brother! He deserves to rot in there." Pulling a bottle of Jim Beam from between the arm and the cushion, he unscrewed the top and took a swig. Obviously, he'd decided not to bother hiding it from her.

"I killed Rave." She waited for that to soak into his alcohol-slowed brain before continuing. "I shot him because he was about to kill me. Plus, he'd broken into my shop—my *home*—and was stealing from me. I'm not happy he's dead, but I'm not sorry I shot him."

Now there was surprise in his expression for a moment before his scowl returned. "Ian left Zup to the cops, though."

"So Billy did the same to him?" Rory demanded. "Kind of a bitch move, don't you think?"

His grunt could've been interpreted either way.

"Besides, he's your kid. That should trump any of Billy's petty grudges."

There wasn't even a grunt in response to that. He stared at the bottle, as if he couldn't meet her eyes. Although she took it as a good sign that remorse was starting to creep in, Rory got to the point of her visit, not wanting to spend precious time bickering with a drunk Julius.

"When was the last time you noticed Ian wearing his necklace? The one with the Riders' mark on it."

He shrugged, actively avoiding her eyes. "Don't remember."

"Think." Taking a deep breath, she tried to soften her tone, at least a little. "He's been here almost every day for close to two months. Have you noticed the chain around his neck?"

"I haven't seen him wear it since last fall." A robot could've delivered the words less stiffly.

"You're lying." When he didn't deny it but just ducked his head again, she eyed him thoughtfully. "Who told you what to say if anyone asked that question? Was it Billy?"

"No." The answer came too fast to be believable.

"Why are you helping Billy frame your own son?"

His eyes darted to the bottle before he met her gaze defiantly. "Stepson."

She ignored the qualifier, focusing on his initial reaction. "Billy's the one bringing you booze."

"So?" he demanded belligerently. "He understands how much I hurt, now that the love of my life is gone."

"Your son lost his mom," she countered, any sympathy she might have felt for Julius buried under her overwhelming concern for Ian. "He didn't give up and drown his grief. Instead, he's trying to take care of you." She turned to leave. "It's sad."

Rory managed to take only one step before she jerked to a halt. Billy filled the doorway, his smile so menacing that she had to force herself not to flinch. Instead, she plastered on her best impassive expression, reminding herself over and over not to show fear. After selling guns to him for three years, she knew Billy would pounce on any sign of weakness.

"Rory," he greeted, his tone as chilling as his smile. "You're being pretty rough on Julius. I know you pride yourself on being a stone-cold bitch, but the man just lost his wife. Even you could show a little sympathy."

"Billy." She was surprised at the evenness of her tone. The way her heart was hammering, she'd been afraid her voice would shake and give her away. "I'm only asking him to stand up for his son."

He took a step closer. Although he wasn't a huge man, he had presence. Rory had to bite the inside of her cheek to keep herself from stepping back. "Maybe his son isn't worth standing up for."

"That's bullshit." The words came flying from her mouth before she considered the wisdom of antagonizing a scary MC president who already had a grudge against her. "Ian's worth it."

Billy's face went grim, an expression just as menacing as his icy smile. "Ian's a killer."

"So are you." *So am I.*

He didn't flinch. Instead, he took another step closer, looming over her. Rory held his gaze. "Worse, he's a fucking traitor. For years, he's been turning his back on the Riders, and now he killed his brother, tied up another, and left him for the cops."

Making a scoffing sound, even as a large part of her screamed at herself to shut up, she retorted, "No, he's not. You're more of a traitor than he is. You lied so he'd be arrested, and then sent the club lawyer out of the country so he wouldn't even have a chance at beating the charges. He's always been loyal to you and the Riders, and you turned on him—why? Because he killed someone in self-defense? Or because he stood up for me after *I* killed Rave?"

His face over his white beard had turned a dark red. She'd thought he'd looked scary before, but now, in a flat-out rage, he was terrifying. Her legs threatened to buckle, so she automatically locked her knees. He charged forward, his balled-up hand headed toward her face, but she couldn't move. It was as if her body was frozen in place, and all she could do was watch as his fist got larger and larger the closer it got to her eyes.

"Stop!"

Julius's shout broke her paralysis, and Rory stumbled back, leaning away from the blow. Billy's knuckles glanced off her jaw instead of connecting solidly with her cheekbone. His teeth bared, Billy lurched toward her as she shook off the throb the glancing contact had caused. His fist raised again but, before he could strike, she heard the familiar sound of a chambering bullet.

"Billy. Stop."

When Billy went still, his hands falling to his sides, Rory chanced a quick glance over her shoulder to see Julius on his feet. The semiautomatic he was gripping in both shaking hands was a cheap piece of garbage he'd definitely not bought from her shop, and she frowned even as gratitude filled her.

Taking advantage of Billy's immobility, she took several steps away from him, circling Julius until he—and his POS gun—separated her from Billy's fists.

"Get out of my house, Billy," Julius said.

"Ju—" Billy started to speak, his hands reaching toward the gun.

The sharp *crack* made Rory flinch and Billy yelp.

"I said," Julius said surprisingly calmly as Billy examined the new tear in the sleeve of his coat, "get out."

Billy's expression went from placating to furious. "You're done. You throw in with this bitch and your traitor kid, and you're not one of us anymore."

"Fine." There was a slight tremor that belied the word. "Now get out."

Billy's glare moved from Julius to Rory and back again, and she had to dig deep to find her calm expression. Tension-filled seconds ticked past, drawing Rory's muscles tighter and tighter as she watched the stare down between the two men. Finally, Billy pivoted around and stormed out of the house. The front door slammed hard enough to make her jump.

It was several minutes before Julius lowered his gun to his lap. He and Rory stared at each other until she had to break the silence.

"Julius. Where'd you find that piece of crap gun?"

She didn't start really shaking until she was ten minutes out of town. Her trip to Liverton had not done anything useful, except perhaps make an existing enemy even more vengeful.

When she returned to Simpson, she turned her pickup

toward the coffee shop. She wasn't quite sure she was ready to be alone yet. Not after the day she'd had.

The sun was touching the top peak of the mountains to the west, changing the light to a deep orange. Rory pulled into The Coffee Spot's parking lot, relieved to see that hers was the only vehicle. Since the hordes from earlier had gone on their way, she hoped she'd have a chance to talk to Lou without interruptions or curious bystanders.

When she walked into the shop to see someone sitting on one of the stools next to the counter, disappointment flared until she realized it was Callum. Whatever she told Lou would be passed on to him anyway, so Rory didn't mind his presence. She gave them both a nod of greeting before taking a stool a couple down from Callum's.

"Rory!" Lou was positively bouncing in place. "I was just about to call you. North got back to me, and he's flying back to Denver tonight! He'll drive to Simpson really early tomorrow morning."

"That's great." The hard lump that had sat in her belly since Ian had called her that morning dissolved a little. "Thanks, Lou."

"No problem." She started wiping down the outside of the pastry display. Apparently, Lou was physically incapable of standing still. "I'm happy to help Ian, plus I'm glad that all those years I suffered through law classes were worth something after all. I might not have a fancy office or lots of money, but I do have amazing contacts."

"Why'd you get that degree if you hated it so much?"

"Because I was a huge wimp." Lou made a face. "I'll tell you the whole ugly story over a beer sometime. Or not a beer, since neither of us drinks. A nonalcoholic beer? Ugh, that's just disgusting. I'd say coffee, but I get enough of that working here."

"I found out some things," Rory blurted when the other woman stopped for a second to take a breath.

Lou's eyes rounded, and the hand holding the cloth stilled midwipe. "What?"

Although Callum didn't say anything, he straightened on his stool, his expression alert.

"Billy's the one who told the sheriff that the necklace belonged to Ian."

"Pendant," Lou corrected.

"What?"

"Never mind. Billy? MC President Billy?" At Rory's nod, she frowned. "Why would he try to frame Ian? Wouldn't that throw suspicion on the whole club?"

With a grimace, Rory admitted, "It's probably my fault."

"Because of what happened at your shop?"

"Yeah. Billy thought Ian was the one who shot Rave."

"That was you?" Callum asked.

She tried to push the full-color, slow-motion replay from her mind. "Yes."

"Good job."

That wasn't what she'd expected him to say. "Thank you?"

He gave her a one-sided smile, and she had an inkling of what Lou found so irresistible in him. "You did what needed to be done to survive. Besides, from what I've heard, Rave's death was no great loss."

Unsure how to respond, she settled on an uncertain nod. It didn't feel right to dismiss Rave like that, as if his life was worth nothing, but she appreciated why Callum had said it.

"Hang on." When Lou interrupted her unpleasant musings, Rory turned to her in relief. "'Billy thought'? Did you talk to him?"

Rory couldn't hold back her expression of distaste. "Unfortunately."

"When? Where?"

"I just got back from Liverton," she explained. "I was feeling masochistic, so I went to see Julius, and then Billy showed up ranting about how Ian's a traitor for killing Rave. I told Billy that *I* killed Rave, and then Julius kicked him out."

"Whoa." Lou blinked wide eyes at her. "You have some brass balls."

As Callum made a choking sound, Rory said again, "Thank you?"

"What else did Billy say?" Callum asked once he'd recovered from his coughing fit.

"Nothing I hadn't guessed. How Ian deserved it because he killed Rave and left Zup to the mercy of law enforcement. He said that Ian's loyalty to the club had been in question even before now—I'm guessing because of his job with the fire department."

Lou snorted. "Because wanting to help people is such a character flaw. Please. Billy's the traitor here, not Ian."

"That's pretty much what I said." She winced. "Actually, I kind of told him off."

"What'd he say to that?" Callum asked. Although he appeared calm, Rory caught some tension in the way he held himself. She wondered if he was questioning whether he should be around her, in case Billy decided to take her out in a drive-by.

She shrugged, although her stomach twisted with remembered fear. "Not much. He tried to punch me, and Julius pulled a gun on him."

Lou sucked in an audible breath as Callum's expression went dangerously hard.

"It was a complete piece of junk—the gun, I mean—"

"Where are you staying tonight?" Callum interrupted.

At the apparent non sequitur, she paused before answering, "Home."

"Alone?"

Now she could follow his thoughts, because she'd just had a similar discussion with Ian not even twelve hours earlier. "It's the safest place I could be, believe me."

His concerned frown didn't lighten. "I'd be more inclined to believe that if you hadn't had four Riders break in just a few days ago."

The reminder of her failed security made her scowl to hide the anxiety that burned through her. "They broke into the shop. Not my home."

"I thought your shop was connected to your home," Lou said, jumping into the conversation. "Where's your house, then?"

"That's one reason why it's safe," Rory nonanswered. Although Lou grinned at that, Callum still looked unhappy.

"Fudge!" Lou glanced at the clock and hurried toward the door to the back room. "I need to start closing. Keep talking, though, just make it loud so I can hear."

Quiet settled over the shop. Without Lou as a buffer, Rory felt a little awkward, sitting with the watchful, quiet Callum.

"Why did you visit Julius?" he asked, which made

her jump and then breathe a silent sigh of relief that he'd broken the silence.

"I thought he might act like a decent human being." When Callum just waited with a lifted brow, she explained, "I was hoping he remembered seeing Ian wearing his necklace—"

"Pendant!" Lou yelled from the back room.

"Pendant," she corrected, rolling her eyes, "recently. Billy had already coached him, though, so Julius gave me some line about not seeing the neck—I mean, *pendant*—since last fall."

"That is such a lie!" Lou barreled back behind the counter, her eyes lit with such fury that Rory was surprised flames didn't shoot from her ears. "Someone took that pendant just a few weeks ago while he was in the shower at the clubhouse."

"Julius stood up to Billy at the end, though. Maybe he'll reconsider." Rory wasn't too optimistic that Julius's liquor-soaked testimony would hold up in court, though. "Who took it?"

"Good question," Lou said. "The reservoir was frozen until the training exercise, so whoever snagged it must've planted the pendant sometime between when I kicked poor Willard and when it was entered into evidence."

Rory tried to process what the information meant. "How could he—or she—have attached it to the weight?"

Callum shook his head. "Wilt pulled that weight out of the water, and he didn't see anything on it, although it was covered in plants and algae. It's possible he missed it."

"Maybe." Lou frowned. "So someone most likely planted the pendent on dead-guy-discovery day. The scene was so chaotic, though, that anyone could've done it."

"Oh!" Rory sat up straight as she remembered something. "Dep—I mean, *someone* with the sheriff's department told me that there was an issue with the weight's chain of custody. It was supposed to be checked into evidence at the scene, but somehow it got overlooked. It wasn't actually entered into evidence until the next day."

"Whoa," Lou breathed. "That'd make tampering with the weight a lot easier."

"And it had to be someone who was at the clubhouse when Ian was showering," Rory added, watching as the other woman's face brightened.

"You're right! This does narrow it down." Turning toward Callum, who was shaking his head, Lou scowled. "Great. You're about to smash my hopes with some of your obnoxious logic, aren't you?"

"Yes." The smile he directed at her was sweet, and Lou dropped her mock-frown and returned it. Uncomfortable, Rory looked away, feeling as if she were watching a moment too intimate to be witnessed by an outsider. "The person who took the pendant didn't have to be the killer, or even the framer. He or she could've been paid by someone else to get it from Ian."

"There it is!" Lou threw up her hands in pretend exasperation, although Rory could see the smile tugging at the other woman's lips. "There you go with your *facts* and *sensible reasoning*." She looked at Rory. "How annoying is that? I can't tell you how many of my wild—yet interesting—theories he's smashed into bits."

"It's what I do," Callum said, straight-faced, making Lou laugh. Even Rory had to smile.

"That's the key, then," Lou said. "We prove that Ian still had the pendant in his possession up until a few weeks ago, and all the so-called evidence against him goes away. Poof!"

"That's why I wanted to talk to Julius." Rory's frown returned. "I just didn't think his loyalties would be so turned around."

Lou's grin didn't dim. "Julius isn't the only one who's seen Ian over the past six months. The whole fire department would testify that he's been wearing the pendant up until a couple of weeks ago."

Chewing on the inside of her lower lip, Rory shook her head. "I don't know how much weight that would carry. I mean, they'd testify that he was bald and green if it helped him."

With an amused snort, Callum said, "You're right. Who else would have noticed the necklace—someone more impartial, I mean?"

"Pretty much everyone in town," Rory said after a pause. "I just doubt that they noticed or that they'll remember whether or not it was around his neck."

With a frustrated growl, Lou nodded in grudging agreement. "You're right. I couldn't even tell you if he was wearing it when I saw him a month ago, and I was ogling him pretty hard."

Callum gave a grunt of protest, and she reached over the counter to pat his arm. "In a purely objective way, of course."

The antsy feeling was returning, and Rory stood. "I'll let you close the shop."

"Are you going to visit Ian?" Lou asked.

Rory grimaced. "Deputy Lawrence took great pleasure in informing me that visiting hours were on Monday nights."

"Deputy Douchebag," Lou muttered, making Rory laugh.

"You headed home, then?" Callum asked, that concerned look returning.

"No." If she did, she'd just pace and fret and jump at every shadow. "Station One. I'm going to see if the guys have any ideas. I've joined Ian on his shift for the past two nights, so I'm feeling wide awake right now."

"Good idea."

"I'll let you know when North arrives tomorrow morning," Lou said.

"Thank you." There was that word, once again. It felt like the hundredth time she'd used it in the past eight hours or so. "I have more information to pass on to North before the arraignment."

"Yeah?" Lou said with interest, leaning forward. She looked ready to leap over the counter and shake the information from Rory.

"Later," Rory said, turning toward the door. "If I don't leave now, we'll be here until midnight, and you still won't have gotten all your closing done. Call me tomorrow morning, and we'll talk. Early is fine—I doubt I'll be sleeping."

"You're going to make me wait all night before telling me what you know?" Lou practically wailed. "That's so cruel!"

"Rory's right," Callum said. "Start closing. You'll survive a night of curiosity."

"Fine. I'll talk to you tomorrow then, and it had better be good!" She softened the threat with a smile.

With a wave, Rory left the shop and headed toward her truck. Outside, it was fully dark, and the warm yellow glow from the coffee shop window made the shadows even more ominous. Something rustled on the far side of the parking lot. Her head whipped around even as Rory told herself to quit being twitchy. Worry about Billy's possible vengeance was making her imagination go into overdrive.

Was there something there, though? She thought she saw a shape that was slightly darker than the surrounding shadows. Walking faster, as quickly as she could manage on the slick surface of the lot, she stared at the form, straining her eyes to distinguish reality from her nervous fears.

The wind picked up, bringing with it the smell of body odor and pot, and her shoulders relaxed slightly.

"Jim?" she called, peering harder into the darkness, trying to pick out Smelly Jim's skinny form. The man had been a common sight around town until a few weeks ago. He'd shared his conspiracy theories with her on numerous occasions. Even though she'd refused to sell him any weapons, on account of his mental instability, he hadn't seemed to take offense. It had been a while since she'd seen him, long enough that she'd been worried something had happened to him. "That you?"

The shape merged into the shadows and disappeared. Rory stood still for another few seconds until she realized how exposed she was, standing alone in the middle of the parking lot, an easy target for someone hiding in the surrounding blackness.

She hurried to unlock the truck and climb inside. As she started the engine, she realized she'd been holding her breath for who knew how long. When she released it, her exhale was shaky.

"Silly," she scolded herself, glad that no one was

around to see her acting like a frightened little kid. Even as she told herself she was overreacting, her hand reached for the glove box, and she pulled out her Smith & Wesson Sigma. Rory wasn't a huge fan of the Sigmas, considering them to be Glock knockoffs. Once she'd switched out the spring to lighten the heavy trigger pull, though, it was a reliable, inexpensive pistol to keep in the truck.

Once she was holding the gun, she felt calmer, the familiar weight and coolness restoring her confidence. After a few more moments, she tucked the gun back into the glove compartment and drove out of the parking lot.

The second she entered the station, everyone descended on her. There were twice as many firefighters there as were on the night shift normally. Rory didn't know if she'd arrived at shift change or if no one wanted to leave without getting an update on Ian's situation.

"What's going on with Ian?" Soup asked.

Before she could answer, Junior jumped in. "Have you seen him? How's he holding up?"

Question after question was thrown at her, until the chief whistled sharply. When everyone quieted and looked at him, Early said, "Give her a chance to speak, guys."

Their eyes turned to Rory.

"I wasn't able to see him," she started with the bad news first. "Deputy Lawrence said that visiting hours were only on Monday nights, and he wasn't in the mood to break the rules."

There was a smattering of grumbles. Judging by the

large number of disgusted looks, pretty much everyone had had the dubious pleasure of dealing with the deputy.

"Asshole," Junior muttered.

Steve was too far away to smack Junior, but he did send a stern glare his way. "Watch your mouth."

"Well, he is."

Although she didn't say it out loud, Rory had to agree with him on that. "Lou lined up a lawyer for him, though, and the evidence is looking pretty shaky. It all centers around the pendant that Ian used to wear."

There were nods from several in the group.

"I remember that thing," Soup said. "I always saw the chain, so I asked to see what was on it one day, and he showed it to me. Said it used to be his dad's."

"Was that sometime this winter by any chance?" Rory asked hopefully, then deflated a little when he shook his head. Of course it couldn't be that easy.

"It was last year sometime—late spring or summer, maybe." He gave her a curious look. "Why's that important?"

"Because it was found with the body in the reservoir," Rory explained. "Billy's trying to say that Ian stopped wearing the pendant last fall, when it actually went missing just a couple of weeks ago."

"*Billy* was saying that?" Steve asked.

"Billy's turned on Ian, thanks to what happened during the break-in at my shop."

"Still, Billy?" Steve frowned. "I thought he was like a father to Ian."

"Yeah," she muttered sarcastically, anger and fear still lingering from her encounter with Billy. "Some father." Rory closed her eyes for a second, refocusing her thoughts on what was important at the moment.

There'd be plenty of time later to stew and be bitter about Billy's betrayal. "What I need from you guys is confirmation that Ian was still wearing that pendant up until recently. Do any of you remember seeing it over the last few months?"

They shifted and glanced at one another.

"Not specifically," Junior admitted, looking pained. "I knew he always had it around his neck, but I couldn't tell you for sure when he stopped wearing it. Sorry."

There was a dismayed chorus of agreement. With each admission, Rory's hope withered a little more.

"Hang on," Soup said as he hurried toward the offices. Everyone, looking baffled, watched him go. Soup returned shortly, grinning and waving a photograph in his hand. "There!"

He thrust the photo toward the group, and they all circled around him, jostling for a better position. When Rory wiggled in next to Soup and managed to catch her first glimpse of the photo, she actually threw her arms around him in relief. As he turned bright red, she released him, surprised by her uncharacteristic show of affection.

"This was taken just last month," Soup said.

"That's great, Soup," Rory said, with another look at the picture. In the photo, Ian was glaring at the camera with an exasperated expression. It looked as if he'd been sitting on one of the locker room benches, leaning forward with his arms propped on his knees. The best part was that he was shirtless. It was great not only because a bare-chested Ian was a sight to behold, but also because the pendant, clear and easily recognizable, dangled from a chain looped around his neck. "How can you prove it was taken in February, though?"

"Look." He pointed at the wall behind Ian. "The locker room was painted just six weeks ago. Now they're blue, but before, they were this nasty yellow."

"Baby-shit yellow," Junior clarified before dodging Steve's slab of a hand.

"Language," Steve growled, although he didn't sound too serious. Everyone was staring at the picture with huge grins on their faces.

"Can I have this picture?" Rory asked. "I'll give it to the lawyer when he arrives tomorrow."

"Sure." Soup handed it to her. "It's on the computer, too. We just printed it off on photo paper to bug Ian. He hates it when we tell him he should be the fire department poster boy."

"The lab geeks can probably get a date stamp off the digital file," Junior said.

Moving toward his office, the chief said over his shoulder, "I have a copy of the dated invoice for the locker room painting. I'll print that for you, too."

"Perfect. Could you send it and the picture to me, as well?" she asked. "I put my email address on one of the volunteer forms."

"Sure," Early called as he disappeared into his office.

"You guys are the best," Rory said, fighting the urge to squeeze the photo to her chest.

"Soup got a hug. Don't I get one too?" Junior asked, stepping forward with his arms outstretched.

Grabbing the back of the smaller man's shirt, Steve yanked him back. "You hug her, and either she'll shoot you, or Ian'll do it when he gets out of jail."

Junior appeared outwardly unconcerned by the threat, but Rory noticed he stayed where Steve had put him.

The door swung open, and she looked over to see Joel Becker enter. The other guys gave him nods in greeting, which he returned.

"What's going on?" Joel asked, eyeing their huddle. The chief returned from his office, the printed invoice in his hand.

"We found evidence that'll get Ian out of jail," Junior said. Rory had to hold back a snort at the way he'd taken partial credit for Soup's discovery.

Joel's expression stiffened, but he just silently headed to the locker room. Rory noticed the chief, his forehead knotted in an uncharacteristic mess of worried wrinkles, watch him go.

"You working tonight, Rory?" Soup's question pulled her attention away from Early's sober regard.

"I was planning on it." She sent a glance toward the chief, whose attention had returned to their group. "If that's okay?"

"Sure you're up to it with everything that's going on?" Early asked.

"I'd rather stay busy. I wouldn't sleep tonight anyway, and I would just stew about everything and drive myself crazy."

"Well, okay then." The chief gave her a stern look that didn't fit on his cheerful face. "But if you find you're too distracted, go home."

"I will, Chief."

His typical jolly grin appeared. "Good job on that." He tilted his head toward the photo she clutched carefully in her fingers. "Ian's lucky to have you."

"He doesn't exactly have…um." She stopped her protest halfway when everyone leaned closer to catch her words, their faces alight with gossip-loving glee. Instead, she finished with a weak, "Thanks, Chief."

To her frustration, the night was agonizingly slow. They had one call, which was for a vehicle off the road. When they arrived on scene, they discovered an orange tag that indicated the car had been abandoned. Although Rory was happy that no one experienced an event that required the assistance of the fire department, she was also wishing for something to take her mind off of the thought of Ian spending the night in jail.

Even though she had the photograph, doubt began to creep into her mind. She wondered if it would be enough, or if Billy had manufactured some other bogus evidence that would point to Ian being the killer. It was upsetting and almost unbelievable that there was at least one person who'd disliked Ian enough to steal and plant the pendant, framing an innocent man for a crime serious enough to send him to prison for the rest of his life. As Rory had said earlier, Ian was a hard man to loathe.

To distract herself, she cleaned. Once she couldn't find anything else to clean, she organized the disaster of a storage room. As she was arranging the coats by size, Soup glanced in and shook his head.

"Callum did this once, and now he's banned from this room," he told her, eyeing the newly ordered shelves.

Without pausing, she said, "It desperately needed organizing. How did anyone find anything in here? It took hours for me to dig out bunker gear that fit. Look, now you can actually see the floor."

"The chief says he knows exactly where everything

is. He's going to be grumpy about this." After another head shake, he retreated from the doorway. He was probably trying to get as far away from the room as possible, so he didn't have to experience the fallout when Early saw its newly organized state.

Rory folded another coat and put it with others of the same size. She wished longingly for a label maker. Glancing around the room, she had a feeling of satisfaction at the difference between the former chaos and the current order. Although the chief might disagree, it was so much better now.

As Rory took a moment to stretch her back, Ian popped back into her head. He never left the forefront of her thoughts for long, but she still attempted to bury her worry in her current cleaning binge. If he didn't get out of jail soon, Station One would never be the same.

And neither would she.

Chapter 16

North Butterfield was nothing like what Rory had expected.

She and Lou waited for him at The Coffee Spot, since there were limited meeting places in Simpson, especially those that were open at seven in the morning. When a tall, thin man in a really nice suit walked into the shop, Lou jumped to her feet.

"Nutter Butters!" she cried, grabbing him in a hug.

He groaned, although he hugged Lou back. "I thought we decided you'd retire that nickname."

"*You* suggested it, but I don't remember agreeing."

As the two exchanged friendly greetings, Rory studied North. He looked so *young*. His floppy, thinning hair was light blond, and his trendy, black-framed glasses just made him look like a kid playing dress-up. Lou thought he was Ian's best chance, though, so Rory decided to withhold judgment and give him the benefit of the doubt.

"Rory Sorenson"—Lou grabbed the lawyer's arm and dragged him the few feet to their table—"meet North Butterfield. Rory knows guns, and North wins cases. There. You've been introduced."

As Rory shook his hand, North smiled. She was struck by how sweet his expression was. From Lou's description, Rory had expected him to be smooth and sharklike.

“Thank you for coming,” Rory said.

“Glad to help.” His gaze flicked toward Lou’s boss, Ivy, who was currently manning the counter and overtly listening to their conversation. “Should we all head over to the sheriff’s office together? That way, we could talk during the drive.”

“Sure,” Lou agreed. “But it’s going to have to be someone else’s vehicle. Callum dropped me off this morning.”

“We could take mine, but it’d be a tight fit in my standard cab.” Rory followed the other two toward the door. “Haven’t you replaced the pickup that burned yet?”

North stared at Lou. “Burned?”

“Long story.” Lou patted his arm. “We’ll catch up after you take care of Ian.” She looked over her shoulder at Rory. “Callum and I are having a little disagreement about that. I have my eye on the cutest 1952 International pickup, but Cal is whining about safety and the lack of air bags, and claiming that I gave him veto rights. I don’t remember saying that, but, then again, a lot of words leave my mouth. It’s hard to keep track of them all.”

“Who’s Callum?” North asked as they made their way to a smaller, new-looking SUV. Apparently, there had been an unspoken agreement that they were taking his car rather than all squeezing into the front seat of Rory’s truck.

“That question falls under the tell-you-later umbrella,” Lou said. “Want me to drive so you can take notes?”

“Please.” North climbed into the back seat. Once the doors were closed, he pulled a notepad from his briefcase and said, “Now tell me what I need to know.”

Eyeing the pad of paper, Lou said, “You’re rocking it old school.”

"Paper can be burned," he said, uncapping his pen. "Electronic files, on the other hand, can always be recovered."

Rory could relate to that—her life had been full of those types of rules. The fact that he was thinking along those lines made her trust him a little more. "Okay. Where do you want me to start?"

"How about with Lou's murder victim?"

"Hey!" She shot him an irritated glance before returning her gaze to the road. "Just because I kicked him doesn't make him mine!"

"You kicked a dead guy?" There was no horror in his tone, only mild interest.

"Not important. Rory, you start, and I'll interrupt if I think you've missed anything."

Taking a deep breath, Rory began.

It took a long time. North filled page after page on his legal pad as Rory talked, with Lou interjecting something every so often.

"Who would've thought a sleepy little mountain town could be such a hotbed of murder and intrigue?" North asked after Rory finally fell silent. Since Lou didn't add anything else, Rory assumed that they'd covered everything North needed to know. They'd been sitting in the SUV in the sheriff's department parking lot for the past twenty minutes. For a while, the only sounds were North's pen scratching against the paper, the rustle of turning pages, and his mutterings.

"Okay," he finally said, making Rory jump. North opened the door and unfolded his lanky frame as he exited the SUV. "Showtime."

Watching as he slipped and slid across the snow-packed surface of the parking lot toward the main entrance, Rory bit the inside of her lower lip. "He didn't say anything about whether he thinks Ian has a strong defense or not. Do you suppose that's a good sign or a bad sign?"

"It's a sign that North is in the zone," Lou said, turning to face Rory so she could give her a level look. "When North is in the zone, he's pretty much unstoppable, so Ian's as good as free."

Despite Lou's confidence, Rory still had a niggling feeling of doubt trying to choke her. "He looks so young."

"Ror." Lou put both hands on Rory's cheeks, turning her head so their eyes met, and, in the process, squishing her cheeks together. "Stop fussing. Ian shouldn't have even been arrested with such flimsy evidence. He'll be fine."

"I'm not..." Her voice was muffled from Lou's hold on her face, so Rory shook off the other woman's hands before continuing. "I'm not fussing. Oh, I forgot to tell North that Chief Early emailed me the picture and the invoice, so we have electronic copies as well as the printed ones I gave him. Do you think I should run in and tell him?"

"No." Lou reached for Rory's face again, but Rory leaned back out of reach. "I think you need to settle down and let North do his job."

"Okay." Rory had to agree that she was acting more like one of her chickens than her usual calm self. It was just that it was *Ian*. "Okay. Can you stay here and wait with me?"

"That's the plan." After a few moments of silence, Lou asked, "Want to play I-spy or something?"

Rory gave her a confused look. "I spy on what?"

"No." Lou laughed. "It's a kids' travel game. You know, I spy with my little eye…something green."

"What?"

"Never mind. It's not that much fun anyway."

Rory felt like she'd just failed some sort of social-interaction test. "We never traveled much when I was little." *Or, you know, ever.*

"Really?" Lou leaned forward, and Rory watched the other woman's hands carefully, wondering if Lou was going to grab her again. "What was it like for you growing up? You never say much about your family, so all I have to go on are crazy stories from The Coffee Spot customers, and I never trust the accuracy of those. In fact, I usually believe the opposite of the rumors floating around Simpson. The local gossip mill is not known for its accuracy."

"By the local gossip mill," Rory said, "do you mean the fire department?"

With a laugh, Lou agreed, "Pretty much, yeah. And I include the dive team in that."

"That's how you met Callum, right?" Although Rory really was curious about the odd pairing, her main motivation was deflecting the topic of conversation away from her.

"Yeah." Her eyes went soft. "I figured he couldn't stand me at first. For whatever reason, he was always there to witness my most embarrassing moments, and he had this *look* he would give me."

Rory knew that look. It was one of the most intimidating things about Callum.

"But then he volunteered to help me with the HDG—I

mean, the Willard Gray case. When everything started happening—my stalker and the fire and my stepfather and everything—he was always there. It kind of freaked me out."

Rory hadn't been expecting that. "Freaked you out? Why?"

"I grew up pretty sheltered and spoiled," Lou explained with a grimace. "I had to learn how to take care of myself once I moved into that little cabin up here. And Callum, he'd wrap me in blankets and pull me around on a little sled if I let him."

Blinking, Rory said slowly, "O-kay."

"That sounded crazy. Sorry." Lou laughed again. "I guess I was just afraid of slipping back to being that soft, dependent person."

It was Rory's turn to laugh—just a dry bark of a sound, but a laugh nonetheless. She was glad Lou was waiting with her. If she'd been alone, Rory wouldn't have lasted two minutes before storming the jail. "I don't think there's any danger of that."

"No?" Lou's usually confident expression was unsure. "It's just so easy to let him take care of the unpleasant stuff."

"No. You're definitely not helpless in any way. I've heard you stand up to Callum several times, and he kind of intimidates me," Rory admitted.

Lou looked shocked. "Seriously? I didn't think anyone intimidated you. You run a business by yourself, hold your own with macho mountain men who think you have to have a penis to know anything about guns, *and* you even went Dirty Harry on armed bikers breaking into your shop. You kind of kick ass and take names, you know."

Flushing, Rory looked out the windshield at the building in front of them. "That's the simple stuff. I wish I could talk to people as easily as you do."

"Please," Lou snorted. "Most of what comes out of my mouth is just straight-up embarrassing. I just keep talking, hoping that whoever's listening will forget the stupid thing I just said."

Rory wondered with amazement if, at the ripe age of twenty-five, she was having her first girl talk. "Well, I don't think you have to worry about being soft or useless, that's for sure."

"Thanks." After a moment of quiet while they both stared at the entrance to the sheriff's department, Lou said, "I wonder what's going on in there."

"I can't think about it." The possibilities were making Rory sick to her stomach. "Can we talk about something else?"

"Of course." A slow grin lit Lou's face. "We talked about my relationship status—how about yours?"

"My what?" She turned a blank face to Lou, who rolled her eyes.

"Your relationship," Lou repeated slowly. "The one with the currently imprisoned bundle of hotness, with the tattoos and bunker gear? Oh, and those *eyes*. How do you even get within ten feet of him without forgetting your own name?"

Her cheeks warmed to an inferno level of heat. "I don't…um, what?"

"Fine. I'll put it bluntly. What's the deal with you and Ian?"

It appeared that girl talk was a lot more uncomfortable than it had seemed in the books she'd read. "No deal, really. He just feels…protective, I guess? Because of what happened in the shop."

"Uh-huh." Skepticism bled from Lou's tone. "I don't think so. I think he's had a thing for you for years, and you're the reason he stays away from the club women."

Rory felt like she'd been pistol-whipped. He turned down other women…for her? They hadn't even kissed yet. They'd been on one non-date date! "Why would you think that?"

"He told us. Well, he implied it."

Her mouth was open, but she was having trouble speaking. In fact, she was having trouble breathing. "He actually said he had a thing for me?" she asked when she finally managed to force out some words.

"Not exactly, but he pretty much admitted he avoids the women at the club because he has feelings for someone, and you're the only woman he voluntarily spends time with. I'm no math genius, but even I can add one and one and make two."

Rory blinked. "It's just so…implausible. I mean, someone like me with someone like *Ian*? He could have anyone he wanted."

"Well, you're the only woman I've ever seen him take on a date."

Although Rory considered denying knowing what Lou was talking about, she'd run their dinner at Levi's over and over in her head enough times that she was pretty sure she couldn't lie about it convincingly. "That was a non-date date. Ian and I agreed."

After staring at her for a long, open-mouthed moment, Lou burst out laughing. "Sorry!" she gasped once she could speak again. "I'm not laughing at you.

I'm just laughing because I had a 'non-date date' at Levi's, too! Maybe they should market their restaurant as the place to go when you're uncertain about the status of your relationship."

Something about the confines of the SUV, coupled with the stress of the past twenty-one hours, made Rory want to confide in Lou. "I've never had a boyfriend," she blurted before she could reconsider.

Lou shrugged. "So? A lot of people just date casually until the right person comes along."

"No." Shaking her head, Rory felt her stomach clench as she clarified. "I've never even gone on a date—except for the non-date date with Ian."

"Never?"

"No." She couldn't look at Lou, afraid the other woman would be staring at her as if Rory was a freak—which she kind of was.

"Wow. How'd that happen?" The casual friendliness had returned to Lou's voice, so Rory dared a glance toward the driver's seat. She was relieved to see that Lou's expression matched her tone. "I mean, you're really nice, and you like guns, which I imagine is a turn-on for a lot of guys. Plus, it's not like you never meet anyone, since people—mostly male people—are in and out of your shop all day. It's like a dating buffet line for you."

That startled a choked laugh from Rory. "I was homeschooled."

"So? I've known a lot of homeschooled kids, and they managed to meet people. School isn't the only place to mingle."

With a frown, Rory realized the conversation had circled back around to her upbringing, despite her attempts at redirection. How had Lou managed that? But this time she felt comfortable enough to admit, "My parents didn't trust many people—or any, actually, so I wasn't allowed to have friends come over to our house. As I grew older, Mom and Dad got more and more paranoid, so eventually they stopped going to anyone else's homes, too. Or anywhere, really."

"Whoa, and I thought my parents were crazy, with my homicidal stepfather and all." Lou winced. "Sorry for calling your parents extra-crazy. Didn't I warn you about my whole 'talking' thing?"

"It's fine." Although she wanted to reassure Lou, Rory couldn't manage a smile. "I know they were nuts. It was pretty obvious when they—" She bit down hard on the next words, not letting them escape. As friendly and easy to talk to as Lou was, there were things too private, too painful, to share.

"Well," Lou said when it became clear that Rory was not going to finish her sentence, "if it's any consolation, my mom encouraged a creepy family friend to stalk me."

"Really?" Although she'd known about Lou's stalker burning down her house, and her stepdad trying to kill her and Callum, Rory hadn't known about Lou's mom's involvement. "That's...not right."

Lou laughed, although it had a hard edge of recent hurt. "Definitely not right. Okay, enough serious talk. Tell me more about guns. I want to bring Callum to your shop and blow him away with my extensive knowledge."

"I can do that." Rory felt her shoulders lower as she relaxed. She'd hadn't even noticed how tensely she'd been holding herself during the conversation. "What do you want to know?"

~

Although their gazes often strayed to the building in front of them, the time passed fairly quickly, considering. Lou was a quick study, as Rory had noticed during the other woman's visit to the shop, and she picked things up easily. The sun was out, warming the inside of the SUV, and talking about guns soothed Rory almost as much as handling them.

"Shoot," Lou muttered, glancing at her watch. "I'm going to have to leave soon, or I'll be late for work. Ivy's not a pleasant person to deal with on the best of days, so she's a real b—uh, bear when I'm not on time."

Rory cocked her head curiously. "Why doesn't anyone want to swear in front of me? Ian corrects himself, too, and Steve hits the guys—Junior, mostly—when they curse while I'm in hearing range."

"I'm not sure." After regarding her closely, Lou said, "I think it's because you have this young, sweet, and innocent look going. You know, since your eyes are so big and the rest of you is so small. It makes me feel like I'm swearing in front of a kid."

"Thanks?"

"I can swear if it makes you feel better—darn, crap, suck."

Shaking her head, Rory felt a smile tug at the corners of her mouth. "Those don't count."

"I know. I just couldn't do it. See if Ian'll talk dirty to you."

That brought the flaming blush back with a vengeance. "He doesn't…we wouldn't…I mean…argh!"

"Sorry!" Lou laughed. "You're just really fun to tease."

"Did you want me to take you back to the coffee shop?" Rory asked, desperate to change the subject. She didn't want to leave their vigil, but Lou had been kind enough to stay with her in the SUV all morning. The least she could do was make sure she got to work on time.

Glancing at her watch again, Lou bit her lip and looked at the sheriff's office. "Let's give it a couple more minutes, and then I'll really need—hang on!"

One of the main doors was opening, but the sun reflected off the glass, making it impossible to see who was emerging. The tall, skinny form of North came out first, his head turned so he could talk to the person behind him over his shoulder. Rory held her breath as she watched the second man step outside—it was Ian!

She was out of the SUV and half running, half sliding across the parking lot toward the men before she even realized what she was doing. Self-consciousness set in when she was five feet in front of them, and she tried to stop, but her boots couldn't find traction on the ice. She tipped forward, the ground rushing toward her face, and she braced for the impact. Instead, a hard hand latched around her upper arm and hauled her back to her feet.

"Thanks," she said breathlessly, staring at Ian. He still held her arm, although his grip had softened.

"No big hug and kiss for your favorite man fresh out of the slammer?" he teased, grinning.

The ever ready blush reemerged. "Not now that you made it all weird," she muttered, making him laugh. "Are you out for good?"

"All charges dismissed," North said cheerfully. "The evidence against him was pretty tenuous, and the picture helped immensely, Rory. Nice work. I got the impression that the sheriff wouldn't have even made the arrest if he hadn't been getting so much pressure to make headway in the case."

"I don't want to break up this get-out-of-jail-free party," Lou called from where she was hanging out of the SUV window, "but if I don't get to work right now, Ivy is going to carve designs in my skin with a razor blade and then shove me into a vat of salt water." When the other three just stared at her in horror, she made a move-along gesture with her hand. "Let's go. Nutter Butters, you're staying at the coffee shop with me. Between attacks of caffeine-deprived hordes, we'll catch up. Do you have a vehicle here, Ian?" When he shook his head, she waved him forward. "Rory's truck is at The Coffee Spot. We'll take you there, and you can ride off into the sunset or find a place to celebrate your newly regained freedom or whatever. Right now, though, I need you all to *move*!"

They hurried to the SUV as fast as the slick parking lot surface would allow. When Ian slid into the back seat with Rory, she glanced away from him, feeling suddenly and inexplicably shy. Apparently, he didn't suffer from the same reservations, since he immediately reached over and took her hand.

"Thank you," he said quietly, and she bobbed her head in acknowledgment, still not making eye contact. "I mean it. North told me how hard you worked to get me out of there."

With an awkward shrug, she said, "Lou got North here. That was the biggest thing. The guys at the station really came through, too—Soup was the one who remembered the photo." She risked a glance at his face, and was even more flustered by his serious expression, so she babbled onward. "Next time the guys want to take a half-naked picture of you and hang it up at Station One, don't give them a hard time about it. It might come in useful."

His laugh was more of a snort. "Apparently." He squeezed her hand, pulling it into his lap. "And you were the one who brought it all together. Did you have a chance to call Carrie?"

"Yes." At the mention, she dug her cell phone out of her coat pocket with her free hand. "I should call her. She'll want to know that you're out." Finding Carrie's number in her recent-call list, she tapped the screen and held the phone to her ear.

"You have Carrie's number on your cell?" he asked.

"Yeah," she answered distractedly as she waited for Carrie to pick up on her end. "She's nice. We bonded." Carrie's voice mail kicked in, and Rory left a brief message, letting her know that Ian had been released and the charges against him dropped.

"We bonded too!" Lou called from the driver's seat. "Rory and me, I mean, not Carrie. I don't think I know Carrie."

"You've been busy in the past twenty-four hours," Ian teased. "Proving my innocence, finding me a lawyer, female bonding..."

"Plus, I cleaned the storage room at Station One." Rory dropped her phone back in her coat pocket.

His eyes widened. "*The* storage room? The one that looks like a tornado blew through it?"

"Not anymore." She gave a satisfied smile. "It

would've been better if I'd had a label maker, but it's still much improved. You can actually see the floor now."

"What'd the chief say?" he asked, scratching his jaw with the hand that wasn't holding hers. His two-day stubble highlighted the hard angles of his jaw and cheekbones. Just when she thought he couldn't be any more handsome, Ian managed to surprise her.

She moved her gaze away from his face. Looking at him was too distracting.

"Um…I left this morning before he arrived, so he hadn't seen it yet."

Ian groaned, but it sounded amused. "That'll be interesting."

Pulling into the coffee shop parking lot, Lou glanced in the rearview mirror at Rory. "Callum will kiss you on the mouth when he sees that storage room. The mess was making his soul itch."

"He will not," Ian said, his words clipped, his grip tightening.

"Ow," Rory said mildly.

He looked at their joined hands and instantly lessened the pressure. "Sorry." Lifting her hand to his lips, he brushed a kiss on the back of it. As he opened the door, Rory stared at him, her mouth slightly open. She stayed frozen until he gave her hand a tug, pulling her out of the SUV after him.

As she straightened, she saw Lou was grinning at her. "Yeah. You're totally the reason." After that cryptic statement, she hurried toward the front door of the shop, towing North behind her.

"What does that mean?" Ian asked, still keeping hold of Rory's hand as they headed for her pickup.

"No clue." That might have been a lie. Rory had a *slight* clue what Lou meant, but there was no way she'd manage to explain without completely dissolving into a stammering, bright-red mess. Changing the subject seemed like the best tactical decision at that point. "Did you want to stop by Station One to let the guys know you're out?"

"No." He finally released her so he could circle to the passenger side of the truck. "You drive, and I'll call."

"Where are we going?" Rory dug her keys out of her coat pocket.

"Your house or mine, I don't care."

After a moment of consideration, she left the lot and headed toward her house. She needed to spend more time there, to reclaim it as hers. Plus, if she didn't open the shop soon, her customers would think she was closed for good. Who knows what rumors were currently being ground by the Simpson rumor mill?

Since Ian was busy calling people and spreading the good news, Rory was able to stay quiet. She appreciated not having to make conversation, since that slight edge of tension had returned now that they were alone. Instead, she concentrated on driving, letting the familiar route home soothe her nerves. When she stopped at the locked gate, Ian extended his hand for the keys. Once she pulled them out of her pocket and handed them to him, he hopped out of the truck.

Jack was waiting for them, quivering with excitement as Ian unlocked and opened the gates. As soon as there was an opening big enough for him to squeeze through, Jack hurled himself at Ian, twisting and wriggling as he tried to get as close to the man as possible. Laughing,

Ian paused with only one side of the gate open so he could affectionately ruffle the dog's coat.

Stacking her hands on top of the steering wheel, Rory rested her chin on her hands and watched the two, smiling a little. For some reason, Jack was positively in love with Ian. Her smile slipped away as she studied the object of her dog's affection. She couldn't blame Jack, really. Somewhere along the way, her childish crush had morphed into something else, something so big it scared her when she thought about it.

With a start, she realized that Ian had opened the other side of the gate and was watching her with an amused expression, waiting for her to drive through. She checked for Jack's location and spotted him curled around Ian's legs, so she eased the truck through the opening. Instead of waiting for him to climb back into his seat, she continued to the pole barn. The time it took to store the pickup and secure the building allowed her a moment to collect her unbalanced and frayed thoughts.

Ian and Jack both waited for her on the back porch. The upward curl of Ian's mouth made her wonder for a panicked moment if he could read her mind. She gave herself a sharp, mental reprimand and regained some of her composure.

He didn't say anything as she unlocked the door and deactivated the alarm. The silence continued as they shed their outerwear and left it next to the back door. His coat hanging next to hers, and his boots lined up by her much-smaller pair made a homey, comfortable picture, a startling contrast to her normal, lonely life. Once again, she was forced to talk firmly to her brain, reminding herself that she liked her life as it was—no Ian required.

When Ian remained quiet while she moved the bookshelves and opened the steel door, she felt tension creeping in ropes up the back of her neck. Her fingers fumbled as she relocked the door. He was standing much too close to her, and she didn't know if she could actually feel the heat from his body warming hers, or if that was her imagination. No matter how many stern talks she was giving her brain, her thoughts flew out of control.

At the base of the stairs, she couldn't take another second. After flicking on the lights for the living area, she turned to glare at him. "What?"

He just raised an eyebrow in question.

"You haven't said anything to me since we started driving here. What's the deal?"

"I knew if I opened my mouth," he said, "I was going to say things I don't think you're ready to hear."

She blinked, started to speak, and then closed her mouth again. After a long pause as they stared at each other, she asked, "Are you hungry?"

His laugh filled the space. "Yes. Starved."

"Sit." She jerked her chin at the kitchen table. "I'll cook."

Ian did not sit. "I can help. I'm not much use in the kitchen, but I could, I don't know, chop stuff or something."

With a huff, she rested her fists on her hips. "You are hopeless at following orders. I'm not picking you for my partner for the next zombie-invasion drill."

Although he laughed, he did pull out a kitchen chair and lower himself into it. "Happy?"

"Yes." She wasn't thrilled with how he was smirking at her, but at least now she had the run of the kitchen without worrying about bumping into whatever rock-hard part of his body was blocking her way. Rory was wound up enough without adding unintentional contact to the mix. Digging in the freezer, she pulled out some beef stew and a loaf of bread. "Stew and bread sound good?"

"Is that your version of a frozen dinner?" he asked, nodding toward the container.

"Yeah. Since it's just me, I make big batches of everything—stew, bread, soups, casseroles, whatever—and then I freeze them in smaller portions. That way, I don't have to eat goulash for two weeks straight."

"That's homemade bread?" Ian eyed the loaf covetously.

"Yep." She put the stew in the oven. "Neither of my parents could bake, so I figured out pretty young that I was the only hope for having anything like that. With the high altitude, it took me forever to figure out how to make good bread, but I was determined. I love fresh bread."

"Me too."

Rory could've guessed that by the way he hadn't taken his eyes off of it. Instead of cutting the loaf in half, as she'd planned, she wrapped the entire thing in foil and put it in the oven next to the stew. Dusting off her hands, she said, "Done cooking."

Grinning, Ian kicked the chair across from his so it slid away from the table. "Take a load off. That was some pretty intense work."

With a shrug, she sat. Now that she didn't have anything else to focus on except Ian, that strange, buzzing tension had returned. "After a busy day in the shop, it's nice not to have to worry about actually making something." Her legs twitched, and she couldn't stop herself from jumping to her feet. "I have some venison sticks from Carson Beatty. Ever since I gave him a good deal on a Beanfield Sniper rifle, he brings me a big bag of it every year. I don't have the heart to tell him I'm not a huge fan of venison. Want some to tide you over?"

"That's okay. I can wait until the stew's ready."

Pausing in the middle of the kitchen, she shifted from foot to foot, unable to bring herself to return to her chair.

"Ror." His voice was gentle, but the way he stood and stalked toward her made alarm rise in her chest. As he approached, she couldn't stop herself from backing away from him. He advanced, his eyes fixed on hers, and she retreated until her lower back bumped against the counter.

Ian closed the last small bit of space between them in two strides. His hands cradled both sides of her face, tilting up her head so she couldn't have looked away even if he hadn't been holding her gaze captive. Leaning down, he rested his forehead against hers.

"You were pretty much all I thought about last night." He huffed out a breath, and he was so close she felt the warm brush of air. "Hell, you're pretty much all I think about even when I'm not in jail. I'm like a nervous kid around you, and you're all composed and remote, so I never figured I'd really get a shot with you. When North told me everything you'd done, how you were fighting for me, even going to see Julius and being threatened by Billy—which made me insane with worry, but we'll discuss that later—I was...floored. Floored and so fu—flipping happy. After more than a decade, that was the first time you didn't seem like some unobtainable dream."

"Oh." As he waited, his forehead on hers, his gaze holding steady, she scrambled for words—any words, although the right words would be preferable. "I… I'm sorry. I don't know how to do this."

"Do what?"

Think, for one, with him that close. "Any of this. I've never dated, never really had close friends. I'm socially backward."

His chuckle brushed her skin, making her close her eyes. In the darkness, she felt him even more, the press of his forehead, his palms and fingers. "No, you're not. You have friends—half of Simpson, in fact. You just don't realize the impression you make."

Her eyes opened again so she could give him a skeptical look.

"It's true. And the whole not-dating-before thing… well, that's a plus for me."

"What do you mean?"

His mouth thinned to a straight line before he admitted, "This way, I don't have to kill all of your exes."

Rory frowned. "I know I'm inexperienced, but that doesn't seem like an emotionally healthy statement."

"Fu—forget that. I never claimed to be emotionally healthy." He leaned in so close that their mouths were just a hair away from touching. "For whatever it's worth, though, I am crazy about you."

Chapter 17

It was surreal. Ian Walsh was almost kissing her in her kitchen, telling her that he was crazy about her. This was not the normal life of Rory Sorenson.

As she stared at him, this beautiful man so close to her, she made a decision. She wanted to keep him. If it could only be for a short time before he realized he was a poster-boy-hot fireman who could have any woman in Field County, and she was just…her…that was okay. She'd enjoy it while it lasted and deal with the fallout when it ended. Rory had been trained her entire childhood to deal with apocalyptic situations. She could survive a breakup. For now, though, she rose on her tiptoes and closed that infinitesimal space between their lips.

For a second, they both froze. It felt incredible, his mouth on hers…but she wasn't sure what to do next. Ian quickly snapped out of his paralysis, and then she didn't have to worry about her next move, since he took over completely.

His lips pressed against hers, pulled away, and then returned, dropping gentle, chaste kisses on her upper lip and then her lower, followed by a touch to each corner of her mouth. They were sweet and innocent…until he started adding a little wickedness, a nip of his teeth or the dart of his tongue. That made it even better, and Rory shivered.

His teeth closed on her lower lip, and a shock of heat

rippled through her. She gasped, her lips parting, and his tongue entered her mouth, playing with hers before retreating. It was incredible, how wonderful this kiss made her feel. With a low sound of longing, she pressed closer, shyly letting her tongue seek out his.

The spark of her touch lit a fuse in him, and the whole tone of the kiss changed. Instead of light and teasing, it turned urgent. One of his hands slid around to the back of her head, pulling her more tightly against him, while his other slid over her shoulder and down her arm before finding its way to her hip.

When he groaned, low and desperate, she shivered with a surge of power. *She*—plain, odd Rory Sorenson—had caused that sound. The thought made her brave, and she let herself explore. Her hands settled tentatively on his biceps, marveling at the size and strength and sheer *aliveness* of the muscles moving under his skin. When she'd thought about kissing Ian, she hadn't expected it to be so intense. Rory felt like she'd been swept up in a tornado, emotions and need swirling around them.

She began to imitate his movements—a kiss or a nip or a touch of the tongue—figuring that whatever felt good to her would feel just as incredible to him. When her teeth scraped lightly over a tendon in his neck, he visibly shivered. Rory realized that turning him on was upping her own excitement, to the point that her knees had turned to jelly, and she had to lean on Ian for support.

He didn't seem to mind. Without pausing in his exploration of the spot just under her right ear, he backed up to a chair and sat, pulling her onto his lap in the same fluid motion. When Rory realized she was straddling him—straddling Ian Walsh in her underground-bunker kitchen—she pulled back, the complete implausibility of the situation shocking her out of her lust-filled daze.

Before she could wrap her mind around the thought that, yes, she was *indeed* straddling Ian Walsh in her underground-bunker kitchen, he'd pulled her back into another hard kiss. Coming to grips with reality quickly lost its importance, and she melted against him once again.

Her hands stroked his sides. She loved the way it made him groan and then go still, as if awaiting the next sweep of her fingers. One pass went lower than before, and her hands slipped under the bottom hem of his shirt on their next upward stroke. When her fingers came into contact with the bare skin of his torso, they both froze.

"Ror," he groaned before diving into an inferno of a kiss. Her fingers flexed as his mouth took over hers. The arm wrapped around her hips pulled her tight to him. His other hand slipped under her shirt, and his palm pressed against her lower back.

As soon as his hand flattened against her spine, she forgot all her newly learned skills. Every nerve, every brain cell, was focused on that skin-on-skin contact. With a whimper of need, she pulled her hands free just to knot them where his shirt covered his back. Yanking him closer, she met his kiss with a newly found ferocity.

He actually growled as he intensified the kiss even more, sliding both hands up her back and then down over her butt. She was so caught up in the heat of their kiss that she didn't realize his hands were cupping her ass until he squeezed, his fingers digging into her flesh. Pleasure rippled through her, building into a pulsing mass in her lower belly. With a gasp, she jerked back hard enough to nearly send herself sprawling on the floor.

Ian caught her and pulled her back to the safety of his lap, looking almost feral with need. Closing his eyes, he dropped his forehead to her shoulder and took several deep breaths. "Sorry," he finally rasped, sliding his hands away. "I didn't mean to get carried away. You just feel really good."

"It's okay." If she'd known how amazing making out with Ian Walsh would be, she'd have pounced on him years ago. As her breathing slowed, however, self-conscious thoughts wiggled their way into her brain. "Uh, what's the timeline on this?"

That made him raise his head so he could look at her. "Timeline?"

"As far as…um." Gesturing between them, she felt the dreaded blush creep into her face. "When we do what."

For a moment, he just stared at her, and then the corners of his mouth started twitching. "A timeline for when we do what. You know, to really plan this out right, we'll need to borrow Callum's whiteboard."

Her flush deepened, and she dropped her eyes.

"I'm just teasing." Wrapping his arms around her, Ian gave her a tight hug. "Sorry. You're just so fu—flipping cute. There's no timeline. If you feel comfortable with something, we do it. If you don't, we hold hands and watch a movie." He glanced around the televisionless space. "Or talk or something. What's important is that we're together. Finally."

"So we are? Together? Officially?" She seriously needed to stop making statements into questions.

"Yes." His firm tone did not allow for any doubt.

"Okay," she said, cautious happiness taking hold, but then a thought occurred to her. "What if it…uh, takes a while? To build up to…that?"

"That's fine." When she kept looking at him skeptically, he grinned at her. "It's *fine*. I'm not saying I wouldn't love to go fast, but just kissing you is more than I'd ever thought I'd get to do, so I'm happy to go at your pace." His smile degenerated into a smirk. "Besides, I think you need to be able to say the word 'sex' before you actually have sex."

Pulling back, she glared at him. "I'm fully capable of shooting you, you know."

"Oh, I know." Despite his words, he didn't look too concerned. He did look happy, though, which pleased her. "Now that your kitchen duties are complete, what did you want to do?"

Although he had his neutral, give-away-nothing expression in place, she knew he was hoping she'd suggest they make out some more. It was a tempting idea, but there was one thing they both needed more than even this. "Sleep."

"I can definitely do that. The Field County jail is not really a restful place." Glancing toward the oven, he asked, "Is there time for a nap before the food's ready?"

She nodded, getting up and heading toward the hallway with Ian following close behind her. Now that the adrenaline and endorphins and whatever else his kiss had kicked into high gear had settled, exhaustion pressed down on her, reminding her that she hadn't slept in over twenty-four hours—twenty-four *stressful* hours. After she opened her bedroom door, she paused, eyeing Ian over her shoulder.

"What are you doing?"

"Heading for bed."

Glancing in her room and then back at him, she felt her heartbeat kick up a notch. "My bed?"

"Yes." When she didn't move, he gave her a beguiling smile. He even batted his stupidly long eyelashes at her. "Please? We can put a row of very pink pillows between us. Or, you know, a row of pink stuffed bunnies. They'll be like fuzzy pink soldiers on a mission of chastity."

Once again, she wished she wasn't so clueless when it came to male-female interactions. They'd been officially together for less than five minutes. Was sleeping together—actually sleeping—right now too soon? But then her eyes met his, and her heart gave a near-painful thump. Frustrated by her own waffling, Rory marched into her bedroom. "Fine. Whatever. I'm too tired to worry about it."

Grabbing pajamas—which were just long underwear so she could quickly throw jeans or BDUs on over the top in a nighttime emergency—she headed for the bathroom.

"You could change in here," he said, sounding like he was about to laugh. "I'll turn my back."

Sending him a glare over her shoulder, she didn't even slow her steps. "Yeah, I saw how well that worked when you walked in on me in the closet."

"It worked pretty well for me."

She walked through the doorway, but then stuck her head back into the bedroom. "Watching me change is far away on the timeline, buddy." She managed to hold her stern frown until she was in the bathroom, when a giddy grin took over. If this bubbly, excited feeling was standard when having a boyfriend—or starting to date, or whatever she and Ian were doing—she understood why everyone else started pairing up much younger than she had. This—whatever it was—was fun. In fact, it was even more fun than when she shot a Desert Eagle .50AE, and that was saying something.

When she reentered the bedroom, she glanced at the bed and stopped. There were two reasons for this. The first was that Ian had indeed created a tiny wall down the center of the bed, a pink-and-white blockade made up of decorative pillows and Mr. Hoppity, her plush bunny. The second was that Ian was sitting on one side of the barricade, covers pulled up to his waist and his chest completely bare.

He was…whoa. Her throat went dry, and she had to lock her jaw so it didn't fall open. His tattoos scrolled across his chest, over his shoulders, and down his arms, emphasizing the contours of his muscles. He was like a living, breathing anatomy lesson. No fat obscured the lines of his biceps, his deltoids, those incredible pectorals…

Rory finally realized that she was staring, and he was grinning, most likely because it was obvious she was barely able to keep from drooling. A little flicker of panic started in her stomach. What was she doing with Ian? She was like a preschooler trying to do calculus.

"I can move the bunny if you want to cuddle," Ian offered, his eyes teasing but also lit with a banked fire.

A part of her, a part she hadn't even known existed until she saw Ian's bare chest in the flesh, wanted to take him up on his offer. The rest of her was a mess of want and uncertainty and shyness, mixed with a good-sized dollop of terror. It was that last bit that made her say, "Don't touch Mr. Hoppity."

"Mr. Hoppity?" he echoed, but her glare must have warned him that she was on the edge, and any sort of mockery would push her right off the cliff.

Another thought occurred to her, and she looked from Ian to the empty side of the bed. "I'd rather be closer to the door."

"Me too." He didn't budge. Instead, his arms crossed over his chest, making his biceps bulge in a distracting way. "And I was here first."

"Fine." Now that the initial shock of his half-naked beauty was waning, her bone-deep exhaustion returned. At least her bed was in the middle of the room, so she wouldn't be trapped between Ian and the wall. Circling to the vacant side of the bed, she crawled beneath the covers. As she lay on her back, Rory firmly closed her eyes. Bright illumination made her eyelids glow orange-red. "Could you get the light? The switch is on your side." As soon as the words left her mouth, the strangeness of them struck her. Ian had a side in her bed. It was hard to wrap her brain around that fact.

After an affirmative grunt, the glow behind her eyelids went dark. "Thank you," she said.

"You're welcome." A pause. "Can I hold your hand?"

"No. Respect the bunny wall."

His laugh was soft and so appealing that she almost reached over the pillows to take his hand anyway. Rory caught herself just in time.

"Good night, Ror."

"Good night, Ian."

"I'm glad I get to kiss you now."

Rory was glad the darkness hid her blush. Turning onto her side, she could just make out his dark shape looming above the wall of pillows in the dim glow of the hall's security lights. When his shadow shifted, she thought it was a trick of her vision until his lips brushed the side of her face, touching her jaw right in front of her earlobe. Her shiver had nothing to do with being cold.

"Good night, Rory."

"Didn't we already do this?" Although she'd intended her words to be sharp, they came out softly, her voice almost husky.

His quiet laugh was his only reply.

The timer brought her out of a deep, syrupy oblivion much too soon. Habit brought her into a sitting position, while her brain was still begging for more sleep.

"What is it?" Ian sat up when she did.

"Food." The word was muffled in a yawn. Beating away the urge to sink back into the cozy nest, into that space still warmed by her body heat, she swung her legs out of bed and stood.

"Not hungry anymore," Ian muttered, settling back under the covers. "Too tired. Eat later."

"Still need to turn off the oven, or everything'll burn." She shuffled toward the door, but a hand on her arm made her stop.

"I'll get it. Go back to bed." As he passed her, disappearing into the hallway, Rory blinked. She'd been on her own for three years. Before that, her chores and responsibilities were just that—hers. No one had ever stepped in to help her just because she was tired. The gesture was so small, yet it shocked her.

Rory was still standing in the same place when he returned from the kitchen.

Backlit from the dim hall lights, Ian said in a voice rough from sleep, "Thought I told you to go back to bed."

She smiled. "Thank you."

Ian came to an abrupt halt. "For what?"

As she closed the gap between them, he didn't move. His eyes stayed fixed on her face. "For turning off the oven." Going to her tiptoes, she dropped a kiss on his chin, the highest spot she could reach.

His palm cupped her neck, his thumb brushing a sensitive spot under her jaw. "You're welcome. If that's the thanks I get, I'm going to start doing more stuff around the house. Who knows what you'd do if I vacuumed."

She was still smiling when he kissed her. Like the first time, it started soft and gentle, but quickly deepened, until Ian pulled back with a groan. "Bed." His voice was even growlier now. Turning her around by the shoulders, he started her on her way back to bed with a pat to the bottom.

"Can't keep your hands off my rear, can you?" It amazed her that she'd just teased him, especially about her butt, and she hadn't even blushed a little.

"Nope. I dream about that ass."

Now her cheeks did redden. "Really?"

"Oh yeah."

She didn't know what to say, but she still didn't regret starting this. Knowing that Ian thought about her made her smile return. "Thank you?"

"You're welcome." Laughter had returned to his voice, but she didn't care. Her chest still glowed with warmth.

As they settled into their respective sides, the motion of the mattress made one of the pillows topple over onto her arm. She straightened it and then kept her hand there. "Ian?"

"Yeah." By the sound of his voice, he was facing her, lying very close to the plush wall.

"You can hold my hand, if you still want to." Her face flamed. Put that way, it sounded like something an eight-year-old would say. Her teeth closed on the inside of her lower lip. She'd expected a verbal answer, so she jumped when Ian linked his fingers with hers.

"Thanks," he said quietly, sounding even closer than a moment before.

Her heart bounced in her chest, and she tried to slow her breathing. If holding hands made her react this intensely, she'd probably have a stroke when they did…other things on the timeline. The warmth from his palm soaked into hers, and his stillness helped her to calm herself. His breathing deepened until she could tell he'd fallen asleep, and she felt herself drifting, relaxed and even smiling a little. She'd already figured out that being with Ian could be fun. Now she knew it could be…nice, too.

After another four hours of sleep, Rory was left wondering how she had ever thought Ian was anything but a dictatorial, rude jerk.

They stared at each other across the table. Earlier, they'd woken reluctantly and eaten the re-rewarmed stew. Ian had demolished almost the entire loaf of bread on his own. Now their bowls were empty, and only crumbs remained of the bread.

"Just sleep on one of the cots at the station. You don't have to go on any of the calls," he said.

"Why?" Standing, she reached for their bowls, but he beat her to it, grabbing the dishes and depositing them in the sink with a little more force than necessary. "I have a perfectly good bed here. And I know I couldn't keep myself from going on calls if I'm there."

Leaning against the counter, he stared at her, his jaw set. "I don't like leaving you here by yourself."

"Ian. My home is secure. You can't babysit me all the time."

"North told me that Billy threatened you."

Shouldering him aside, she started washing their few dishes. "He couldn't get down here, even if he wanted to."

"No." That didn't seem to make Ian any happier. "But I know you. If anyone sets off one of your alarms, you'll be upstairs and outside in a second."

She paused in the middle of rinsing suds off a bowl to look at him. "Well, yeah. That's what you do when someone invades your property."

"And *that* is why I don't want to leave you here alone." He almost violently grabbed a dish towel hanging on the oven door and held out a hand for the bowl.

"Do you want me to stay down here if someone tries to break in?" She gave him the dish and absently reached for the second. "I don't know if I could do that—just watch on the cameras as they take all of my inventory."

"Call the sheriff's department."

That honestly hadn't occurred to her. She'd grown up learning that she took care of herself and her property. Calling for help just seemed...unnatural. She offered the cleaned bowl to Ian and said, "It takes them a while to get here. Plus, I'd still have to go out to unlock the gate."

"Rory." Instead of taking the bowl, he closed his hand over hers where she held it. "Nothing you own is worth your life."

"But that is my life." She gestured toward the ceiling. "I need to protect it."

"Everything up there can be replaced." Placing the bowl on the counter, he cupped her chin, tilting her face so she met his eyes. "You can't. You need to protect yourself first. This is my last shift, then I'm off for four days. Just come with me to the station tonight, so I don't go out of my mind worrying about you here by yourself."

Rory shook her head as well as she could with him still holding her chin. "I can't tag along everywhere you go so you can protect me. I'm really good at protecting myself, whether from Billy or zombie hordes." She tried to smile, but his grim expression didn't change. "I like you." Her blush returned in a wash of heat, but she plowed on. "I like whatever this is that's starting between us. But this—the house and shop and property—is my life, and I want to keep it, too."

After a long moment, he gave a short, hard exhale. "Fine. At least promise me you'll stay down here if anyone comes on the property."

Regret clawed at her throat, but she had to be honest. "I want to tell you yes, so you don't have to worry, but I'm not going to lie. I wouldn't be able to just sit here and hide."

His jaw muscles worked as he stared at her. Finally, with a short, silent jerk of a nod, he tossed the dish towel onto the counter and headed for the stairs. He was halfway up them before she realized he'd set off the alarm in the back room, since he didn't know the code. Also, his Bronco was still parked at his house.

"I'll give you a ride home," she offered, hurrying after him.

"I'll call Soup for a ride."

"That's stupid. I'd have you home before he even gets here. Besides, you need my keys to unlock the gates."

He paused, staring at the steel door. "Fine."

She was silent. They'd fought before, both of them stubborn to a fault, and then things had cooled, and they'd been okay. But this was the first time she was left uncertain about her place in his life; there had been too many changes between them, too quickly.

She swallowed her questions, her worry, and drove him into town. She didn't say a word.

By the time she sat in her idling pickup, watching Ian open his own side door after a silent trip to his house, she was in turmoil. The door closed behind him, hiding him from view, and the back of her eyes and nose started to burn. Had they broken up? Was it over after two kisses and some sleepy hand-holding?

She didn't know. She didn't know how any of this worked.

When she realized she was staring at his house like an unbalanced stalker, she eased the pickup away from the curb. Without thinking too hard about where she was going, she pointed the truck toward The Coffee Spot. If someone had a question about a gun, they came to her. Now Rory needed the advice of an expert—or at least the closest thing to an expert she knew.

Chapter 18

After she barged into the coffee shop, she stopped just inside the door, barely avoiding squashing her nose against the back of the last person in a long line. Not only was every chair in the place occupied, but Callum had taken his usual position on the stool closest to the wall. Her plan for a conversation with Lou was blown to bits.

"Rory!" Lou shouted as she poured steamed milk into a cup. "Get over here and sit."

Eyeing the occupied stools, Rory didn't move.

Handing over the drink and taking the proffered money in the same gesture, Lou said, "Gary, you've been on that stool for three hours. It's time to go home and face Veronica."

"But..." the occupant of the seat next to Callum whined.

Shaking her head, Lou pointed toward the door with the hand not pulling change from the register drawer. "Home. Apologize. She'll yell and then forgive you. It's a ding in her car door, not a visit with a hooker. Go."

Although his face was sullen, he slid off his stool and headed for the door. When an early twenty-something man in skinny jeans sidled toward the vacated seat, Lou turned her pointing finger toward him. "Don't even think about it. Keep your hipster ass off that stool. Where are your manners? Stealing a seat from a lady?

Didn't your mother ever teach you better?" When the man slunk away toward the other side of the shop, Lou grinned at Rory. "Hurry up before someone else tries to grab it. That's prime real estate next to *Caliente* Callum here."

Although Callum just looked slightly pained, Rory blushed as she slid onto the stool. "Thanks, Lou, but I shouldn't stay long. I have to get the chicken coop closed up for the night."

Lou hurried away to take the next person's order. As she bustled around making drinks, Callum leaned a little closer so she could hear him. "No shift tonight?"

The mention touched a little close to a very raw nerve, and she moved her gaze to the top of the counter. There was an empty plate and a napkin folded with extreme precision. Even if it hadn't been in front of him, she'd have guessed it was Callum's work. "No."

"Heard you were the one who cleaned the storage room."

She had to smile a little at the deep satisfaction in his words. "Yeah. It was slow last night, and I had some nervous energy to spare."

"Thank you. I saw it today. A huge improvement."

"What he means," Lou broke in as she pulled a large cup from the stack, "is that he can actually step foot in there now without curling into a whimpering ball."

It was still strange to see someone brave enough to tease Callum. When Rory glanced at him, though, he was calmly sipping his coffee, eyeing a grinning Lou over the top of his cup. He even looked a little amused. Their easy interaction made her feel even more inept. She couldn't imagine a conversation between the two of them disintegrating into whatever had just happened between her and Ian.

"You okay?" Callum asked, and her eyes jerked to his. She hadn't realized she'd been projecting her feelings onto her face for everyone and his mother to see.

"Yeah." Although Callum just sipped his coffee, Rory couldn't meet his gaze. She felt strangely guilty for the lie, tension building in her chest until she felt like she had to say something or her lungs would explode. "No. I don't know."

There was more silent coffee-sipping on Callum's part. Rory reached for the folded napkin, needing something to do with her hands, but Callum slid it out of her reach.

"Sorry." Grimacing, she knotted her fingers together to hold them in place. "I'm not usually so fidgety."

"It's okay. What's up?"

"I think..." She paused, unable to believe she was about to confide in Callum, of all people. Lou was busy, though, and Callum was there and listening as if he was really interested, and Rory was pretty sure her brain would explode if she didn't figure out what exactly had just happened, so Callum it was. "I think Ian and I broke up. Maybe. Or we might have had a fight. Or I might have just refused to obey him, so he's cranky, but everything will be fine once his shift is finished. Or maybe I won't ever see him again."

"I doubt that last one," Callum said evenly. "You both live in Simpson, after all."

"You're right." Horror-stricken, she stared at him. "I won't ever be able to go to Station One or the grocery store or the post office without being worried that

I'll run into him. When he starts dating someone else, they'll be together, and then I'll run into *both* of them. I bet she'll be gorgeous. It's going to be so awful and awkward." With a groan, she let her forehead rest on her stacked hands.

"You probably need to figure out if you have actually broken up before worrying about the aftermath." His voice was so matter-of-fact, it calmed her panic, and she raised her head. Rory could see how he'd be a good dive-team leader.

"I know." Taking a deep breath, she prepared to expose her secret humiliation. "I just haven't done this before, so I don't know if this is just a normal spat, or if we're done."

"What was the fight about?"

"He wanted me to go with him to Station One tonight." When Callum nodded, she continued. "But I need to reopen the shop, so I told him I was staying home. He didn't like that, so we argued about it for a while, and then he wanted me to promise to hide and call the sheriff if anyone tried to break in again."

"That sounds reasonable."

She stared at him. "Hide and call the sheriff? Could you do that if someone broke into your house?"

After considering this for a moment, he said, "No."

"So why would you expect me to be able to do that?"

A small smile played at the corners of Callum's mouth. "Good point. But I can understand why Ian would be concerned, too."

Lou snorted. With a half-prepared drink in her hand, she leaned over the counter toward Rory and Callum so she didn't have to yell over the chatter of the crowd.

"What he's not saying is that he refused to let me stay alone when my stalker was"—she winced a little before smoothing out her expression—"well, not dead. Not that I complained." At an eyebrow lift from Callum, she amended that. "Too much."

"So," Rory said after Lou returned to finish the latest drink order, "what do I do? Wait for him to call? Call him? Apologize?" She scrunched her face. "There's not really anything I'm sorry about, though, except that we fought—or argued or broke up or whatever we did."

Callum was looking a little uneasy. "I don't think I'm the best person to be giving relationship advice."

There was a snicker from the vicinity of the cash register. With all the noise in the shop, Rory wasn't sure how Lou was hearing their low-voiced conversation, but she didn't seem to be missing a word of it.

"You're not going to help?" She stared at him, panicked. "But I don't know what I'm doing!"

"Fine." He placed his travel mug on the counter and aligned it perfectly with his empty plate. Rory wondered what his closet looked like, but then she decided she had a pretty good idea. Callum's closet would definitely have the floor space for a makeshift bed. "Have another conversation with him after his shift—actually, after he sleeps after his shift. Just tell him straight out what you told me, and then ask if that means you two are done. Right now, you're guessing, and he's probably guessing, and it's nothing that can't be solved by ten minutes of talking."

Rory studied her clenched hands as she considered this. The thought of him saying that they were definitely over made her stomach twist like a wet towel. On the other hand, not knowing was horrible. Could hearing the confirmation that they'd broken up be any worse than that? She suspected yes, but she still wanted to know for sure. "Okay."

"Really?" Callum sounded surprised.

"Yes. It makes sense."

"It does?"

Reaching across the counter, Lou squeezed his hand. "Look at you. Cal, the relationship sensei. You'll need to start an advice column in the *Simpson Star* newspaper."

He made a scoffing noise, but still looked a little pleased.

Hopping off the stool, Rory started for the door.

"Are you going to call him now?" Lou shouted after her.

Pausing with one hand on the door handle, Rory said, "Chickens first, then feed Jack, and then I'll stop by the station. I'd rather do this face-to-face. Listening to long pauses on a phone call will make me lose my nerve."

Lou approved. "Good idea. Serious conversations should be face-to-face. Besides, that way, he'll be right there so you can make up afterward." She lifted her eyebrows in a goofy gesture that made Rory laugh, despite her blush.

"Thanks," she called as she pushed open the door and stepped into the cold night.

During the drive home, the roads were dry, but small snowflakes whirled in front of her truck's headlights. The chickens had tucked themselves into the coop already, so she just had to close the door and collect Jack. After he ate, she loaded him into the pickup and started for the station.

The flurries were thickening, and snow was sticking to the road in random patches. The traction was still good, but she slowed anyway, telling herself it was because she was being careful rather than because she was delaying her conversation with Ian. The drive was short, however, and she reached Station One much too quickly for her peace of mind.

When she let Jack out of the truck, he bounded to the door. Rory followed more slowly, although the small bits of snow stinging her face kept her from dawdling too much. As she entered the station, bringing Jack and a gust of cold, snow-filled wind with her, she quickly shut the door behind her. The warm air was a relief, and she felt her shoulders relax a little, only to seize up again at the sound of male laughter coming from the break room.

Jack had already disappeared, galloping toward the smell of food and his new favorite group of people. She followed, poking her head inside to see the usual nightshift crew sitting around the table, the remains of a mostly eaten cake in front of them.

"Rory!" Soup was the first to greet her. "We got you something." He leaned back in his chair until he balanced on its two back legs and could reach something on the shelves behind him. Rory, like the big chicken that she was, kept her eyes on him so she wouldn't have to look at Ian.

"You're going to break your head," Al scolded, although without much heat. "Don't let the safety officer see you doing that."

"Joe ruins all our fun," Soup sighed, straightening so all four chair legs connected with the floor. He held out a box to her. "Here."

Rory accepted it, eyeing it cautiously. "Gloves?"

"Extra-small for those tiny doll hands of yours." Tipping back in his chair again, he grinned and winked at her. "Now, for me, I take extra-large…in *all* my latex coverings."

Steve reached past Al to slap the back of Soup's head, knocking him forward so his front chair legs clattered against the floor.

"Ha!" Junior crowed. "For once it wasn't me."

The rest of the guys laughed, and then Al turned to Rory. "Want some cake? We're having a little 'we're glad you're out of jail' celebration."

"We were going to put a metal file in the cake," Soup said, not seeming too ruffled by Steve's reprimand, "but the only one we had was really dirty, so it didn't seem hygienic—or tasty. Who wants a grease-and-dirt flavored cake?"

"No, thanks," Rory said. "I was just…ah, hoping to talk to Ian for a minute?" She finally managed to work up the nerve to glance at him, although his expressionless face didn't reveal anything. Her stomach twisted tighter.

Without a word, Ian stood and made his way around the table toward her. As he escorted her out of the break room, he stayed close behind her, although he didn't touch her. Rory wasn't sure if this settled her nerves or wound her tighter.

As they made their way down the hall, she heard Junior whisper in a voice meant to carry, "Did any of you guys notice the tension? Are Mom and Dad fighting?"

"Mind your business," Steve said gruffly.

The other men's chuckles followed them until they

entered the training room. When the door closed behind them, an awkward silence fell.

Rory glanced at the closed door they'd just passed through. "Can we maybe go to a different room? I just have this feeling that Junior and Soup already have glasses pressed to the door so they can listen."

With an amused snort, he moved toward the storage room she'd just reorganized, herding her in front of him. It was a little unnerving to have his silent, possibly angry bulk looming behind her, so she hurried into the room.

"Did the chief mind that I cleaned up a little?" She glanced around the space. Even though she'd done the work, it was still odd not having the mountains of gear piled everywhere.

"From what Al told me, the chief stared at it for a long time when he got here this morning. All he said was that he needed to have a little chat with you."

Nibbling on the inside of her lip, Rory sent him an apprehensive glance. "That doesn't sound pleasant."

"Probably not."

They both grew quiet.

Rory knew she needed just to get this done. Straightening her shoulders, she said, "I talked to Callum." That wasn't how she'd intended to start, but at least she wasn't silently staring at the shelves anymore.

After opening his mouth and closing it again, he finally responded, "Okay. I didn't expect that. Why were you talking to Callum?"

"Why?" The question threw her a little. "Um…I guess because I went to see Lou at The Coffee Spot, since she's really the only person in a solid relationship who I know well enough to talk to about this." After a pause, she amended her statement. "She's really the *only* person I know well enough to talk to about this, solid relationship or no solid relationship."

Ian looked confused. "Okay."

"She was really busy helping customers, but Callum was there." Since she wasn't exactly sure how she'd managed to dump the entire mess in Callum's lap, she fumbled her words a bit. "He...uh, well, he had this *look*—not the scary one, but the calm, I-can-handle-anything one—and he asked if I was okay. Since I wasn't, I told him why."

"And why weren't you okay?"

For some strange reason, it was so much easier to tell this to Callum. With Ian, the outcome seemed to matter so much more. "Because we argued. And you left."

His expression unreadable, he watched her silently.

"And I didn't know if that was normal, or if it was a huge fight, or if we were broken up."

That cracked his impassive look. "Do you want to break up?"

"No." She frowned. "I really don't. I just don't know the rules."

"We could add them on the whiteboard with the timeline."

Shooting him an irritated look, she snapped, "Don't make fun of me. I know I'm stupid when it comes to this." She waved a hand between the two of them. "Everything else has been easy for me—lessons and guns and drills—so I'm having a really hard time not knowing what to do. I feel dumb."

A genuine smile curved his mouth as he took a step closer. Reaching out to touch her face, he tucked a loose strand of hair back under her hat. "You're not being dumb. You're actually being up-front and mature about this. I shouldn't have stormed out of there earlier. I was just"—the smile faded, and he blew out a hard breath—"frustrated."

"Frustrated?"

He started to pace. "I'm not trying to take away your freedom. It's hard being here when I know you're home alone, when there's someone out there who wants to hurt you. Billy's pissed at you—and me—and he's a vengeful fu—guy. I love this job, but right now, all I can think is that I'm out helping strangers instead of protecting you. It makes me absolutely crazy sitting here, imagining your pretty head getting blown off by Billy's shotgun."

Rory blinked. "I've trained all my life to deal with situations like that. Well, that and others, like a nuclear winter and deadly viruses and zombies. But you have to trust that I know how to handle myself."

He took three quick strides until he was right in front of her, moving so fast that she jumped. Cupping her face in his hands, he said, "I know you can. But you can't win every fight. It takes just one bad day—one bad second—and then you're gone. I've been chasing you for years, and I've barely grabbed hold of you. I can't lose you now."

Staring at him, mesmerized and terrified in equal parts by his words, by the intense, almost desperate look in his eyes, she opened her mouth. "So, we're not broken up."

His hollow expression eased, and he gave a short laugh. "No. Definitely not."

"Good." The knots in her stomach eased for the first

time since their argument. "Do you need me to stay here for your shift? So you can eat cake without imagining splatters of my brain matter?"

"No." Leaning closer to her, he kissed the corner of her mouth. "But thank you for asking. You'd never be able to ignore the calls"—he kissed the other side of her lips—"and then you wouldn't get any sleep"—his mouth touched her upper lip—"and you'd be useless in the shop tomorrow." He scraped his teeth gently over her bottom lip.

By this time, she wasn't comprehending any of the words that came out of his mouth. "Uh-huh," she murmured blankly, staring at him. His brown eyes were so sweet and warm, and just wicked enough to put off any Bambi references. "Are we making up now?"

"Yeah." His thick fringe of eyelashes lowered halfway as his gaze turned scalding. "We're definitely making up." With that, he kissed her for real. This time it was even more explosive, even more consuming and addictive than before. His hands roamed, changing the feel of the kiss, like dialing the oven temperature from three-fifty to broil.

His fingers found her sides beneath her coat, and then one hand slipped behind her, running up the length of her spine and back down to the small of her back. His touch, even with several layers of fabric separating them, made her skin tingle. With a shiver, she tried to burrow closer.

Her own hands reached around him, gripping handfuls of his thermal shirt so she could tug him closer. With a groan she felt more than heard, he took the kiss deeper. He was getting rougher, nipping at her lips with enough force to sting. At first, she was a little startled, but each soft bite flared with heat, that tiny pain morphing into a sweet pleasure.

With a moan of her own, she closed her teeth on his bottom lip, hoping to give him the exact amount of pleasurable pressure he was giving her. When he sucked in a quick, startled breath and then attacked her mouth with renewed urgency, she was pretty sure she'd done it at least halfway right.

Her hands flattened so she could feel the contours of his back through his shirt. Although she knew he was muscled, the unyielding flesh beneath her palms surprised her just as it had the last time they'd done this. It was like caressing a marble statue—a warm, moving statue who could kiss *really* well.

Ian seemed to appreciate her tentative exploration, his breathing quickening and his kiss becoming almost frantic. His excitement made hers flame even higher, building with each touch and kiss and press of his body against hers. They were fully clothed, with their hands restricted to the PG zone, and even so, Ian was acting like this was the sexiest experience of his life. It truly *was* the most intense and wonderful thing to ever happen to her, and she didn't want to stop touching him.

Rory burrowed closer, seeking his heat and touch, even while mentally cursing all of their layers of clothes. She forgot where they were, forgot about the group of firefighters eating cake just a few rooms away, forgot everything except for Ian. As he dropped a line of biting kisses down the side of her neck and then back up again, she closed her eyes and groaned. The sheer carnality of the sound would have startled her if she hadn't been so caught up in Ian's spell. By the way he tightened his grip, her groan affected him too. With a pleasurable shiver, she tilted her head back so he'd have easier access to that spot under her ear—the place that was quickly becoming her favorite.

She didn't know how long they would have continued—or how far they would have gone—if the radio hooked to his belt hadn't blared. They both jumped and let out simultaneous disappointed groans.

"Of course," he muttered, adjusting the volume on his portable as the tones sounded. "No calls when Junior was telling that stupid story about his friend's first visit to a strip club for the fortieth time. No calls when Soup was showing me how he could hang a spoon on his nose. But *now*, of course there's a call."

"Can't everyone do the spoon-on-nose trick?" Rory asked, then quieted as the dispatcher's voice replaced the tones.

"We had a report of a structure fire on Goat Hill Road in Liverton. The caller believes the residence is occupied."

They both froze.

"Goat Hill Road?" Rory repeated. "Isn't that where…?" She trailed off, not wanting to finish the thought. From the look on Ian's face, she didn't have to.

"Julius." He whirled and ran for the door.

Chapter 19

The patchy slick spots she'd dealt with driving to the station had worsened. Now, flakes thickened into an opaque, wind-blown sheet, and the entire surface of the highway was icy. Soup had taken one look at Ian's frantic face and shoved him into the center seat of the engine, taking over driving duties. Steve and Junior were following in the main tender, with Al far behind in the second tender, a slow beast of a truck. Al's voice was tense as he requested mutual aid from the surrounding districts. Although all of the neighboring fire departments were quick to offer help, their estimated arrival times were dismal, thanks to the weather and sheer distance.

"Ian," the chief's voice barked over Fire's dedicated channel. "You are on support only on this call. You will not be entering the structure, do you copy?"

Ian didn't respond. Instead, he stared grimly through the windshield. Rory wasn't sure if he was oblivious to Early's words or if he wasn't going to promise the chief anything.

"Walsh, do you copy?" Early's voice was harsh.

Giving Ian's stonelike profile a glance, Soup reached for the radio mic. "He copies, Chief. We'll make sure he keeps his head."

Ian didn't react outwardly to Soup's promise. Her insides churning with worry for Julius and Ian and all the firefighters about to pit themselves against a house fire, Rory tentatively reached for Ian's hand. She closed her fingers around his, anxiety gripping her when he remained unresponsive. Worried that she'd reacted wrongly—again—she was about to pull away when he caught her in an almost painful grip that contrasted with his expressionless face. Rory clutched his hand just as firmly, trying to put all her understanding and worry and desperate hope into that one squeeze. Neither of them let go until the engine was pulling up in front of Julius's house.

For an endless second, Rory stared. She'd expected the cartoon version of a house fire, with flames climbing the walls and leaping from the roof like a crown. This was darker, with only occasional red glows from the lower-level windows giving hints of the inferno inside. A movement by the garage caught her attention. As she turned her head, she saw Junior and Steve rushing to hook up hoses, and she was viscerally reminded of why they were there.

She scrambled out of the truck. By the time she'd rounded the front and rejoined Soup and Ian, both men had donned SCBA gear, and her heart tried to pound from her chest.

"Chief said you were supposed to stay out of there," Rory yelled over the noise of the engine.

Ian looked at her, appearing calm. Only his eyes were frantic. "He's my dad, Ror."

"What are you doing?" Steve demanded. Although Rory was sympathetic to Ian's need to help, a wave of relief crashed over her when she heard his implacable tone. He'd keep Ian from running into a burning building.

"He's going in." Soup was the one who answered.

"We can try to stop him, but it'll take at least four of us even to slow him down, and that's a fu—flipping waste of manpower, if you ask me. He's holding it together, right, Beauty?"

Ian gave a short nod, adjusting his mask. His hand trembled the tiniest bit, making Rory's breath catch.

Although Steve barely paused, it felt like forever before he blew out a hard breath. "Fine. But if you start losing it, you get out, got it? If you don't, you're putting your brothers' lives on the line."

Holding Steve's gaze, Ian nodded.

"I need to hear it."

"Yes sir. If I start to lose it, I'm out."

"Okay. Go."

As Ian grabbed the nozzle end of a hose and jogged toward the front entrance of the house, Rory stared after him, frozen.

"Rory!" Steve's bark made her jump, breaking her paralysis. "I need you on the pump controls with Junior."

"Yes sir!" Once again, zombie training came to her rescue. If left alone, she would have stood uselessly, silently begging for Ian not to die—but with an order to follow, she could trust her instincts to carry her. She hurried over to climb the steps behind the cab to the top of the truck.

"Hey, Rory." Junior gave her a hand up. Although he appeared calm at first glance, his face was flushed, and his eyes were wider than normal. Rory wasn't the only one feeling the rush of adrenaline. A clear cord snaked from the portable radio hooked on his coat to his earpiece. "Let's give these guys some water."

Junior shouted out explanations each time he turned

a knob or flicked a switch, but Rory found it almost impossible to concentrate. From their perch on top of the truck, she could see Ian opening the front door. Nearby windows lit with flames as oxygen rushed inside. For a bare second, Ian was silhouetted in the doorway before he stepped into the fire.

Rory must have made a noise, since Junior turned his attention from the controls to her.

"Beauty will be fine," he said loudly, giving her a hearty pat on the back that nearly knocked her off the truck. "Soup, too. They're old hands at this." Despite his words, Rory saw the sweat streaking from beneath his helmet, and vapor rising from his skin. It was too cold, and they were too far from the fire for it to be anything but nerves.

Forcing her gaze off the front of the burning house, Rory made herself pay attention to what Junior was telling her. It wasn't doing Ian any good for her to stare at the house, waiting with her heart squeezing painfully for him to reemerge. The best thing she could do was help on the outside. She had to trust that he knew his job and could take care of himself. Soup was with him, too, she remembered with a feeling of relief. Despite his joking manner, Soup would die for Ian.

Al arrived with the second tender, taking over scene command from Steve. The lieutenant paced, his gaze never leaving the burning structure as he spoke into his radio.

"This shows the pressure of the—" Junior broke off, jerking up his head to focus on the house.

"What? What's happening in there? Junior, tell me!" Rory demanded.

"It's fine." His tight expression told her things were

anything but fine. He went silent, obviously listening to the radio through his earpiece. Frustration and tightly restrained panic flared in Rory, and she balled her hands into fists.

"Junior, if you don't tell me what is going on in that house right this second, I'm going to go home, get one of my many guns, come back here, and *shoot you*. So start talking."

He really focused on her for the first time since she'd joined him on the truck. "Whoa. You sound really serious about that."

"I am." She was shaking with nerves and aimless fury, her gaze shifting between Junior's wide eyes and the burning house holding Ian—*her* Ian. "Tell me what they're saying."

"Uh…they're just at a…delicate point."

"What does that mean?"

"The smoke's darkening, and they're seeing some ghosting on the ceiling."

It was like he was speaking in another language. Rory wanted to scream, but forced herself to speak calmly. "Ghosting?"

"Isolated flames moving in the hot gas layer."

"Junior."

His mouth twisted unhappily. "It's a possible indication of impending flashover."

"Flashover?" Although she didn't know what it meant, the word sounded scary.

"There's basically four stages of a fire. Flashover is when it goes from the growth stage to the fully developed stage really fast."

She flinched. "That sounds dangerous."

"It is." After pausing to listen to another radio transmission, he continued. "The burning gases can cause a lot of pressure, enough to blow out windows or doors—"

"Okay!" she interrupted. Now that she knew what was happening, each detail just fired her imagination. Rory pictured Ian's limp body flying through the air, wrapped in flames… With a hard shake of her head, she shut down the images. "Okay, so they just need to get Julius and get out of there quickly."

"Right!" Junior's agreement came too quickly. "They'll be out of there in no time."

The seconds ticked by, turning to minutes, and even Junior's stream of chatter slowed and eventually stopped. A furious-looking chief arrived and stomped over to talk with Al. Rory caught herself staring at the house again, gripping the metal bar in front of her so hard her fingers ached.

"How long can it take?" she finally burst out. "Julius never moves from that chair. How long can it take to get him and get out?"

"It's hard to see." Junior stared toward the house, but his gaze was far away. "Even if you think you know where you're going, it's easy to get disoriented."

Bolting to her feet, she stared at him in horror. "You think they're lost in there?"

"What? No! Of course not." He looked at the controls and fiddled with a valve she was pretty sure didn't need fiddling with. "I'm just saying that they have to move slowly. That's all."

"Rory!" Chief Early was gesturing for her. As she turned to climb off the truck, Junior bumped her arm lightly.

"He'll be fine, Rory. They both will."

She studied his face for a moment, judging his sincerity. He looked more earnest than she'd ever seen him, so she gave a slow nod. "Thanks, Junior."

As she hurried over to where the chief waited, her gaze kept getting drawn to the house. Even though Junior had retracted his words, they'd left a looping track in her brain. She kept picturing Ian lost in the fire, separated from Soup and the fire hose, wandering from room to room in the flames and smoke until the dreaded flashover blew him into oblivion.

"Sorenson!" bellowed Early, and Rory realized she'd stopped moving, her horrified gaze fixed on the house and her feet locked in place. She forced herself to move, dragging her eyes from the now-flaming front of Julius's home and focusing firmly on the chief.

"You okay?" he asked, his normally cheery face tight with concern.

"Fine." It seemed crazy for him to be concerned about how she was doing when two of his men were inside a blazing house.

"You're not thinking of following him in there, are you?"

She looked at him in surprise. "Could I?"

"What? No!" His brow drew down in confusion. "You haven't been trained in SCBA, or even passed basic firefighter courses."

"Then why are you suggesting it?" Frustration and frantic worry made her voice snappy.

"I'm not *suggesting* it, I'm saying—"

Both of their attentions were drawn by a shout from Junior, and their heads jerked around toward the fire. A form stumbled out of the front entrance, and Rory sucked in a breath and held it, her heart pounding in her ears. The dark shape wasn't quite right, though—it wasn't Ian. Then the form materialized, showing it wasn't one person or even two, but three. Ian and Soup were supporting a limp Julius between them.

All the tension leaked out of Rory's muscles. She felt like Mr. Hoppity would after all his stuffing was removed.

"Thank God," Early muttered.

Rory would've echoed the sentiment if she'd been able to speak. As it was, she had a hard time not crying with sheer relief. She bit the inside of her lower lip until she tasted blood and the tears had been forced back to where they belonged.

With excellent timing, an ambulance pulled up behind the second tender. Soup and Ian changed course to haul Julius in that direction, and the EMTs jogged to meet them. Although Rory knew she should stay out of the way, she couldn't seem to stop herself from hurrying toward Ian.

By the time she reached him, they were loading Julius into the back of the ambulance.

"Ian!" She wanted so badly to throw herself at him, to wrap her arms around him and feel the steady beat of his heart. When he turned toward her, though, she jerked to a halt. His gear was blackened, and his face was streaked with soot where it hadn't been covered by the mask. His face was drawn, and he looked like a stranger—a stranger about to snap.

The ambulance turned, siren blaring and lights flashing, and headed toward the highway. It passed a car parked a block from them.

An oddly familiar-looking car.

Rory squinted to get a better look at the vehicle until an audible inhale from Ian snapped her back to the present situation. He was staring after the ambulance, looking lost.

"Aren't you going with him?" Rory asked. "What did they say? Will he be okay?"

"No." His voice was calm—too calm. "I promised him I'd stay and try to save Mom's house." As if he'd just remembered the burning building behind them, he turned and took a step toward it. He stumbled slightly, and Rory reached for him but pulled back before making contact.

"He was talking, then?" she asked carefully, watching to make sure he wasn't going to topple over.

"He tried a few times—he was in and out. We took too long to get him out because I couldn't find him. We had to look through the whole damn house before we tripped over him in the bedroom."

"At least he finally got out of his chair." She closed her eyes. Those had not been the right words. In fact, they were probably the furthest from the right words she could've managed.

Ian's sharp crack of laughter startled her into opening her eyes. "True." The blank look melted away, leaving him looking scared. "Fuck, Ror. What if he dies? I lost my mom, lost the club… He's all I've got left."

The fear in his face was flat-out wrong. She'd never seen Ian Walsh frightened—not driving in a blizzard on ice-slicked roads or facing armed burglars or running toward the scene of an accident. Rory was determined to take away that terror. She had no idea how to do it, but she'd get it done. Somehow.

Taking the tiny step forward required to bring their bodies into contact, she wrapped her arms around his middle. His coat was bulky, as was hers, and she felt like she was trying to hug Paul Bunyan. Despite that, she clung to him the best she could.

"I don't know if he'll be okay," she said, figuring she'd probably say the wrong thing yet again but unable not to at least *try* to give him comfort. "If he does die, though, you are *not* alone. He's not all you have left. The entire fire department would lay down their lives for you…well, maybe not Joel Becker, but everyone else would for sure. And uh, me."

"What about you?" His arms were still hanging at his sides, but she refused to let self-consciousness steal her nerve.

"You have me."

"Yeah?" His voice was rough. Finally, *finally*, his arms wrapped around her, hugging her back. Although their gear was too thick and bulky to share body heat, Rory felt so much warmer than she had just seconds earlier.

"Yeah." They stood in silence as Ian's brothers in all but blood fought to save his mother's house. "I still hope Julius doesn't die, though."

With a shuddering sigh, Ian tightened his grip around her. "Me too."

Chapter 20

"I WISH I COULD KICK HIS A—AH, BUTT INTO A treatment center," Ian grumbled.

Rory grinned at him.

He regarded her happy expression with suspicion. "What?"

"You're switching out your swears again." She shrugged. "I know you're feeling better."

After they spent a long, sleepless night in the hospital waiting area, the verdict was that Julius was not going to die—at least not from smoke inhalation. The doctors were concerned about the effects of his drinking, however. After the he'll-live-for-now update, Ian and Rory were able to relax a little for the first time since the previous evening's call had come over the radio.

Reaching over, he took her hand and pulled it into his lap. "Yeah, I am. Although now that I know Julius is going to live, I can be pissed at him again."

She sighed. "It wouldn't work, anyway."

"What wouldn't?"

"Forcing him into treatment." She leaned against his shoulder, looking at their hands rather than his face. "If he's determined to drink, then he'll find a way to drink. It's like when he was suicidal. If he'd really wanted to kill himself, he would've found a way." Although she felt his gaze, she didn't look up to meet it. Her nerves were too raw and exposed for eye contact.

"Your parents… They found a way, didn't they?"

With an affirmative shrug, she focused even harder on their intertwined fingers. Ian had nice hands, strong hands with enough scars and callouses to prove that he was useful. "They'd made up their minds that the end was near, and that it was going to be horrible. All that training to survive an apocalypse, and they didn't even try to see it through."

His thumb stroked from the side of her wrist to the bottom of her thumb. "I'm surprised they left you to face it alone."

Her choke of a laugh sounded pained, even to her own ears. "They tried not to."

She felt his body jerk, but when he spoke, Ian's voice was even. "How?"

"They tried to make me see reason. For weeks, they talked and talked, trying to wear me down. I didn't get it, though. If the world disintegrated into a mess of misery and horror, then I would take stock and decide if I should continue living. They didn't even wait to see if that terrible event even happened, though. When I wouldn't bend, they decided to force me to bend."

His arm was like iron under her cheek. Again, his steady voice didn't match the tension in his body. "What did they do?"

"Drugged my venison stew." She could still taste the bitter edge of the already gamey food. "Luckily, I never really liked venison, so I'd pretend to eat it but end up sneaking most of it to Jack. I barely ate any of it that night, since it tasted especially bitter. When Jack wobbled to his feet, ran headfirst into the table leg, and passed out cold, it wasn't hard to figure out what they'd done—and what they still intended to do."

"What'd you do?"

"Took Jack's unconscious body and ran." She still had nightmares about that trip up the stairs and through the steel door into the shop, juggling the dog's dead weight. The locks had stiffened under her shaking hands, and she was certain her parents would catch her and drag her back down the stairs to the bunker they'd intended to turn into a coffin for three. "I didn't go far, just spent the night hiding in the pole barn. By the next morning, I'd talked myself into thinking they hadn't really meant to kill me. They were my *parents*. They loved me—I knew that. It's why I stayed for so long, despite their craziness. I figured the stew had probably just been bad or something." Her laugh was hard and humorless. "I went back down to talk to them. I found their bodies in their bedroom."

"Your mini Costco?"

"That's the one."

"How'd they do it?"

"Poison. Belladonna. Like Belly said, they went old-school."

Ian gave another little start. "She said that? That seems…not very tactful, even for Belly."

"That's just Belly." She shrugged. It hadn't bothered her, although she'd been so numb immediately after her parents' deaths that nothing seemed to affect her. "The poison thing was strange, though. It wasn't the original plan. Dad's SIG-Sauer P226 was next to them. I think they were planning to do a murder-suicide, but neither of them could shoot the other, so they went with the backup plan."

"So they were going to shoot you?" His voice wasn't quite as calm and even anymore.

Her mind flinched away from the question. "I have to believe that they couldn't have done it." It would hurt too much to think anything else.

His hands sandwiched hers tightly. "I don't think they would've gone through with it, either."

Narrowing her eyes, she gave him a look. "Thanks for the support, but how could you say that? You didn't even know them."

"Because I know you." He met her gaze and held it. "I don't think anyone, much less your parents who loved you, could bring themselves to destroy someone so brave and smart and amazing."

His logic was faulty, but she was too flustered by his words to say anything. Pressing her forehead against his shoulder, she hid while she regained her self-composure. "Thanks. Rave wouldn't have had a problem putting a big hole in me, though."

"He was a useless assh—uh, piece of sh—garbage." He huffed out a quiet laugh. "It's hard not to swear when I'm talking about Rave."

"Yeah." The movie of his death began looping in her mind. It had been a few days since she'd last dealt with the bloody replay, and Rory wondered if a lack of sleep and overabundance of stress had left her brain tired and vulnerable.

Breaking into Rory's morbid thoughts, the doctor reappeared—a tall brunette who radiated confidence and competence.

"Mr. Walsh, would you like to see your father now?"

He stood. Since he still held Rory's hand, he pulled her up with him.

The doctor's gaze flicked to Rory. "Family only, I'm afraid."

Slightly relieved, Rory tugged her hand free. After her last confrontation with Julius, she didn't think seeing her at his bedside would be the healthiest thing for the injured patient. He'd probably have a stroke just at the sight of her. When Ian's lips flattened into a hard line, Rory knew he was about to argue. Shaking her head, she put a hand around his forearm and gave a gentle squeeze.

"It's fine," she said quietly. "I'm not his favorite person right now, anyway."

Although he didn't smile, the harsh cut of his mouth softened a little. "And I am?" he muttered, leaning close so only she could hear him.

"I don't think Julius would be happy to see anyone, unless that person had a flask in their back pocket."

"True." His eyes emptied, and Rory regretted saying that. In apology, she slid her hand down his arm and tangled her fingers with his.

"Ian. Even if he pretends otherwise, he'll be glad to see you. When I went to see him the other day, he was disappointed you weren't with me."

His expression remained skeptical, but his fingers tightened around hers before releasing her hand. He turned to the doctor, who gave him a smile that was a little more flirtatious than Rory cared to see.

"I'll call the shop while you're visiting Julius," she said, a little too loudly. "The *gun* store. That I *own*."

Rory focused a flat, warning look on the doctor, who appeared a touch startled.

Ian, however, seemed to be amused again. He brushed a quick kiss across Rory's cheek before returning to the doctor's side. The doctor kept any more smiles to herself as she escorted Ian out of the waiting area.

Once they disappeared, exhaustion hit Rory hard. She slumped into a chair, allowing her head to rest on the back of the seat. Everything that had happened—the intruders, Rave's death, Ian's arrest, Julius's accident—swirled around her brain, and she didn't have the energy to lock all the bad thoughts away in their assigned mental closets.

The burning behind her eyes and nose grew worse, until tears began to leak from her closed eyelids and draw wet lines down the sides of her face. With an impatient sound, she sat up and roughly scrubbed at her cheeks. Rory didn't cry. It was pointless and weak and wasted time. There was no solution to any problem that could be found in tears.

Taking a shaky breath, she closed her eyes again and mentally began to fieldstrip and reassemble a Ruger Mark III. Her hands moved slightly with her thoughts as she allowed the process to fill her brain, driving out the muddled chaos. Over and over, she repeated the familiar motions, until she was calm again.

"Ror?"

Ian's voice made her jump and snap open her eyes. "Hey." She tucked her fingers beneath her thighs, a little embarrassed he'd caught her messing with an imaginary gun. "How's Julius?"

"Pretty doped up." He grimaced. "He wasn't making

much sense. Kept accusing me of burning his house down and other crazy things. A couple of times, he even thought I was Billy."

"He's confused. He'll realize you saved him once he's off the painkillers."

"Maybe." Sinking into the chair next to her, Ian groaned. "Can we go home now?"

"You tell me." Rory examined his tired face. "Did you want to stay in Denver so you can be here if Julius needs you?"

"Nah." Grimness stiffened the lines of his face. "He'll be here at least overnight, and Squirrel said he'd come get him."

"Okay. I can probably manage two hours of driving without falling asleep and killing us, but you'll need to stay awake to make sure I don't start drifting. You up for that, or should we get a hotel room?" Her face went hot. "Hotel rooms, I meant. Rooms. Plural."

Although his chuckle was rough, it contained honest amusement. "If you'd kept it at one room, I would've taken you up on it. Let's head back up the mountain. I'll drive, though."

"Sure?" Rory eyed his face as they both stood.

"Yeah." He stretched before reaching for his coat.

As they walked toward the exit, Ian kept a light hand on the back of her neck. If this kind of casual touching was part of being in a relationship, Rory decided she could easily get used to it. When he pulled his hand away before they exited the main doors so he could don his gloves and hat, she frowned at the loss. Shaking off her disappointment, she pulled on her own gloves and reminded herself not to be clingy.

"I'm sorry I dragged you into my mess," she said.

"What?"

"With Billy." She turned toward the street where the Bronco was parked. Even in the predawn darkness, the temperature in Denver felt almost tropical after being in the frigid mountain storm the previous evening. "I feel like I robbed you of your family."

Slinging an arm around her shoulders, he pulled her against him in a sideways hug. "No, you helped me see who my real family is. The Riders have changed. It's not the same club anymore. I just wish I could protect you better."

"I'm pretty good at protecting myself." Rory nudged him teasingly with her elbow, trying to lighten the conversation. "I'm a better shot than you, remember?"

"Oh, I remember." With his encircling arm, he gave her a playful shake. "What I remember is kicking your cute little butt on the range."

"Uh-uh. Your male ego must be affecting your vision."

"Didn't you promise me a rematch?"

"Anytime," she said as he climbed into the Bronco. "Well, anytime if things ever calm down so I can get back to the shop and the range."

He pulled out into the unusually quiet street. That was the advantage of driving during the predawn hours, Rory supposed—less traffic.

"I'm the one who should be sorry for sucking you into all of the club drama," Ian said, concentrating on the red light in front of them.

"I started it," she admitted. "You helped me during the burglary, so if anyone should be apologizing for sucking, it's me." The double entendre struck her after the words had already emerged, and she was grateful for the sketchy illumination from the streetlights so Ian couldn't see her blush. She knew he'd caught her slip, though, because he was grinning.

"Never apologize for that," he said, and she reached over to smack his upper arm. That just made him laugh.

"Hopefully, things will settle down and go back to normal soon. We're due for some boring normality."

"We are due," he said, his smile slipping off his face, "but that doesn't mean we'll get it."

By the time they reached Simpson, the sky was barely lightening in the east, but the sun hadn't made an appearance yet.

"My place or yours?" Ian asked.

With a sigh, Rory said, "Yours. If we stop by the station for my keys, the guys will want to know all the details about Julius. Even though I already told Al the basics when I called him, it'll still take us an hour to get away from that bunch of Nosy Nellies." Sleep was pulling at her so insistently that an hour seemed like an impossibly long stretch of time.

"Don't sound so excited about staying at my place," Ian teased lightly, turning the Bronco in the direction of his house.

"It's just"—she made a face—"those *windows*."

"Did you want the closet again?"

She did. She just didn't want to admit it.

"You do, don't you? That's fine. Your bed's still set up in there." He grinned at her, and his teeth flashed whitely in the grainy dawn light. "We'll have to put a real bed in there if you keep sleeping over."

Rory was blushing but not sure why she was embarrassed. It might have been talking with Ian about beds. "The sleeping bag's fine. I'm not picky."

"Maybe not, but I like a real mattress."

"So?"

"So"—he drew out the word suggestively—"I'd eventually like to sleep in the same bed as you again. Sometime in the future. When we reach that spot on the timeline."

"Oh." Whatever was flying around in her stomach felt too big to be butterflies. Bats, maybe. Or pterodactyls.

His gaze slid toward her as he backed his SUV into his driveway. "Unless we're already at that point on the timeline?"

Her body enthusiastically answered in the affirmative, bringing a hot flush to her face and warmth to other parts. During that horrible, interminable time while she waited for him to come out of Julius's burning house, something had clicked inside her. She wanted Ian. For as long as she could have him, she wanted him, and she was sick of wasting time. "Yes."

The SUV jerked as he hit the brakes harder than necessary. "What? Really?"

"I'm there." His flabbergasted expression brought back her uncertainty. "Unless you're not there? Because we don't have to do anything you don't want—"

His happy laugh interrupted her. "Are you kidding? I've been there for *years*."

Ian turned off the engine and leaned toward her. Startled, she leaned away from him.

"What's wrong?" he asked, stopping midlean. "Didn't we just agree we were *there* on the timeline?"

"We're not at the kissing-in-front-of-the-neighbors point, though."

"It's okay. They're not awake yet."

Rory stopped his forward advance with a hand on his chest and looked pointedly at the dashboard clock. "They're awake. It's not *that* early."

"My neighbors are lazy."

"All of them?"

"It's an epidemic in this neighborhood."

"An epidemic of laziness."

"It's sad."

"You're a liar."

"Hey!" Ian sounded offended. "This accusation from the woman who denies that I'm a better shot?"

"No way you're getting a kiss now."

"Shi—oot." He backed off a little. "Not even a tiny one?"

Reaching behind her, she pulled the handle and opened the door. "You're punchy. Get inside and go to bed." As she jumped out of the Bronco, she had to smile. Punchy Ian was kind of cute.

He was waiting for her when she rounded the back of the Bronco. Although Rory was half-expecting him to tease her more, he just wordlessly escorted her to the side door. As he unlocked it and held it open for her, his phone beeped.

"It's Steve," Ian said as he checked the text message. "He's headed over to your place for chicken duty, and he'll leave Jack there." There was another beep. "Afterward, he'll swing by my house and leave the keys in the mailbox."

A ripple of relief coursed through her. "Tell him thanks."

His fingers moved over the screen before he returned the phone to his pocket. "Done."

"I owe him one." She stepped out of her boots. Her legs felt like they weighed a hundred pounds each.

Helping her out of her coat, Ian suggested, "He's always in need of babysitters."

"Uh..." She let him pull off her coat as she stared at him in horror. "Would it be rude if I told him I owed him one but not to ask me to babysit?"

"Not rude, just very...specific."

She groaned. "I don't know how to take care of kids. I'd probably lose one or accidentally kill it. He'd be smart to keep his offspring as far away from me as possible."

"Don't worry about it today." He tugged off her stocking hat and leaned to kiss the top of her head. Just that small touch erased her exhaustion. She tilted her head back, hoping for more now that they were out of the neighbors' sight. By the look in his eyes as he backed her against the wall, her hope was about to be realized.

He leaned toward her, his mouth getting closer and closer until her eyes slid shut and her heart thundered. Her breaths were quick and shallow, and she knew he could feel them against his lips. There was a pause before his kiss landed on her chin.

Her eyes popped open. "What are you doing?"

"Kissing you," he answered between pecks, following the line of her neck.

"You missed my mouth."

"I do miss it." He started back up her throat, nipping when he got just under her jaw. "Every time I'm not kissing you."

She groaned, goose bumps spreading from where his teeth had connected.

"Sorry. Too cheesy a line?"

"What? No." Her answer was distracted. "I just really like it when you bite like that."

With a growl, he flattened her body against the wall, wasting no time in finding her lips. Her arms looped around his neck as his hands roamed, stroking along her back and cupping her ass, lifting her off her feet and holding her sandwiched between him and the rough plaster.

There was no fear this time, no nervousness. Rory threw herself wholeheartedly into the kiss, allowing her hands to explore his perfect physique. Watching him do his job—fighting fires and helping accident victims and pulling people out of burning buildings—made her appreciate his body even more. He wasn't just beautiful. He was *useful*. The beautiful part was just a bonus. The other guys teased him about being their cover model, but he honestly didn't seem to care much about his looks. His body was a tool he used to help him do what he loved.

His hips pressed into hers, tearing her from her reverie. She had experience at the kissing and touching part, but anything beyond that was still a mystery—a slightly nerve-racking mystery. As she hesitated, Ian started kissing her favorite place under her ear.

"Um..." She wiggled and then froze at his groan. "We're moving through the timeline pretty fast."

Ian went still, his teeth locked lightly on her earlobe. He released her, exhaling in a light puff against her ear. That made her shiver, too, and she wondered why she'd stopped him. Everything he did felt so *good*. She wished she could stifle that part of her brain that went into panic mode when his hands and mouth went to certain places, and her center went all gooey.

When he pushed away from the wall, caging her in the brackets of his arms, her body felt chilled at the loss of his body heat.

"You're in control of the timeline," he said, his eyes steady on hers. "When you say stop, we stop. When you say go"—his eyes went molten—"we definitely go."

"Okay." It sounded good in theory, but she didn't trust her body not to get carried away.

"Okay?"

She nodded.

"Does that mean go?"

Catching the inside of her bottom lip in her teeth, she hesitated and then nodded again. As soon as her head made the barest motion, his mouth was on hers again, fierce and hungry. This time, there was no gentle lead-up to passion—the kiss exploded in an immediate conflagration.

Her hands locked around his biceps, her clenching fingers barely denting the hard flesh. She kept them there as all her attention focused on the feel of his lips and tongue and teeth, and all the marvelous things he was doing with them. His mouth dropped to her neck again, and she twisted her chin up and to the side to give him access to her vulnerable throat.

She became aware of her hands locked around his upper arms, and she softened her fingers, sliding her palms over his fabric-covered biceps. A sudden urge swept over her to see him bare-chested, to run her hands directly over his skin without the barrier of his shirt blocking her touch. Without hesitating, she slid her fingers up his arms and over his shoulders before grabbing two handfuls of his shirt and pulling.

His head came up, and he looked at her, as if checking to make sure she really wanted what her tugs were asking. When she hauled at his shirt again, he shifted back so her grip on his top pulled it over his head, and he lifted his arms so they slipped from the sleeves as well.

When his shirt was completely removed, it dangled from Rory's nerveless fingers as she studied his bare torso, shock and lust and anxiety fighting in her stomach. He really was perfect, as calendar-worthy as the guys at the station teased him of being. As he stood there, so gorgeous and muscled and hot, Rory suddenly felt unworthy, thinking of her small breasts and slim figure, her average features and inexperience.

"You're so beautiful," he said, contradicting her thoughts as if he could read her mind. Reaching toward her face, he smoothed her hair away from her cheek. "Sometimes, at the station, I'll be working on an engine or rolling hose or whatever, and you'll pop into my head." One corner of his mouth turned up in a grin. "I have to quickly think about something else—something really not sexy, like Chief in a Speedo—before I embarrass myself. The guys would never let me live that down."

Heat rose in her cheeks, and she couldn't help but smile. Keeping his hands on either side of her shoulders, Ian lowered his head until his mouth met hers. As they kissed, she first kept her hands at her sides, straight down by her hips so she wouldn't accidentally touch his bare skin. Soon, though, the temptation proved to be too much.

Tentatively, she brushed her fingers against his forearms, exploring the texture of the prominent veins and the tickle of hair before sliding over his elbows to the biceps she'd discovered earlier. They felt different without a fabric covering, harder and softer at the same time. She moved to his shoulders and neck and back again.

As she explored, his kiss changed. Rory matched his reaction to what she was doing, learning where he was sensitive and what spots were a little ticklish. It was a powerful feeling to make his breath catch in his chest, all without touching anything below his waist.

"Wait," he finally rasped, pulling away and tightly closing his eyes. Rory leaned back against the wall and watched him in concern as he dragged in one quick breath and then another. When his panting finally slowed, he opened his eyes and smiled at her look of concern. "Just got a little wound up. Ready to go again?"

Despite the coolness of the room, he was sweating, the moisture catching the light and making his skin gleam. Rory bit back a smile, thinking of how much he looked like an oiled-up model right now, and how much he'd hate that if he knew. Her hand reached out as if it had a mind of its own and traced the convex lines of his abs. His skin rippled under her touch.

"I'll take that as a yes," he muttered, before diving down to claim her mouth again.

It felt like forever and, at the same time, merely seconds that they kissed. She'd started sweating, as well, and her top felt stifling. When she pushed at his chest, he rocked back with a reluctant groan.

"Too much?" he asked, his voice rusty.

Shaking her head, she grasped the bottom of her shirt

and tugged it upward, stopping around the bottom of her ribs when Ian grabbed her hands and held them still.

"Sure?"

Pulling out of his grip, she yanked the shirt over her head and tossed it aside. "Yes."

He stared at her for so long her fingers twitched with the desire to cross her arms over her chest. Glancing down at herself, she held back a groan of dismay. Her white bra was home-sewn, old and utilitarian. Even in its heyday, it hadn't been a sexy piece of lingerie. Now it was stretched and faded. The urge to cover herself grew stronger.

"Whoa." He cleared his throat. "You're so…" When his eyes lifted, meeting hers, the pupils were dilated, and the lids heavy. "I can't believe I'm finally seeing you this way." When his hand reached toward her, Rory could see a faint tremor making his fingers vibrate. Then he touched her skin, and she couldn't think about his reactions. Everything in her was concentrated on how he was making her feel.

His touch, as light as it was, almost burned. When she glanced down at the spot where his fingers had brushed, Rory half expected to see a singed mark on her skin. Leaning closer, Ian allowed his lips to follow the trail of his hand. She jumped, as if he'd given her a static shock. With his mouth still on her collarbone, he smiled against her skin.

At Ian's nudge, she leaned back, her eyes sliding closed so she could fully concentrate on what she was feeling. His hand and mouth stayed on her upper chest and then moved to her belly, skipping over her breasts. Despite the lack of R-rated action, she couldn't imagine feeling more aroused than she was at that moment. Wanting to see him, she opened her eyes.

This time, when he pulled back, chest pumping with his breaths, she gave a quiet moan of disappointment. The air quickly chilled her mostly bare skin, and she gave in to the renewed urge to cross her arms over her front.

"Okay." Instead of returning to his explorations of her upper half, he took a step back. "Enough of that for tonight."

"Really?" Even she could hear the clear disappointment in her voice, and she blushed.

"Really." Despite his stern tone, his eyes still locked on the exposed skin not hidden by her crossed arms. "I'm about to turn the trip along the timeline into a bullet train, so it's time to sleep. Want the bathroom first? When you're done, I need to shower." He rubbed a hand over his face, frowning at the black residue still clinging from the fire.

After studying him for a second, she pushed herself away from the wall. Her shirt was halfway across the room where she'd tossed it, so she slipped around Ian and hurried over to retrieve it. Instead of pulling it back on, she just held it in front of her chest.

"Need something to sleep in?" Ian asked. Even though they were separated by several feet, he still looked as intense as when they'd been locked together. "You can borrow one of my T-shirts."

"That's okay." For some reason, he seemed disappointed by that. Giving him a baffled look, she took a backward step toward the stairs. "I'll just sleep in my clothes." Although Ian seemed to accept that, she was curious. "Did you *want* me to wear your shirt to bed?"

"Yeah." He advanced a couple of steps, and she retreated, keeping a semisafe distance between them.

"Why?"

"Why?" he repeated, cocking his head. He paused, as if considering it. "I don't know. I just like the thought of you in my shirt."

"Huh." It was her turn to pause. "Is that a normal thing, or just a strange quirk of yours?"

His laugh sounded a little choked. "I don't know. I could do a survey of the guys at the station if you want, though."

"No!" she blurted, then flushed when he laughed again. "Don't you dare mention this to them."

"I wouldn't." Taking several quick steps forward, he closed the gap between them before she realized what he was doing. He kissed her lightly on the nose. "I was just teasing. Go change."

"Okay." She turned but hesitated. "I'll take one of your shirts."

"Yeah?" At the pleased hum in his voice, her blush deepened, but it also made her happy.

"Yeah. Now that we're…dating, I think it's my responsibility to humor your fetishes, as long as they don't get too weird."

"Fetishes?" Picking up his abandoned shirt, he held a corner and snapped it across her seat. Even though it didn't hurt, she yelped and hopped away from the fabric whip, quickly darting toward the stairs as he chased her.

When she was safely inside the bathroom with the closed door between her and her pursuer, she realized she was actually giggling. Rory didn't remember ever *giggling* before in her life. It was actually kind of fun to act like a silly, giggly girl. Hugging herself, she leaned against the door and smiled. With everything that had been happening with Billy and Rave and Julius, she hadn't really had a moment just to enjoy what was developing between her and Ian. Worries started to crowd her brain at the thought, but she shook them off. She could stress about everything tomorrow. For now, for once, she was going to be happy.

Chapter 21

"How are you still tired?" Ian asked, a baffled expression on his face as he watched her yawn for the fifth time in two minutes. "You slept for ten hours."

"It was eight, and I have lots of missed sleep to make up," she explained, interrupting her own words with yet another yawn. "You don't have to stay with me, you know."

"I know." Despite his words, Ian still matched her steps as they trudged through the snow away from the chicken coop. Jack danced in excited circles around them. "I want to. Besides, I need to get back on a non-vampire schedule. Next shift, I'm on days."

"That must be hard." She stopped abruptly for a moment to avoid tripping over Jack. He galloped away, and she started walking again. "Switching back and forth like that."

Ian shrugged. "We have four days to adjust. I'd rather do that than work only days or only nights."

"Aren't you tired at all?" She eyed his face in the weak light. The sun had disappeared behind the mountains, leaving only a gray dimness.

"I could sleep a little more," he admitted.

Rory interpreted that as manly man speak for "I'm still exhausted but won't admit it."

As they climbed the back steps, he asked, "Are you opening the shop tomorrow?"

"Yes." She dug out her keys from her pocket and unlocked the dead bolts. As soon as Ian caught the edge of the door, Rory moved to disarm the alarm. "I'm tempted to keep it closed one more day so I can clean"—they both glanced around the still-bloodied back room—"but I've been shut down too many days already."

"I can help you clean tomorrow," he offered.

"Just what you want to do on your day off," she mocked, heading straight for the bookshelf hiding the steel door. "Scrubbing brain matter off the walls."

"What I want to do"—he'd done that thing again, where he snuck up behind her and spoke quietly into her ear—"is to stay with you. I don't care what I have to do to get that. I'm fine with dealing with biohazards if I can do it with you close by."

Flushing, she ducked her chin and concentrated on punching in the correct code. It was harder than it should've been. Rory wondered if this mixture of giddiness and shyness was normal. "Lock the back door, would you?"

"Already done." His breath tickled the edge of her ear, and she hunched a shoulder as goose bumps prickled her skin.

To her relief—and disappointment—the last of the locks gave way, and she escaped through the steel door. It was only a brief respite from her tumultuous feelings, since Ian followed her.

"I'll get the lock," he said, turning back to the door.

She didn't argue. Instead, she scampered down the stairs, needing a second alone to compose herself. In the kitchen, she leaned her forehead against the wall and took a deep breath. She didn't recognize this fluttery, needy twit she'd become, and she wasn't sure what to think. Practical, straightforward Rory was someone with whom she was comfortable. Swoony, googly-eyed Rory, not so much.

"You okay?"

"Yeah." Pushing away from the wall, she headed for the fridge. "I'm going to feed Jack. Did you need anything?" After the huge meal they'd just had at his place, she would be surprised if he was hungry again.

"I'm good."

When he yawned loudly, she gave him a narrowed-eyed look. "Don't start." Rory bit back her own, answering yawn. "It's catching."

He grinned. "Sorry." As she put Jack's food in a bowl and set it on the floor, Ian remained quiet. There was a weight to the silence, though, that made her look at him curiously.

"What?" she finally asked.

"Can I sleep in the pink bed? We can even set up the bunny wall again."

Rory forced a scowl, even though she really wasn't annoyed. Having him in her bed had felt cozy and comforting. She'd expected sharing a bed would've been weird and sleep-disrupting, but it was nice—*really* nice—having Ian with her while she slept. "I suppose it's the least I can do if you're going to be scrubbing disgusting things off my walls tomorrow."

"Darn straight." A small smile played around his mouth as he leaned his shoulders against the wall. "So what do you do in the evenings, since you don't have a TV?"

She shrugged. She felt a little awkward standing in front of the fridge, so she imitated his stance and leaned back against it. "Depends on what needs doing. I'll clean and oil my own guns, or do bookkeeping stuff for the shop. Sometimes I'll just mess around on the internet, clean the house, cook, read, sew…whatever."

When he pushed off the wall and stalked toward her, she froze. If he were ever to attack her, she'd be a goner for sure, since he seemed to erase all her flight-or-fight instincts. He stood in front of her, too close as usual, and caught her arm gently at the elbow. His hand traced the length of her forearm, across her wrist, and finally tangled his fingers with her own.

Stepping back, he tugged her with him. Rory followed, as if she were the rat to his Pied Piper. His eyes stayed focused on hers as he drew her into the living room toward the couch. "You still tired?" he asked.

"Uh…no." With her heart pounding as it was, sleepiness was the last thing she felt.

As if he could read her thoughts, he smiled, a wicked and slightly smug tilt of his mouth. "Good."

Ian sat, pulling her down beside him. Her heart started pounding in anticipation of what was to come. Now that she'd experienced what it was like to make out with Ian, she wanted him, wanted that closeness.

Instead of kissing her, though, Ian just sat back against the couch, stroking his thumb over her hand. "This is nice, just having a minute to breathe. Lately, I feel like we're either in the middle of a crisis or exhausted from the aftermath."

At the word "breathe," Rory did, exhaling the air she hadn't realized she'd been holding. Her shoulders settled against the back of the couch as she relaxed. "It is," she said. "Nice, I mean."

"Want to go to Levi's after the shop closes tomorrow night?" He stretched out his socked feet and got comfortable. With a gentle tug, he pulled her against his side. She slowly relaxed against him. Releasing her hand, he wrapped an arm around her shoulders and closed his eyes.

Once her heartbeat settled a little, she recalled the question he'd just asked. "Um, I don't know. Everyone will be staring and crawling into our booth and asking questions. I mean, even before everything happened, we still had half the restaurant at our table."

"True," he agreed without opening his eyes. "Might be good to get it over with, though. Just deal with everyone at once while we eat some good barbecue."

She made a noncommittal sound. Eating in the midst of those rapacious eyes and needling questions sounded a little hellish to her. Ian was right, though—sooner or later, whether it was at the post office or grocery store or coffee shop, the citizens of Simpson would corner her. At least at Levi's, she'd have Ian at her back. "Let's see how we feel tomorrow evening."

From the way his grunt sounded, he was more than halfway to sleeping. Soon, his breathing changed, grew deeper and slightly louder, and his arm weighted more heavily on her shoulders. Rory melted against his side, turning slightly to get more comfortable. He was angled into the corner of the couch, and she curled against him, resting her hand in the middle of his chest and her cheek in the hollow beneath his shoulder.

His heart beat under her palm, slow and strong. His chest rose with each breath, lifting her hand and head with it. She smiled. Although she'd never been to either coast, she imagined that was how it felt to be brought up and lowered by ocean waves. Soothed by the motion, Rory didn't even have to mentally fieldstrip any guns in order to fall asleep.

Rave and Billy stood by her bed, looking down at her paralyzed form.

"Poison or bullet?" Billy asked in a conversational tone.

"Shoot her." Rave had cloudy, dead-man's eyes. "I want to watch the bitch bleed."

Rory woke and jumped to her feet in the same jolt.

"What's wrong?" Ian was standing next to her almost instantly, his voice sounding wide-awake.

"Nothing." She was sweating and breathing hard. There was no way to control the perspiration, but she made an effort to slow her inhalations, counting to four before she allowed the air to escape. "Just a bad dream. Sorry."

"Sh—oot." He blew out a hard breath and wrapped his arms around her in a hug. She must have startled him, because she could feel his heart pounding at twice its normal pace. "No need to be sorry. You couldn't help having a nightmare. After everything, it'd be strange if you were dreaming about ponies and ice cream."

Pulling away from him enough that she could see his face, she raised her eyebrows. "Ponies and ice cream? Is that what your happy dreams are about?"

He grinned, his eyes lighting with that wicked spark. "Nah. My best dreams are more along the lines of—"

"Okay!" she interrupted, having a feeling his words would result in some serious blushing if she allowed him to finish. "What time is it?"

"Without windows, it could be noon, for all we know." He glanced at his watch. "Or it could be one in the morning."

Tipping her head to the side to stretch her neck, she winced when vertebrae popped. "Probably good that I woke us before we spent the whole night on the couch. We'd have been stiff and sore tomorrow."

His hands slid up her back and landed on her shoulders, where he began to knead the tight muscles.

"Oh!" She was startled at first, but then she relaxed into the massage. "Oh, that feels really good."

"You sound surprised," he said, his voice husky. "Haven't you ever had a shoulder rub before?"

Rory closed her eyes and leaned back into his touch. He hit a knot at the base of her neck, which made her jump and then moan in pleasure as it loosened. "No. It hurts a little, but it feels incredible at the same time. No wonder people pay for this."

"Sometime when it's not the middle of the night, I'll have you lie down on the bed so I can do it right." The heat in his voice sent a shock of desire through her, so strong it startled her, and she pulled away. His hands slipped off her shoulders, and she swallowed a regretful whimper at the loss.

"Right," she said, jittery with want and not knowing how to act. All her feelings were so new and huge and overwhelming, and she knew she was screwing up everything. "It's night. So…bed?"

"Bed." His hands returned to her shoulders, this time to turn her toward the bedroom. She resisted begging him to resume the shoulder rub.

Ian headed for the bathroom, so she quickly changed

into pajamas. As she automatically headed toward "her" side of the bed, he returned, stripped down to his underwear. Rory averted her eyes so she wouldn't stare. She was struck by how easy it was to fall into the pattern of sleeping with Ian. It had just been a short time ago that the idea of even bringing him into her underground bunker had scared the bejesus out of her, and now it felt like he fit. Crawling under the covers, she glanced over to where he was stacking pillows between them.

"Don't worry about it," she said, rolling onto her side.

"Yeah?"

"Yeah."

"Okay." He sounded pleased as he tossed the few pillows aside. "I won't try anything."

Her face flamed, and her throat locked, keeping her from responding. To her relief, he didn't seem to expect an answer. When he reached to turn off the light, his muscles were clearly delineated under his skin, and she watched them stretch and flex with his movement. Swallowing hard, she forced herself to turn over onto her other side so her back faced the mesmerizing show.

Darkness settled over the room, and the bed moved as he settled. "Good night."

"'Night."

After several minutes of silence, Rory's eyes were beginning to close again. As she drifted into a half sleep, she vaguely felt him shift before a wall of heat pressed against her back. It felt wonderful. She wiggled a little closer to that source of warmth and heard his breath catch. His hand touched her waist almost tentatively, and she went still, suddenly wide-awake. When he started to withdraw, she grabbed his hand and held it in place.

"Ror, are you sure?"

"Positive." Her voice shook just a little.

"I can wait." Despite the words, his fingers curled around her hip. "We don't have to do this tonight."

"I don't want to wait anymore." Her heart crashed against her ribs in a flurry of nervous excitement. The feel of him pressed against her back and his hand smoothing over the curve of her hip made her feel a strange combination of safe and cared for and so aroused she didn't think she could wait another second.

Twisting her head, she kissed him before her nerve could fail her and self-consciousness return. It was rough and clumsy for only a split second before they both found their footing and the kiss smoothed into a thing of beauty. There was a difference to this kiss, though. It was more intense, as if they both knew the decision had been made. She turned onto her back, and he moved above her, never breaking their contact.

He kept it at kissing, though, catching her hands when they attempted to stray. The anticipation was killing her, shredding her patience and her confidence. In a state of frazzled nerves, she bit down on his bottom lip. He jerked and then moaned, pressing her back against the bedding, his kiss turning frenzied.

A wave of need rushed over her, drowning out any rational thoughts. He knelt, his knees braced on either side of her waist, and lifted the hem of her pajama shirt. Without hesitating, she raised her upper body and then her arms, allowing Ian to pull off her top. When the cool air hit her bare breasts, she paused, testing her own response. Although she should've been freaked, she realized she was mostly feeling relieved. She had wanted Ian for so long; no amount of inexperience could make her retreat now. This was happening, and Rory was glad.

Her nerve bolstered by that realization, she reached for the waistband of Ian's boxer briefs.

"Whoa." His hands covered hers, stilling them. "That's kind of like the abandon-all-hope-ye-who-enter-here point, understand?"

Although she was too tense to actually laugh, her snort was amused. "Understood."

Watching her carefully, he slowly lifted his hands. She tugged down the fabric to his thighs, and the heat in his eyes flared red-hot.

"Okay," he breathed, and then he was kissing her again.

If she'd thought he was out of control earlier, he was beyond restraint now. Without moving his ravenous mouth from hers, he stretched out on top of her again. Rory braced for his weight, but Ian caught himself on his hands before he crushed her.

The kissing continued, and, at one point, Rory realized that he'd removed the remainder of both of their clothes without her noticing. She had a moment of self-consciousness at being naked beneath him, but that slid away quickly. His hands were everywhere, leaving their usual trail of fire. Hers were locked around his neck, holding on too tightly to explore.

He kissed his way over her sternum and between her breasts. Her body vibrated with tension, waiting for him to go left or right, to find the aching center of either of her breasts. Instead, he went directly to her belly button and she made a disappointed sound.

"Did I miss something?" he asked with put-on innocence.

"Yes," she said, tugging at his hair in a futile effort to make him shift to her needy breasts.

He laughed, an almost soundless, husky chuckle. "Where did I miss? Here?" Dropping a light kiss on her lower ribs, he looked at her teasingly. She resisted the urge to growl in frustration.

Releasing his head as an idea occurred to her, she brushed her hands over her chest. "Here." Her voice came out throaty and unintentionally sexy. Her breasts lit with pleasure, and she ran her fingers over their peaks again, arching into her own touch.

"Rory," Ian hissed, right before sucking a nipple into his mouth. He definitely wasn't teasing anymore. His touch was so much more intense than her own. Burying her fingers in his short, unruly black hair again, she pulled him tighter to her, completely unable to control the hungry noises she made.

Pushing himself up so he hovered above her, he stared down at her. "God, Rory. You're so beautiful, so perfect."

Flushing under the compliments, she couldn't manage a response beyond an awkward smile. His attentions had left her worked up and able to think about only one thing. After a gentle but thorough kiss, he left her for a minute to dig a condom from a wallet in the pocket of his abandoned pants, but his weight was pressing her into the mattress again before she could even get chilled.

This is it, she thought, bracing herself, but he just started kissing her again, as if he had all the time in the world. Supporting his weight on one elbow, he used his other hand to explore, finding all the places that made her skin ignite.

By the time his fingers slipped between her legs, she was sweating and squirming and more than ready. Still, though, he kept his touch careful. Rory began to worry that he was *too* relaxed. How could he be kissing her in that leisurely way while she was ready to explode? She turned her head away, and he pulled back so he could look at her.

"What's wrong?"

She met his eyes—his heavy-lidded, passion-filled, smoldering eyes—and her worries instantly dissolved. It was obvious he was just as excited as she was, but he was being patient for her sake. "Nothing. I'm just… I'm ready."

"Sure?" he asked, gravel roughening his voice, and she felt a flare of last-minute nerves and doubt. He waited, though, watching her evenly, until she nodded. Then his eyes lit with happiness and heat, and he carefully entered her.

It hurt at first. She stiffened, and Ian froze in place, sweating and wild-eyed, until she gave him a shaky, "Okay." Then he moved, holding her gaze the entire time, and it was painful, and then less painful, and then just strange feeling, and then it was almost…nice. He shifted positions slightly, and then it started feeling *really* nice.

"Oh!" The pleasure startled her. Ian paused at her outburst to study her face more closely. He must've seen her enjoyment, because he bared his teeth in a grin and started moving again. Heat grew in her belly as his mouth descended on hers. She dug her fingers into the muscles connecting his shoulders to his neck as she returned the kiss fiercely. Why had she waited so long to feel this amazing connection with Ian?

He pulled back again so he could watch her. With each minute change of speed or angle, he examined her expression, as if learning what she liked and what she didn't. Having him direct such focused attention on her, showing that he cared so much how she felt, was intoxicating. Then the pleasure increased, stealing all her conscious thoughts.

The sensations started to build, growing and growing until her skin couldn't contain them any longer. It felt so good, so intense, that it frightened her a little, but Ian held her eyes as her pleasure sharpened to a peak. Despite his reassuring gaze, the explosion that radiated through her took her by surprise, making her shout and clutch him until she slowly returned to earth.

He finished just after she did, and it was her turn to watch his expression as he came. It was a powerful feeling, to make someone experience such intense pleasure. He rested his forehead on the mattress above her shoulder, and she massaged his scalp as he panted for breath.

After a short time, he lifted his head so he could meet her eyes. "You okay?" he asked.

Rory smiled. "That was fun."

He gave a startled bark of laughter and then rolled them so she was on top of him, straddling his waist. "Good."

Feeling extra naked and exposed, she tried to cross her arms over her chest. Ian caught her hands before she could and kissed both palms, one at a time.

"Don't hide," he told her sincerely. "You're perfect."

She snorted. "I'm not even close to perfect."

"You're perfect," he insisted, pulling on her hands until she leaned down for a kiss. When they finally came up for air, he met her eyes. "I've thought so ever since the day I gave you that cupcake."

Giving him a shy smile, Rory said, "You're pretty perfect yourself. I'll never forget that cupcake."

"Yeah?"

"Yeah." Unable to hold his gaze anymore, she dropped her eyes to his throat. "Why do you think I like the color pink so much?"

When he was quiet, she snuck a glance at his expression. His eyes were on fire. "I fu—freaking love you, Rory."

Her throat locked before she could return the sentiment, and then he was kissing her desperately, as if he would never be able to stop. She didn't mind—an eternity of kissing Ian was acceptable to her.

Chapter 22

"I've got this," Ian told her the next day, blocking the doorway to the back room. "Just stay up front and run the shop."

Setting her jaw, Rory said, "That's not right. I have to at least help."

"No, you don't." Using his bulk, he moved her back a few steps. "Your nightmares are bad enough already. Besides"—he looked over her shoulder at something behind her—"I have help."

"Hey, Ror," Soup said, and she spun around to face him. Her argument with Ian had distracted her enough that she hadn't even heard the beep of the door alarm. Soup was grinning as he crossed the shop. When he reached her, he slung an arm around her shoulders and pulled her into a sideways hug. "I'm here and ready to clean. Put me to work."

She opened her mouth, but before she could say anything, the door opened again, and Junior bounced through it. "Morning, Rory! You're looking fine today."

"Watch it," growled Steve, who'd followed the other man at a more sedate pace.

"It was a *compliment*," Junior said with an exaggerated sigh, even as he kept his eye on Steve's big mitts.

"There's a fine line between your compliments and disrespect," Steve grumbled before looking at her. "Hey, Rory."

She blinked at him. "Between taking care of my animals, and now this, I'm not going to get out of watching your kids, am I?"

He gave her a rare grin. "Nope. Don't worry, though. The sitter usually survives."

"I'm not worried about *my* survival," she muttered, but her words were drowned out by the guys' chatter and Al's entrance. "Is everyone coming?"

"Everyone who's not on duty," Ian said, his voice a little tight. "Soup, if you don't get your fu—flipping arm off of her right now, I'm going to rip it off and beat you with it."

All the guys, including Soup, laughed, but he lifted his arm off her shoulders and even took a few steps away from her for good measure, holding his hands in a "don't hurt me" gesture.

As they moved toward the back-room door, Rory started to protest again. "I really shou—"

Ian's short, hard kiss stopped her midword. The men hooted and catcalled, but she barely heard them. He pulled back and grinned at her stunned face before disappearing into the back room with his crowd of firefighters. She stood frozen in place.

"Whoa," she muttered, her fingers touching her mouth. Finally shaking off her Ian-induced stupor, she turned to start her day.

The shop was busy. Rory figured it was a mixture of the nice weather, the shop's hiatus, and morbid curiosity that brought in what seemed like the entire population of Simpson to look at guns. Within just a few hours, all her patience and saleswoman skills had been sucked dry. When the front door opened yet again, her head whipped around so she could glare at the newest arrival. Once she saw it was Chief Early, her expression softened into something that wasn't quite a smile—she'd lost that ability an hour earlier—but was as close as she was going to get at the moment.

"Chief," she called over the buzz of chatter coming from the other customers. "Are you here to check out that Peacemaker?"

He made his way over to the counter before speaking at a normal volume. "Actually, I'm going to help clean up in back, but since I'm here..."

Her frown returned. "You don't have to clean, Chief."

"Sure I do." Leaning one arm on the counter, he grinned at her, unfazed by her scowl. "I never want to be the type of chief who sits back and makes my men do all the dirty work. Besides, I know that you've been the reason Doris has let me in the door after I bought a new gun—several times, in fact. I'm happy to do this for you, Rory."

Embarrassment made her cling to her glower. "If I didn't encourage you to buy guns, Doris wouldn't have a reason to toss you out onto the lawn. You don't need to do this, Chief."

"Yes, I do." With another quick, completely unoffended smile, he headed for the back.

"Well, you're getting an extremely discounted price on that Colt, then!" she yelled after him. Early waved as he closed the door behind him, and she stared at the spot where he'd disappeared. When an easily identifiable smell wafted toward her, she sniffed at the air.

"Are they painting?" she asked out loud, wondering if she'd go into the back room at the end of the day to find a completely remodeled space. That wouldn't be a bad thing. Neither was having a shop full of guys who would have her back if necessary, she admitted to herself. Everything that had happened with the attempted burglary, and Rave and Billy, had her on edge. It was reassuring to have reinforcements nearby, just in case.

"Um, Rory?" She reluctantly turned her attention to Phil. To her surprise, he didn't have a new trophy girlfriend hanging off his arm this time. "Wilt keeps telling me I should replace my Glock with a Springfield XD. What do you think?"

"Well, first off, I think that it's good you're concentrating on arming yourself rather than the blond of the month. As far as the Springfield goes, it is a good gun—reliable, really smooth trigger, and a pleasure to shoot. The most important question, though"—she unlocked the display and pulled out the XD, placing it in its case—"is which *you* like better." Rory got out a Glock 22, as well, and pushed both cases toward him, along with two boxes of ammo. "It's a beautiful day. Go out to my range and kill some paper."

He grinned, his face lighting up at the thought of doing some shooting. Rory could relate. Following him out the front door, she pointed him toward the range and called for Jack. When he trotted toward her, she held the shop door open.

"C'mon, Jack," she said, and he bounded into the store, brushing against her legs on his way. Even though the dog would probably stay by his chickens, Rory would rather he not be roaming the property when someone was shooting. Jack immediately trotted over to his dog bed in the corner and lay down.

Dodging customers, she made her way over to the back-room door and pounded on it with her fist. When Junior stuck out his head, she told him, "The range will be hot in about five minutes. Could you let the guys know not to get excited when they hear gunfire?"

"Got it. I'll pass it on."

"Thanks." Rory attempted to peek around him, but Junior blocked her with his body. For a slight guy, he could sure make himself into a wall when he wanted. "How's it going in there?"

"Great." Still keeping his body in her line of sight, Junior closed the door before she could see anything.

"Excuse me," the male half of a couple she didn't recognize said. "Which gun would be best to take with us hiking, in case we run into a bear?"

"This one." Rory moved to the other side of the room, the couple following, and pulled it out of a display.

The man looked nonplussed. "Pepper spray?"

"It's the big can of the strong stuff, so it's called bear spray." She set it on the counter, since the customer didn't seem inclined to take it.

"I'd feel more comfortable with a gun."

"You wouldn't after the bear attacks you."

"I'm a good shot," he huffed. "I'd hit it before it reached us."

"Doesn't mean the bear will go down before it can do some damage." Rory nudged the bear-spray canister closer to the couple's side of the counter. "When bullets are fired, there's a greater chance of injury to the humans involved than when bear spray is used. U.S.

Fish and Wildlife even did a study. You know what's even more effective?"

"What?" the woman asked.

"Avoiding bears altogether. They'll generally stay away from you as long as they know you're there. Make lots of noise when you hike. Don't rely on bear bells—they're not loud enough. And don't carry smelly food in your packs."

"If you stumble over an animal carcass," Grace Wiltshire piped up from across the room, "don't hang around to check it out. A bear or mountain lion might not be done with their dinner." Of course all the locals were listening. It was like Simpson television—and no one could ever resist tossing in their own two cents.

"You'll want to hike during the day," Bob, Grace's husband, added. "Wildlife is out and about between dusk and dawn, usually."

"Don't climb a tree to get away from one. Black bears are great climbers." At George Holloway's contribution, Rory looked at the big, bearded man in surprise. He rarely said more than two words to her. If he wanted to handle a particular firearm, he'd generally point and grunt.

"Since all of you seem to have this information session handled," Rory said, not at all reluctant to hand over the customers to the locals' care, "I'm going to order lunch for my volunteer work crew."

"What are they doing back there?" Bob asked immediately, as if Rory mentioning the firemen working in her back room opened the floor for questions.

"Making some improvements," she hedged before picking up the phone. To forestall any questions, she kept it pressed to her ear as she looked up the phone number for Levi's.

After she tapped in the number for the restaurant, the female half of the couple brought the bear spray to the register, while her significant other sulked on the other side of the room. Rory rang up the spray while giving Bonnie her order. She hesitated, glanced at the back room door, and then doubled the amount of food. If all the firemen ate as much as Ian, then she would need a mountain of barbecue to feed the group.

Once the couple left, the other customers gradually made their way out of the shop. A few bought odds and ends, and George got three-inch Magnum shells, but most shuffled out empty-handed. Rory wasn't too surprised, since she'd figured most of the people there wanted information, not anything she was selling.

As George paid for his shells, Rory asked, "How are you liking your Saiga-12?"

His grunt sounded positive.

"Did you do some modifications on it?"

This time, the grunt was accompanied by a nod. His earlier loquaciousness had apparently been short-lived. Despite his usual silence, Rory liked George. According to local gossip, his father had been as much a hermit as Rory's parents. Except for his volunteer work with Search and Rescue, George didn't seem to have any social interactions—no friends or girlfriends, at least as far as any of the townspeople knew. Rory didn't really pay attention to the gossip. She just knew that George seemed like a kind man who really liked guns. That was good enough for her.

"Bring it in sometime. I'd like to see what you've done."

She chose to interpret his wordless response to that as an "okay."

"The price has shot up on those, so you were smart to get it when you did." She handed him his receipt and the bagged shells. "Guess you're a trendsetter."

Although it was hard to tell beneath his beard, Rory was pretty sure a corner of his mouth ticked up for a second. She was rather proud she'd managed to get George Holloway to smile.

They'd eaten everything.

Rory blinked at the empty containers spread over the counter that had held an obscene amount of food less than an hour earlier. It was a good thing she'd doubled the order. She had a feeling that she could have tripled it and the guys still would have consumed everything. Since she still wasn't allowed in the back room, they'd spread out around the front of the shop, sitting on stools or the floor to eat.

An arm wrapped around her from behind, and she resisted her instinctual reaction to drive an elbow into the belly resting against her back. When Ian's voice spoke quietly in her ear, she was glad she hadn't assaulted him.

"Did you get anything to eat?" he asked.

"Barely." She stared at the empty cartons, still flabbergasted by the crew's ability to eat. "I had to dodge stabbing forks, and I think Junior tried to bite me when I reached for the mac and cheese."

Overhearing this, Junior winked at her. "I'll bite you anytime, baby."

As Rory felt Ian's body stiffen, Steve whacked the

back of Junior's head. Thrown off balance by the unexpected blow, Junior had to stumble forward a few steps so he didn't fall on his face.

"Hey!" he yelled, indignant, but Steve just shook his head.

"You're lucky it was me and not Walsh who did that," Steve told him. "He'd have used a two-by-four."

"Or a crowbar," Ian growled. Although the others chuckled, Rory was pretty sure that Ian wasn't joking.

"So, how's it going in there?" She jerked her head toward the still-closed back-room door.

"It's shaping up nicely," Al said, wiping his mouth with a paper napkin. "I think you'll be happy with it."

"I'm sure I will." This confirmed her impression that they were doing a full remodel, rather than the general hose-down she'd initially expected. "You guys didn't need to do all this."

"Of course we did, little sister." Soup patted her on the head. "You'll be right there with us when we help Junior move, or paint the LT's house. It's just what we do."

"Well, thank you." The heat at her back felt nice, and she leaned into Ian before she realized what she was doing. When she tried to pull away, he tightened his grip, so she relaxed again, accepting that she was participating in her first PDA—well, second, after the earlier kiss.

"Back to work," the chief barked, gathering paper plates. "Thanks for lunch, Rory."

There was a chorus of thanks from the other guys.

"I'll clean up." This time when Rory pulled away from Ian, he let her go. She took the stack of plates away from Early. "It's the least I can do."

As the other men disappeared into the back room, Ian hung back. "Sounded busy out here earlier. How's the grand reopening going?"

"Good." She shrugged. "I do better with a few customers than a big crowd, though. I tend to get…cranky."

With a laugh, he brushed back a strand of hair that had escaped her ponytail. "It's part of your charm."

When she just rolled her eyes at that, he laughed again. "Better get back to work." Before she realized what he was doing, he leaned in and kissed her. She immediately worried that she must taste like the barbecue she'd just eaten, and then all rational thought dissolved. By the time he pulled away, her brain was fuzzy.

Judging by his heavy-lidded eyes, he was in a similar state, although he had the presence of mind to back away from her. If it had been up to Rory, they would've spent the entire afternoon kissing, while the other firemen finished up the back room.

"See you later," she said, giving an embarrassingly goofy wave as he pulled open the door.

"Later." Ian imbued the single word with so much suggestive promise that she blushed. With a grin and wink, he was gone.

After watching the closed door for much too long, she shook off her silly giddiness and went to work cleaning up the remains of lunch. As she separated the burnable trash from the plastic, she tried to think of something other than Ian. It didn't work. Her crush had swollen to elephant size, and she was fully in its grip.

When the front door opened, she looked up with relief. She'd rather deal with customers than her own soppy thoughts. Once she recognized the two men who'd just entered, however, she changed her mind.

"Anderson," she greeted the first man, hoping her poker face was hiding how much she disliked him and his brother, Wilson King. They were obviously related, with the same pale skin and receding hairlines. Anderson was the older of the two, and slightly...*more* than his sibling—a little taller, broader, more outgoing, smarter. Wilson seemed content to trail behind in his brother's shadow.

"Rory." Anderson's eyes swept the shop with a covetous intensity that made her uncomfortable. "Heard you had some excitement here a few days ago."

She made a noncommittal sound before asking, "Can I help you with something?"

"Yeah." King's pale blue eyes met hers. "We were hoping to take a look at that back room of yours."

"Not sure why you'd want to see that." Leaning on the newly cleaned counter, she feigned a casual stance. "Besides, it's out of commission today. I'm getting some remodeling done."

The lines on his face sharpened with irritation. "Everyone knows you keep your 'special' inventory back there."

"Not sure what 'everyone' is talking about." She kept her voice even, her words slow. "That's just where I do my cleaning and repair work."

His jaw tensed and then relaxed as he forced a smile. "I heard you're not going to be doing business with the Riders anymore. I thought we could come to an... arrangement. Maybe we could help to fill that gap."

"There's no gap." That came out with more of a snap

than she'd planned, so she took a breath and mimicked his fake smile. "Were you looking for something in particular? If you don't see it here"—she gestured around the shop—"I can probably order it." Since there was no way either King brother would pass the background check required to purchase a firearm, she was safe from having one of her guns end up in Anderson or Wilson's meth-dealing paws.

Anderson didn't even glance around at the displays. "I was thinking about something a little more…ghostly."

Keeping a blank expression locked in place, she shook her head. "What you see out here is what you get."

"I see," he said, biting off the end of each word. He wasn't even trying to hide his fury now. "You'll deal with MC trash but not with us."

Rory hid her flinch. It seemed like she hadn't even dealt with one threat before another came crawling out of the woodwork. The King brothers were bad news. With them as an enemy, there'd be nowhere safe left in Simpson. "Like I said, what I have available is out here."

"Dumb bitch. You're picking the wrong side. From what I hear, Billy's losing it, the Riders are a fucking mess, and the members are turning on each other like a pack of starving dogs. We're picking up all the pieces they're dropping. Soon, we're going to be the most powerful men in Field County. You really don't want to piss us off." With a menacing look, he stormed to the door. After Wilson stared at her for a few seconds too long, he followed his brother. When the door banged shut behind Wilson, she let out a breath and flicked on her computer screen so she could watch the camera footage of the parking lot. The two men got into a Jeep and left abruptly, the tires flinging melting snow and gravel behind them as they roared through the open gates. Long after they'd disappeared, Rory sat and watched the empty parking lot, her stomach churning. With an abrupt motion, she pushed the power button on the monitor, darkening the screen.

It was probably hypocritical of her, but she'd had no problem selling to the Riders before the burglary. Although she'd known they weren't saints, their criminal actions had been vague and unconfirmed. The King brothers, on the other hand, would never leave her shop with one of her guns in their hands if she could help it. Meth was a dirty business, and she didn't want to be responsible for arming the brothers. She just needed to figure out a way to remain neutral.

Jumpy from the Kings' visit, she started when Phil barreled through the front door, his face glowing from the still-brisk temperature and the joy of shooting.

"The Springfield is awesome, Rory."

"Obviously." She glanced at the clock. "You've been out there for almost two hours."

"I came in when you were picking up food and grabbed some different ammo," he said, putting some empty boxes by the register. "I wanted to see if I could get it to jam."

"Did you?"

"Nope. I put five hundred rounds though it, and it just kept firing."

"What'd you think?"

"It's great. I like the trigger even better than my Glock."

"You going to make the switch, then?"

"Nope."

"No?" She eyed him with slight surprise. "I thought you were in love."

"It's a nice gun." Pushing the Springfield's case toward her with some reluctance, he shrugged. "My Glock's a nice gun, too. I trust it. I know I could drop it in a mud puddle, and it'd still fire. We have a relationship. I like how comfortable and familiar it feels in my hand. If I replaced it with the Springfield, I feel like I'd be leaving a faithful, reliable wife of many years. How would I know that the new woman—as great as she seems—would stand behind me like my wife would? No." He gave the case a final, slightly mournful pat. "I'll stick with my Glock."

Sliding the Springfield's case out from under Phil's possessive hand, she set it behind the counter to clean later, once her back room was hers again. "I think you've made the right choice for you, Phil. I commend you on seeing past the seductive new gun and sticking with your faithful partner."

"Thanks." He gave her a quick grin. "By the way, I took your advice and asked Donna out."

Rory blinked, pausing in the middle of ringing up the ammo he'd used. "I advised you to ask out Donna?" It had been a rough few weeks, but she didn't remember giving any relationship advice to anyone. That would be like a turtle giving tips on how to high-jump.

"Not Donna specifically," he clarified. "You said to quit trying to turn the women I date into something they're not. Donna moved here from Connor Springs a few months ago. She's hot, *and* she can outshoot me."

"Sounds like the perfect woman," Rory said, a little thrown by the conversation. Was he expecting more relationship advice? She hoped not. She hadn't even known she'd given the first batch.

"She really is." Phil's grin grew dreamy around the edges. "Thanks for giving me that push."

"You're welcome?" Clearing her throat, she gave him his total.

Phil paid and left, thanking her another several times. When the door closed behind him, her breath left her lungs in a relieved rush. The silence of the empty front of the shop was wonderful.

For a while, she cleaned the displays and counters. The quiet was occasionally broken by thuds, swearing, and laughter coming from the back room, making her curiosity grow until she was itching to sneak a peek through the door. Rory managed to resist the urge, and she redoubled her cleaning efforts.

The front door swung open, and, for the second time that afternoon, her smile died when she saw who entered. This time, it was Billy, Zup, and another Rider she didn't know by name. His ruddy, broad face looked familiar, though.

"Billy," she greeted flatly, resuming the faux-casual stance she'd taken when the King brothers were in the shop. It seemed to be the day for visits from dangerous men.

"Rory." Billy strode toward her, his face impassive. The other two silently spread out to other parts of the shop, checking out the displayed guns with exaggerated interest. Rory didn't like that. It was impossible to keep watching all three at once. This wasn't like when they used to come in to check out the back-room merchandise. They, even clueless Zup, were moving with a sense of purpose that scared her silly. Her heart beat too quickly, and she barely managed to keep her fear from showing on her face.

"Hey, guys!" she yelled, trying to keep her voice casual despite the volume. "Billy's here to visit!"

It wasn't even a full three seconds before Ian was charging through the door, followed by the other firemen. Zup and the unnamed Rider dropped their pretense of looking at the display cases and faced the six men. There were a few moments of stillness so tense that Rory half-expected a tumbleweed to roll through the shop.

"Billy." Ian was the first to break the silence. "What do you want?"

"Just came to talk to one of my suppliers, Ian," he said smoothly, holding his hands in a gesture of innocence. "Wanted to make sure there weren't any hard feelings because of all the recent…unpleasantness between us."

It was strange hearing words better suited to a politician coming out of Billy's mouth.

"There are," Ian said, crossing his arms across his chest. "Lots of hard feelings."

Zup shifted, drawing Rory's attention. "What are you doing?" she asked, making him turn in her direction.

"What?" he asked defensively, and her eyes narrowed.

"Did you just steal something?" She pushed away from the counter and started to circle around to the other side. Anger rushed through her, pushing aside the fear. What right did they have to invade her shop and try to take her guns, leaving her feeling scared and helpless?

"No!" He moved toward the door, holding his hands open to show they were both empty. "See? I didn't take anything. We'll just leave."

Backing toward the door as well, Billy shook his

head, feigning regret. "Guess we'll just have to find a new supplier."

"You do that," Rory said flatly, stopping her forward charge when Ian put his hand on her arm.

The third MC member was also heading for the door, and the Riders exited under seven pairs of watchful eyes. As soon as the door closed behind them, Rory leaned over the counter to turn on her monitor, twisting the screen so she and the firemen could watch the three figures hurry toward an SUV.

"They're in a rush," the chief muttered.

"What's he doing?" Soup asked, leaning closer to the screen, watching as Billy pulled something out of his pocket. "Is that a cell phone?"

"Isn't Billy the head honcho?" Al asked, also getting closer to the monitor. "I wonder who he's calling?"

The nameless Rider got into the driver's seat, reversing the SUV out of its parking spot within seconds.

"Everyone's flying out of here today," Rory muttered. Her stomach twisted with unease. The Riders' visit seemed strange and pointless, but Billy wouldn't have risked coming to her shop without a reason. She moved toward the area where Zup had been acting squirrelly. There was a Taser display there, but it didn't look disturbed.

Although…there was something off about it. Cocking her head, she took another couple of steps closer. The corner of a small box stuck out from behind the display. It hadn't been there before. "Why would he leave something…?"

Suddenly, everything clicked. The answer flashed in her brain, lit up with bright warning lights, but she couldn't get the words out fast enough.

"Out!" she yelled, whipping around to start shoving the guys toward the back, and closer, door. "Go! Billy's cell phone—move! Bomb!" She finally shouted the important word, but they weren't responding right. Unlike a normal group of people, the guys didn't panic and rush for the nearest exit. Instead, they all concentrated on getting everyone *else* out of danger first, and she found herself propelled forward until she was at the front of the pack and closest to the door.

Ian! her brain screamed. *Get Ian out!*

"Ian!" The terror in her voice echoed through the room, mixing with the shouts and commands from the guys. Hands and bodies pushed her toward the exit, and she fought them, trying to turn, unable to leave Ian behind. He'd just yanked her, kicking and screaming, from her self-imposed hermit shell. How could she return to life without him? "Ian!"

"I'm right behind you!" His voice, though tight with tension, eased the panic rushing through her. "Go, Rory! Now!"

Her zombie-drill training kicked in, and she automatically reached for the door. Just as she yanked it open, she remembered.

"Wait! We forgot Jack!" she yelled, twisting around to see him. Jack lifted his head from the dog bed where he'd returned after lunch, his belly full from all the bits of food the guys had slipped to him.

"Rory, go! Get out!" Ian's frantic voice shouted as her panic returned. She couldn't leave her dog, the last remaining member of her family, the one who'd almost given his life for hers three years ago. She couldn't run outside like a coward and allow her faithful companion to be blown to bits. Rory ducked around the men, dodging their well-meaning, grasping hands, until she was at the outside of the circle again.

"Everyone out!" the chief bellowed. "Go! Go! Go!" All the guys except Ian followed his command, rushing through the door in a well-ordered stream.

"Rory!" Ian yelled, reaching for her.

Twisting out of range, she slipped by him and ran toward the dog. "Jack!" He stood up and stretched. Panting with terror, Rory lunged for him, grabbing his collar and a handful of scruff, ignoring his yelp as she hauled him toward the exit. "C'mon, Jack!" she cried. Her breaths weren't coming out right, sounding perilously close to sobs. She didn't cry, though. Rory never cried. Making small noises that were definitely not sobs, she dragged her dog toward the door that suddenly seemed so far away.

Ian grabbed her from behind, his hands latching around her upper arms. He shoved her through the door. Pulling out of her grip, Jack jetted ahead, streaking through the back room and out the exterior door the guys had opened. Everything slowed, every movement of her legs felt like she was moving through thick syrup. Only her thoughts came in fast-forward, stupid thoughts like *please let Ian and Jack be okay* and *I don't want to die, not yet* and *please, God, I'd like to kiss Ian again, at least one more time*.

"Let's go!" the chief shouted from his position outside the back door.

Rory ran toward it, her muscles moving too slow but her heart racing too fast, feeling Ian pressing her from behind, urging her to increase her speed. She pushed, trying to go just a little faster, because Ian was behind her, and if she died, so did he, and she really, really didn't want Ian to die.

Just as her foot touched the porch, the world went blindingly bright.

Suddenly, Rory was flying.

Chapter 23

SHE FLOATED IN GRAY SPACE, NOT WANTING TO WAKE completely. If she did, she knew the dull pain throbbing around the edges of her consciousness would sharpen. The rise and fall of conversation was niggling at her, though, not letting her sink into total oblivion.

"...shouldn't all be in here." The female voice was unfamiliar.

"You are an angel to make an exception. Well, multiple exceptions."

Rory frowned. Was that Soup talking?

"I didn't see this," the unknown woman spoke again. "Just...stay quiet and don't touch anything."

There was a light thud of a door closing, and then a few seconds of silence before another, different whacking sound broke the stillness.

"No. Touching." That was definitely Steve.

"Ow!" And there was Junior. "I was just looking! I wasn't actually going to press that button. Besides, I'm a medical professional. I know what I'm doing!"

Despite the potential for pain, Rory decided she needed to wake completely, before Junior messed with something on the wrong machine and killed her. Her eyelids felt like they weighed a thousand pounds, but she managed to force them open a slit.

"Hey, Rory." Junior's face looked huge as he leaned

over her. "You're awake again. You going to stay with us this time?"

She swallowed against a dry throat and then rasped, "Quit pushing buttons."

Junior scowled. "I didn't touch anything! I was just looking!"

There was laughter behind him, and then Soup and Steve were leaning over her, too.

"How're you feeling?" Junior asked, his expression switching to a clinical competence that contrasted oddly with the goofiness of just seconds earlier.

"Head hurts." She checked in with her body parts. "Face hurts. Ribs hurt. Everything else hurts, but not as much."

"That fits." He smiled. "You have a concussion, a bruised jawbone, and a couple of cracked ribs. Ian landed on you pretty hard."

"Ian." Her whole body clenched, making everything hurt even more, but the pain didn't matter. "How's Ian?"

"He'll be fine," Junior soothed. Rory checked out Soup and Steve's expressions to get confirmation. Their calm nods allowed her to relax her muscles a little. "The doctors were more worried about your injuries than his. He's just a few rooms over."

"Can I see him?"

"Nursezilla wouldn't like us taking you on field trips," Soup said. "We're already pushing it by the three of us being in here with you. Let them check you out first, and then we'll see if we can round up some wheels for you."

"What happened?"

The guys exchanged glances. "Do you remember Billy and his boys visiting?" Soup asked.

"Yeah." The images of their rushed exit flipped through her mind. "Did everyone get out? Is anyone else hurt?"

"Yes and no." At Rory's startled expression, Junior clarified, "Everyone got out, and no one else has anything but minor injuries."

She narrowed her eyes, suspicious that they were sugarcoating things for her. "How minor?"

"Chief had a few nicks and scratches, but the explosion was mostly contained to the front of the shop, and Walsh blocked the shrapnel that came through the open door with his brick-house body," Soup explained.

"Shrapnel?" she repeated sharply. "Just how badly is Ian injured?"

"I'll be fine," a new, achingly familiar voice said from the doorway. "You were the one who kept losing consciousness on us."

Forgetting her own aches, she tried to shove herself to a sitting position, yelping when pain clamped around her chest.

"Easy," Steve ordered, stilling her with a broad hand on her shoulder. Once the initial pain eased, she pushed against his hold, and he helped her to a semisitting position.

Rory craned her neck to see around his bulky form. "Ian?"

"Here." Soup and Junior stepped back to give Ian a spot next to her bed. When he came into view, she ran anxious eyes over his face. Except for a red-and-purple lump on his forehead, he looked surprisingly unharmed.

"Hey," she said, lifting a hand toward him.

"Hey, Ror." He grabbed her fingers and locked them in the warmth of his.

"Nice gown, Beauty," Soup mocked, although he gave Ian's upper arm a squeeze at the same time. "I'm surprised you don't have a trail of doctors and nurses behind you, checking out the rear view."

With a scowl, Ian reached back with his free hand and twitched his hospital gown into place. Although his wince had barely crossed his face before he erased it, Rory still caught the pained grimace.

"Shrapnel?" she asked.

"I'm fine."

"Liar." She eyed him as he swayed slightly. "Sit before you fall on your face."

Steve moved a chair behind Ian, who lowered himself into it. By his expression and stiff posture, sitting wasn't much of an improvement to standing.

"What did you hit your head on?" she asked, checking out the goose egg on his forehead.

"Your head." He ran his thumb over the back of her hand. "Sorry. I was the cause of your concussion."

"And her bruised ribs," Junior added. "And, indirectly, her bruised jawbone, although that was mostly caused when her chin hit the ground. Your weight on her probably didn't help, though."

Steve grabbed Junior by the back of his shirt and hauled him toward the door. "We'll let you two have a minute," he said. "Soup." Steve jerked his head toward the door, and all three men filed out of the room.

"Bruised ribs?" Ian repeated when they were alone. "Ouch. Sorry for that, too."

"They'll heal." Although she started to shrug, she felt the pulling ache of the ribs in question, so she quickly returned her shoulders to their original position. "And don't apologize, when you took the brunt of the explosion for me."

He gave an aborted shrug very similar to hers. "As you said, I'll heal." He used his free hand to stroke a strand of hair out of her face. "You scared the hell out of me when you went back for the dog."

"Is Jack okay?"

"Yeah. Squirrel's taking care of him. And the chickens."

"Tell him thank you from me."

"I will." Ian kept his hand cupping her cheek.

"The shop's probably in pretty bad shape, huh?" Rory didn't want to ask, but she needed to know.

"I didn't see. Once the blast went off, I was focused on you."

A nurse with brown hair pulled back in a ponytail entered the room. "You're awake," the female voice from earlier said, "and *you*, Mr. Walsh, should not be out of your room." She gave Ian a stern look, but he just set his jaw and tightened his fingers around Rory's hand. "Those bandages need changing. C'mon. I'll escort you back."

Giving a final squeeze, Rory pulled her hand away from his. "Go on. We'll talk later."

With a grumpy huff, he pushed himself to his feet. Leaning over her bed, Ian brushed his lips over her cheek. "Later." As always, the one word was more of a promise than a standard good-bye. He wavered a little when he straightened, and the nurse reached to take his arm. He shook his head, refusing help.

As he headed for the door, Rory bit the inside of her cheek to hold back a gasp. His hospital gown gaped open, revealing a wide expanse of gauze pads covering the majority of his back. In several places, the white bandages were marred by red and yellow stains, as blood and other fluid seeped through the gauze. She stared until he reached the doorway, the nurse close behind him. When he turned, she forced down her horror at the extent of his injuries and smiled, lifting her hand in a small good-bye wave. The corners of his mouth quirked up in return, and he looked at her intently for a long moment before leaving.

Rory was dozing a few minutes later when the nurse returned, along with a couple of doctors. She was relieved that neither were the attractive blond doctor who'd cared for Julius after the fire. If that woman was around, Rory would have to sneak into Ian's room to stand guard so he wasn't molested in his sleep. Instead, there was a tall woman with steel-gray hair and a no-nonsense expression, as well as a round-cheeked, younger man.

They checked her and told her that, barring complications, she'd be free to go after a night of observation. As soon as she was alone, she slid out of bed, wrapping one arm around her sore ribs. The room tilted alarmingly when she first made it upright, as blood rushed and pounded through her brain.

After a few seconds, her body accustomed itself to standing, and she shuffled toward the door. A peek into the hall showed that it was clear of stern yet well-meaning firemen and nurses. Since there were no other rooms to her left, she turned right. The first room next to hers was empty. The second contained Chief Early and Al, so she knew she had the right place even before she saw Ian in the bed.

"Hey," she said, slipping into the room. The two standing firemen turned toward her, looking startled.

"Hey," Al said in surprise. "We were just about to go see you."

"Should you be out of bed?" the chief immediately demanded.

"Probably not." She gingerly made her way over to Ian's side. "But I figured if they really wanted me to stay in bed, they would've tied me to it."

Early frowned. "That could be arranged."

"Then Ian would just come to my room, and his wounds would open up again," she said, eyeing the new bandages covering his back. The white wasn't marred by any blood yet. Ian was on his stomach, his face turned toward her. When he made to prop himself up on his elbows, she pressed a hand to his uninjured shoulder. At the same time, she bent to kiss him on his temple. "I'm out of here tomorrow. Did they tell you when you'll be released?"

"Today, most likely."

Al slid a chair toward her, and she accepted it with a smile of thanks. Her arm curled around her ribs again as she gingerly lowered herself onto the seat. All three men watched her with concern. "Today? Really?"

"Yeah." He caught her hand in his. "It looks bad, but most of it's superficial."

The chief snorted. "Yeah. Especially the burns. Oh, and the one hole in your back that took five staples to close."

"Burns?" Rory repeated.

Even lying down, Ian's glare had power behind it. "I said most. And the burns are just first- and second-degree."

Rory rested her head next to Ian's so they were eye to eye. "I wish I'd been the last one out."

"I know." He smiled, a sweet, gentle curve of his lips. "That's one reason I love you so much."

She couldn't smile back. "I don't like when you're hurt."

"I don't like when you're hurt, either. Especially when it's because I landed on you."

"You were protecting me. Bruised ribs are nothing compared to that." Her eyes flicked toward the bandages covering his back.

"Okay," the chief said, too loudly. "I think we should take a little walk around the halls. Al, feeling like stretching your legs?"

Both dove for the door like a naked Letty just appeared on the bed. Rory finally smiled. "We really know how to clear a room, don't we?"

"We'll have to remember this, next time we want to get rid of the guys. Just get mushy, and they scatter."

She inclined her head a little closer as her smile widened.

"There you are." Rob Coughlin's voice startled her, and she sat up abruptly. Her ribs protested, and she hissed out a breath.

"Watch it," Ian snapped, rolling to his side so he could glare at the sheriff.

"I'm fine." The stabbing pain had settled back to its regular steady ache. She didn't want Ian and Rob fighting, for several reasons. "What can we do for you, Sheriff?"

"I need to get your statement." He took a couple steps into the room, keeping an eye on Ian. "I stopped in your room, but it was empty. I figured I'd talk to Ian first, but here you are."

Rory braced herself for another grueling round of questioning and winced at the pull on her ribs.

"She's injured," Ian almost growled. "Statements can wait."

Instead of looking angry, Rob appeared almost rueful. "I wanted to talk to you for another reason, too, Ian."

His glare didn't lighten, but Ian didn't order the sheriff to leave, either.

"I wanted to apologize," Rob said, making Rory sit up straighter in surprise. This time, she managed to hide her pained wince before Ian noticed. "I knew you weren't behind Willard Gray's murder, but I gave in to pressure from the state investigators and others in the department. They saw that pendant as a smoking gun. Outsiders tend to prefer physical evidence to gut feelings." He grimaced. "I should've stuck to my guns and refused to arrest you. I'm sorry for that."

Although Ian kept his face impassive, Rory could see the sheriff's apology had been unexpected. "Thank you," Ian said stiffly. Before he could add anything else, the door opened.

"Now *you*'re in here?" the ponytailed nurse snapped at Rory as she entered. "I'm going to borrow this nice cop's cuffs and chain you two to your assigned beds. Let's go, missy!"

"Come see me before you leave?" she asked, stretching out a hand.

He caught it and gave it a kiss. "I'm not going anywhere once I'm discharged, except down the hall to your room. We'll go home together tomorrow."

Blushing, she couldn't hold back a grin. "See you later, then."

"Later."

True to his word, Ian returned to her room in a couple of hours, planted himself in a chair, and didn't budge. Since they didn't need to split themselves between two patients anymore, firemen filled Rory's room until nursezilla snapped and kicked out everyone except Ian. There was a steady trickle of other visitors, too—Belly, Lou and Callum, other firemen, regular customers, and a bunch of people who'd made the trek from Simpson to check on them.

"The sheriff said the shop is in pretty rough shape," she told Ian once the last of the visitors had been chased from the room. "He showed me some pictures." The sight of the shattered display cases and blackened walls had made her chest hurt in a way that had nothing to do with her ribs.

Ian rubbed her upper arm, one of the only places on her body that didn't hurt. "What else did Rob have to say?"

"Just that he'd arrested Billy, Zup, and the other guy who was with them."

"Rucker."

"That was his name?" When Ian nodded, she continued, "I gave him my statement, but it wasn't like last time, with the same questions over and over. I think it helped that the chief and the other guys had already told him what had happened. Well, that and the fact that we hadn't shot anyone this time."

Ian let out a short, unamused laugh. "Yeah, I'm sure that helped."

"Were you surprised he apologized for arresting you?"

"Yeah. That was unexpected. It was good of him, though. It would've been better if he hadn't arrested me at all, but I'll take what I can get."

"He said he'll put some deputies on my shop, so no one tries to do any looting. That's nice of him, I guess. And they'll keep an eye on the Riders, so no one retaliates." Sleep was pulling at her, but she didn't want to end the conversation. Swallowing a yawn, she asked, "How are you doing?"

His shoulders flexed, as if checking the status of his injuries. "Back hurts, but I'll live."

"No, I meant…uh, with the whole Billy thing." She'd never be a therapist. Asking Ian about his feelings was making her twitchy and uncomfortable.

His eyes left hers, and he glared at the wall for long enough that Rory started to think he wasn't going to answer. "Even after I found out he'd thrown me at Rob, even when he left that glowstick, I still had a soft spot of doubt. A part of me hoped he was just making empty threats, that he cared about me too much to actually hurt me—or you. If he'd come to me, apologized, explained, then maybe I'd have forgiven him. I think I didn't want to give up that connection with the Riders. After this, though… When I was stabilizing your head and neck, keeping your airway open, and you were limp in my hands, that cord holding me to Billy and the Riders just snapped. I'm done. Even if Billy came to me, begging for another chance, told me the best fu—flipping excuse ever created, I'd just kick him in the face. So, in that way it was good. Him planting that bomb…" His jaw flexed. "That was the end. The last soft spot is gone. Billy killed it when he tried to kill you."

Lifting a hand to the back of his head, she pulled him down to her. When he was close enough, she kissed that tendon that stood in relief on his jawline. He blew out a long, shuddering breath and bowed his head, tucking his face in the curve of her neck. They stayed like that until Rory lost the battle with sleep.

Chapter 24

"IT WAS TOO MUCH, ANYWAY," LOU DECLARED, wiping the already clean counter at The Coffee Spot. "I mean, a fireman *and* a motorcycle-riding, leather-wearing badass? It's a dangerous excess of hotness. Our heads could've imploded from hotness overload."

Rory blinked at her. "First, I don't think the laws of science really work that way. Second, he's keeping the motorcycle. And the leather."

"Be careful, then." With a mock-concerned frown, Lou rinsed the cloth in the sink. "You're in danger of hotness-induced head implosion every time you're around Ian Walsh."

"I'll keep that in mind," Rory said dryly, unable to quash her grin. The bells on the front door jangled.

"And speak of the devil..." Lou grinned at someone behind her. "Hey, Beauty. How are the battle wounds?"

Ian gave his usual shrug before sliding a hand across Rory's back, making her shiver. "Ready?"

"For what?" Lou's eyes shone with open curiosity.

"Levi's." Try as she might, Rory couldn't hold back a grimace. She was dreading the meal, but Ian was right. It was better to deal with the curious citizens of Simpson all in one go—especially now—rather than being swarmed at the grocery store or having people run into the road and wave her down as she was trying to drive to Ian's house.

"You don't look too happy about that," Lou observed.

"I'm not." With a sigh, she slid off the stool, still moving carefully, although her ribs were not nearly as sore as they'd been a week ago. "At least I get good food during the inquisition."

Lou laughed. As Rory and Ian made their way to the door, she called after them, "Watch out for implosions!"

Ian frowned at her, but Rory just rolled her eyes. When they were in the Bronco, Ian said, "What'd she mean?"

"No idea." Hoping he'd think her blush was due to the recent cold snap, she shrugged. "It's Lou."

He eyed her closely, but then seemed to accept her nonanswer. "How'd things go today at the shop?" A doctor's appointment in Denver to recheck his injuries had kept him away all day.

"The insurance company investigator was there."

"Yeah?" He exited the lot carefully, since the melted snow had refrozen, turning the pavement into an ice rink. Rory noticed he still kept a few inches of space between his still-tender back and the seat. "How'd that go?"

"It was surprisingly painless." She'd been dreading dealing with the insurance company, but everything had gone smoothly so far. "There doesn't seem to be any structural damage, and I've been able to salvage some of my inventory, too. Look." She pulled the SwissMiniGun from her pocket. "I even fired it after they left. It's undamaged."

"Great," he said dryly, glancing at the pistol with amusement. "The tiny gun still works."

With a mock sigh, she tucked it back in her pocket. "You don't have any appreciation for this marvel of engineering."

"Nope," he responded unapologetically. "I still have

another week at least before the doctor will clear me to go back to work, and the guys just started their days off." As he swung onto Second Street, the Bronco's back end kept turning, slipping sideways on the ice. Rory's hands clenched on her thighs, but Ian just eased out of the skid, straightening the vehicle as if nothing had happened. "We'll be able to lend a hand at the shop."

"You don't have to do that," she protested, but he just ignored her objections, as usual.

"I want to help."

"Fine." She threw her hands up in the air. "But you know what happened last time you guys all helped in the shop."

Lifting one hand from the steering wheel, he found the tight muscles connecting her neck to her shoulder and started massaging. "Yeah, well, if there are going to be explosions, I want to be there."

Despite her instinct to melt under his ministrations, she shot him a sideways look. Was he being literal or suggestive? His fingers digging into her muscles felt too good, so she quit analyzing his words and just enjoyed the massage.

When they pulled up to the curb a block from Levi's, Rory almost groaned in disappointment. It seemed an unfair trade—an end to her neck rub for the stares of gossipy Simpsonites. She stayed in her seat until Ian circled the SUV and opened her door.

"Out, Ror. The sooner we get in there, the sooner we can leave."

"Fine."

As they walked toward Levi's, Rory noted the vehicles lining both sides of the street and stifled a sigh. It appeared that everyone and their grandma was eating at Levi's tonight. When Ian caught her hand and laced their fingers together, however, her dread of the upcoming evening eased.

"Ready?" he asked, releasing her hand so he could open the door to Levi's and gesture Rory through the entrance.

Her answer was an unintelligible grumble, but she braced herself and walked into the restaurant.

"Surprise!" the crowd filling Levi's shouted.

Rory took a startled step back, bumping into the wall of Ian behind her, and started to reach for the gun in her pocket.

Ian's fingers closed around her searching hand. "No shooting your party guests," he said quietly, close to her ear, an audible smile in his voice. "Happy Birthday, Ror."

All she could do was stare at the smiling crowd and blink. She'd actually forgotten it was her birthday. They'd always been subdued events growing up, and she'd never even had a friend to invite over to celebrate, much less a party...until now. "How'd you even know it was my birthday?" she asked Ian, keeping her back pressed against his front. She knew if she took a step into the crowd, she'd be swarmed.

"Chief," Ian said, loudly enough that Early stepped forward, his cheerful face wreathed in smiles. "He got it from your paperwork."

"That seems...unethical," she muttered, and felt Ian's chest vibrate with a laugh. Forcing a smile, she took a deep breath and stepped toward the waiting horde. Just as she'd feared, the crowd swallowed her whole.

~

"Well?"

"Well what?"

Smirking, Ian looked down at her as he unlocked the side door of his house. "How was your first party?"

"How'd you know it was my first party?" she asked, more to avoid answering his question than anything. She couldn't really answer, because a dozen conflicting emotions twisted in her gut, and she hadn't had a chance to sort through them yet.

"The way you reached for your gun when everyone yelled, 'Surprise!' was kind of a clue."

"I was startled," she said defensively, ducking under the arm he was using to hold open the door.

He snorted a laugh as he followed her. "Besides that first moment, what'd you think of the rest?"

"It was…more okay than I expected." She stripped off her boots and coat before walking over to lean against the counter. "I think I had fun at parts."

"Parts?"

"Like when Belly juggled steak knives. That was… oddly fascinating."

"It was."

"Once everyone stopped focusing on me and just talked in small groups, it was better. Just hanging out with the guys from the station, and Lou when she got there, that part was easy. The whole singing at me thing, though…that was unpleasant."

He muffled his laugh with a cough.

"And the presents." Her huge pile of gifts was still packed in the Bronco. "I have to admit that I liked getting presents."

"I got you something, too." Grabbing her hand, Ian pulled her toward the living room.

The idea of another present was exciting enough to muffle the unease of entering the room of glass walls. "You didn't have to."

He gave her a look. "I know. I wanted to. Here." Stopping in the middle of the living room, he swept his arm in a wide gesture. "Happy Birthday."

It took her a second to realize what was different, but when she did, Rory started to smile. "You covered the windows."

"Steel-core shutters." He grinned proudly and grabbed her hand again. This time, he pulled her up the stairs and into his bedroom. "Here, too."

The bedroom windows were shuttered, as well. Rory ignored the fact that a bullet could easily pierce the drywall surrounding the protected windows and focused on the generosity of his gift.

"I love them." Fighting down a surge of awkwardness, she took a step closer so she could give Ian a quick hug. She carefully avoided pressing on his still-healing back. "Thank you."

When she tried to step away from him, his arms locked around her and kept her close. "You're welcome. No more closet sleeping for you."

Tilting her chin so she could meet his eyes, she raised an eyebrow. "Ulterior motives?"

"Definitely." His voice was a raspy growl that made her shiver. Leaning down, he touched his lips to hers. Just that light contact made her heart hiccup. When he deepened the kiss, she pressed closer, looping her arms around his neck. Her fingers burrowed into the silky short strands of his hair, giving gentle tugs and lightly scratching his scalp.

Being with him like this made her feel so secure, so safe, she wouldn't even have needed the shutters covering the windows. Making a pleased sound against her mouth, he cupped his hands under her butt and lifted her. Startled, she wrapped her legs around his waist to help keep her aloft and pulled her lips from his. Ian burrowed his face into the side of her neck, dropping light kisses and leaving a trail of goose bumps.

Rory didn't even realize he was carrying her to the bed until her back touched the comforter. Her eyes went wide as he followed her down, pressing her to the mattress with his weight.

He kissed her, and her body immediately woke, heat flaring under his touch. All her self-consciousness evaporated, leaving only desire and so much love her heart ached with it. Her hands explored with more freedom than ever before, although she avoided his still-sensitive back.

He kissed her carefully—too carefully. Rory clutched his head, trying to pull his lips harder against hers, but he kept his touch gentle. With a low growl of frustration, Rory nipped his lower lip.

Guilt set in when he pulled back, looking startled.

"Sorry," she muttered.

"What was that for?" he asked, although there was a humorous glint in his eyes.

"I just wanted you to be a little"—her gaze darted around before finally settling on his chin—"um, rougher."

His body jolted slightly, and his amusement morphed into heat. "I want to be careful with your ribs."

She felt her breaths come quickly, her arousal feeding off his. "I'm fine. My ribs are fine. I don't need careful." Although she might feel it in the morning, right now she needed anything but gentle. She wanted him wild and uncontrolled, so caught up in his passion for her that he was oblivious to anything else in the world. Pulling his head down toward her, she caught his lip in her teeth again, tugging at it teasingly.

It was his turn to growl. His mouth found hers, and she instantly knew that any form of "careful" had disappeared. They kissed each other as if the world was ending and all that existed was the two of them. With a groan of relief and pleasure, she lost herself in that passion, where injuries and angry MC members and meth dealers didn't exist.

Her hands slid under his shirt, tracing his abs upward until she could lightly score her nails over his pecs. He pulled away just long enough to yank his shirt over his head and toss it away before returning his lips to hers.

They scrambled out of the rest of their clothes. In the heat and passion, Rory forgot to be self-conscious, forgot everything except the man above her. His mouth and hands explored her body, finding the places that made her shudder and cry out his name. Unable to take another second of pleasure, she rolled them both over so she was on top, forgetting about his still-tender back until he hissed a breath through his teeth. Quickly turning them so they were on their sides, facing each other, she started an exploration of her own. She loved finding his ticklish spots, the sensitive places, the ones that made him groan and shiver under her touch.

Once they were both shuddering and sweating with need, he rolled on a condom and slid into her, and they fit like matching puzzle pieces. Rory locked her legs around his hips, unable to tear her gaze from his. His face was even more beautiful to her now than the first day they had met. He was Ian, and he was perfect.

"I love you," she blurted, unable to hold in the words for a second longer.

His face lit with happiness, and he lowered his head to touch his lips to hers. They continued to kiss, and pleasure flowed through Rory, the physical peak driven even higher by the surge of love and comfort and peace being with Ian gave her.

As they caught their breath afterward, neither one letting go, despite healing ribs and burns and shrapnel wounds, Ian kissed that favorite spot beneath her ear.

"This was a good birthday," she whispered, barely loud enough for him to hear.

"Good." His breath warmed her neck and all the cold spots left inside her. "I love you too, Ror."

That new feeling of security and contentment flowed through her again. "Could you open the shutters?"

He went still. "Are you sure?"

Surprisingly, she was. "I think I'd like to see the stars."

"You're amazing, Rory." Giving her a hard kiss, he rolled out of bed. "Let's look at the stars, then."

Rory woke early, her body accustomed to being on chicken duty, a chore taken over by Steve as his birthday present to her.

Turning onto her side, she could barely make out

Ian's sleeping form. His breathing was deep and even, lulling her into a half doze. She smiled drowsily, thinking of the night before, the maybe-fun party, and the definitely fun lovemaking session afterward. Her stomach warmed with a slow burn at the memory, and she reached toward his dim shape. Her hand found his arm first, and his breathing immediately changed.

Although he'd obviously awakened, he didn't move. After a moment of hesitation, Rory stroked a line from the inside of his elbow to his shoulder and then back down again. He was shirtless, so there was no barrier between her fingertips and his skin.

"'Morning," he said, his voice raspy.

Scooting an inch closer, Rory propped her head onto her free hand and reversed the course of her fingers, ending up at the top of his sternum. "Good morning."

"Very good morning." A shadow shifted, and his hand settled on her blanket-draped hip. "I like waking up this way."

She made a sound of agreement. Thinking back to even just a month earlier, her life seemed so...lonely. Plus, the nights had been a lot colder without this furnace of a man in bed next to her. As she moved her fingers, intending to explore his chest, a pounding noise made her sit up.

Grumbling, Ian slid out of bed and turned on the lamp. Rory squinted until her eyes adjusted.

"What's that?" she asked as the pounding started again.

"Someone—who will soon be a dead someone—is knocking on the door." He stomped over to where his pants lay in a heap on the floor and bent to pull them on. Rory watched, fascinated by the way his black boxer briefs hugged his tight rear end. When she realized she was gawking at him, she flushed and turned her head.

If someone was at the door, she figured she should probably get dressed as well. Rory got out of bed before remembering what she was wearing—and what she wasn't. Although Ian's T-shirt almost reached her knees, she still felt extremely pantsless.

"You don't have to get up," Ian protested, fastening his BDUs. "I'm just going to get rid of the annoying assho—uh, jerk who's knocking on the door way too early in the morning, then I'm coming back to bed."

He turned to look at her once his pants were buttoned, and he went still. Only his gaze moved, following the length of her body from her feet to her face. A slow grin curled his mouth. "That shirt looks good on you."

Her face was so hot that Rory knew it must be flaming red. "Weirdo."

He laughed. "Don't change out of it." His eyes dropped to her legs again, before he visibly shook himself and turned toward the door. "I'm just going to shoot someone really quick, and then I'll be back."

She hesitated for a minute after he disappeared, but she felt too naked in just his shirt and her underwear. After she'd dressed, Ian hadn't returned yet, so she headed downstairs to see who the loud knocker was.

Halfway down the stairs, she caught a glimpse of the visitor and stopped on the step. Julius, looking ill and uneasy, was standing in the living room with Ian. Rory half-turned, intending to return upstairs and let the two men talk privately, when Julius started to speak.

"It doesn't feel right, doing this," Julius said, his gaze darting around the room, landing on her for a very brief second. In just that quick glance, Rory thought she saw contrition. "The Riders have been my family—*our* family. It's not the same club it used to be, though. Something's wrong with Billy. They destroyed our home. Suze was so proud of that house."

Ian visibly startled, rocking back a step. "The Riders burned your house? They almost killed you!" His voice rose to a shout at the end. The strength left Rory's legs, and she sank to sit on a step.

"When you were in jail, Rory came to see me. Billy showed up, threatened her, and I kicked him out. The night of the fire, he came to visit." He ducked his head, looking ashamed. "I should've known something wasn't right, that Billy would've never really forgiven me for pulling a gun on him. He brought a bottle of Black Label, though, and I let him talk me into having a drink with him. Last thing I remember is Billy telling me what a shame it was, that I used to be an asset to the Riders, and now I'm just a sentimental drunk who picked a traitor over my brothers." Julius's voice cracked on the last word, and he blinked rapidly several times. "Then there were flames, and I couldn't breathe, and you were there, dragging me out."

Fisting his hands at his sides, Ian strode two paces away from Julius and then returned to his original spot, like the rage inside him wouldn't allow him to stand still. "That asshole tried to *kill* you!"

"Yeah, and he's gunning for the two of you now." Julius's expression was almost fierce as he met Ian's fuming stare. "Tack's back. He got all three of those guys out on bail because he has some dirt on the judge. Billy's planning something. Squirrel came to me this morning, said he and Carrie were getting out. The club's gone rotten, he said. I got here as quick as I could. Whatever the Riders were to me all these years, you're my *son*."

"What's he planning?" Ian's voice had gone soft.

Her neck prickling with alarm, Rory rose to her feet.

"Your girl. Rory." Julius flicked a glance at her again. "They want the guns—"

Suddenly, the door flew open, smashing against the wall behind it. Zup and six other men, all carrying weapons ranging from shotguns to baseball bats, rushed inside and circled Julius and Ian before any of them could move. Even in the shock of the moment, Rory recognized several of the guns she'd sold them. Billy entered last, his scarred face fixed in a falsely amiable smile that was cold enough to freeze Rory's insides.

"Julius," Billy greeted. "You're turning out to be an even greater disappointment than I thought."

Although he was visibly shaking, Julius thrust out his chin. "I know the feeling, Billy."

Rory took a soundless backward step, mentally reviewing what weapons were available upstairs. The options were dismal. She swore to stock Ian's house as soon as they got out of this mess.

"Boss," one of the men said, jerking his head toward Rory.

Billy looked up at her and gave that bone-chilling, false smile. "Rory! How good to see you. Come down and join us, won't you?"

For a second, she hesitated, until the Rider to Billy's left racked his shotgun and pointed it at Ian. Her feet started moving down the stairs even before she made the conscious decision.

"Rory, run!" Ian ordered, and his tone of command made her pause. Another Rider swung his bat toward Ian's back.

"Behind you!" Rory shouted. Ian turned and tried to dodge, but the bat caught him in the side. As Ian stumbled back, Rory ran down the rest of the stairs. Before she could reach Ian, Billy grabbed her arm, yanking her away. She fought him, twisting and punching and scratching, until Billy grabbed a Glock 19 from one of his guys and aimed it at Ian.

"Keep going, Rory, and I'll put a few new holes in Beauty." The way he said Ian's nickname was so different from the teasing, fond manner which the Fire guys used that it made Rory cringe. She stopped fighting, the sight of Billy's gun being pointed at Ian bringing her to complete stillness.

"Much better." He started backing toward the door, keeping the Glock aimed at Ian while pulling Rory with him. She couldn't look at the gun, so she focused on Ian's face—his rigid, furious face. When he started to take a step toward her, she stopped breathing, imagining the bullet tearing through his center mass, taking out his vulnerable, vital organs as it went. Her fear for Ian distracted her from Billy until the cold press of a gun barrel to her temple regained her attention. Ian abruptly stopped, eyes blazing.

"Dean, cover Walsh," Billy ordered, keeping his gun tight to Rory's head. "We're going to go do some gun shopping."

"You call us traitors, but you're the fuckhead turning on your brothers." Julius sounded shaky, but his glare was solid. "Burning my house—*Suze*'s house—and threatening to put a bullet through my son? If this is what the Riders are now, I'm glad I'm out."

"Shut up, you useless drunk," Billy snarled, grinding the barrel of the gun against Rory's head.

Ian didn't seem to notice Dean's shotgun aimed at his chest. All his attention was focused on Rory. She tried to smooth her expression, to reassure him that she'd be all right, that they'd both be all right, but as terrified as she was, she wasn't sure if she'd managed to pull it off.

"Take me instead," Ian demanded.

Even as Billy snorted, Rory was shaking her head. "I'll take you. He doesn't know where the special inventory is."

When Ian frowned at her, she glared right back at him. She wasn't about to let him sacrifice himself for her.

"So he's useless to me." The oily satisfaction in Billy's voice set off all kinds of alarm bells in her brain.

"Don't you dare shoot my boy," Julius shouted.

"If you kill him," she warned Billy, her expression as flat and cold as his, "I will never show you where those guns are. I won't care what you do to me."

"Rory..." The terrified fury in Ian's voice made her eyes burn, but she forced away the tears. If she lost it now, they were both dead.

"Fine," Billy said. "I won't kill him as long as you hand over everything in that back room of yours. I'll know if you're holding back. All I have to do is call Dean, and your fuck buddy here gets a bullet in the belly. Won't bother me to make that call. He's as good as dead to me, anyway."

"What happened, Billy?" Ian demanded, turning his livid gaze on the MC president. "You were like a father to me. I would've done anything for you—I fucking *killed* for you. How could you turn on me like this?"

"You turned on me first!" Billy shouted, his fingers tightening painfully around Rory's upper arm. "You stood by this bitch even after she killed Rave—your *brother*—and sold guns to those fucking King brothers. Anderson King was already making noise about taking over the Riders' territory, and *she's* arming those bastards. You humiliated Zup, told Julius lies about the club, turned your back on us over and over until we'd had enough. Enough! Dean, if he moves, shoot him in the gut."

The Rider with the shotgun didn't respond except to grip the weapon pointed at Ian more tightly. Billy, his false amiability gone, yanked Rory the last few steps to the door.

"Wait!" she cried, trying to dig in her heels to stop their forward progress. "I need my coat and boots."

"You'll survive a little cold, princess." Billy didn't even pause.

"Maybe." She caught the closet doorknob with her hand. "But the neighbors will notice if I'm stumbling through the snow in a shirt and socks."

That brought Billy to a stop. "Fine. But I'll be watching. You try for anything except your boots and coat, and I'll end Walsh."

Her breath was coming too quickly, making it hard to think. She tried to slow her inhales and pretended calm. "They're in the kitchen."

Scowling, he scanned the room. Apparently satisfied that his seven men could control Julius and Ian, he hauled Rory toward the kitchen. As soon as she'd jammed her feet into her boots and put one arm in her coat, Billy forced her outside, holding the gun in his coat pocket where the casual observer wouldn't notice it.

She stumbled, almost dropping to her knees in the snow.

"One call," he warned, jerking her upright. "One call, and he's dead."

Barely restraining the panic wanting to overtake her at the threat, she concentrated on wading through the snowdrifts that had formed on Ian's driveway during the night. Billy's vehicle was parked on the street, behind another SUV that was blocking both Ian's Bronco and Julius's borrowed Oldsmobile in the driveway. Her feet slowed unconsciously as warnings blared through her mind. *Never let them take you. If you get in their vehicle, you're as good as dead. Do whatever you have to in order to avoid getting in that car.*

"Quit messing around," Billy snapped, giving her arm another jerk. The sound of a truck engine stopped her heart, and then made it restart at a frantic pace. A plow truck rounded the corner, and Billy swore.

"Get in," he ordered, almost dragging her across the last few feet of snow to the SUV. His grip pushed her over the edge into panic, and she started to struggle, yanking back against his grip. "Stop! Stop or he's dead!"

The words penetrated, bringing a different form of anxiety. What if she'd just caused Ian's death with her loss of control?

The plow truck slowed as it grew closer, and Rory recognized George Holloway in the driver's seat. She remembered that he occasionally subbed for the county plow driver.

"Wave," Billy gritted, jamming the barrel of the gun against her back. "Wave and smile, or Ian's fucking dead."

She did. Plastering on a giant fake smile, she waved like a contestant in a beauty pageant. As the plow truck grew closer, Rory saw George's frowning face. Although he watched them the entire time he passed, he didn't stop. Disappointment squeezed Rory's stomach as the plow truck continued on its way.

"Good," Billy grunted, hustling her around to the driver's door. "You're driving. I have Dean on speed dial. You fuck up again, and I'm making that call. Got it?"

When she didn't answer immediately, he jammed the gun into her back again.

"Yes," she managed to say, anger flaring out of her helpless fear.

"You'd better, or your boy is dead."

The drive to her shop felt like it took forever while, at the same time, it went by in a flash. A couple of times, she thought she saw another vehicle following in the distance. One of Billy's men? Or had the King brothers caught word that their enemies were about to get the upper hand? Was she about to get caught in the middle of a war for real? Her stomach twisted, but she had no choice. She kept driving.

Billy got out with her at the gate and held the gun on her while she started opening the locks. The surrounding silence almost made her wish Jack wasn't with Steve and his kids for the day. When Billy gave her another hard nudge with the Glock, she was thankful her dog was safe elsewhere. Billy had almost killed him once—that was more than enough.

The rev of a heavy diesel engine made her frown and

look behind them. She expected to see Anderson King's ruthless face twisted in a snarl—she never expected *George*. The plow truck was headed toward them, moving fast. Rory gawked at the rapidly approaching raised blade of the truck before diving to the side, painfully scraping her hip and palms as she skidded across the frozen ground. Twisting her head, she stared at an immobile Billy.

"What?" he squawked before turning and reflexively raising the gun, squeezing off a few shots. Sparks flew as the bullets ricocheted off the pickup, making Rory duck instinctively. She raised her head in time to see the windshield cobweb and collapse in on itself as a shot burrowed through the glass. With a crashing squeal of metal against metal, the plow truck rammed into the back of her pickup. Her truck lurched forward, smashing into the still-frozen Billy and pinning him against the gates.

He looked down at his crushed lower body, shock on his face. Then he looked at her, and his expression went hard with hatred and fury.

As blood ran from his nose and forehead into his white beard, he raised the Glock, his intention clear on his face. Slipping her hand into her coat pocket, Rory held his gaze as she closed her hand around a marvel of European engineering. Billy started to smile, his cold, ruthless smile that always made her stomach clench with fear, and his finger found the trigger.

Rory yanked out the SwissMiniGun and shot him twice in the throat.

Shock covered his face, his mouth opening and closing in wordless protest. Blood poured from his neck, and the Glock dropped to the ground. His now-empty hands raised to futilely attempt to stanch the blood flowing out of his body. Within seconds, though, his eyes went blank and lifeless. Billy's body slumped forward, held only somewhat upright by his pinned position between the gates and Rory's truck.

"Okay?" a growly bass voice asked as a hand extended toward her.

Blinking at the bear of a man towering above her, she accepted the hand up. Except for shaky legs—well, an entire shaky body—Rory was surprised to find she was still in one piece. "Yes. Thank you."

"Saw you smiling." He scowled at Billy's limp form. "Knew something was wrong."

Despite everything, a laugh bubbled out of her. "I figured you would call the sheriff or something. I didn't think you'd go for the solo rescue."

"Radioed dispatch, too."

Another engine, this one pitched differently than the snowplow, was growing louder. Rory tensed.

"We should get inside," she said, turning to work the locks as quickly as she could. "I don't know who's coming, but Billy had seven guys with him." Her heart clenched at the thought of Ian being at Dean's and the rest of the Riders' mercy.

Without saying anything, George turned and started walking toward the snowplow.

"George!" she called, dropping the lock she was frantically trying to open in order to run after him. The big man didn't hesitate.

Once she ran past the plow, she saw a motorcycle flying toward them over the snow-packed road, and she slid to an abrupt stop. Ian was astride in only his BDUs, no coat or shirt or helmet or even any boots. All he had was a look on his face that told her he'd blast through hell to get her back and keep her safe.

As soon as he'd stopped the bike, barely keeping it upright as it tried to slide out from under him on the slick road, she hurled herself toward him. He caught her and clutched her to his chest.

"Fuck, Ror," he repeated over and over, his hands sliding over her as if checking for injuries. "Are you okay? Fuck, Rory."

"I'm not hurt," she assured him, holding him just as tightly. "Are you? You must be freezing! How'd you get away from those guys?"

His laugh was short and choked. "Daisy was watching through the window and called the cops. Rob already had some deputies headed to my house, since he figured Billy'd come after us. When they pulled up, we used the distraction to take out the Riders."

"All of them?" Her heart raced in retroactive panic at the thought.

He pulled back just enough to smooth her hair out of her face. "We took them by surprise. Besides, they're pretty out of shape." He grinned. "I found out that Julius can still kick some ass. Once those guys were out, I took off after you, but my Bronco was blocked. The bike was my best option. I needed to get to you." He glanced around at the mess, his eyebrows drawing together. "What the fu—freak happened here?"

"George Holloway saw me smiling and waving in your driveway. He knew something was really wrong." She noticed red-and-blue lights approaching in the distance. The rest of her new family was coming to her rescue. She'd gone from hermit to an entire town of heroes having her back. It was mind-boggling and overwhelmingly wonderful.

Ian frowned. "George Holloway? The Search and Rescue guy who doesn't talk?"

"He might not say much," Rory defended the big guy, "but he knows how to drive a plow."

Eyeing the wreckage the snowplow had caused, Ian pulled her close again. "Thank God he does."

Epilogue

"Ready for tomorrow?"

"I guess." Rory shrugged, looking around the shop. It was hard to believe that just three weeks earlier, the place had been a mess of charred walls and broken glass. "This is only my second, but I'm already sick of grand reopenings."

Ian grinned, leaning against one of her new glass display cases. "I bet you'll really get a crowd in here."

"Yeah." Even to her own ears, she sounded grumpy, but Ian just laughed and slung an arm around her shoulders.

"I'll do chickens if you want to lock up," he offered.

Despite a small pang of guilt for dumping the chicken chores on him, she agreed. As she turned off all but the security lights and secured the front door, she thought about Ian. He'd returned to work since his back had healed, leaving angry pink shrapnel and burn scars that were sensitive but not, according to Ian, painful. Between him and the other firemen, the post-explosion remodel of her shop had been finished in record time. When she'd offered to pay them, they'd looked at her like she'd just drop-kicked a kitten.

The Riders were a leaderless, chaotic mess, according to Squirrel. Zup had tried to take the reins, but that had almost immediately been a disaster. It was going to be a long time before the MC regained its position in

Field County's criminal underworld, if it ever did. Rory was just relieved she no longer had to keep looking over her shoulder for vengeful bikers.

Yeah, just vengeful meth dealers, she thought with a humorless laugh. Her life would never be boring, but at least she had someone to watch her back now. She wasn't alone anymore.

As she waited for Ian to return from the chicken coop with Jack in tow, she opened the steel door and leaned against it. Rory realized that she was smiling. They'd been pretty much living together, switching off between their houses, and each night they'd gotten closer. At the memory of those nights, she gave a pleasurable little shiver just as Ian walked through the back door. Embarrassment made her flush and drop her gaze. He gave a low laugh as he engaged the locks.

"What are you thinking about?" he asked in a husky voice that told her he'd made a pretty close guess.

With a defensive scowl, she tossed back at him, "Shouldn't I be asking you that question?"

Her attempted insult just bounced right off his thick hide. He didn't even stop grinning. "Do you think anything about our relationship is typical?"

After thinking about that for a moment, she said, "No."

"C'mon." He nudged her toward the stairs. "I'm hungry."

Although she knew perfectly well he was talking about food, another shiver rippled through her, and she bit off a sigh before it could escape. What was it about Ian that had turned her into a lust bunny? She busied herself with relocking the steel door behind them.

"We have some of that chicken casserole left." She

dragged her mind off Ian and what he'd done with his mouth the previous night. "Is that okay?"

"That's great." He gave her his best puppy eyes. Even though she'd never admit it, Rory would do pretty much anything for Ian when he looked at her that way. "Can we have bread, too?"

Feigning nonchalance, she shrugged. "Sure."

Ian grabbed her around the waist, lifting her as he pulled her into a backward hug. "Have I mentioned lately how much I love you?"

Her heart took off like a racehorse out of the starting gate, and she swallowed. No matter how many times he'd said it, it still knocked her for a loop that Ian Walsh loved her. He squeezed her tightly before releasing her.

Trying to keep from jumping him, she hurried toward the kitchen. Just that small gesture had heated her body to the boiling point. Blowing out an unsteady breath, she refocused on heating dinner.

"Now I really want to know what's spinning around in that brain of yours." Unbeknownst to her, Ian had crossed the kitchen and was standing right behind her. His breath brushed the back of her neck as he spoke. Goose bumps prickled up her nape, and he touched his lips to the spot his breath had just warmed.

"Nothing too interesting," she said, closing the oven door and turning.

When she came face-to-face with Ian, she immediately forgot what she was doing. His eyes were such a warm, rich brown, she just stared into them.

As if he were in the same speechless boat as she was, he didn't say a word as he leaned closer. Rory tipped her head willingly, but he only brushed her lips softly with his before stepping back. Rory swayed, a little off balance by his quick retreat.

"How long do we have?" he asked, his voice sounding a little hoarse.

She looked blankly at the stove. "Uh…an hour?" She actually had no idea if that was correct or not, but whatever Ian had planned for the next hour would almost certainly be worth a little burned food.

"Good." Taking her hand, he tugged her toward her bedroom. She followed easily, wondering where the resistant, contrary Rory had gone. As soon as they entered her room, he was kissing her, and everything else except for Ian left her mind. There was the usual urgency, the one that spun Rory into a cyclone of desire.

They tumbled onto the pink bed, sending pillows and Mr. Hoppity flying. Rory laughed against Ian's mouth, making him lift his head.

"What's funny?" His mouth curled as if prepared to smile at her answer.

"Nothing specific." She tugged him back down so their lips almost touched. "I'm just happy."

"Good." His breath warmed her skin. "Making you happy makes me happy."

"You know what would make me extra happy?"

"What?"

"If we stop talking and go back to kissing."

It was his turn to laugh, but he quickly fulfilled her request, taking her mouth hungrily. As always, his passion fed hers, making her feel desired and even beautiful under his hands and lips. His mouth trailed to her favorite places, making her moan and shiver unself-consciously.

They undressed each other, playing a sort of mutual

striptease as they unfastened buttons and zippers, finding the sensitive skin beneath. By the time they were both naked, Rory was desperate for him.

"Please," she begged, making him groan. His hands stroked over her sides and her breasts. Rory twisted against him, wanting him inside her. Finally, *finally* he entered her, connecting their bodies in the way that always overwhelmed her with feelings of belonging and pleasure and sheer, absolute love for this man.

She wrapped her legs around his hips and pulled him tightly against her. His strokes quickened, grew rougher and harder, and she reveled in the force of each one. Clutching him with all of her limbs, she held him close as she came, not planning on ever letting him go. Ever since he'd given her that pink cupcake, she'd been his. Now he was hers, as well.

As if he shared her thoughts, he didn't let her go even after their breathing slowed and their bodies cooled. Instead, he rolled so she was on top of him, straddling his waist. Being on top was still a little disconcerting. There was no way to hide her nakedness from him. He noticed, too, judging by his dilated pupils and the way his hands began once again to explore. Running his fingers down both of her arms, he caught her hands and brought them to his mouth, kissing her palms one at a time.

"You're going to marry me someday," he told her. Despite his lingering happy grin, his tone was serious.

She tried to force a frown. "Bossy."

"Yeah, I am." He didn't sound too bothered by that. "Which house did you want to keep?"

Her frown turned thoughtful. "Your house is growing on me since you put in the shutters. If a few more security measures were installed, I could live there. We could keep mine for emergency use only."

Ian grinned. "The zombie apocalypse?"

"Sure." Pulling her hands free of his, she braced them on his chest as she leaned down to kiss him. "Or just when I'm mad at you."

With a laugh, he tugged her down the rest of the way, wrapping his arms around her in a hard hug. "I think I'd prefer the zombies."

Rory would've smacked him, but her arms were locked in place by his tight hold. Instead, she rested her cheek against his chest and smiled.

The man didn't look familiar, but his expression made Rory tense.

Working her way through the last stragglers of the re-reopening crowd, she crossed the shop to stand next to the stranger eyeing the new Taser display. "Do you need help?"

He jumped, his face tightening even more as he turned toward her. "I need protection."

"Home protection?"

"*Personal* protection. I think there's someone after me," he blurted, then closed his eyes and shook his head. "No. That's not right. I *know* it. He killed Gray Goose and cut off his head and tossed him in the reservoir, and now he's coming after me."

"Okay." Rory studied the man's face. He was probably in his early sixties, and he'd shaved off whatever hair had been left on his head. Although he was average in height and weight, he practically vibrated with a nervous energy that made him seem bigger. His eyes darted around, not holding hers or landing on anyone else for very long. She knew crazy. She'd grown up with crazy. This guy was setting off every alarm bell in Rory's head, and they were all ringing with the same tune—this man wasn't stable. "What's your name?"

His gaze flickered to the door, around the room, and back to her face. "Does it matter?"

She considered that question for a moment, never looking away from him. "Yes. It matters."

Still, he hesitated. Just when she was sure he'd dart for the nearest exit, he said, "Baxter. Baxter Price."

"I'm Rory Sorenson." It was her turn to glance around the room, but she had a purpose. Her gaze landed on Ian, who was talking with Soup next to the register. He turned his head to look at her, as if he'd felt Rory's gaze. She couldn't help but smile at the sight of him, but then she quickly remembered her immediate goal. "Watch the place?" she mouthed, swinging a hand as if to indicate the shop.

Although the corners of his mouth curled down with concern, he nodded.

"Baxter"—she turned back to her twitchy customer—"can we go in the back to talk?"

"Yeah." His shoulders dropped a little. Rory assumed it was relief that he could escape the still-crowded shop. When she waved him toward the door to the back room, he didn't move. Although she hated to turn her back on anyone, especially unbalanced strangers, she set her jaw and walked toward the door. Keeping her head turned slightly, she watched in her peripheral vision as Baxter followed her, his gaze still shifting from side to side.

In the back room, Rory stepped to the side so Baxter could enter, and then she closed the door most of the way. Away from the other people, Price seemed to settle a little, although he was still visibly tense.

"What's going on?" she asked. When he hesitated, she leaned back against the wall, forcing at least an illusion of calm. "Unless I know the situation, I can't help you figure out the best way to protect yourself."

He nodded with several bouncy jerks of his head. "Okay. Okay. Just...you won't call the sheriff on me, will you?"

"I'm not planning on it." She gave him a wry, reassuring smile, wondering if the guy had the cops called on him a lot. "Poor Rob has been here way too much lately. I was hoping to have a sheriff-free month or two before the next incident."

Although he didn't return her smile, the muscles in his face eased slightly. "Okay, then. I...okay. I need protection from them. They've been following me. I can hear... I know they've been watching."

Rory spoke slowly, carefully choosing each word. "Do you know who they are?"

"King. Anderson and Wilson King. I know he sent them after me." The tension was creeping back into his wiry frame, and he started to pace.

Casually shifting position, Rory made sure the heavy worktable separated them. Why were the King brothers after him? A drug debt? Was Baxter a meth addict? That could explain his erratic behavior. But what was the connection between the Kings and Willard Gray, the headless man found in the reservoir? "Who is 'he'?"

The question brought a flurry of frantic head shaking.

"No, no, no, no. He knows I know. It'll just get worse if I tell. I can't, can't..."

"Okay." Rory raised her hands so the palms were facing outward. "You don't need to tell me. What do you need?"

"I don't...I don't know." He paused, pivoted a full circle, and then resumed his pacing. "They took his gun. Said they won't let me have a weapon." His laugh was short and bitter. "They taught me how to use them and then said I couldn't have them anymore. How can I protect myself? How? How, how, how?"

"Easy." Keeping her tone low and even, she kept her eyes on Baxter's progress, back and forth behind the worktable. "If you can't legally buy a gun, there are other ways to protect yourself."

"I heard...I heard..." He stopped pacing, meeting her eyes with a hopeful expression. "Can you get me one? I heard you could. Get me one and just not tell them." His eyes went to the ceiling as he said "them," making Rory wonder if he meant the government or some celestial beings.

"Maybe," she hedged. There was no way on God's green earth that Rory would hand this man any type of weapon in his current mental state, but she was still trying to figure out how best to help Mr. Baxter Price. "First, I need to know more. Tell me who 'he' is."

"But, but...he'll know. He'll know I'm talking." The pacing started again, and Rory had to force her muscles to relax so Baxter didn't pick up on her tension. He didn't need any additional stress.

"I won't tell." Rory held his gaze evenly. "I swear to you that I won't tell anyone."

Baxter stilled. Like magic, his eyes steadied and cleared. He opened his mouth, and Rory knew that whatever he was about to say would be the sane truth as he knew it.

"You okay, Ror?" Ian asked from the shop doorway.

She turned toward him. "I'm fine. Give us a minute?"

Ian's gaze flicked over her shoulder as he frowned. She twisted around to see Baxter slipping through the back door.

"Wait!" she called, running across the room.

"What's going on?" Ian asked, following her through the door.

"The King brothers are after Baxter Price." She hurried onto the back porch and looked around. The only things moving were the thick flakes of falling snow.

"Who's Baxter Price?"

"The guy who was just here. He was Willard Gray's friend."

"His friend?" he repeated. "Is he Gray's army buddy, the one who realized he was missing?"

"I think so."

"What do the King brothers want with him?" he asked thoughtfully. "Are they connected to the murder?"

Peering through the gloom, she said, "No idea. Baxter didn't say before he bolted. I wouldn't be surprised if the Kings were capable of murder, though."

Ian rested his hands on her shoulders. "How would they have gotten a hold of my pendant?"

"I don't know." Sagging a little as the adrenaline left her system, she leaned back against his chest.

She wouldn't find any answers staring out at the silent, snowy emptiness. Baxter Price was gone.

Keep reading for an excerpt from the next book in the Search & Rescue series

GONE TOO DEEP

ELLIE ALMOST DIDN'T TAKE THE CALL. IF HER DATE hadn't been so completely, utterly, and excruciatingly boring, she would've let it go to voice mail. Thanks to Dylan's never-ending monologue about his triathlon training, she seized the opportunity to escape when her phone made her tiny purse vibrate under her hand. Ellie didn't care who it was—a reminder from her dentist would have been better than listening to Dylan talk about how brick workouts affected his lower GI tract.

"Please excuse me," she interrupted with an apologetic smile as she pulled the phone from her purse. "I have to take this."

Sliding off her barstool, she booked it as fast as her stilettos would take her toward the ladies' room. On the way, she tapped the screen to accept the call.

"Hello?" She fully expected it to be a telemarketer, since Ellie didn't recognize the number. The seven-one-nine area code covered a big chunk of South-Central Colorado.

"Eleanor?" a male voice asked.

"This is she." Definitely a telemarketer. No one

who knew her well called her by her full name. It was worth listening to this guy's sales pitch, though, just to get away from the brain-sucking boredom that was her date.

"Eleanor."

The voice sounded familiar. She frowned, trying to place how she knew the caller as she ducked into the bathroom. It was empty and blessedly quiet compared to the loud music and chatter filling the main part of the club. "Yes?"

"Just…just wanted to say sorry to you, baby."

As recognition hit, Ellie's fingers went numb, and she almost dropped the phone. When she tried to speak, only a faint wheeze emerged from her throat.

"They're coming for me," he continued, his words fast and urgent. "I've managed to get away from them so far, but I wanted… I wanted to tell you, just in case. I'm sorry. Sorry, sorry, sorry."

"Dad?" she finally managed to squeeze out of lungs compressed with shock.

"Yeah, baby girl. It's me. I haven't… I haven't been a good dad. I know that. I know. But I wanted to say I'm sorry. I love you, baby. I've always loved you, but things are just not right…not right in my head. If I could've been a better dad, I would have. I would."

Her knees felt wobbly, and she slid her back down the wall until she was sitting on the floor. "I know, Dad." Her voice shook as badly as her knees. "I know you can't help how you are. I love you, too."

"They're trying to kill me, baby. Trying to keep me quiet. I can't, I can't… *He*'s trying to keep me quiet. I'm going to hide, though. I'll do my best to stay alive. I want… I want to try again with you, try to be better this time. Will you…would that be okay?"

"Yeah, Dad." Tipping her head back against the wall, Ellie closed her eyes. "That would be great."

"Good. Good." His words slowed for just an instant before the anxious patter started again. "I'm going to Grandpa's cabin. I took you there that one summer, do you remember? The cabin? We had fun, didn't we? You had fun?"

"I remember." Her voice broke on the last word. "We did have fun." She'd been ten, and they'd had a great time—at least until Baxter had had an episode and barricaded them both inside the cabin. Getting them out had required the efforts of a SWAT team and several law enforcement agencies. That had been Ellie's last unsupervised visit with her father.

"No one else knows about it. I should be…should stay hidden. They won't find me there. As soon as it's safe, I'll come find you, okay? We'll try again. I'll be a better dad this time. I promise. Promise, promise."

The alarm bells going off in her head finally penetrated her shock and sadness, and she sat up straight. "I believe you, Dad. Why don't you come to me right away? You don't need to go to the cabin." The thought of her mentally ill and obviously unmedicated father wandering alone in the wilderness was terrifying. "I can pick you up. Where are you?"

"At Gray Goose's house. They killed him, baby girl. Chopped off his head and dumped him in the reservoir. They'll kill me, too, if I don't hide. Need to hide. Can't die, can't die. If I die, I'll never get to try again with you, baby, and I know I can do better. I'll do better."

"I know you will, Dad, but you don't have to hide. I'll come get you. I'll keep you safe, okay? They won't be able to get you if you're with me. What's the address?"

"No, no, no. Don't come to Simpson, baby. They can't get you. Not you, not you. Stay away from them. They'll kill you, too. Not you, not my baby girl." He grew more and more agitated with each word.

"Dad, it's okay. They won't get me." The monsters in Baxter's head only tormented him. "I'm safe. I need to get you safe, too."

"I'm going to the cabin. I'll hide there. You stay away. You stay away, baby. You need to stay far away."

"Dad..." Her phone gave the double beep of a lost signal. "Dad!"

She fumbled to call the number, but it immediately went to an automated message telling her that the voice mail was full. A sob caught her by surprise, and she pressed a hand over her mouth as if to physically hold it back.

The restroom door swung open, and a pair of laughing women walked inside. When they saw her, their smiles immediately died.

"Are you okay?" one of them asked.

Ellie suddenly realized how she must look, makeup smeared, sitting on the bathroom floor in a dress that definitely wasn't designed for that. Taking a shaky breath, she tried to force a reassuring smile.

"Yes, thank you." Ellie climbed awkwardly to her feet, flattening her hands against the wall when her legs shook, threatening to send her back to the floor. "I just got some bad news. A family issue."

"Oh, I'm sorry." Both women looked at her

sympathetically. Now that she was on her feet, they must've decided she wasn't in need of their assistance, because they headed for the stalls. Ellie took tentative steps to one of the sinks. Her face looked pale, her skin undershot with green, and her hazel eyes were huge. She did a cursory job fixing her makeup, took several deep breaths that weren't any less shaky than the first one, and left the restroom.

Dylan was waiting where she'd left him. Although it felt like the phone call had taken hours, it had probably only been ten minutes, tops, since her cell had vibrated. She wove her way through the crowd until she was next to him and plucked her sweater off of her stool.

"Dylan," she said, leaning close to his ear so he could hear. He wrapped an arm around her waist, and she couldn't stop herself from flinching. Even shielded by the barrier of her dress, her skin felt oversensitive, as if every nerve was exposed. Ellie resisted the urge to shove his arm away, reminding herself that he was her boss's friend. Later, when her father was safe, she could gently give him the brush-off. "I'm sorry, but I have to go. Family emergency."

"Oh, that's too bad." He knocked back the rest of his drink and stood. "I'll drive you home."

She cringed inwardly. Over the past hour, she'd watched him drink two and a half martinis, and he'd just finished off the third. "Thank you, but I'll catch the L. There's a stop right by my apartment building."

"Sure?" When she nodded, Dylan sat down again. "Okay. It's been fun. I'll call you, and we can do this again sometime." When he leaned in as if to kiss her, Ellie twisted free of his arm. Boss's friend or no, he wasn't getting a kiss. Diplomacy had its limits.

"See you." After giving him a wave and a forced smile a few feet out of groping reach, she hurried toward the exit. Before she'd even left the club, Ellie had forgotten about Dylan. Her mind was filled instead with worry for another man.

The chilly air smacked her in the face as she stepped outside, and she hurried to pull on her long sweater. The fine, soft knit didn't offer much protection from the cold Lake Michigan wind, but it was slightly better than just the thin material of her dress. Turning right, she skirted the line of people waiting to enter the club. It was still early for a Saturday night, not even eleven, and Chicago's downtown was thick with both pedestrian and vehicle traffic.

Instead of heading toward the nearest train station, Ellie decided to walk home. It was less than a mile northwest to her condo building, and she needed to move, or her anxiety would boil over. Her shoes weren't the most uncomfortable ones she owned, although they were close. She'd been walking in heels for a decade, though, so she'd had years of training in ignoring discomfort.

Ellie realized she was picking at her cuticles and quickly yanked her hands apart. She thought she'd rid herself of that nervous habit, but it apparently took only one phone call from her dad to reduce her to the anxious teenager she'd once been.

Walking wasn't enough. She needed to do something productive, or she was going to run down the street, screaming. Digging her phone out of her purse, she stared at the time on the screen for several seconds before pulling up her contacts and tapping her mom's number.

As she held the cell phone to her ear, she realized her

hand was creeping up toward her mouth. Ellie dropped it to her side and made a disgusted sound. The only thing worse than picking at her cuticles was chewing on her hangnails.

"El?" Her mother's voice sounded worried. "What's wrong?"

"Hi, Mom. Sorry I'm calling so late. Did I wake you?"

"It's not quite nine here." Her mom had moved to California a few years before. "I'm not *that* old yet."

Normally, Ellie would have laughed at that, but the tight ball of nerves in her stomach wouldn't allow it. Instead, she stayed silent.

"Did the date with Chelsea's friend not go well?" her mom asked, the sharp edge of worry in her voice fading to general concern.

"No. I mean, it wasn't great, but that's not why I called." Taking a deep breath, she blurted, "Dad's in trouble."

Silence greeted her announcement. As she waited for her mom to speak, Ellie counted her footsteps, heels clicking on the pavement. *One. Two. Three. Four. Five...*

"Honey." There it was—*the tone*. Ellie had forgotten about the way her mom's words came out slow and heavy, thick with a mixture of fatigue and condescension, whenever she talked about her ex-husband. "You can't let him pull you into his drama."

"It's not drama, Mom." Her hand hovered by her mouth again, and she impatiently yanked it away. "He's sick, and he's scared, and I need to go get him."

"He'll just drag you down with him." The *tone* had sharpened with added irritation. "I know you love him, sweetie, but you can't fix him. You can't make him take his meds, and, without them, he's not safe to be around."

"He's never hurt me." She closed her eyes for a

second, ashamed at the sullen cast to her voice. Why did interacting with her parents reduce her to a thirteen-year-old? "I just want to bring him to a safe place. He's trying to get to Grandpa's cabin."

"Scott's cabin?" Her mom sounded startled. "In Colorado?"

"Yes. The one he took me to when I was ten." When Ellie heard the inhale on the other end of the call, she grimaced. It had been a mistake to bring that up. After their extraction from the cabin, her mother hadn't let Ellie out of her sight for days, and any mention of Baxter had turned Ellie's mom blotchy red with rage.

"What is he doing? That place isn't even accessible by car until June at the earliest. He'll have to hike—no—" Her mom interrupted herself. "I can't do this. *You* can't do this. El, you need to separate yourself from him."

"I can't just leave him," Ellie said softly, stopping at the entrance of her building. Tilting back her head, she stared, unseeing, at the layers of metal balconies above her.

"Yes." Her mother had her stern, you-will-listen-to-me voice going. "You can. You have to. Think of all the times we tried to help him and just got sucked into his mixed-up mess. For your own sanity, you need to stay clear of him."

The balconies grew blurry, and she scrubbed away tears with the hand not holding the phone. "But I haven't. I haven't tried to help him, *ever*. He'd visit for an hour, looking so lost and desperate, and I'd be polite to him. When he'd leave, I'd feel relieved. If you'd heard him on the phone… Mom, he's so scared."

"There's no real threat, El. It's in his head."

"But there is a threat!" She brushed at her cheeks, but her tears flowed faster than she could wipe them away. "You said it yourself. He'll have to hike to the cabin. There's no running water, and who knows if Dad will bring food, and he's going to hide there until he feels safe. The monsters are always with him, though, so he'll *never* feel safe."

Her mom sighed loudly. "You can't save him, El."

"Not from his brain." Her breath left her lungs on a hiccup. "But I'm going to find him, and I'm going to take him somewhere where he won't freeze to death hiding from the boogeyman."

"El..."

"I'm sorry, Mom, but I have to do this. If I don't, and something happens to him, I won't be able to live with myself."

"I lived with the man for fifteen years, El. I tried, over and over, to fix him. You're just inviting heartache."

"Better heartache than regret." Ellie took a deep, shuddering breath. "Can you give me directions to Grandpa's cabin?"

"I'm not helping you chase after him, El." The *tone* was back. "I can't stop you, but I'm not going to encourage this."

Ellie was silent as she resisted the urge to whine. "Okay," she finally said. "I'll figure it out. Bye, Mom."

"El..."

Hearing a lecture approaching, Ellie ended the call.

That night, she lay in bed and ran the conversation with her father through her mind, over and over. When she'd asked him where he was, he'd said "Gray Goose's house." What did that mean? Was it just nonsensical rambling, and she was being an idiot for taking it literally?

He'd also mentioned "Simpson," telling her not to come there. That sounded more logical than *Gray Goose*. She reached for her phone and pulled up the Web browser. After entering Simpson, she hesitated, then typed in "Colorado."

When the results appeared, she saw that Simpson, Colorado, was a tiny mountain town in Field County. Her heart jumped in excitement and nervousness as she stared at the small screen. There it was, the starting point for finding her father—the place that would either be the scene of a heartwarming, father-daughter reunion…or a grim tragedy.

"You're going to do *what*?" Chelsea stared at Ellie, her mouth open. Even with her current shocked expression, Ellie's redheaded boss was beautiful—tall, slender, and perfectly polished.

"I'm going to Colorado to find my dad." Ellie focused on keeping the box-cutter blade straight, slicing a perfectly even line across the packing tape. "Since I'm off tomorrow and Tuesday, I shouldn't have to take any vacation time."

"But…" Chelsea's mouth closed with a click of teeth. "Isn't your dad, well, crazy?" She hissed the last word in a loud whisper, even though no one else was in the store with them.

"That's why I need to get him," Ellie explained, pushing back the instinctive urge to defend her father.

"He's too…vulnerable to be wandering around in the middle of nowhere. I'm going to bring him back here and hopefully talk him into staying at a mental health facility in Chicago until he's back on his meds and stabilized." Saying it out loud made Ellie realize how many "ifs" were in her plan—if she found him, if she could convince him to return with her, if he'd be willing to get treatment… It was a definite long shot, this plan of hers.

"Wow." Chelsea leaned against the jewelry display case as Ellie pulled out a stack of cashmere scarves. "That's intense. I call my dad crazy, but that's just when he wears two different-colored socks, not when he runs around in the mountains, thinking the aliens want to suck out his brain or something." Reaching over to the stack of scarves, Chelsea stroked the top one. "These are gorge."

"Yes." Although her eyes were on the newly arrived merchandise, her thoughts were still on the town of Simpson.

"Hey!" Chelsea's hand left the scarf to slap Ellie on the shoulder. "You never told me how your date with Dylan went! Spill, chicklet! How was it?"

"Uh…" *Horribly boring*. "Short. My dad called early into it, so we barely got past introductions."

"Well, short or not, he liked you."

Ellie gave Chelsea a confused look. "How do you know?"

"He texted me when you were in the bathroom or something." Chelsea pulled her cell out of her pocket and tapped at the screen. "Here." She held up the phone so Ellie could read the text.

UR frnd is HOT. Lks like chick usd 2 B on Vamp Dairies.

Her nose wrinkled involuntarily.

"What?" Chelsea demanded, turning the phone so she could read the text. "It's sweet. He thinks you look like Nina Dobrev."

"He used text-speak. And he spelled 'Diaries' wrong—unless there's a new show about bloodsucking cows that I haven't seen yet. And I look nothing like Nina Dobrev."

"Don't be such a snob." After tucking her phone back in her pocket, Chelsea put her hands on her hips. "Dylan's awesome, has a good job *and* a great body. If I hadn't stuck him in the friend zone, like, a year ago, I'd so be all over that. And you have Nina Dobrev's hair."

"It's just..." Ellie tried to smooth out her scrunched face. "He talks about his triathlon training a *lot*."

"So? That's what he's interested in."

Chelsea's tone had sharpened, and Ellie suppressed a wince. She wasn't handling the conversation well. "I know." She tried to make her voice placating. "He seems like a great guy. I was just distracted by that call from my dad."

After a long look, Chelsea's glare softened slightly. "That was probably it. Because Dylan's amazing. If you were focused on him, you'd see that."

"Sure." Normally, Chelsea was a fun boss and roommate, but she had definite opinions and got a little contrary if she didn't get her way. Occasionally, she required careful handling. Today, with the whole Baxter situation hanging over her head, Ellie was fumbling. A subject change was in order. "You're right about these scarves—they're beautiful. How much do you want to charge for them?"

Chelsea switched topics willingly enough, but Ellie couldn't keep her mind from wandering to her upcoming rescue mission. She'd mapped the route from her condo to Simpson, and it was just over a thousand miles. If she drove, it would take sixteen hours—without breaks. She definitely needed breaks. As much as she hated to spend some of her savings on a plane ticket and rental car, driving all that way just seemed crazy. Besides, didn't everyone in Colorado need to drive Jeeps and Hummers to navigate the mountain roads? Her beloved, middle-aged Prius probably wouldn't cut it.

"El!" Chelsea's sharp tone cut through her tumbling thoughts. "Are you listening?"

"Of course I'm listening, and you're absolutely right, Chels," Ellie soothed with the ease of long practice, her mind still running over travel plans.

Chelsea's irritated frown smoothed into a smile. "So you think that's a good idea?"

"It's brilliant." Ellie had no idea what the other woman was proposing, and, honestly, she didn't really care. Her father was lost, and Ellie was going to find him—no matter what it took.

Squinting against the glare of the sun reflecting off snow, Ellie fumbled for her sunglasses. In Denver, the tulips and daffodils had poked their heads out of the ground already, and the day's temperature was supposed to hit seventy degrees. Who knew the mountains still had snow?

Then again, the peaks were white, which could've been a clue. She slowed her rental car as she approached a curve at the base of the pass where a flashing sign warned of possible ice on the road. It felt as if she'd reversed time two months during the two-hour drive from Denver. Maybe she should've splurged and rented an SUV at the Denver Airport rather than the more economical compact.

She sped up again as the road straightened. Although she'd been tempted to head to Simpson as soon as her shift at the boutique had ended the evening before, Ellie had gritted her teeth and bought a plane ticket—at a price that made her wince—for a flight leaving early the following morning. After being on the road for close to three hours, she was desperate to stop. It was already past noon, though, and she had only another day and a half to find her father and return them both to Chicago. Besides, there wasn't anywhere to stop. The high plains stretched in waves of white in all directions, the barren landscape unbroken until it bumped up against the surrounding mountains. Ellie carefully kept her gaze on the road so the emptiness, the feeling that she was the only person alive in this achingly lonely place, wouldn't reduce her to a useless, terrified heap.

Steering around another looping turn, she saw signs of civilization just as her GPS announced that she'd arrived at her destination. She slowed as she started passing structures—a feed store, a gas station, a ratty-looking motel—and then she abruptly turned the rental into the parking lot of a small building. A large sign above it introduced it as The Coffee Spot.

Her body craved a shot of caffeine almost as much as it desired a restroom, and this place would most likely offer both. She parked the car between two pickup trucks. As she got out of her rental, she eyed the vehicles that bracketed her. They loomed over her, making her car look miniature.

The air was thin and cold, despite the sun. Shivering, she wrapped the open sides of her cardigan around her. The single-button style was cute, but she would have appreciated several more buttons at the moment.

She closed and locked her car, then took a step toward the shop. Without warning, her heeled ankle booties slid out from under her, flying up in the air and sending her crashing onto her butt. The blow jarred her tailbone painfully, and she took a moment to shake off the shock of the fall before taking inventory. Except for her throbbing coccyx, all her other body parts seemed to be unharmed. She shifted to her hands and knees on the slick, packed snow.

An enormous hand appeared in front of her face. Startled, she glanced up at the person connected to the offered hand, first taking in his booted feet and working her way up his legs and torso before finally landing on his bearded face. He wasn't a man; he was a mountain.

The mountain was frowning, and Ellie realized she was rudely staring at her would-be helper. "Thank you," she rushed out, grabbing his gloved hand. As her fingers curled around his, she took in how small her hand looked in comparison to his oversized mitt. It reminded her of how her car appeared next to the pickups.

He pulled, easily lifting her to a standing position, and she scrambled to get her feet underneath her. The icy footing was unforgiving, and her free arm swung wildly until she latched onto the stranger's other hand. When she finally got her balance, she still clung to him, not wanting to let go of her anchor and start flailing again.

After several seconds passed, though, it started to feel a little awkward. "Sorry," she said, reluctantly loosening her grip. "And thank you. I'd be flat on my back again if it weren't for your help."

He didn't release her now-limp hands. Ellie looked from his frowning face to her captured fingers and back again.

"Uh...I think I'm okay now. You can probably let me go."

Apparently, the mountain didn't agree. Still gripping her hands, he dropped his frowning gaze to her booties.

"I know." She grimaced, interpreting his look as silent criticism of her footwear. "These were the closest thing I had to winter boots, though."

His hands finally dropped hers, and Ellie pasted on a polite smile, ready to give the giant a final thank-you and very slowly shuffle her way to the coffee shop door. Before she could open her mouth, though, his hands latched around her waist, and he lifted her as if she were a doll.

Her thank-you turned into an indrawn shriek. "What are you...? Put me down!"

Ignoring her order, he took several sure-footed strides toward the entrance of the shop and set her on the mat in front of the door. Then, without a word, he turned and walked to one of the trucks.

Openmouthed, Ellie watched as he got into the driver's seat and drove out of the lot, not even giving her another glance. When the truck disappeared, she blinked and turned toward the door. A small group of people crowded around the glass door and window, staring at her. Startled, Ellie took a step back, and everyone inside hurried to turn away from her.

Ellie waited another few seconds as the people inside the shop pretended like they hadn't been watching the whole time she'd been carried to the door by a mountain.

"This is a weird town," she muttered, and pulled open the door.

About the Author

A fan of the old adage "write what you know," Katie Ruggle lived in an off-grid, solar- and wind-powered house in the Rocky Mountains until her family lured her back to Minnesota. When she's not writing, Katie rides horses, shoots guns, cross-country skis (badly), and travels to warm places where she can scuba dive. A graduate of the police academy, Katie received her ice-rescue certification and can attest that the reservoirs in the Colorado mountains really are that cold. A fan of anything that makes her feel like a badass, she has trained in Krav Maga, boxing, and gymnastics. You can connect with Katie at katieruggle.com, facebook.com/katieragglebooks, or on Twitter @KatieRuggle.